WHAT CAN SAVE US NOW...?

FATHER EDMUND MORAN...Last in the line of priests chosen to safeguard the world from the horrifying secret of the Grail.

DR. LAUREN BLAIR...The incredible truth revealed by her scientific testing of the Grail heralds the doom of mankind.

INSPECTOR FRANK DONNELLAN... Entrusted with protecting the Grail, his most desperate concern is protecting Lauren Blair.

DR. PERCIVAL LEECH...To possess the Church's most treasured relic, he is willing to destroy the future of our world.

CARDINAL DI STEFANO...Devoted to strengthening man's faith in God, he has unleashed an ungodly force beyond his comprehension.

GRAIL

PHILIP MICHAELS

AVON
PUBLISHERS OF BARD, CAMELOT, DISCUS AND FLARE BOOKS

GRAIL is an original publication of Avon Books. This work has never before appeared in book form.

Cover illustration by Mark and Stephanie Gerber

AVON BOOKS
A division of
The Hearst Corporation
959 Eighth Avenue
New York, New York 10019

Copyright © 1982 by Isis Literary Productions
Published by arrangement with the author
Library of Congress Catalog Card Number: 81-69278
ISBN: 0-380-79921-9

First Avon Printing, July, 1982

Printed in the U.S.A.

WFH 10 9 8 7 6 5 4 3 2 1

ACKNOWLEDGMENTS

The author wishes to thank:
Dr. Irving, Department of Archaeology, University of Toronto, for expert advice provided on the dating of historical objects,

and

James A. Lowden of the Geological Survey of Canada, Ottawa, who gave generously of his time and his knowledge of the technical procedures of geochronology.

PROLOGUE

"If it be possible, let this cup pass from me...."

—St. Matthew

Britain...in the year A.D. 926

THE MONK who was called Matthew pulled back on the reins, stopping the horse at the crest of the hill. As he leaned forward in the saddle his gaze moved slowly across the vista below.

The valley was swathed in early-morning fog. The fields glistened with dew as the mist swirled across the tall grasses, wending its way through the majestic oaks standing like heralds along the perimeter of the meadow. The wind shifted and suddenly the abbey of St. Gallen came into view. Matthew could see the entire chapel, save the short spire. Beside the chapel was a low long barrack, constructed of the same stone as the abbey proper, weathered and black from years of inhospitable climate. At the end were the stables and animal pens, built from the same oaks that guarded the approach to St. Gallen.

The wind shifted again and the abbey was gone, as though it had never been there at all. The horse drew back, shaking its head, pawing the earth. Matthew leaned forward and spoke to the animal, stroking its neck with his great hand. He was a giant of a man, six and a half feet tall, generous of girth, with immense shoulders and a powerful torso. Beneath the damp curly hair was a gentle face, with green eyes flecked with brown. Gentle, concerned eyes. Sorrowful eyes.

"It is time for morning mass. I do not hear any bells."

Matthew turned to the speaker, who had ridden up behind him. He was the papal legate, Tractus,

the envoy sent to this land from Rome by the Holy
Father, John X. He was also the man Matthew had
been commissioned to return with. Behind them was
the legate's escort: twenty armed soldiers provided
by Robert de Baron. Ordinarily even men with weapons did not travel these lands in daylight unless the
journey was necessary. By night only the wretched
or the mad ventured out of doors. Yet this cohort had
ridden half the night, each man carrying a torch so
that their numbers could be seen by anyone lying
in wait. The swords had been unsheathed, the thongs
of battle axes wrapped tightly about the wrists, the
blades swinging gently to and fro.

"I beg his Excellency to remain here. I will ride
down alone."

"That is not prudent," the legate observed. "You
should take some men with you."

The monk shook his head. "I thank his Excellency
for his concern. But if one man is not enough then
five or twenty will not suffice."

He clicked his tongue and the horse moved forward.

I have returned too late.

As the mists embraced him he looked back. The
men upon the hill disappeared. He unsheathed the
short-handled battle axe, twice the size and weight
of a normal one, forged by himself, a weapon other
men needed both hands to hold. He handled it easily,
as though it was nothing more than a stick. A stick
with which he could cleave a man in half in one blow.

I have come too late.

The silence was oppressive. He heard nothing. Not
the warble of a morning bird, not the rustle of a fox,
the lowing of the cattle, the bleating of the sheep.
He rode past the oaks, stained black from the mists,
the wind shaking the water off the leaves onto his
face and neck. He paused in the clearing before the
abbey then turned his horse to the left and slowly
rode past the stables. There was a dank smell in the

air, coming from behind the barred doors. For an instant he thought of dismounting and entering the stables, then thought better of it.

Matthew rode past the low barrack where the monks slept and worked. He heard nothing from within at an hour when everyone should have been awake, finishing the morning chores before mass. The mass. The legate had said it: there should have been the sounds of bells rising above the soft litany in the chapel. The smell of tapers should have infused the air, mingling with incense. It was as though all life, not only human life, had fled this place. The very stones of the abbey of St. Gallen, sanctuary to all those who lived here or passed through this land, seemed to have died. The spirit of holiness that imbued this consecrated ground was no more.

Matthew brought his mount before the abbey doors and slipped from the saddle, the great axe held out in one hand. With the other he pushed open the abbey door. It swung back easily, bumping gently against the wall. The monk stooped and passed under the archway, then straightened up, looking to either side. The vestibule was empty.

The sunlight broke through the mists, streaming down the corridor ahead of him. With the axe held before him, Matthew proceeded down the hall. The tapers must have been burning all night, for nothing remained of them except stubs. The shaft of sunlight guided him as far as the first of the stone-hewn pews. Because of the angle of the archway, it travelled no farther. Matthew stood very still, allowing his eyes to expand into the darkness. Then slowly the sun began to penetrate the tall lead-lined windows behind the sacristy... and those on either side of the rearmost stone pews. With exquisite slowness, as though it dared not reveal the whole at once, the sunlight unveiled the furious terror that had visited the abbey of St. Gallen.

The two novices, Augustine and Luke, were impaled on rough-hewn saplings on opposite sides of the altar. Their bellies had been ripped open and their entrails disgorged. Flies buzzed around the corpses. There were rats at the base of the saplings, lapping at the blood, worrying the tender wood, clawing frantically to get at the corpses. They darted their heads at him, squinting as though he was the intruder, and went back to work. This was their domain now. Matthew beheld the scene like one possessed. His head snapped to the right. There, in the second rank of pews, were the bodies of his four brethren, pressed tightly together so that one supported the other. Their heads had been cut off, the heads of goats and sheep set upon their shoulders. As radiant light bathed the abbey in life-giving warmth, the stench of death began to choke Matthew. He looked at his feet and saw pools of red-black blood.

Too late! I have come too late!

Then he remembered the abbot Palinurus. The holy elder of St. Gallen. Matthew looked to his right at the two confessionals. Both were empty. Could Palinurus have survived the onslaught? Had he managed to reach the catacombs in time, those tunnels that had been painstakingly constructed beneath the foundation of the abbey, leading all the way to the other side of the copse? If God had any mercy...

The monk heard a sound behind him. He whirled about, his axe blades flashing in the light, to see the front door closing slowly. There was no one, nothing, pushing it. The door was falling back on its own momentum. Matthew took a single step. Suddenly his fist was in his mouth and his teeth were clamped on his knuckles, drawing blood. As the door gently closed off the sunlight, Matthew saw, impaled to its wood with long hideous nails driven through his hands and feet, the body of the abbot Palinurus, eagle-spread, his head twisted completely around his neck so that the agony poured forth from his lifeless eyes into Matthew.

The great axe slipped from his fingers, the iron sparking off the stone floor. With a low moan the last survivor of St. Gallen fell to his knees, the heels of his hands pressed against his eyes as though he would push them into the back of his head. The scream that came from his throat was heard all the way to the hill where the legate waited with his men. When they heard the cry they too knew they had come too late.

The legate watched as Matthew raised his arms high over his head and drove the cross into the head of the last grave. For a moment he remained like that, both arms resting atop the cross, his body heaving from exhaustion, the face and hands caked with dirt and sweat, the eyes glazed, madness dancing behind them. The monk worked like one possessed. While the legate and his company had stared open-mouthed at the horror that had overtaken St. Gallen, Matthew had uprooted one of the stakes by the altar and laid the novice's body upon the stone floor. He pried the corpse off the stake then turned to the next one. He removed the animal heads from the shoulders of his brothers and carried their bodies into the barracks. At last he wrenched out the nails that held the grotesquely crucified Palinurus to the door. Matthew guarded the bodies of his fallen brothers as an animal would its wounded. He worked alone and in silence, washing the corpses, then wrapping them in clean white linen. Only after this was done did he allow other men to dig the graves while he fashioned the crosses. Throughout the requiem that preceded the interment he did not say a single word.

The legate came over to the monk and bade him stand.

"What happened here?" he asked. "Who could have done this to them?"

Matthew did not answer him. Instead he looked up at the sky, at the sun that stood in the center of the heavens.

"You have a long journey, Excellency. If you leave now you can still reach Ictus by nightfall."

"But my vessel does not sail until this time tomorrow!"

"There is no tomorrow, Excellency," the monk said softly. He looked about himself, his penetrating stare searching the hills and woods for something. "There is no tomorrow," he repeated.

As Matthew turned to go back into the abbey the legate grasped his arm.

"In the name of the Holy Father I command you to tell me what has happened here," he said coldly. "I promise you whoever did this—Franks, Saxons, Norsemen—they will be found. And punished."

The monk regarded him sadly. "Not who, Excellency. What." He walked away.

Back in the desecrated abbey, Matthew moved past the altar to the sacristy. The large, heavy stones he himself had hewn had been ripped up from the floor, flung aside as though they were nothing more than pebbles. The entire wall behind the sacristy had been shorn away. The destruction was methodical. Whatever had eaten the abbey of St. Gallen had not been content with murder and destruction. It had been looking for something. Something it had not found. The furious devastation around him spoke of thwarted desire.

Matthew came to the altar. It had been ripped from its foundation and moved to one side but the ledge upon which it rested remained untouched. For good reason: the ledge appeared nothing more than a large boulder rising smoothly from the earth. It wasn't that at all. Picking up an iron pike, Matthew twisted its point into the earth beside the rock. When it had gone deep enough he leaned back, prying the rock up from the earth, working his way around the edge of the stone. When he had gone around once he felt the stone give way. A final effort raised the slate cover from the earth. A sharp twist of the massive arms moved it to one side.

Groaning with effort, Matthew pulled the ledge back. Then, lying on his belly, he reached into the pit and removed a canvas sack.

"What is it you have there?" the legate asked him.

Matthew did not answer him. Instead he carefully unwrapped the canvas, placing two objects on the stone beside him. He then stripped away the oiled skin covering the first to produce a rolled parchment.

"This is what the abbot Palinurus would have shown you had he lived," Matthew said. "This is why he wanted you to come. The parchment records everything we know of the knight Brideshead. Some of the writing is in his own hand, the rest recorded by myself from the knight's own words."

Matthew reached for the other object. Carefully he untied the leather jerkin that enclosed it.

"Mother of God!"

The legate could not help himself. The leather had fallen away to reveal a chalice of the purest gold. It was not large, in height twice that of a man's palm, perfectly round and shallow, standing on a base that flared out in four soft curves. The legate approached Matthew, his gaze upon the cup, lips parted in astonishment.

"It cannot be!" he whispered.

Matthew held the chalice aloft in his hands. The sun streaming through the lead-lined windows poured into the cup. When the legate gazed into its depths, the fine whorls seemed to move, wave back and forth, shiver, dissolve, then move together again.

"You recognize this, Excellency," Matthew said.

"I do. But it cannot be what I think it is."

Matthew nodded. "It is the Holy Grail, the chalice

used by Our Lord at the Last Supper. The cup from which He drank, which caught His blood during His last agony upon the Cross. This is why Palinurus sent me to Ictus: to return with you so that you would convey the cup to his Holiness in Rome."

"How did you come by it?" the legate demanded.

Matthew placed the cup on the floor and drew the leather jerkin about it.

"The story of the chalice—as much as we know of it—has been written down by Palinurus," he said, handing the legate the parchment.

"You must tell me—yourself!" the legate commanded. "You must tell me everything, from the beginning." He paused. "You said there was a knight. Yet we found only the members of the order."

"He was taken," Matthew said quietly.

"Taken! By whom? Why should the invaders take him but kill the others?"

"The knight died the morning I left for Ictus. A crypt was being fashioned for him. But as you saw, the vault is empty. There is no body."

"What in God's name would they want with a body?"

"It is all in the parchment," Matthew repeated softly. He rose, towering over the legate. "You must go now, Excellency. You must take the chalice and the parchments and reach Ictus before evening."

The legate reached out and clasped his hands about the chalice. Even through the leather he could feel its warmth, its smooth perfect roundness.

"This is a miracle," he said. "I have seen drawings of the chalice, have heard it described.... Still, it is difficult to believe that it exists."

"It does, Excellency. This is the Grail."

"You will come to Rome with me," the legate said at once. "The Holy Father will want to speak with you." He looked around. "There is nothing left for you here."

"I will not go, Excellency," Matthew told him. "My place is here."

"You have no choice in the matter," the legate said crisply. "I order you to come with us."

"Then I must disobey, Excellency," the monk said. "I beg of you, allow me to remain with my brothers. Do not force me to raise my hand against you or our men."

The legate looked upon the giant incredulously.

"You would defy the command of one who speaks in His Holiness' name?"

"I would disobey Rome itself if need be."

"But why! You yourself said that whoever brought such carnage upon the abbey will probably return."

"And I shall defend my church as best I can. My place is here. I was spared only because the abbot decreed that I should be the one to travel to Ictus. Perhaps had I remained we might have stopped them."

"You cannot stop these savages alone!" the legate protested.

Matthew held out the parchment and the chalice. "I beg of you, Excellency, take them and leave. Ride hard and fast to Ictus. Whatever followed the knight here, whatever overwhelmed the order will not rest until it has the chalice. Read what Palinurus wrote, what the knight told him before he died. Read it and protect the chalice with your very life. Only in the most holy place on this earth must the chalice rest. Only in Rome it will be safe from them."

"Madness!" the legate whispered. "You are jabbering like some idiot child!"

But Matthew had already turned away. As he heard the last of the legate's words he was disappearing into the green stillness of the forest.

He knew the woods well and was able to hide from the men the legate sent after him. They never came close to discovering him. After an hour the hunt ceased. From his vantage point he heard the shouts of the soldiers as they saddled their horses and prepared to leave. He waited until he saw them moving up the crest of the hill before slipping back into the cloister. Matthew climbed into the bell tower and gazed out upon the procession. One by one the men and mounts disappeared over the hill. The last one to vanish was the legate. The envoy paused for an instant. Matthew thought he saw him turn in his saddle and look back at the abbey, his arm raised in a farewell gesture. Then he too was gone.

Matthew returned to the abbey. He washed the blood from the stone and cleaned the pews where the novices had been placed. He scrubbed the door of the abbot's blood until his hands were raw, then buried the carcasses of the slaughtered animals. This done, he went to the monks' quarters and gathered up every religious object, all the crosses, the prayer palimpsests, and bibles. From the abbot's quarters he removed the vestments, coarse wafers, and sacramental wine, and brought these with him to the abbey. He gathered the broken crucifixes and ikons and arranged them around the altar. By the time he finished his work, daylight was fleeing from the sky.

Matthew returned to his quarters, washed himself, and donned a fresh cassock. When he returned to the abbey he entered the confessional and cleansed himself of his sins. He drank the wine he had left for himself and took communion. Then as the last song of the birds faded into the forest he began to say mass.

He prayed for the souls of Palinurus and his brothers, that God would grant them eternal rest and peace by His hand. He prayed for the knight Brideshead whose body was no more. At last he prayed that the Lord give him strength to face this night, endow him with courage to face the terror that even now was sweeping over the night, descending upon the land, slithering toward the abbey like some hideous unstoppable force from Hell.

"The Lord is my Shepherd; I shall not want.
He leadeth me beside the still waters...."

He heard the chanting, an evil wind rising out of
the pitch night. He felt their presence around him,
surrounding him. He sensed their lust after his flesh
and hot blood.

"He restoreth my soul; He leadeth me in
the paths of righteousness for His name's sake.
Yea, though I walk through the valley of the
   shadow of death,
I will fear no evil: for Thou art with me...."

The hooves of a thousand horses trampled the
earth, causing the entire abbey to shudder. Fissures
appeared in the mortar, splintering the wall. The
inset stones began to glow until Matthew could
actually feel the heat emanating from them. Then
one by one they began falling out of the wall, spitting and hissing. Something obscene, which had no
fear of holy ground, was literally pulling the abbey
apart.

Matthew was on his knees, his arms flung around
the altar, head pressed hard against his shoulders,
eyes squeezed shut. The upheaval around him was
deafening. In his terror he imagined himself one of
the Philistines caught in the Temple where Samson
had pulled the pillars apart.

When he finally dared to open his eyes, he found
himself looking up at the evening sky. Yet in spite
of the season, he felt as though he were standing in
the antechamber of Hell. Then he looked over his
shoulder and gazed upon the ferocity climbing toward him, moving over the burning stones so effortlessly, a feral grin upon its face. He stared at it,
then whirled around as the fiendish legions pushed
their way over the rubble of the four walls.

"Surely goodness and mercy shall follow me
all the days of my life; and I will dwell
in the house of the Lord—"

Matthew took a step back, retreating up against
the altar, standing in the center of the circle formed
by the crosses and crucifixes.

"You shall not have it, infernal progeny!" he spat
out. "I command you, in the name of all that is holy,
return to the depths whence you came!"

The horror shambled forth, pausing at the foot of
the pit.

"You did not find it!" Matthew whispered, his face
shining, voice triumphant. "It is gone!"

A terrible silence descended on the church. The
horror stood perfectly still, seemingly transfixed by
the sight of the empty pit. A long slow hiss, like that
of a nest of snakes disturbed, was heard.

"Get thee behind me!" Matthew thundered, his
voice a clarion within the church. "You dare not
strike me upon holy ground!"

"It is our ground, priest," the horror rasped. "It
is foul and corrupt with our stink now."

"Be gone!" Matthew screamed, thrusting the crucifix toward the onslaught.

A searing pain drove into his brain. When he
opened his eyes Matthew saw that the hand holding
the cross had been shorn away. Then before he could
utter another word of prayer, they set upon him and
he was no more.

PART ONE

Follow, follow, follow the gleam
Banners unfurled o'er the world
Follow, follow, follow the gleam
Of the chalice that is the Grail.

—SALLIE HUME DOUGLAS,
  Follow the Grail (1923)

CHAPTER ONE

E VEN THE FIRST TIME, the dream frightened him.
Not because of what he saw but because he could
not wake up from the vision, no matter how he struggled.

Arturo Cardinal Capellini, curator of the Museum
of Pagan Antiquities, was standing on the bank of
the River Styx, the last barrier in the soul's journey
from Life to Death. In the distance Charon, the grotesque ferryman and servant of the Underworld, was
rowing his punt to the opposite shore. On the bank,
Capellini saw three figures waiting for the ferryman.
They were clothed in robes. Their hoods prevented
him from discerning their faces. Their hands were
hitched into the sleeves of their cassocks.

Who can they be? Capellini asked himself. Why
would the ferryman bring them back to this side, to
the living, if they are already dead?

Mesmerized, Capellini watched as the figures
stepped into the prow of the boat. They stood there,
looking across the motionless gray waters. He could
feel their gaze upon him.

They are coming for me, he thought fearfully. I
must flee.... Yet he remained rooted on the far bank,
unable to move, unable to tear his gaze from those
who were watching him.

They are coming for me. They are coming back!

At that instant, Arturo Capellini began to scream.

He did not stop until his servant ran in and shook him awake.

March twenty-first.

Winter had come to an end. The wind sweeping across Saint Peter's Square bore the scent of lilac, willow, and roses, carried from the freshly turned Vatican gardens. Even at this early hour, six o'clock, the sun felt strong, warm, and life-giving.

Urban IX, Vicar of Christ, Bishop of Rome, looked at the empty *piazza* from the balcony of his apartments. The Holy See was stirring to life. Far below him, where yesterday thousands had stood to receive his blessing, sweepers were cleaning the pavés, fishing the debris from the Bernini fountain. Even from this distance he could smell the fresh bread rising in the Vatican bakery near the Via della Conciliazione wall. The silence pleased Urban, the tranquillity and repose gave him a measure of confidence for all he planned to accomplish this spring and summer. Above all else, there was the Tour, the hallmark of his rule.

The Holy Father raised his hand and silently made the sign of the cross over his domain; then he uttered a few words of prayer for all the people across the world who kept the True Faith.

Breakfast was spartan but nourishing—tangerines, grapefruit sections, bread, butter, and rich strong coffee. Two places had been set at a small table in an alcove whose windows opened onto the gardens. Dominic Cardinal di Stefano, the papal secretary, rose when the pontiff entered. He knelt and pressed his lips against the ring of the Fisherman. Urban gestured for him to be seated.

"We trust you have procured the opinions of the various departments," the pontiff said. A slight, ascetic man, Tuscan-born and -bred, Urban had the stamp of his native province upon his face: a wide, creased fore-

head, sharp agate eyes, a proud hawklike nose overlooking bloodless lips. He had little patience with the
more contentious members of the Curia, none with
those who believed their approval was a necessary imprimatur to papal proposals. He was forthright in the
extreme, disdaining loquacity and verbal peregrina-
tions.

"The reports from the Congregation for the Propagation of the Faith, Vaguozzi at the Finance Minis-
try, and the curator of the Vatican museums were
delivered to me last evening, Holiness," di Stefano
said.

The secretary watched as Urban broke bread with
his blue-veined hands. They were disparate men,
this Tuscan aristocrat and the man from the South.
Di Stefano was a child of the Naples docks. As a man
he had retained the sinewy leanness of youth, the
sharp, suspicious movements of the streets. Yet he
was graced with a face Michelangelo would have
envied: clean sharp cheek lines that spoke of his
authority, proud serene eyes of the palest blue, a
nose that might have been beaten into a Roman coin.

"Their views concur with your own," di Stefano
added.

The pontiff ran a slice of lemon rind along the rim of
his cup and sipped his coffee. He knew there were those
in the Curia who disliked di Stefano, were displeased
by what they considered his undue influence upon the
Papacy. It was true that di Stefano, by the authority of
his position, decided who gained access to Urban,
which projects should receive his attention, what pol-
icies were to be considered over others. He could not
please all petitioners. Yet Urban trusted his judgment
completely. He and di Stefano had been friends for
many years. The prince and the pauper had studied in
the same seminary, taken their vows together, worked
within the same organizations of the Church. Over the
years they had become like right and left hands, coop-
erative, complementary. Urban paid no attention to

the voices of dissatisfaction. Not once had his friend failed or betrayed him, or even given him the slightest cause to question his fealty.

"We are pleased that at least this one time these august men have agreed upon something," Urban said dryly. He dipped a crust of bread into his coffee and chewed it for a moment.

"Faith is a curious thing," he continued. "Like an underground stream which may flow silently for centuries, unseen and unheard, it at once rises into its spring. We are living in the age of religious revival. In this revival the Mother Church must hold her own, especially against the rising force of Islam. The Muslim world is experiencing a resurgence unprecedented in a thousand years. The message has gone out to the faithful: return to the teachings and ways of Allah. That must be our message to Catholicism: the Rock of Peter has endured. The faith lives, and in it all men who believe. *This* is the reason we have conceived the Tour, to show every Catholic, every Christian, his heritage. When he witnesses the glory of the past, the conscience will stir from its sleep, the flame of faith will rise true and strong."

Although di Stefano had heard many variations on this theme, he was still gripped by the passion behind Urban's words. For this pope was about to do what no other in history had ever done: take a living faith to his people across the world.

Urban had never revealed how or when the idea had come to him. It was staggering in its implications, limitless in its scope. The Vatican would scour its museums, cathedrals, monasteries, and churches, and put together an exhibition of its most priceless treasures for a world tour. Of the countless paintings, sculptures, tapestries, mosaics, and other objets d'art—the incredible full spectrum of Vatican treasures gleaned through almost two millenia—only the best would be selected. Only those that reflected man's greatest artistic and imaginative sentiment, the embodiment of his struggle to reach out to his God, his declaration to his Creator of all that was good in him, would go forth.

A spectacle unlike any other, the Tour would stagger and astound. The much-vaunted Tutankhamen exhibit would pale beside it.

"Have you an estimate of the number of pieces in the composition?" Urban asked.

"Sabatini at the Museum suggests no more than two thousand. Logistically and in terms of selection that is a sound figure."

"What of the arrangements with museums abroad?"

"These are all in place," the secretary said. "The exhibit will open in Boston at the Bennett Museum. It will travel west across the United States, moving north twice into the provinces of Quebec and Ontario. From the West Coast it will turn south, into Mexico and South America, then across to the African continent, north again to Poland. From there it will proceed throughout Europe."

"How will the exhibit be protected?"

"The diocese liaisons in each city will make suitable arrangements with the local police."

"The final cost?"

"All told, some seventeen million American dollars."

"Revenues?"

"One hundred million—at a minimum."

If Urban was impressed by this figure he gave no sign of it. He had already worked out an estimate of the Tour's final income. Di Stefano's estimate was only slightly higher than his own.

Urban never blushed when speaking of money. He fiercely cherished and fought for the independence of his faith. He had inherited a Church wavering on bankruptcy. The pragmatic politics of Paul VI had been left to wither by the generosity of John Paul II and his successor. Obligations to international bankers had grown while revenues from the faithful and their numbers had dwindled. The Tour would bring much-needed—desperately needed—funds as well as return the strays to the flock.

"It seems to us we are ready to issue the directive to our museum curators," Urban mused. "Have you the Letter of Instruction?"

"Sabatini is satisfied with the draft I presented him. It awaits your approval, Holiness."

The pontiff reached out and was handed the one-page directive his secretary had drawn up, instructing the directors of the Vatican *gallerias* to open their vaults for inspection by a panel of experts approved by Urban—fourteen men and women, lay and ecclesiastical, selected from leading universities, foundations, and museums across the world, whose responsibility would be to insure that only the greatest treasures in the Vatican repository were included in the Tour.

"This is good," Urban pronounced. "Dominic, you will tell the museums we have officially agreed to proceed. They are to make the necessary arrangements with their governments for the Tour's safe and unobstructed passage. Keep us informed of any difficulties."

Knowing from habit that the command signaled the end of their interview, di Stefano rose, then knelt and kissed the ring of the Fisherman. But he was wrong. The pontiff motioned him to sit.

"In all the discussions you and I have had about the Tour, something has been absent."

"Holiness?"

"Not in your organization, Dominic," Urban smiled. "That is unimpeachable. No, what we refer to is the intangible. We need a unifying theme for the exhibit, something that will serve not only as a centerpiece, physically, but be the one object that best captures and reflects the Tour's theme."

"Is your Holiness suggesting that we include a relic, perhaps the Shroud of Turin?"

"Yes, but not the Shroud. There is still doubt as to

its authenticity. We need an object that all of Christendom recognizes as being Holy, whose venerability is beyond question. Something that will inspire our people to reaffirm their commitment to the True Faith."

Di Stefano rose and walked over to the French windows, watching the gardeners remove the burlap sacks from the fragrant hedges.

"A miracle," he said, his voice tight, grim. Di Stefano was a man who solved the insoluble. He felt a personal stake in any directive given him by Urban, even if he must move heaven and earth to fulfill it. Sometimes he'd had to.

"Exactly. Find us that miracle," the Fisherman told him. "Scour every cellar, every vault. Bring us the treasure that has been overlooked. Yes, a miracle!"

That afternoon, under the imprimatur of Urban IX, the Letter of Instruction was delivered to the director of every *galleria* of the Vatican museums: Dominic Cardinal di Stefano would be leading a group of experts through the exhibits with the intention of collecting the finest pieces from each for the Tour. The following morning both the Vatican State Radio and *Osservatore Romano* devoted the majority of their time and space to a lengthy announcement of the Tour as prepared by the secretary.

Leaving the experts to their task, di Stefano set out on his own mission. He made a point to ask to see the *gallerias'* vaults and storage rooms, questioning the curators about objects that were not part of the public displays. The bewildered custodians complied with his requests, standing by puzzled as di Stefano rummaged through one century after another, whispering to each other that not even di Stefano knew what he was looking for. That much was true.

Whatever di Stefano was searching for he did not find it in the Picture Gallery, or in the Chiaramonti

Wing, or even in the august Court of the Belvedere. The enormous catalogues in the Museum of Christian Art yielded nothing. But he persevered, following the evaluators from one museum to the next, working eighteen hours a day for the ninety days it took to canvas what lay in the Vatican City proper. June passed into July, the height of tourism and chaos in Rome, the worst time to venture beyond the Vatican walls. But he had yet to visit the cellars and vaults of the papal summer retreat, Castel Gondolfo, the selected churches and cathedrals that lay as far apart as Ajaccio and Venice. The pace would have crippled another man, but Dominic Cardinal di Stefano kept on, seemingly tireless, ever alert, his eye keen, his questions succinct. He had received his instructions and as of that moment he had vowed to deliver his pope a miracle.

The last day of August. Still nothing.

The air was oppressive, laden with moisture from the thunder shower that had engulfed Rome that day and did not break until the early hours of the next. Dominic Cardinal di Stefano adjusted the air-conditioning unit in his study, then slipped into the high-back leather chair behind his desk. It was three o'clock in the morning, but he had at least another two hours of reading left.

He had travelled the width and breadth of the country and still he did not have his miracle. He had even prayed for it, but his prayers, like his efforts, seemed to have gone unrewarded.

But di Stefano did not surrender. Once again he pored over the computer printouts that detailed the known holdings of the Vatican museums, his third time through the lists. Somewhere, something had been overlooked. He sensed it clearly, felt as though he could almost reach out and touch the key that had thus far eluded him. Almost...

At half past five the papal secretary turned out the twin lamps on his desk. Dawn had broken, pur-

PHILIP MICHAELS

ple, pink, rimmed with a dazzling white, the promise
of another hot day. He was almost through the printout, with only the inventories of the lesser *gallerias*
to go, beginning with the Museum of Pagan Antiquities. He let his hand fall back against the leather
padding and closed his eyes. The pieces were all
there. He just couldn't put them in the proper order.

Pagan Antiquities...

At that instant, logic, reason, and memory came
into perfect equilibrium in di Stefano's mind. The process known as discovery was underway, the translation of the intuitive and speculative into a firm deduc-
tive course. Di Stefano was completely unconscious of
the process. He did not know how or why the discovery
took place, what chemical reactions within his brain
were necessary before it was born. He, like most men,
would have attributed the mystery of discovery to yet
another mystery: the hand of God, the leap into the
void, something that had no human attributes, which
descended upon man from a force greater than himself,
altering his life without the slightest regard for him,
using him as a mere vessel, an instrument toward an
end of which he is completely ignorant.

Di Stefano sat up abruptly, his eyes scanning the
mounds of paper on the desk top. As though guided by
an invisible hand, his fingers searched beneath the
stacks, withdrawing three separate items: the computer printouts for the contents of the Museum of Pagan Antiquities; the Museum's provenance catalogue;
and a two-page report he had unearthed from the Secret Archives:

The object that he had suddenly remembered was
listed as number 734 on the printout: A GREEK OR
ROMAN CHALICE OF THE PERIOD 50-100 B.C. The entry
was marked with an asterisk that meant the cup
was not on display. Di Stefano circled the entry and
placed the marked sheet to one side.

He checked the index of the provenance ledger and
turned to the designated page. The provenance for the

25

chalice consisted of a single entry: a copy of the original provenance, the accuracy of the translation certified by a long-deceased Museum director, attributed the testimony to the legate Tractus. It had been entered into the Archives of the Holy See in the year A.D. 926. According to Tractus, the cup had been given to him by an abbot of a monastery somewhere in Britain, to be taken back to Rome as a gift for the Holy Father, John X. There was no clue as to either the abbot's or the abbey's identity. No location. No hint as to whether the cup had been manufactured in Britain or had found its way to the Isles via traders. Nothing at all . . . except that the chalice existed.

Di Stefano marked this page and placed the ledger to one side.

The report. Dating back to 1767, written by Emilio Boglidaccio, the first director of Pagan Antiquities, it referred to the chalice held by the Museum.

I break with the oath of my office in committing such words to paper. Better that I should cease at once and burn everything I have thus far written. But I cannot permit such an event to go unrecorded. Those who follow me must be apprised!

The construction of the Museum of Pagan Antiquities has been complete for almost six months now. I, with several aides, have been bringing treasures to their new home from various other *gallerias* within the Vatican Library. It is a proud moment for us all, for although it is small, the display is truly remarkable. Of course certain special relics shall be kept in the vault. I have inspected the stronghold myself and found it complete in every detail. The construction, done to my particular specifications, has rendered it impregnable. Yesterday the locksmith instructed me in the method of opening and closing the door. He is returning to England within the week. The mold for the keys has been broken. I am the only one who can open the vault.

Thus today time came to bring these objects that we do not show into the safe. I saw to this task myself for no one, save my successor, may know what it is we are custodians of. I had removed all the items before I reached for the cup...I tremble as I write this. But I must continue. My joy is as great as my fear....

I took the iron box in which the chalice rests and immediately felt a warmth emanatihg from the metal. The heat grew stronger the longer I held the cup, so much so that I had to lay the box down. Without thinking I broke the seals on the box and opened it. Surely I couldn't have believed there was anything amiss inside the box—such an absurd notion! Still, for whatever reason, I broke the seals....

The instant I beheld the chalice I knew it could only be a holy relic. I knew that I, a humble and unimportant servant of the Lord, had been graced by His presence. Although it was dark in the stronghold, with no light except for a very small lamp, the cup glittered. It blazed as though a tiny piece of the sun itself had been imbedded within it. I swear by all that is Holy that I witnessed the cup shimmer, its metal turning molten...the miracle of transformation.

Smitten by such power I fell to my knees and prayed, prayed as one possessed, as only one who has set his eyes upon the Holy Grail could....

"The Holy Grail..." di Stefano murmured.

Was it *not* possible? On what stone tablet was it written that the Grail did *not* exist?

Di Stefano looked from the printout to the provenance ledger to the Boglidaccio report. Without the report he couldn't have understood the significance of the other material. The printout had told him the piece existed. The provenance confirmed this while at the same time informing that the chalice had come from Britain, the reputed resting place of the Grail, to Rome. Boglidaccio's words forged the two.

The Holy Grail.

Di Stefano read over Boglidaccio's words once more. Would they be enough? To start with, yes...But he would need more. He would require a paradox: irrefutable proof that the chalice was not a forgery. He needed proof of a miracle.

Di Stefano carefully confronted the awesome volume of material on his desk. Proof...In four days the Tour was to open in Boston, at the Bennett Museum. He recalled reading something about the Bennett, quite recently, in fact. Nothing to do with what he required. But something. He reached inside the left-hand drawer and pulled the file on the Bennett.

There it was.

A six-page bulletin from the Bennett Museum detailing another project to which Doctors Lauren Blair and Isaiah Webber, co-directors of the Antiquities Department, had successfully applied their latest dating analysis, a method far more accurate than the commonly used carbon-14 process.

Dominic Cardinal di Stefano was tempted to call the Holy Father immediately. But he knew better. Intuition told him that he had done the impossible. By sheer hard work and some logic and reasoning—and the grace of God—he had found a miracle for his pope. Of this he was certain. But intuition was not enough. It had to be supported by fact. There were several critical steps to be taken before di Stefano could even consider going to Urban. He did not dare to be wrong. Not this one time...

The cardinal rose and took a deep breath. Despite the hour and his lack of sleep, he felt vital, alert. At that moment the sun appeared over the horizon, flooding the study with light. Warmed by its radiance, the prelate turned toward it, and bowed his head in prayer.

CHAPTER TWO

MONSIGNOR ARTURO CAPELLINI, curator of the Museum of Pagan Antiquities, shivered. Brows arched up, eyelids snapped back, eyes that were usually calm and thoughtful stared up at the ceiling. His stare was of that of one confronted with stark terror, powerless before it. This time the monsignor awoke without screaming, but only because he had heard the persistent rapping on the door. His servant.

Arturo Capellini sat up, swinging his feet over the edge of the bed. His skin crawled as the cold morning air swept over it. As was usual after waking from the recurring dream, he was bathed in sweat. He reached for his robe and, drawing it tightly about himself, opened the door to admit the servant, the ancient Calabrian peasant, Bruno the Cat.

At first glance Monsignor Arturo Capellini appeared an aloof, distant man. Of average height, his pewter grey hair was cut *en brosse*. This, coupled with a lean, almost gaunt profile that ended in a jutting chin made for a severe countenance. But his blue eyes sparkled and danced behind iron frames and the smile below a nicotine-stained moustache remained fixed even when he was alone, as though he was recalling a particularly amusing anecdote.

You are not smiling this morning. He regarded his fading reflection as the steam rose from the copper tub, coating the mirror. *You have forgotten how to smile.*

The dreams had become more frequent. From once every few weeks to every second night.

Arturo Capellini had spent thirty-seven of his fifty-four years in the priesthood, two decades of that in the Department of Antiquities, ten years as director. As a trained archeologist, he had travelled to the remotest corners of the globe. His intellect spanned seven languages, four thousand years of history. Yet none of this was any defense against the dream. It pursued him relentlessly, shaking his soul as the terrier does the rat. In these cool nights of early October, not even prayer provided solace against the dread that had crawled upon him.

Capellini scrubbed himself with a rough sponge, shaved, and took a breakfast of juice and coffee in the morning room, overlooking the magnificent Spanish Steps. Bruno the Cat had placed three green and yellow pills in a tray beside the water glass, a silent reminder to obey the physician's directive. Shortly after the dreams had started, Capellini had undergone a medical examination. It yielded nothing. His constitution was that of a man ten years younger. The medication prescribed was a mild depressant, designed to prevent him from overtaxing himself. The curator was aware that Bruno was watching him. He felt a mild pang of guilt as he reached for the medication, which were actually sugar pills he had put into the vial in place of the real ones.

By half past eight he was at the *galleria*. Over another coffee, Arturo Capellini perused the morning mail and several newspapers. When the ormolu clock on the mantelpiece of his cluttered office chimed nine, he rose and walked along the balcony to the marble staircase. By now the anxiety of the night had all but melted away, the images of the shadows gathering in the boat only a vague memory.

The curator thought it a shame the Museum was

located next to the Vatican Library. Visitors usually
began their meandering at the Chiaramonti Gallery,
passing through the Round Hall and the Gallery of
Statues and slowing down at the Cabinet of Masques
before coming to a dead stop in the magnificent Court
of the Belvedere, which housed two of the most prized
pieces in the Vatican collection: the sculptures of Lao-
coön and the Apollo Belvedere. Once the visitor had
come out of his reverie he generally passed quickly
through the Museum of Pagan Antiquities to the Sis-
tine Hall. As a result, much that should be seen was
ignored.

Designed by Luigi Valadier on the command of
Clement XIII, the Museum of Pagan Antiquities was
completed in 1767. It resembled a private eighteenth-
century salon more than it did a *galleria,* housing
Etruscan bronzes and Roman ivories. The center-
pieces of the *galleria* were a chryselephantine statue
of Athena (Greek, circa fifth century B.C.) and the coin
collection, which drew numismatists the world over.

Arturo Capellini was justly proud of his museum.
Over the years he had added a piece here and a piece
there, gleaned either from the immense storage
rooms of uncatalogued material or brought to him
from digs across Southern Europe and the Near East.
For the last ten years he had reserved three hours
each morning—except when he was away on a dig—
to combing the storage holds.

"Arturo!"

The curator paused in mid-step, glanced down the
hall, and saw Dominic Cardinal di Stefano coming
toward him. The two men were not friends, in fact
barely nodding acquaintances. Capellini's work seldom took him near the papal offices while di Stefano
had no particular interest in pagan antiquities.

So why does he address me by my first name?

"Eminence," Capellini said, re-establishing for-
mality and, with it, distance.

"I was on my way to see you. Have you an appointment to keep?"

Although he had washed and shaved, the papal secretary could not rid himself of fatigue. His eyes were red, burning, his hands trembling as much from caffeine as nervous anticipation.

"No, I am going to the holds. Cataloguing. However if the matter is urgent—"

"A fortuitous coincidence. What I came to see you about concerns the vaults."

Capellini smiled. "Don't tell me you've had a change of heart and will include something from my modest collection in the Tour?"

Capellini had been mildly disappointed when the papal evaluators took nothing from Pagan Antiquities for the Tour. True, the museum's collection did not reflect the Tour's intent and theme, which was the propagation of the faith. Nonetheless the curator thought one of the exceptional pieces might have been selected. Even a portion of the coin collection. But he had not pressed the issue.

"You may be closer to the truth than you think," di Stefano told him.

"Then you should be looking through my display cases, not the vaults." Capellini led the way to a private elevator whose door opened with a magnetic key. He looked askance at the papal secretary.

"I regret I am not here to revise the evaluators' opinions of your *galleria*'s collection," di Stefano said tactlessly, looking directly at the stainless-steel sheets of the elevator door.

Then why have you come? What is it you expect to find in the vaults?

Deep, deep in his soul a wisp of uneasiness rose, the embers of an undead woodland fire.

"Nor to see anything that the evaluators saw or knew about."

"I'm not sure I understand, Eminence."

Di Stefano changed the subject.

"The usual method—and until recently the most effective—of dating historical objects has been the carbon-14 process. Is that correct?"

"Yes."

"You noted I said: *has been*."

"I did. The latest process is the Blair-Webber Spectrum Analysis, developed by Doctors Lauren Blair and Isaiah Webber of the Bennett Museum in Boston. According to independent evaluations, the process is effective and totally reliable."

"I am glad your observation concurs with mine," di Stefano said dryly.

The elevator came to a smooth halt. The doors opened on an enormous warehouse, a full two stories high. On the left-hand side were metal shipping containers, piled four high. On the right, in five rows running the length of the warehouse, were crates, six high, each one measuring the standard twelve cubic meters. Di Stefano stepped into one aisle, looking up and down, shaking his head.

"None of this has been catalogued, I suppose."

"Very little," Capellini admitted. "Not enough time, not enough hands..." Capellini shrugged.

"It is the same story everywhere," di Stefano acknowledged. "The Vatican Library has enough cataloguing for at least three hundred years. The other *gallerias* have as much if not more material." He turned to the curator. "Think, Capellini, of the trove we may be looking upon. I assure you that after the Tour, changes will be made. I will see to it you get your hands—the evaluators, instruments, funds...."

"Eminence, I am grateful for your interest in—"

"I have come to examine a specific object in your vault," di Stefano interrupted.

"I assure you there is nothing in the vault that would be of interest to you." The tone gave him away: harsh, flat, tinged with fear. A rebuke.

"So you would presume?" di Stefano asked, his voice a stiletto.

33

"I have been curator of this gallery for twenty years," Capellini said quietly. "The first and only time I was in the vault was on the eve of my predecessor's death. Since then the vault has been sealed. Nothing has been added, nothing taken out. If you wish I can show you the inventory ledger."

"Is there something in the vault you would rather I didn't see?" di Stefano asked.

What are you driving at?

Arturo Capellini willed himself not to voice the question. He had to lead di Stefano away from what he had come for... gently. Very gently.

"Eminence, this is the Museum of Pagan Antiquities. The artifacts placed here have been associated with heathen rituals. They have come down to us through the ages by way of pilgrimages, crusades, explorations in the New World, confiscations by the Inquisition. There is very little, if any, provenance for such objects. We know only what the old ledgers contain, impressions and opinions of those who first placed them in the custody of the Church. And their reports, I might add, are sketchy.

"There are also relics that are 'allegedly' holy, said to have belonged to saints and prophets. Scrolls, urns, tablets, that sort of thing. Two lances as well, attributed to Longinus, if I remember correctly. In short, even if there was an object of rare beauty to be found within the vault—and there isn't—it could scarcely be in keeping with the theme of the Tour. Which is to promote the Catholic faith."

"And this is why you are afraid, because some of the relics have a history of heathen worship?" di Stefano queried, his sarcasm mocking the curator.

"No, Eminence," Capellini said firmly. "I simply find it odd that you should concern yourself with objects of questionable worth."

"I concern myself, curator, because you have in your vault an object that could well become the centerpiece of the entire Tour."

34

Di Stefano looked keenly at the curator, the gaze boring into the other man's consciousness.

What has he come for? Dear God, what?

But Capellini said, "I believe, Eminence, you have been misinformed."

The papal secretary deposited his calfskin briefcase on one of the crates and snapped the locks. He withdrew the Boglidaccio papers and handed them to Capellini.

"Written by the hand of your earliest predecessor, confirmed by your own inventory sheets and provenance index. The cup that may be the Holy Grail."

The curator accepted the material and scanned the words. His eyes froze when they caught the reference to the Grail. At that instant the smoldering fears in his mind ripened into hot flame.

He dreamed with his eyes open, seeing himself standing on the shore of the Styx. Far out, in the gray-green mists broken by light that was not light, he saw the ferryman of the River that runs between Life and Death, making ready to row to the side of Life. He believed he knew now who it was Charon was bringing over, the group of hooded figures who stood at the prow.

I can save myself, he thought, *I can save all of us with a few words from my lips.*

But the warning died in his throat and he said nothing. He understood but did not want to believe that it was already too late.

Arturo Cardinal Capellini knew of the chalice that was in the vault of the Museum of Pagan Antiquities. He had never seen it but he knew it existed. His mentor and predecessor, the Jesuit archeological historian Father David Burney, had brought his pupil down to the vaults only days before his death.

Educated in England and France, Burney had worked on archeological digs around the world. Arturo Capellini, then a young priest, had been his assistant. From the arid plains of Syria, Iraq, and Turkey to the vast emptiness of the Gobi Desert, from the Serengetti Plains of Africa to the rain forests of the Amazon, they traced the path of Christian missionaries and priests with one objective: to unearth records of their encounter with religions already existing in a region when they brought Christianity there. In the thirty years he worked in the field before returning to Rome to assume the post of curator, Father David Burney increased the *galleria*'s collection threefold. But equally important, he devoted his later years to the drawing up of a set of texts that detailed the relationship between the Christian Church and the pagan religions it encountered. It was this knowledge and respect for the pagan that he passed on to Capellini.

David Burney returned from his last expedition a dying man. The Vatican administration, not unaware of his condition, pressed him for the appointment of a successor. The Jesuit called for his pupil and bade him sit and listen to what he had to say. He started by asking that Capellini remember all he had learned on the various expeditions, that he remind himself of the writings he had helped Burney compile. This would help him understand what was to come. Then David Burney revealed a secret he had been preparing his pupil for since the beginning of their collaboration, a notion so fantastic that it defied belief, knowledge held by no other man in the world. Swearing the younger man to holy secrecy, he told Capellini about the Fisher Kings of which he was the latest in a line. He spoke of the chalice that lay in the vault of the Museum of Pagan Antiquities, the cup that the Fisher Kings had guarded for over a millennium. He now bequeathed that responsibility to Arturo Capellini.

He urged Capellini to start searching for *his* successor at once, seeking out a man, just as Burney had done, who possessed the attributes to maintain the lineage and protect the Grail, the holiest of fonts, the only existing link between man and his Lord, even at the cost of life itself. He warned Capellini against those in the Church who might seek the chalice. They were to be dissuaded, no matter by what means. The Church was eternal but some of her servants were not above venality. He prophesied that scientific development relating to archeology and geochronology might one day drive the curious deeper and deeper into the vaults of the Vatican museums. One day they might even investigate the holds of the modest Museum of Pagan Antiquities.

The prophecy had come true.

By a chance intersection of one man's desires and his investigations and the existence of the Bogli-daccio notes, a secret preserved for one thousand years was about to be revealed.

The Boglidaccio notes... His predecessors suspected something like that could have existed. Boglidaccio's successor heard tell of an astounding final confession the first curator had made on his deathbed, a confession that was looked upon as the ramblings of a demented man, his brain consumed by the madness raging within his body. The confession had been dismissed. Nonetheless the Fisher King made passing mention of what he had heard, that Boglidaccio had allegedly witnessed some miraculous event and had committed details of it to paper somewhere.

Written of it. As Boglidaccio himself admitted: how could a Fisher King have even dared to *think* of putting down such thoughts on paper? No matter how awesome the alleged miracle! And why, in the name of everything that was holy, why hadn't the notes been included in Boglidaccio's formal diaries? So that his successor could have destroyed the testimony!

"I would like to inquire as to where you came upon this material," Capellini said softly.

"In Boglidaccio's own writings," di Stefano said. "Fifty years after his death an archivist discovered

these two pages sealed into a third, close to the end of
a volume. He simply added them into the body of the
text without any consideration of their possible significance."

The prophecy had come true.

An oversight on the part of Boglidaccio's successor, who, with what he knew, should have examined
all of Boglidaccio's papers meticulously. An oversight compounded because this Fisher King had not
left even a hint of anything untoward for his successors to find. So by caprice, a stroke of ill chance,
the beginning of the end.

And I too am guilty.

Burney had mentioned Boglidaccio, a good man
but overwhelmed by his task, a man who had been
too loose with his tongue. He'd warned Capellini
never to stop searching for errors among those who
might have succumbed to the temptation the first
curator had. To scour the works of Burney's predecessors, even his own writings, for the vaguest hints
about the Grail, words that were vague, ambiguous,
yet still clues set down by the unconscious desire to
share what could never be shared. In case an error
had been made. This too was part of his responsibility, to continually re-examine the past so that
what lay there would have no future.... And now he,
like those before him, had failed.

The prophecy had come true.

The dream of the chalice had stirred within a man
and he had come to Capellini demanding what he believed to be his by right, by virtue of his office and ti-
tles.

And I dare not give it to him!

"You agree there can be no question as to the authenticity of the seal of Boglidaccio's signature," di
Stefano said, not bothering to mask his impatience.

"No, I do not question that," Capellini said. He
paused because what he had to say next pained him.
Yet he had no choice.

PHILIP MICHAELS

"I would ask you to look at the date on that seal,"
he said. "Boglidaccio died the following day. Don't
you think, Eminence, that these are the words of a
man not in full possession of his faculties? Surely if
they had been believed then such a claim would have
been investigated? Furthermore, there is no evidence whatever to indicate that the chalice in the
vault is the Holy Grail. If you like, I will secure the
provenance so that you may study it. I'm certain our
conclusions will be identical."

"Curator, do you really believe I would be here with
you if I thought that?" di Stefano demanded. "I have
spent over a month investigating the Grail legend. I
have read *everything* on the subject, from the Song of
Songs to the most recent interpretations of the Galahad story. And my conclusion, based on the provenance you mention *plus* Boglidaccio's notes, is that
what the papal legate carried from Britain to Rome
in the year A.D. 926 was the Grail."

Di Stefano was amused at the curator's obvious
surprise.

"Yes, Capellini, I had the text of the legate's report
to John X brought to me from the Secret Archives.
When I read his words, I was convinced he had looked
upon the Grail and that *he* knew as much. Why is
it so difficult for *you* to believe? Can you understand
what authentication of the Grail will mean? The
Church will be able to offer profound proof of its role
to the faithful: that of the keeper of Mysteries, the
custodian of the Christian lineage. The discovery
and display of the chalice will be a symbol of the
Church triumphant—that from its history it can,
after almost two thousand years, summon up a miracle that defines its existence. The faithful will come
to see not only a relic from the past but an embodiment of the true faith. Think of the belief that will
be rekindled, the lives that will be transformed!"

But there was another aspect, Capellini thought.
Attendance at the exhibit will multiply tenfold if not

39

more. Extra bodies would mean extra wealth, the coffers of the Tour would be emptied and replenished, like the miracle of the loaves and the fishes.... The fact that he was even thinking this horrified him. Yet he was reacting to the nuances in di Stefano's words, to an undercurrent of which he was certain the secretary was unaware, the faint murky presence of corruption.

"Authentication," Capellini murmured. He had to try another tack, had to keep the waves of helplessness at bay.

"The Blair-Webber process. Do you not understand?" di Stefano cried. "Their geochronological process is effective beyond question. Both of them are at the Bennett Museum in Boston. The Tour *opens* at the Bennett. That is where the tests can be performed! It's as though Providence was guiding us!"

Providence...but which one? Capellini said inwardly. *You say you have read the legate's report. There are writings you know nothing of. The Palinurus parchment. The texts of my predecessors. You know nothing! Least of all that the cup cannot be removed from this consecrated ground!*

Even as these thoughts flashed through his mind Arturo Capellini realized he could not deny the papal secretary. If he did not open the vault for di Stefano on the secretary's authority, di Stefano would return with a papal directive. The only immediate course was to allow di Stefano to *see* the cup. If Providence was benign, the prelate would conclude for himself that the chalice was not what he imagined it to be.

And if it was?

"Very well," Capellini shrugged. "I will show you the cup. But I'm afraid you will be disappointed."

"Let us hope not."

The vault was at the far end of the storage room. Constructed by Chubb of London at the turn of the century, it was the size of a large walk-in refrigerator. Several years earlier, the security-alarm mechanisms had been updated, the door removed and replaced with one containing an *in situ* computer. Arturo Capellini inserted a key that released a small console and punched in the appropriate combination. When the computer accepted the information the second half of the sequence was entered. Unlike the door of most other vaults this one did not swing open. With a hydraulic sigh, the two-ton armor shield rolled slowly away to the right. The lights came on automatically. A rush of stale air swept past the two clerics, mingling with the pungent odor of the lubricating grease on the rollers.

The interior of the safe was ten meters by six. Humidity and temperature controls kept the air dry and cool. Imbedded in the ceiling were spigots for a dry-powder sprinkler system. Running from floor to ceiling were rows of shelves, separated by a large worktable. Several tools rested on the scarred wooden surface; chisels, a small hammer, a crowbar.

Di Stefano looked over Capellini's shoulder at the crates. They were short—no more than a foot high—most of them rectangular in shape. Two hundred, he reckoned. Perhaps more.

"Do you know what you have here?" he demanded softly, trying to move beyond the threshold.

"Yes," Capellini told him. "If you would wait here I will bring the chalice."

Capellini closed his eyes and summoned up an image of the exact location of the lead box. He moved down the center aisle, paused, then pushed aside two small crates. He grasped a lead box with both hands and, holding it against his chest, brought it over to the worktable. The curator picked up a chisel, hesitated for an instant, then guided the sharp edge to the first seal. He reached for the hammer. The sound of metal striking metal reverberated in the confines of the vault. Eight lead seals, fixed at each corner of the box three hundred years ago, gave way. With the tip of the chisel he pried one of the sides forward, then another and finally a third. The chalice rested on the last side.

In that instant the rim of Hell appeared over the universe.

Arturo Capellini heard a sharp intake of breath behind him as the chalice was revealed. As his hands reached forward to grasp the cup he also heard the scraping of shoe leather against the cement floor.

Dominic Cardinal di Stefano felt the tremor first, beneath his left foot, which was still on the threshold. Out of the corner of his eye he saw the immense vault door shudder. Then move. In the next second four thousand pounds of hardened steel was hurtling at him. Instinctively di Stefano jumped back. The fine edge of the door brushed his fingertips. The blood it drew cast a thin red stain, stark against the black matte finish.

Capellini turned just in time to see the door shut fast. The echo of steel upon steel resounded painfully in his ears. Had he, as most others would have, covered his ears with his palms, the horror might have been aborted. Instead, Arturo Capellini clamped his hands around the chalice.

Arturo Capellini's flesh began to burn. He tried to pry his fingers from the cup but they remained there, as if fused. The flesh was smoking, its acrid sweet stench filling the air. Capellini was rooted to the spot, his eyes transfixed by the immolation. Then the bone of his fingers appeared, white at first, turning gray then black as the heat charred it.

A new and different echo hurtled about the steel walls as Capellini screamed. Finally the echo and the scream became one and the same.

CHAPTER THREE

THE PRIEST was a young man, tall, ruggedly built, with the shoulders of an athlete. One of several anomalies that separated him from others of the cloth was his recruitment by the Celtics. He had applied to the diocese for permission to play but relented before the bishop's disapproval and returned to scholarly work. His expertise lay in religious art, especially in works that fused mythological elements and Christian teaching. His training had been completed in Rome, at the Museum of Pagan Antiquities under the tutelage of Arturo Capellini. It was in this area that he now lectured at Harvard University as visiting professor.

The priest was midway through his delivery. As usual the auditorium was filled to capacity, for his classes attracted not only those enrolled in Fine Arts and Religious Studies but students from other disciplines. He had charisma, and that rare gift of infusing those who listened with his own curiosity and passion for the subject. Word of mouth about such an instructor spread quickly. His popularity was envied by many of his colleagues.

The priest was speaking about the various levels of meaning ascribed to any particular religious symbol. How was it that an object came to represent a certain element in a religion? How, through the course of the religion's history, had its influence waxed or waned; how, after a time, had it been perverted? Suddenly he ceased to speak. He did not even speak the last word in his throat. His head snapped back and at once his face become mottled, shining with sweat. Those sitting in the front row saw the muscles in his forearms bulge out as his fingers tightened about the edge of the lectern.

I am burning. God help me but I am burning!

He willed himself to look down at his hands. They were hooked around the lectern like talons.

They are burning but there is neither smoke nor fire.

The power flowed from the corded muscles in his arms and chest and he snapped the lectern in two. The splintered wood fell away, clattering to the floor. The fire that was consuming him abruptly vanished.

Several students were clustered around him by now, anxious, holding him by shoulders, demanding to know if he was all right. For a moment he did not lift his bowed head but instead took deep breaths, trying to dispel the dizziness and clear his head. He could not tell them. He had no conception of what had overtaken him. He could not explain the terrible dread that had infused him, literally tried to consume him. The dread was gone now but its residue remained in his bones.

The priest pulled himself away from the anxious students, muttered a few words about fainting spells, and fled through the nearest door.

Arturo Capellini forced himself to eat the light supper of grilled chicken breast and overcooked vegetables brought up by the sister. As he ate, he listened to the faint cacophony of early-evening traffic that filtered through the windows of the private room at Salvator Mundi hospital. Then he pushed away the stand upon which his plate rested and looked up at the crucifix over the door. Then across to the clock on the night table. If he held his breath he could hear the sound of the digital mechanism. The sheets he lay between were warm and smelled faintly of starch. The pictures on the wall opposite the bed were in soothing pastels—yellow, orange, and honey brown. The little details. He had to make certain of the little details.

The prelate glanced at his hands.

He could not remember how long he had stood there, hunched over the cup, his fingers clamped to the metal. But he remembered the stench of roasting flesh and the color of bone as it changed from white to gray to charred black.

He could not recall when di Stefano had found him or how he had opened the door. Only that by then he was on the floor, his arms clutched around his belly, hiding the hands. When the papal secretary had tried to free his hands, the curator had lost consciousness.

Capellini glanced at his hands and brought them close before his eyes. There was no balm upon them nor any bandages. The skin was the color of a shell's interior, speckled with liver spots. The veins showed through the skin like threads of cerulean wool.

The hands were whole.

He remembered waking in this bed. Screaming when he looked at his hands and saw they were whole. Di Stefano had helped hold him down. The doctor was instantly by his side. There had been the momentary whiff of alcohol, the prick of the needle.

The doctor had returned later on in the afternoon with a colleague who wore a smart plus-four suit and smoked odorless brown cigarettes. Di Stefano was there as well. Capellini was asked what had happened in the vault after the door had closed in on him. The curator spoke of his hands burning as though it was an indisputable fact. He stopped short when he caught the others looking at him.

The hands were whole.

On a silent signal the physician and di Stefano departed. For the next hour the psychiatrist was alone with Capellini. He encouraged the prelate to speak about why he *thought* his hands had burned.

By this time the curator knew better. He answered the psychiatrist's questions in monosyllables, refusing to be probed. The damage was done. Although the psychiatrist addressed him with deference and spoke in a rambling way about the phenomenon of spontaneous combustion it was clear to Capellini that no one would believe him if he stood by his premise. His delicate treatment was accounted for by his position. One might consider a prince of the Church mentally unbalanced; one would not dare whisper such an opinion aloud. Even as the psychiatrist departed, murmuring confidently about hallucination caused by trauma and stress, Capellini knew the matter was not closed. In the Vatican, Dominic Cardinal di Stefano waited with his own queries. Behind him, Capellini felt the presence of Urban IX.

The curator of the Museum of Pagan Antiquities drew the covers back and swung out of bed. The linoleum was very cold against the soles of his feet. For a moment he stood by the window, watching the pink-purple twilight gather over the city, like an ink stain upon glass. Along the via Rapeta cars moved slowly, their foglamps a chiaroscuro of pale yellow-orange. Capellini understood what had to be done. He went into the bathroom, stripped, and showered. His clothing had been taken away, cleaned, and returned to the closet. The undershirt chafed because of the starch.

Adjusting the temples of his spectacles over and behind his ears, Capellini opened the door and glanced in either direction down the corridor. The sisters at the nurses' station were eating dinner. Twenty steps and he was in the elevator.

"What do you make of this?"

Urban IX leaned forward in the red-leather wing-back chair, pushing his feet a little closer to the fire that crackled in the grate. He wriggled his toes in the wool-lined slippers, squeezed the bridge of his nose between thumb and forefinger. His gaze returned to the object covered in chamois, standing on the marble coffee table.

"The psychiatrist Monti believes it to be a form of hysteria," di Stefano said.

Urban's voice was rich with irony. "The curator of the Museum of Pagan Antiquities, a man of scholarship and noted achievement—a scientist as well as a prince of the Church—is a hysteric?"

The secretary placed a buff file on the table before the pontiff.

"I took the liberty of procuring Capellini's health records. There seems to be only a single factor of any significance: three months ago he underwent a medical examination. It seems he was sleeping badly. The diagnosis was stress, strain from overwork. A mild medication was prescribed."

"And you say he was convinced that his hands burned when he touched the cup."

"He was. I think he is still so convinced, even though he would not discuss the incident with the psychiatrist when they were alone."

"Why?"

Di Stefano sipped the vintage port, setting the crystal goblet on the side table beside him. The flash of blue flame off crystal reminded him of something. He couldn't quite remember what.

"Capellini was reluctant, to put it mildly, to show me the chalice, Holiness. I believe that had I not informed him I was familiar with its provenance he would have denied the cup existed at all."

"Why do you suspect him of such deceit?"

Di Stefano shrugged. "Perhaps he has certain doubts as to the chalice's provenance."

"Are these warranted?"

"No, Holiness, they are not." Di Stefano dropped his arm and from the satchel at his feet pulled out an accordion folder with the imprimatur of the Secret

Archives across the side. The broken red wax seal slapped against the cardboard as he placed the file on the coffee table.

"Curious and more curious," Urban murmured. "Show me the cup."

Di Stefano rose and lifted the chamois covering from the vessel. The gold was so pure its glare drove straight into the eyes of both men. The flames in the grate seemed to reach out toward the chalice as though magnetically drawn to it. Fire flashed in the secretary's mind. Suddenly he was back on the threshold of the vault, the murderous door thundering down upon him, threatening to dismember him, the rollers hissing like serpents in their greasy track. He felt the razor edge slice into his finger. He stared in horror as the blood poured out of his flesh. The spell was broken. Realizing what had happened, di Stefano tried to pull the door back. He had placed both hands against the opaque face and strained. He screamed out for Capellini. Finally he had stepped back, staring at the silent barrier...until of its own accord, the door had rolled back.

The interior of the vault was filled with the stench of roasting meat. Di Stefano knew the smell well from the Naples abattoirs. He saw Capellini on the floor, kneeling, hunched over, his hands clutching his stomach, rocking from side to side. But he did not move toward him. His gaze was captivated by the chalice. Standing on the worktable, its brilliance reached out and drew him to it. He came to it somnambulistically and gazed into the depths of the bowl. The hundreds of whorls, so finely tooled he could not believe them to have been fashioned by a human hand, swam before his eyes, fragmenting, blending together, then dissolving until the cup was but a sheen of polished metal. For an instant, before he backed away, di Stefano thought he had discerned red flecks in the very center of the cup.

But he mentioned none of this to the pontiff. The

door had closed because of a defective mechanism. It had opened when Capellini, inadvertently or otherwise, had tripped the interior emergency release. He had not stared into the chalice at all but gone immediately to the aid of his brother...

"It is magnificent."

Out of the corner of his eye di Stefano saw the pontiff lean forward, his hands moving toward the cup.

My hands are burning!

"Exquisite..." Urban muttered, taking the cup in both hands and holding it before him, high, as though he were offering benediction.

The hands were unaffected. Just as di Stefano's had not burned when he had touched the chalice.

"I am grateful it pleases your Holiness."

The pontiff looked across at him. "You have brought us the miracle. The Tour is complete. We tell you, speaking from the very heart and soul, that this is the Holy Grail." Urban set the chalice on the veined marble table but his gaze never wavered from it. "What do you propose now?" the pontiff asked. "As far as the chalice is concerned?"

"Holiness, I have given the matter much thought. Today is the sixth of October. Tomorrow, two Alitalia air freighters will convey the Tour to Boston. The gala opening is scheduled three days from now. I would like to suggest the following: permit me to inform Leech that the Church is sending over a relic for testing. I have investigated the Blair-Webber geochronological process. It is fast, accurate, and utterly reliable. Naturally I would not even hint to Leech as to what we believe the chalice is until the last possible moment.

"On October 10th, I would convey the cup to Boston. But I will not stay. In my opinion my presence would cause undue speculation. Instead I will speak to Father Moran."

"Moran...a priest?" Urban queried.

"Holiness, it is true that on the face of it Edmund Moran does not have standing within the Church. But he is a Baldarese."

"Ah, yes. I keep forgetting his Baldarese connections. Of course I know of the boy."

"He calls himself what he wishes," di Stefano said. "But the upshot is he is a Baldarese. His discretion and integrity are beyond reproach. To date he has done a splendid job of co-ordinating the Tour while it is in Boston. I have no qualms about entrusting the chalice to his care.

"Further, Holiness, Moran is a scientist, an archeologist. He will, again in a discreet way, be able to oversee the testing, keep the Holy See informed as to exactly what is happening."

"How many people are to be told about the chalice's true identity?"

"Leech, Moran, Doctor Isaiah Webber, the co-discoverer of the process, and the man whom I will insist do the testing."

"Their silence is assured?"

"Without question, Holiness. The Bennett Museum has a vested interest in the chalice in that should the test prove—"

"*When* the tests prove..." Urban corrected him.

"Of course. When the tests prove that the chalice belongs to the proper geochronological era then both Leech's and the Museum's names will be associated with the discovery. Likewise Doctor Webber. I would think that is reason enough to agree to any conditions we might stipulate prior to the actual testing and final announcements. Furthermore, any premature speculation would be detrimental to their scientific inquiries."

"Indeed you have thought this out carefully," Urban commented. "A final question: what of Connelly, our venerable cardinal in Boston? Protocol would dictate he be informed."

"Not necessarily, Holiness. You may recall Connelly is almost eighty years old. He has petitioned for retirement from his post and spends most of his time at his home outside the city. It is Moran who actually conducts the day-to-day affairs of the diocese. I see no need to disturb his Eminence unduly."

"Of course," Urban murmured. He sat back, eyes riveted upon the chalice.

"We have the provenances of the legate Tractus," he said softly. "The notes of Boglidaccio. It is almost enough."

"If we have the scientific evidence, our claim to the chalice's identity would be indisputable," di Stefano finished for him.

"We ask you to inform us of the exact details involved in the testing," Urban said. "The cup must not be damaged in the slightest." The pontiff paused. "There is a final matter: Capellini. The chalice was found in his Museum...."

"Holiness, may I suggest that owing to his rather...indeterminate condition, Capellini not be informed of the Holy See's intentions. As soon as we have the conclusive proof I will tell him what has happened. It will be a great moment for him and for the *galleria*."

Urban considered the suggestion. "Very well—"

The soft whirr of the telephone interrupted him. Di Stefano rose and answered the call. Urban noticed his secretary's fingers turn white, so tightly did di Stefano grip the receiver.

"That was the attending physician at Salvator Mundi," di Stefano said, his voice harsh. "Capellini is gone. He was not discharged but simply left. The sisters think he slipped away during dinner. The hospital has tried to reach him both at home and at the Museum—to no avail."

"Find him!" Urban commanded. "Find him and bring him here. Until it has been proven that the cup is the Grail no one else is even to suggest the chalice exists!" The agate eyes glittered. "Find him!" he whispered.

Di Stefano reached for the telephone and jabbed at the raised digits. The duty officer in charge of Vatican security answered on the first ring.

Arturo Cardinal Capellini entered the Vatican through the gates on the Viale Vaticano. He made small talk with the sentry who examined his pass and asked after the health of the Swiss Guard who escorted him the length of the Vatican museums to Pagan Antiquities. When at last he was alone, the curator descended into the storage holds and quickly made his way to the vault. He inserted the key that released the computer console and entered the combination. Only when the vault door rolled back, as smoothly as it had that same morning, an eternity ago, did he feel himself tremble. He stared at the door, the reflection off the lamps above creating a crescent of light across its opaque face. It was mocking him, daring him to enter. If he tried it would kill him. It told him that.

Arturo Capellini did not have to cross the threshold. The interior lights had come on automatically. The hammer and chisel lay exactly where he had left them, to the right of the three lead plates of the box in which the chalice had rested.

The cup was gone.

A terrible anger seized Capellini. For an instant he wanted to rush to di Stefano and demand by what right he had removed the cup from a collection that was not in his custody, without the permission of the curator.

The door started to move toward him as he stood on the threshold, the wheels in the trough lapping up the grease like some hungry animal.

Capellini knew what di Stefano would say: he had acted on behalf of the pontiff. It was Urban who wanted the cup.

Capellini stepped back and the door sighed to a close inches from his face. He heard the faint clicks as the tumblers fell into place, the first and second combinations sealing the door in place. He backed away from the door, not trusting it. A moment later he was on the staircase moving swiftly toward his office.

He had no choice. Not really. Even though he was a prince of the Church, a figure who commanded respect even before the Holy Father, he would never be able to convince Urban to return the chalice. Not without revealing its true provenance. Even then would Urban believe him? Believe the writings of Burney? Of all the Fisher Kings who had come before him? No. He would be outraged that such a treasure had been hidden from him, from his predecessors throughout the centuries. He would accuse Capellini of usurpation. The chalice would move from the Fisher Kings to a man who did not understand it.

May God forgive me...

For the first time in over a millennium the chalice was on the verge of leaving consecrated ground. What would happen when that came to pass? What ancient horror that was *already stirring within the cup even as it rested in the Church* would return to life? Plague, pestilence, famine...

Capellini unlocked the door to his office. In the semidarkness he rifled the drawer of his desk, taking out his red Vatican passport, an envelope of office money, several credit cards.

Would Urban listen to him even after he returned? Listen to a cleric who had fled the hospital only hours after being attended to by a psychiatrist...a cleric who disappeared telling no one his destination or purpose?

From the closet he removed a black overcoat, red scarf, and gloves. It would be cold in Geneva at this time of year.

Arturo Capellini glanced at the luminous dials on

the clock face. The hospital would have noticed his absence by now. An alarm would have been raised, di Stefano informed. Then the pope. The curator didn't bother to lock the door on his way out.

Capellini entered the Via della Conciliazione just as a security team arrived at the Museum of Pagan Antiquities. He got into the first taxi in the rank, giving Leonardo da Vinci Airport as his destination. The prelate prayed his memory was accurate and that airline schedules hadn't changed. The last flight for Geneva should be leaving in just over an hour. He knew of a quiet, very private hotel on the outskirts of the city. Discretion was the byword. Just as it was in the Grand Banque de Genève where he would present himself tomorrow morning. There was another vault. Where the Palinurus manuscript was kept, and the records of the Fisher Kings.

The alarm would have been sounded by now. They would be looking for him. Arturo Capellini leaned forward and told the driver to hurry.

CHAPTER FOUR

THE STORM had started around midnight. At seven o'clock in the morning the sky was still dark, the rains tapering off to a hard steady drizzle. At Logan Airport jets were stacked, some holding up to forty minutes. But the flight Father Edmund Moran waited for was arriving on schedule. Standing a few feet away from the archdiocese's black Chrysler, the young priest turned his umbrella into the wind and watched as the Vatican Grumman Gulfstream touched down at the far end of runway.

On this, the day of the gala opening, Father Edmund Moran was five days shy of his thirty-sixth birthday.

He had been born in Rome, a stone's throw from the Vatican. His father had been an American, a wartime operative for the OSS; his mother, the beautiful and equally brave Therese Contessa Baldarese, eldest daughter of one of Northern Italy's ruling families. Both parents died when he was less than a year old. The wires connected to a cable car carrying twelve people up the Zurmatt had snapped, the car plummeting into the gorge. The bodies were never recovered.

Edmund Moran was raised by the patriarch of the Baldarese clan. His mother tongue was Italian, which he spoke in the staccato manner of a Roman born and bred. English, French, and German followed, the spectrum completed by Arabic and Mandarin Chinese. His intellect was matched only by his physical prowess. The boy who could argue the finest points in theology and philosophy was also a champion archer and equestrian. But there was a third, seldom seen, side to him, the contemplative, which, in the spring, bade him wander out into the rolling hills of the Campo Florio estate and there listen to the spring wind as it coursed through the wild flowers and heather.

On the boy's seventeenth birthday, the old Marchese Baldarese came to him and told him he must choose a calling. The boy asked if the Marchese would grant him his time for two days. The old man was puzzled but curious. No sooner had he assented than the boy had them packed and off in the car.

Edmund Moran's journey took them in a rough circle around Rome, some two hundred miles in circumference. They stopped for lunch at the magnificent Baldarese palace, where a kinsman had reached accommodation with Paul II, dined with monks from an abbey a thousand years old, and drank fresh young wine from their presses. The great houses of cousins once, twice, thrice removed opened their doors to them. The museums and churches they supported welcomed their visit with deference and respect.

When they returned to Rome, Edmund Moran said to the old man: "You have made me a part of the living past. Everything we have seen, touched, tasted, has become part of me. To belong to this family is to belong to the custodians of civilization. To belong to civilization is to recognize the source of all life: the Lord God. Therefore I shall devote my life to the study of civilizations, helping to unearth what came before us and preserve it. I shall do this for you and because I recognize the work of the Lord's hand."

The old man embraced him and wept. He had sons who would maintain and expand the empire he had inherited, who would swell the coffers of the Baldarese banks and lend greatness to the name. But he had only this one boy who truly understood *what*

he had tried to preserve during his life, to pass on
to the next generation, to teach by example. In these
young hands the spirit of the name of Baldarese
would be preserved.

Edmund Moran chose to attend Boston Seminary,
this in spite of the fact that he had never seen the
land he was still a citizen of. At age twenty-one he
took his vows and a degree of advanced standing in
theology. Upon presentation of a thesis on the history of the Baldarese family's art treasures, the
University of Bologna granted him a master's degree. Three years later, Harvard bestowed upon him
the doctorate for his work at archeological digs in
Israel, Syria, and Iraq, the basis for his dissertation
on the relationship between Christian and pagan
mythologies.

The combination of priest and scholar was the true
expression of his spirit. Every progression in his
work as an archeologist was balanced by the intense
wonder he felt about Creation. With every discovery
he experienced a sense of timelessness and a surge
of faith; each item he patiently removed from the
dust of the past reaffirmed his faith for the present,
his hope for the future.

It was only natural that such a personality should
come to the attention of the Vatican. Encouraged by
Antonio Cardinal Santini, a Baldarese cousin, Father
Edmund Moran left his work in the field and presented himself before the Vatican Discipline Committee. No less than seven museums and *gallerias*
had already petitioned the Committee for the services of the young, influential cleric who, although
he called himself Moran, nonetheless wore the signet
ring of the Baldarese. The Committee suggested to
Father Moran that he put his experience in the field
to work in Rome. In a rare gesture the Committee
permitted him to choose among the contenders.
When presented with the list, Father Moran asked

if he might select yet another *galleria*: the Museum of Pagan Antiquities.

Arturo Cardinal Capellini had known of the young priest. There was even a thin folder of correspondence between them in his files. But although their fields and interests coincided, Arturo Capellini did not, upon hearing of Edmund Moran's return to Italy, submit a request for his service. He was certain Moran would choose one of the bigger, more prestigious *gallerias*. The morning the young cleric called upon him at his office with his request to be permitted to work there was a turning point in both their lives.

The twenty-year difference in their ages hadn't the slightest effect on their relationship. Arturo Capellini's vast knowledge of his *galleria*'s treasures was itself a trove, one Edmund Moran mined with vigor. In turn, the young cleric's energy and enthusiasm infected the curator. They came to work as one, both in the field and in Rome, their goal to make the Museum of Pagan Antiquities a proud jewel in the Vatican crown. In the two years that had passed since Capellini's health had made further excavation projects impossible and Moran had accepted the Harvard post, letters and phone calls spanned the geographical distance at regular intervals. It was a comfortable pattern, highlighted by Moran's frequent trips to Rome. Until a week ago, when the pattern had been shattered.

Something is wrong, Father Moran thought to himself. Dreadfully wrong...

As the ramp was wheeled up, the hatch was drawn back and a steward stepped out, unfurling an umbrella. Dominic Cardinal di Stefano, gripping an aluminum carrier about the size of a Gladstone bag, appeared and quickly descended the steps.

"Eminence," Father Moran said.

"Father..." The papal secretary brushed past him, ducking into the car. Even before Moran settled beside him di Stefano had raised the electronically operated partition between the driver and passenger compartments.

"I am honored to meet you, Eminence," Moran said as the car started off.

"And I you," di Stefano replied. "I trust you have made suitable arrangements, according to my instructions."

"I have, Eminence. Archbishop Connelly is staying at home today. He has difficulty in such weather. He suffers from rheumatism. We will have complete privacy in his office at the cathedral."

"Very good. I'm sure that when you hear what I have to say you will understand the reason for this subterfuge. In due course I will make my apologies to Connelly."

"Does his Eminence wish to stop at a hotel first, to freshen up? The diocese maintains a suite at the Ritz."

"As I mentioned to you over the phone, Moran, my stay here will be very brief, just long enough to pass along to you your instructions."

"Whatever your Eminence desires," Moran murmured.

"Tell me, have you been to the Museum?" the papal secretary asked.

"Yes, last night, Eminence. The exhibit is stunning."

Di Stefano smiled faintly. "Good. His Holiness will be pleased. You are to be commended for the work you've done on our behalf, as our liaison."

"Your Eminence is too kind. Dr. Leech has outdone himself in the physical arrangement." Moran paused, then added, "It's unfortunate you won't be able to see his work for yourself."

Di Stefano did not rise to the bait. "I regret that as well."

By luck the drive into the city was one step ahead of the morning traffic rush. The bells in the tower of St. John Lateran tolled eight as the stretch sedan turned into the drive at the rear of the cathedral and came to a stop under the portico. Father Edmund Moran stepped out and opened the door to the archbishop's office. The papal secretary followed quickly behind him, the aluminum case swinging gently in his hand.

The priest turned on the twin lamps on either side of the desk.

"Lock the door," di Stefano told him, setting the carrier on the desk, then opening it and removing a rectangular box the length of a shoe box but twice as high. Using a small crowbar, he carefully pried back the sides until Moran saw an object sheathed in chamois. Di Stefano removed the cover.

Even though the light from the twin lamps was strong, the chalice took on a gleam all its own. Moran stared at it, mesmerized by the irrepressible power that streamed from it. Suddenly, in a gesture he could not fathom, his fingers curled round the crucifix hanging at his chest. Father Edmund Moran backed away from the chalice.

"Well, Father, what do you say?" The note of triumph in di Stefano's voice was unmistakable. Hearing no response he looked sharply at the priest. "Father?"

"It's...it's magnificent," Edmund Moran stammered.

"Do you know what it is?"

"Eminence, it reminds me of—" Edmund Moran could not bring himself to say the words. Impossible! It couldn't be!

"It is," di Stefano told him. "It is the Grail."

He heard thunder ringing in his ears, a dull ominous roar that filled his head with pain. He watched as di Stefano reached into the carrier and brought out an armful of books, ledgers, and papers.

"The provenance," he said. "As well as historical

material I have gathered together on the Grail legend."

"But where...?"

Di Stefano covered the chalice with the chamois. Immediately Edmund Moran felt the heat recede.

"You have never seen the cup before, Father?"

"Never, Eminence."

"You're certain, are you?"

"I don't think it would be possible to forget something as—as brilliant, if one had seen it."

Di Stefano regarded him steadily. "No, I don't think so. But I ask because the chalice was found in the Museum of Pagan Antiquities. And you, Father, are closely associated with that *galleria*."

Edmund Moran was stunned. "But if it was found in Pagan Antiquities, why isn't Cardinal Capellini here?"

"A good question. I was hoping you could provide me with an answer."

The young priest shook his head. "I'm afraid I can't, Eminence. In fact I don't understand what it is you're suggesting."

"Come over here," di Stefano said. "There is a great deal I have to tell you and little enough time in which to do so."

In the next hour Dominic di Stefano explained precisely how the cup had been unearthed. He showed Edmund Moran the provenances, explained to him why the cup had been brought to Boston, the secret arrangement, begun by di Stefano, which Edmund Moran would conclude with Percival Leech and Isaiah Webber for the geochronological testing.

"This is all quite incredible," Edmund Moran said slowly. "Has Cardinal Capellini offered his opinion?"

"When was the last time you spoke with Capellini?" di Stefano asked.

"Some two weeks ago, perhaps a little longer."

"You've heard nothing from him since, especially not in the last few days?"

"No, Eminence."

Di Stefano paused. "I know there is a close relationship between you and Capellini. But I ask you to believe me when I tell you that Capellini is not a well man. Last week he suffered a collapse, a mental breakdown. He was admitted to Salvator Mundi for observation and that same evening discharged himself against his physician's advice. He has not been heard from since. I was hoping he might have contacted you."

"Eminence, I don't know what to tell you," Edmund Moran said. "A breakdown! Arturo was in perfect health. True, he couldn't take the strain of expeditions or prolonged digs, but—"

"I realize what you think, what we all thought," di Stefano interrupted. "My point is this: if I myself had not witnessed his condition I would have had a hard time believing it."

"But what actually happened?"

"However I did," di Stefano continued, calmly ignoring the question. "Given his absence, I took charge of the chalice. I am now passing the responsibility for its safekeeping to you. Be very clear on this point: you are answerable only to me, and through me to the Holy Father himself. He has placed enormous trust in you. I have vouched for your ability to carry it. Please do not disappoint me."

Edmund Moran looked at the secretary. "You have paid me a tremendous compliment, Eminence. And if I should hear from Cardinal Capellini?"

"Find out where he is and call me at once, no matter the time of day. His Holiness is very concerned for the curator's well-being. We only want what is best for him. But he is not to interfere with the Tour or the testing of the chalice. *Not in the least*."

"If the cardinal's condition is as bad as you say it is, Eminence, then he needs help quickly," Moran said. "I have to try—"

"You have to stay here," di Stefano told him. "The Holy See will find him soon enough. You know we have the means."

"Will you please call me when you do?"

"Of course. Now if you have no other questions as to what has to be done..."

"Just one point, Eminence. You mentioned Doctor Webber as your first choice to direct the testing. That may not be possible. Isaiah Webber has been undergoing treatment for cancer. In the past year Doctor Blair has been responsible for almost everything to do with the TRACE process."

"I realize that," di Stefano said. "Still, Webber assured me that he can oversee the project. He also spoke very highly of Doctor Blair. Are you familiar with her background?"

"Professionally there is none better."

"And as to her religious beliefs? I don't want antipathy toward the Church to cloud the results."

"I'm certain that will not be the case. But I will inquire as to her religious affiliations."

"Do so. If there is any problem call me at once."

Di Stefano came over to the chalice and gently ran his fingers around the rim.

"I leave this in your care," he said softly. "You realize the meaning this discovery can have for our faith. The Holy Father will be very anxious to hear from you."

"I will see to everything," Moran murmured. "I thank you for your confidence. I shall not fail you."

The young priest kneeled and pressed his lips to the cardinal's ring.

Edmund Moran accompanied the papal secretary outside and watched as the car moved off down the lane. At Boylston Street it paused for an opening in the traffic, then turned and disappeared. For a few moments, Father Moran stared down the lane, seeing nothing but the blur of cars going by. Slowly he turned and went back inside, taking care to bolt the door. Without knowing why, he came over to the desk and lifted the chamois off the cup. He took two steps back and regarded the cup. He had no control over what happened next.

He saw the setting exactly as it had been that morning at Harvard. The sun had cleared the trees in the Quadrangle and its light was sweeping through the windows high in the back of the lecture hall, the glass acting as a prism, creating a spectacular aura over the students. He was standing at the base of the auditorium, facing his class, weight on his left leg, leaning forward slightly, hands on either side of the lectern. A student in the sixth or seventh row up, center, was wearing a beautiful green sweater; the girl below and to her right was chewing her lip while taking notes. There was a stack of 3 x 5 cards on the lectern.... There was...His hands were burning....

He saw nothing but his hands, withering, shriveling, heard nothing but the cracks of crisp flesh being consumed by an invisible fire. The lectern splintered, he collapsed to his knees, somewhere in the distance familiar voices were shouting at him, his students....

He had run from the lecture hall, run like one possessed down the corridors toward the nearest exit, crashing through them, then plunging into the Quad, into the brilliance of the fierce autumn sunshine. Only then did he dare look at his hands. They were whole. He stared around himself, a frightened, quivering animal, and fled toward the church at the foot of Merton Street. There he stayed until prayer dispelled the awful coldness within him.

"What are you?" he whispered, as though he truly believed the chalice would somehow answer him. "Where did you come from?"

He crossed over and jerked the leather covering over the cup, replacing it in the box and pressing the finishing nails into the grooves with his thumb.

And what in God's name had happened to Capellini?

In the course of the day, Father Edmund Moran placed over a dozen calls to the Continent. He sent telexes to various museums Capellini might have retreated to. He spoke with the curator's only relative, a sister in Bologna. The cardinal had not been there. He was not expected. He stopped calling Pagan Antiquities after a voice he did not recognize informed him that the museum was temporarily closed, its curator on a sabbatical. If Bruno the Cat was at the house on the Via di Spagna he was not answering the telephone.

At half past five Edmund Moran returned to his coach house on Chestnut Street in Cambridge. He telephoned Percival Leech at the Museum and told him the object in question had arrived from Rome. By the time he had showered and changed, two plainclothes security men from the Bennett Museum were waiting at his door.

CHAPTER FIVE

LAUREN BLAIR did not mind the rain. It was the kind of slow steady drizzle one associated with the countryside. Today it fitted her mood.

In the morning she made herself tea and settled back on the couch with newspapers and journals, reading, smoking, from time to time gazing out the window. The living room of the split-level thirtieth-floor Harbor Square condominium overlooked the Boston Inner Harbor. Fog rolled in across the Bay, sniffed at the wharves, then moved on into the city. Blasts from the horns of outgoing freighters, shepherded by tugs, punctuated Beethoven and Schumann at regular intervals.

After lunch she retreated to the den, whose windows overlooked the city, turned on the desk lamp and went to work on notes for tomorrow's lectures. Four hours passed before she knew it. She glanced out at the traffic thickening on Atlantic Avenue, then at her watch. While the bath was running she iced a bottle of champagne and two glasses. By the time he arrived the scent of Mitsouko enveloped her. Her jet-black hair lay in a brilliant cowl across one shoulder, the lapis-lazuli eyes setting off the smooth ivory of her skin, her pink lips, her one visible delicate seashell ear. At twenty-nine the promise of girlhood had been fulfilled, a beautiful woman had come into her own.

Then it all went to ratshit, Lauren Blair thought.

She was standing by the bedroom window, looking out onto the city but as oblivious to its detail as to her nakedness. She turned and looked at him in bed. One arm was flung out across the pillow, the other by his side. Strong shoulders, chestnut hair that curled at the nape of the neck, a strong face, chiseled nose, light mouth, pronounced jaw. Strength that was deception, that betrayed the weakness within him, weakness he loathed, fought against, could not bear. A man of striking attractiveness who still could not understand why other things did not come as naturally and easily as his physical beauty. As they hadn't today. When the Finance Committee had turned down approval and funding for his pet project, a South American dig on the north shore of Lake Titicaca in Bolivia. He had been so damn sure he'd get the money! Sure enough to let his classes slide, sure enough not to apply to other foundations for backup grants. Sure enough and lazy. So when what he wanted hadn't been handed to him, he went out and got drunk, on Scotch he couldn't hold, at the Faculty Club where his credit was already overextended and his colleagues' esteem low, on self-pity that became surliness and recrimination. God only knew what kind of scene he had made—and the repercussions that would invariably follow.

Then he comes home to me, she thought, anger flaring. *On the one night that's important to me he arrives blitzed, mutters something incoherent and drops off into oblivion. The one night that was to be ours. But if it couldn't be his as well, no one could enjoy it.*

She rubbed her arms, a shiver working its way down her spine, and came back to bed. She slid in beside him, slipping an arm under his head, pressing it against her breast. Love...goddammit! It tolerated no reason, no logic or common sense. For two years she had lived with it, revelled in it, suffered for it. Love would not let her go. Why?

She was the progeny of the American upper middle class. Both parents had been, still were, practicing professionals. Her father ran an exclusive medical clinic in Los Angeles. Dorothy Blair was chief executive of a holding company whose interests included a nationwide chain of pharmacies and security systems outlets tied into Montgomery Ward. As far back as Lauren could remember, she had been treated as an adult, spoken to as one, expected to conduct herself as a peer of her parents. In turn she received respect and responsibility, growing up fast, striving, always striving to contribute.

All well and good. She *had* succeeded, beyond anyone's reasonable expectations. Her relationships with men were, at worst, satisfactory, at best, delightfully abandoned. But they had always been brief. And they had always been ended by the man.

"You're too much for them, Lauren," a girlfriend had told her. "You move too fast, think too much, demand as much as you give. No one's asking you to play the dummy, but you've got to ease up, give the guy a chance to come to you before you devour him and spit him out."

Unfair, Lauren had thought. And said as much. But was it? She was beautiful and that made her desirable. She never lacked a bedmate. Her invitations out were legion. She had her success, she had her courtship. But not love. Of love she knew nothing at all. That was the one aspect of life in which she had had no instruction. Her parents had never spoken of it. She had to think hard even to recall when she had heard that word pass between them.

So perfectly equipped to deal with the outside world, she understood nothing of what it was to love, how one loved, why, what love offered, what it demanded. If it was so desirable, why did the words "I love you" bring a gleam of fear into men's eyes? Why did the same words, when they were whispered to her, sound so hollow, lies rattling around in passion-consumed mouths, words that scarcely veiled their true intentions?

For a time, because of her work, she could forget about love. Until Tim.

They had met in Chicago, at an archeological seminar. Lauren had gone to accept a prize on behalf of Isaiah Webber. Tim was the keynote speaker. Their attraction had been instant, mutual, and inevitably passionate. The fates appeared kind: both were to return to Boston, she to the Bennett, he to Harvard. Within three weeks of their return Tim had moved into her Harbor Square condominium.

Lauren always found the memory fascinating. Thinking back, she remembered how beautiful the first four or five months of their lives together had been. The next twelve faded in succession, the brilliance disappearing into a shine, the shine into shadows, the shadows into a neutral grayness in which two people merely existed, cohabited, tolerated one another...Where had love fled?

It had fled from his arrogance, which she had mistaken for self-confidence, an assurance she had thought confirmed his intellectual equality with her. Love had withered under his covetous gaze at her possessions, the money that brought elegance and refinement to their home. Love fled from his envy whenever she accepted a speaking engagement or contributed an article to a scholarly journal. That they were professionals in the same field came to work against them, for the disparities of their respective positions could not be hidden, overlooked, or denied: she was the more accomplished one, whose reputation even then was assured, whose future was destined, as though by magic, to be brilliant.

In the later months their lives were cleaved into two separate but unequal parts. The first was the professional, in which they co-existed uneasily, thanks to his skirmishes into drink, and the barbs and taunts that were the inevitable results, whenever his work failed to bring him the rewards he desired so badly, felt himself cheated of. The second, much smaller and falling at increasingly less frequent intervals was the love he turned upon her. Even then she believed he did love her. Or at least did very much want to love her. That was the memory she chose to keep: not the conflict, the rages, the unjust accusations or callous remarks. But the tenderness, those few moments when over a candlelit dinner he would take her fingers into his and caress them, how he would stroke and nuzzle her hair, the secret words that made her close her eyes, the sure gentle touch as he explored her body.

It was as though he knew.... He could deny her so much, punish and ignore her until the breaking point. Then flowers and wine and dinner at the Millcroft Inn overlooking the waterfall and drinks at the River Café. He knew, yes he did, just how much he could hurt her before exquisitely redressing the balance, leaving her sated, helpless, at peace.

Unlike others, Tim did not leave her. He stayed, a presence she loved and was a little afraid of. A man who exploited her one weakness, the love she craved and wanted so badly to give, a man who undeniably satisfied her when she needed satisfaction most.

Looking at herself, she felt the divine fool, fully aware of her condition, unable to bring herself to change it. Or at least that had been the case. Tonight the barrier had been broken. Tonight he had hurt her and offered nothing. Tonight he had forced her to realize that it was really over with, everything except the shouting....

"Better?" She handed him a perfect Manhattan on the rocks.

"Yeah."

The voice gave him away, gravelly, slightly hoarse. As did the marked trembling of the fingers when he reached for the drink. The nap and shower had helped but she was still saddened by what she saw. Suddenly Lauren had the image of Dorian Gray, blessed by eternal youth while in some closet a portrait of excesses rotted away.

They were in the dining room, Tim McConnell in his red Jockey briefs, Lauren in a smooth black evening dress.

"Sorry about that," Tim said.

"It's all right. *I'm* sorry about the results."

"Managed to get that much out, did I?"

The chuckle died in his throat and was quickly replaced by anger: What the fuck did she know about failure? Phi Beta Kappa at Wellesley, Briant Fellow at Harvard, member of the Lukas expedition to Egypt, and neither least and nor last, co-discoverer of the Webber-Blair dating process for historical objects. Piece of cake.

"Listen, I'm sorry," Lauren said. "There's always a chance for next year," she added lamely.

"No way, Stukley's pissed off at me as it is. He'll be digging beside that fucking lake next year, count on it."

"Can't you make some sort of arrangement with him?"

Tim shook his head. "Burned my bridges there, babe."

Pride. She persisted in spite of knowing better. "It's worth a try, hon. Stukley's a professional. He knows you've done a lot of research in the field, as much as anyone else. You'd be invaluable to him."

"So let him come to me! Might be nice for a change not to go begging all over town."

Stukley wouldn't do that, she knew as much. He could use Tim, no question of that. But Faculty would overrule the appointment even if Stukley proposed it. Tim was due to come before the Tenure Committee in January. He had to get his act together at the University, spend more time with his students, write that paper which was still germinating—a publishing requirement unfulfilled after two years.

"I'd better finish dressing," Lauren said. "The car will be here any minute."

Tim nodded and said nothing. When she was gone, he reached over to the buffet and picked up a shallow metal container. "Smoker's Candle." He lifted out the wax by the blackened wick and turned the bottom tray over. A rectangle of clear plastic fell out. Tim unwrapped it carefully and with a penknife extracted four good lines of cocaine, which he laid out on the smoked-glass dining-room table.

"Rock and roll..."

The MacDonald's straw was just the right size. Nice even fit into the nostril, smooth, unimpeded draw.

He felt the rush immediately. The stuff was that good. And from somewhere he'd have to get $2800 for another ounce. It was the best. It was what kept him going. He hung his head back, letting the dissolving crystal flow to the back of his throat, then padded into the bathroom to rinse his nostrils. Tim McConnell wondered how much *pura* he could buy in Bolivia for $2800.

The Bennett Museum, a sedate piece of architecture, dated back, as its discreet founding stone read, to 1910. The wrought-iron gas lamps heralded from the turn of the century and tonight, as every night, they were the only light upon the black-grey granite blocks that made up the façade. Only two police cruisers, with patrolmen in dress uniform, were indications of anything out of the ordinary. The limousines arriving at the front steps were scarcely noticed by the few faculty and students hurrying down the street, huddled under umbrellas. The gala opening of the Vatican Tour was, by design, an understated affair, reserved for Patrons and Money, the two not necessarily interchangeable. Tomorrow would be a different matter.

Because parking was something of a problem on

narrow, cobblestoned Merton Street, the Museum had insisted on providing livery service for its guests.

"Lauren?"

She turned away from her reflection in the limousine window. His eyes were dilated, cheeks flushed.

"I'm happy for you, truly."

He squeezed her hand.

She returned the squeeze and smiled. She had learned the meaning of limitations a long time ago. It would have been perfect had Tim not gotten drunk, if he had made love to her in the afternoon, if he could truly share her joy and pride in her achievement. But he could not, not now, not yet. The completeness of the moment eluded her. But what didn't change was the fact the her work had brought her the reward she needed as much as love: respect.

Lauren Blair had begun working with the Museum Director, Isaiah Webber, five years earlier, toward the end of her work on her doctoral dissertation. She started out in the research assistant pool but quickly proved that her interest in pre-Christian and Christian antiquities was matched only by her voluminous knowledge of the field of archeology as a whole. And if that wasn't enough, she also had a minor in physics and mathematics, giving her a solid base from which to develop new methods of dating historical objects. Webber gave her her head, opened museum vaults for her inspection, procured grants for studies in London, Cairo, and Jerusalem. Under his tutelage, Lauren completed four years of basic field work in two, after which he took her on as associate, his alter ego in the laboratory search for a geochronological process far more accurate than the carbon-14 method.

Isaiah Webber had been working on a new approach to the dating of historical artifacts for over a decade, changing his methods as new and more refined instruments became available. A year earlier, he had admitted he had reached a *cul-de-sac*.

Given the computers, the electron microscopes, and spectroanalysis synthesizers at his disposal, he felt he should have isolated the key to the new process. In fact he almost had—until the cancer bit into him like a reptile, sucking away his strength, denying him the energy to finish his work. At that point he brought in Lauren Blair.

Not at all surprisingly, she literally attacked the problem. His computer time tripled. The library started to complain about the number of overdue volumes. His phone bill—calls to London, Aix-en-Provence, Rome, and Jerusalem—was astronomical. Webber shielded Lauren from these mundane details. He would not permit such a combination of talent and dedication to be concerned about departmental budgets.

Yet the rewards were most tangible. One morning almost six months to the day after she started, a telephone call interrupted Webber's sleep at five o'clock. In spite of his condition the director was out of bed, into his clothes, out the door and at the lab within twenty minutes. Three hours later he too was convinced. Lauren Blair had found the process that had eluded him.

In the aftermath—the excitement of the find, the incredible possibilities that lay ahead—Lauren didn't care that only a tiny fraction of the world knew, much less understood, the magnitude of her achievement. Taking Webber's work to its logical conclusion, Lauren had unearthed the key to time itself. The process Webber had begun and she completed could definitively pinpoint with unerring exactitude the date of any artifact, using literally a smidgen of organic matter. Countless pieces in museum collections, hitherto undated, could now be catalogued. The lamp posts on the road to man's past could be made brighter, the possibilities for his understanding himself, if he so chose, increased a hundredfold.

An awesome contribution, as evidenced by the letters, offers, and invitations that inundated her office from universities, foundations, and clubs around the world. But greater than all they promised or could ever give her was the feeling of wholeness the discovery had brought her. She had contributed to human knowledge. She had tasted immortality, as all men wish.

Tonight it *could* have been perfect, if only Tim...

"Babe?"

She snapped out of her reverie.

"The door's open. We're here."

Lauren shook her head. She gathered up her purse and slipped past the driver. The fresh water-laden air made her gasp, then Tim's arm was around her, an umbrella held close to her hair, guiding her into the elegant crowd that flowed smoothly from sleek cars up the steps and into the night reserved for them.

The beaten copper doors of the Bennett Museum opened on a regal atrium, with soaring vaulted ceilings, white-green-veined marble floors with a Fasano fountain as centerpiece. Beyond the fountain and up a few steps was the Grand Salon: two hundred feet long, seventy wide, forty high. It was here, under the myriad of chandeliers, in display cases of polished mahogany and Lexam armored glass, that the Vatican exhibit came to life.

"I can't believe it!" Lauren breathed as they paused at the small proscenium that overlooked the salon.

Tim McConnell had no answer. The magnificence, the sheer power and glory of what he beheld silenced him.

The exhibit flowed from the left side of the room to the right, in a serpentine fashion, to allow for smooth circulation of the guests. Beginning with sculptures, roped off by maroon velvet cord, the viewer was swept along to the religious masterpieces representing seven artistic traditions, from the earliest iconographers to Leopardi's most recent commission for Urban IX. The vividness of the oils tapered off into magnificent architectural miniatures that gave way to a host of religious artifacts: crosses, chalices, scepters and orbs encrusted with diamonds and the almost unknown lapis lazuli, inlaid with purest ivory, the most delicate shell. In the carefully constructed avenues, moving like wraiths under soft winds of refined conversation and discreet appraisal, were the five hundred notables. It might have been a scene out of the court of Imperial Russia or Vienna at the time of the Hapsburgs.

Tim McConnell had been at Harvard for almost a decade, as student and instructor. He thought he had come to accept the presence of money and power, the sheer weight it carried. But this! The Vice-President of the United States, two Cabinet officers, two Justices of the Supreme Court, the Governor of Massachusetts, and the Mayor of Boston surrounded by a bevy of their officials, luminaries from the arts and letters, science and business, men whose wealth was outstripped only by their power, others whose intellect rivalled that of the machines they conceived and controlled. And naturally the media. But not reporters or commentators. Walter Cronkite and the Chairman of the Board of CBS; their opposites at NBC and ABC represented by John Chancellor and David Brinkley. There were no cameramen on the floor; instead they had been given the gallery above the Grand Salon as their exclusive vantage point.

A glittering world. Fame, wealth, and power compressed, distilled like the essence of rose petals. His world for tonight. He wanted to make it his forever.

"I trust you both are suitably impressed."

Both Lauren and Tim turned round at the same time. The voice, low-pitched but underlined with unquestioned authority, belonged to Dr. Percival Leech, Chairman of the Board of the Bennett Museum, Ambassador Extraordinary to the President, Fine Arts evaluator and patron.

"My dear?"

"I never expected anything like this," Lauren said.

Percival Leech permitted himself a smile. Only a shade over five foot five, with a Napoleonic belly, his commanding presence emanated from the eyes, unyielding agate, reinforced by the thrust of his jaw and his magnificent arched eyebrows.

"I agree: the Church has outdone herself."

He addressed Tim McConnell: "And you sir, what is your opinion?"

Tim couldn't tell if there was any sarcasm behind the words. "It's overwhelming," he said softly, not looking at Leech. "Somehow very familiar..."

Lauren glanced up at him, frowning. How could it be familiar? Tim had been in Rome only two days in his entire life. Even if he had *slept* in the Vatican he couldn't have seen a tenth of what was presented in this room.

"An unorthodox observation," Leech commented dryly. "Well, come along. No, wait, here he is."

"Laurennnn!"

His wiry hair askew, rim bifocals threatening to slip over the edge of his Bergerac nose, the irrepressible, scarecrow figure of Doctor Isaiah Webber bounded up toward them, somehow maintaining his balance on the smooth stone steps.

"Laurennnn!"

Oblivious to decorum, Isaiah Webber hugged her, held her back, smiled, then kissed her on both cheeks.

"You are late!" he scolded. The German accent became slightly more pronounced when he was excited. "I have been telling everyone about you. You must come with me—at once!"

Isaiah Webber favored imperatives in his speech.

"Isaiah, you're marvellous!" she laughed, and kissed him back.

"Tim!" Webber pumped his hand enthusiastically. "I may have her—with your permission?"

McConnell smiled and bowed gallantly. "By all means, Doctor."

As they departed arm in arm into the throng, Tim McConnell heard: "How very droll."

But when he looked around, Leech had vanished.

Webber was on familiar terms with almost everyone and introduced Lauren with a paternal pride. In between pleasantries and snatches of conversation she managed to have five minutes alone with him.

"You're looking much better, Isaiah," she said carefully. "The treatments must be helping."

Webber toasted her. "The *shamans* at that overpriced clinic can't make head or tail of it," he chuckled, Adam's apple bouncing furiously. "I've gained five pounds, Lauren! Can you imagine, *five pounds.*"

Lauren stepped back and regarded him carefully. Isaiah had been rail-thin to begin with. The leukemia, diagnosed sixteen months ago, had reduced him to little more than a skeleton. Even then, when his condition was deteriorating and the outcome starkly obvious, Webber had refused to tell her the truth about the pain he lived in. His levity was the constant mask that hid his torment.

"Oh don't stare at me like that, it's embarrassing," he scolded her. Lauren reached out and hugged him.

"You are getting better," she said softly, squeezing his arm. "God, Isaiah, I'm so happy!"

"God had nothing to do with it," Webber said.

"All right, so He had nothing to do with it," Lauren relented. "You wear your atheism like a badge. Tell me, Isaiah, do you really believe it's root extracts and apricot pits that're helping you?"

The Claybourne Clinic outside of Boston, the retreat Webber had been admitted to, worked strictly with homeopathic medicines. Admission to the program was limited to those patients diagnosed as terminally ill and who had a physician's certificate attesting to their condition. Only in this way could the clinic offer its treatment, taking advantage of an obscure loophole in the Massachusetts health laws that permitted the terminally ill to seek what was considered extramedical treatment.

"You're still skeptical, aren't you?" Webber teased her.

"How can I be?" Lauren shrugged. "Last year the best doctors in the country gave you no more than three months. Even Sloan-Kettering passed on you. You beat the odds, Isaiah. Hell, there were *no* odds! For you, Claybourne provided a miracle. They gave you back your life."

"My life and my work," Webber corrected her. He touched her hand. "You have been a faithful pupil. My dear Lauren...when you made your breakthrough on the TRACE, you did not forget me."

"Isaiah!"

"No, it's true. I do not exaggerate. You picked up the research when I could no longer continue. Without you the TRACE program would have atrophied. Someone else would have continued...everything would have been lost."

"Isaiah, I only put the pieces together," Lauren protested. "You had ten years invested in the development of TRACE."

"Years made worthwhile because you saw the efforts to their fruition."

Webber's eyes were shining. "This is your night, Lauren, not mine."

"Mine? What do I have to do with the Tour?"

"I want you to stay behind after the others leave, yes?" Webber said.

A private party—that was her first thought.

"All right, I'll ask Tim—"

"Not Tim. Only yourself."

Not a party. Business. She could feel it in the quickening of her pulse.

"Isaiah, is anything wrong?"

"No, nothing is wrong," he said slowly. "There is something I must discuss with you—only with you, yes?"

"Sure," she answered helplessly.

"Good." He patted her hand. "We will be done within the hour. I will meet you in the foyer. Make your apologies to Tim."

"Isaiah, the priest, standing near the end of the Pre-Christian exhibit, who is he?"

Webber pushed the glasses up his nose and peered, not at all discreetly.

"You noticed," he murmured.

"I couldn't help but," she said. "He's been looking at me for the past twenty minutes. I'm sure I've seen him somewhere...."

"He is Father Edmund Moran, Vatican liaison for the Tour. He will explain everything."

"Edmund Moran, the archeologist," Lauren started. "Of course..."

He cut a lone figure standing at the corner of Montigue and River Streets. To his left, the evening traffic flowed smoothly around the crescent, tires hissing off wet asphalt. To the right was the park, with its orange lamps vaguely defining cinder paths. A hundred feet away, a small gazebo shimmered as headlights flashed off the wet paint.

The man adjusted his red muffler around his neck, twisted his umbrella slightly and looked at the back wall of the Bennett Museum. The tall stately windows were awash with light. Even at this distance and with the traffic around him he could hear the strains of music being played by the University Chamber Ensemble. He drew back the sleeve of his black overcoat, and looked at the luminous face of his watch. Another half-hour before the gala ended. Not so long. The man lowered his umbrella against the winds and began walking toward the gazebo. He had made one entire circuit of the park already. His legs ached as much from arthritis as from the hard gravel as it dug into the soles of his shoes. But he had to walk. He could not sit still for more than a few minutes. Not now.

Cathy Windsor, her clear plastic umbrella held at an angle, ran across Bayview. Her momentum carried her across the sidewalk. She felt the ribs of the umbrella bump against something.

"Gosh, I'm sorry."

The man smiled kindly at her and moved aside to let her pass.

"Sorry," she called back over her shoulder and continued on, boots crunching over the gravel.

Cathy Windsor had left the Business Administration Library twenty minutes earlier. This week, her boyfriend was working nights as well. The car was in the garage, eating up her overtime. But she didn't mind the walk home, even in this weather. Twelve hours of dry hot air left her drowsy and irritable. Some fresh air, even if she was wet, should help her sleep. Between students and campus police patrols one could walk at virtually any hour. Cabs took half an hour to come even if the dispatcher told the driver he'd be getting a Boston run.

Cathy glanced over her shoulder at the man following her. If she hadn't bumped into him, seen what he was wearing, she might have been worried. Until the police caught that maniac who got his jollies chopping up women... She was passing the gazebo when something reached out, sweeping her off her feet, hurling her against the gazebo railing. Her coat and dress were shredded, her breasts and stomach burned as though a row of knives had passed over them. She couldn't see anything because her eyes were being gouged out. That was when she screamed, and continued screaming, not realizing there was something over her mouth.

Her legs were forced apart, knives burned tracks into her abdomen, deep, so deep. And the smell...the pain in her womb... She was bleeding. God, she was bleeding. Something hissed in her ear. Then she died. In the blinding instant when the razor slashed between her legs.

In a final fury her body was heaved against the gazebo post and was supported there for a second until it dropped in a bloodied, broken heap.

The man in the black overcoat and red muffler saw everything. He could not, did not want to believe what was happening. Nor could he move. The carnage happened so quickly that he was still paralyzed when the horror was finished with the girl.

Now it saw him. And started toward him.

"We have been waiting," the horror rasped. "Waiting for you..."

Then he was running, off the path onto the slippery grass and into the trees. He heard something move on his left and desperately flung his umbrella in that direction. He kept on running, oblivious to the branches snapping across his face, not daring to look back lest he once again see that unholy visage bearing down upon him, its jaws open to shred him and carry him back to Hell with it...

The lights over the left half of the Grand Salon had been extinguished, the exhibit fading as gently as a film dissolves until there was almost no definition to the individual pieces. Over the right-hand side, dimmers had reduced power by two-thirds. Three spotlights brought forth the richness of the tapestry threads, casting a warm glow over the adjoining alcove with its burnt-orange easy chairs and marble coffee table.

The plainclothes security detachment, an elite squad headed by an equally special inspector, discarded its formal attire for more comfortable clothing—black turtlenecks, trousers, and sneakers, the side arms now worn openly in shoulder holsters, two-way communicators clipped to their belts. Throughout the night, they would patrol their assigned areas of the museum in two-man teams. The contingent was headed by Inspector Francis Xavier Donnellan, the only man in the Boston police force to hold that rank.

"All in all, a success," Percival Leech pronounced, lighting a Romeo y Julietta.

They were gathered in the alcove, Percival Leech standing, Webber, Lauren Blair, and Father Edmund Moran seated on the semicircular sofa. The Chairman drew smoothly on his cigar, savoring the flavor, and regarded Lauren.

"For the benefit of our young colleague here I will go over some old ground," he opened.

"A few days ago, His Eminence Cardinal di Stefano, the papal secretary, conveyed a message to me. It seems that a curator in one of the Vatican museums had unearthed a rather interesting piece—a chalice—which, the Church hoped, could eventually be included in the exhibit. However, the provenance attributed to this artifact indicated that it might in fact be something more than an exemplary period piece. His Eminence had heard of the new dating process developed by Webber and yourself and requested that I arrange for the chalice to be tested by this method while the exhibit was in the city. I took the liberty of accepting on your behalf."

Lauren paused, her gaze shifting to the priest.

"I was informed that Father Edmund Moran would be acting as liaison between the Holy See and the Bennett Museum, that he should be kept abreast of every development in the testing no matter how trifling. We're all familiar with the good father's expertise in archeology. I don't believe the Church could have made a sounder choice in this instance.

"Father Moran, if you would continue from this point..."

He was too good-looking for the cloth, Lauren thought, admiring the easy and gentle way he had moved, this in spite of his obvious strength and athletic prowess. As if he had picked up on her thoughts, Edmund Moran glanced at her, a hint of a smile upon his lips.

Edmund Moran had been watching Lauren ever since he had caught a glimpse of her moving among the crowds on Isaiah Webber's arm. He was familiar with her reputation, had read her academic papers and followed the development of TRACE very closely. But even though they worked in proximity to each other, their paths never crossed. In the maelstrom of Harvard that was not all that unusual.

What was it about her? Moran asked himself, conscious that he was still looking at her.

Even though he adhered to the vow of chastity, Edmund Moran nonetheless appreciated and got on easily with women. With more than one he had felt carnal temptation rising. Not so here. The attraction was undeniable, strong, persistent. And, he was certain, mutual. But there was something more, something that lay behind her beauty and intelligence, something that drew him toward Lauren Blair yet at the same time made him fearful, uneasy....

"Thank you, Doctor Leech," he said at last. The voice was mellifluous, with the slightest trace of an accent.

The priest paused, closing his eyes for an instant, summoning back the long conversation in which di Stefano had recounted the history of the chalice. His gift of recall did not fail him.

"I would like to begin by saying that the object in question comes from the vaults of the Museum of Pagan Antiquities. The title is appropriate in that the collection is composed primarily of artifacts that once belonged to the rituals of other religions. Primarily but not exclusively. The chalice is a case in point.

"There is a provenance regarding the chalice, originating in the year A.D. 926. It was written by the papal legate who carried the cup from Britain to Rome, and is the basis for the Church's concern about this piece."

"Concern, Father?" Lauren Blair spoke up.

The priest regarded her calmly, the smile disappearing from his lips. "It is conceivable, Dr. Blair—certain if the provenance is taken at face value—that the chalice is the Holy Grail, from which Christ drank at the Last Supper, which caught His blood when the spear of Longinus pierced His side."

"You're not serious!" Lauren exclaimed softly.

"Very much so."

She rose and paced a few steps, unable to control her excitement. "That's incredible! And the chalice has been in that vault—"

"The Museum of Pagan Antiquities."

"Pagan Antiquities, for over a thousand years."

"Within the Church for that length of time. In the Museum since 1767."

"The implications are phenomenal," Webber murmured. He turned to Lauren, placing a hand on her arm. "I will explain later why you were not informed of this beforehand."

Lauren brushed the apology aside. Her imagination had been ignited, her mind churned. "What exactly does this provenance contain that it leads you and others in the Church privy to this matter to suppose the chalice is the Grail?"

"Let me go over the story of the chalice as it is recognized by the Church," Father Moran said. "The cup used by Our Lord at the Last Supper was crafted in the Holy Land. Who the artisan was and how it came to rest on that table, that particular night, is unknown. After the Crucifixion, Joseph of Arimathea, Jesus' uncle, removed the chalice and took it with him to Britain. Joseph was a wealthy tin merchant who had a profitable trade between Britain and the coastal ports of the Mediterranean and the Near East.

"At this point the story of the Grail begins to fade. We know Joseph established the first Christian mission in Britain, on the site which is now Glastonbury. Obviously this chalice must have been an important focal point for the faithful. However, nothing more is written about it. The silence that falls over the Grail lasts over eight hundred years until the legend of the Quest is born.

"You remember the Arthurian Romances about the quest for the Holy Grail. These recount the exploits of Lancelot, Galahad, and Bors, who sought to find the Castle of Corbenic, the home of the Fisher Kings who were said to be the descendents of Joseph and the guardians of the chalice. Each quest failed save—according to legend—that of Galahad, who found the Grail but never lived to return with it to Camelot.

"There was, however, another knight who has never been mentioned in any of the Romances— Brideshead. He makes his first and, to the best of my knowledge, only appearance in the provenance of the papal legate. From what the legate set down we learn that a wounded knight arrived at the abbey of St. Gallen in the fall of the year 926, carrying with him a chalice. The abbot, Palinurus, had no doubt that what Brideshead had brought with him was the Holy Grail. No reason is given for his certitude. However, Palinurus was so convinced that he dispatched one of his scribes, Matthew, to Ictus, now St.-Michael-by-the-Sea. Matthew was to convince the papal legate, who was departing Britain at the time, to come to St. Gallen."

"Does Palinurus say where Brideshead found the chalice?" Lauren interrupted.

"In the north country, by our reckoning somewhere near the present border between England and Scotland."

"And the knight?"

"Nothing is ever heard from or about Brideshead."

Father Moran paused. "The legate writes that upon his arrival, he and Matthew found the abbey of St. Gallen overrun and sacked by unknown invaders. Palinurus and the rest of the order had been murdered. But the cup, hidden away, had not been discovered. After burying the dead, the legate departed for Ictus. He concludes that Matthew refused to travel with him. A later account, rendered by the abbot Simon of Ictus, states that Matthew disappeared. His body was never found."

"Quite the incredible tale," Isaiah Webber said softly, leaning forward, elbows on knees, long bony fingers intertwined. "And the Church has never made the legate's parchment available to scholars?"

"Never."

Webber put on an elfin grin. "Even though the addition of Brideshead to the Grail myth would bring forth a slew of doctoral theses?"

"In spite of that," Father Moran smiled.

"So the Church is basing its opinion that the chalice is the Grail solely on this record," Lauren murmured.

"I think it would be fairer to say that if your tests prove that the chalice dates back to the period of Christ, then along with other details your method would furnish, the provenance could be the capping stone."

"Has this parchment been dated geochronologically?" Lauren interjected.

"No."

"Would you have any objections to our testing it?"

"The Church does not consider this necessary," Percival Leech said. His tone indicated that the subject was closed. Its force caused Lauren to stare at the Museum Chairman.

Isaiah Webber picked up the slack. "Father, I'm well aware of your reputation and therefore assume you're familiar with geochronological procedures. What is it, precisely, that you require of us?"

"The chalice has never been subjected to any scientific testing," Father Moran said quietly. "As you will see, it is composed of metal and a shell inlay. The Holy See asks that you find an accurate date for the cup based on these components."

"To determine whether or not the cup was made before A.D. 33," Lauren finished.

"Precisely."

"And if that should be the case?" she asked.

"Then I would suggest rechecking its structure against representative pieces of the same period with a view to finding any discrepancies in either design or manufacturing techniques."

"And if everything proves positive then, along with the legate's parchment, the quest for the Holy Grail may at last be over," Webber finished quietly.

The enormity of these last words silenced the group.

"The impact upon the Christian world would be staggering," Leech said. His voice was stern, seemingly untouched by the awe that held sway over the others. He spoke with a strange certainty, a finality that suggested he had glimpsed the future and knew exactly what lay there.

"This is one reason the Holy Father chose this moment to bring the chalice from its resting place," Father Moran agreed. "In this time of uncertainty and doubt, a reaffirmation of the living faith would indeed be a miracle. The Grail would form a new bridge between the Church and her adherents. For the first time in almost two millennia, the faithful would be able to gaze upon, in some instances even touch, that which had been graced by their Savior."

"I would like to see the chalice," Lauren said. "I presume it is in the city."

"It is," Father Moran said. "In fact, it is in the Museum at this moment. There is one more detail I should mention beforehand. Absolute secrecy must be observed with anything having to do with the chalice. The Holy See is most anxious that there be no rumors and hearsay about its existence. I think you can imagine the furor that would inevitably erupt if word got out about such a possibility. Both the Holy See and the Museum would be inundated with inquiries. Speculation would run rampant, your work placed under unnecessary duress. On the other hand, by observing secrecy you will be guaranteed as much time as is required. Then if the results are positive the Holy See and the Museum can coordinate the announcement of your findings. Statements can be prepared and you will have the opportunity to draft your own responses to questions the media will inevitably pose. I trust there are no objections to such conditions." He looked at the two scientists, receiving nods of assent.

"In that case, perhaps we can proceed—" Father Moran started to say.

"One moment!" Percival Leech held up his hand then turned back to the security agent at his side. His expression remained impassive as the whispered exchange continued. "It seems there is a problem," Leech said, addressing the others. "The chalice is in the fail-safe vault which is set on dual combination. I have one. The other is with the director of security who is absent from the premises at the moment."

"What's happened?" the priest asked.

"There has been an accident on the Museum grounds. Donnellan has gone to investigate."

CHAPTER SIX

THE BENNETT MUSEUM jealously guards slightly more than three acres of prime Cambridge real estate. Bounded by Montigue Street, River Street, and the diagonal Merton Street, the property is an almost perfect triangle. Beyond the delivery bays nestled in the northeast corner of the Museum lies a parkland with posted orange lamps that illuminate the gravel paths. To the north, the park borders on Hoyt Field; along its southern perimeter is a quadrangle used for local exhibits in the summer. The small gazebo is frequently in use as a student necking station. Francis Xavier Donnellan later calculated that at least three coats of industrial-strength white paint would be needed to hide the blood splattered along the sides and base of the clapboard structure.

The quandrangle resembled a battle zone. On the perimeter were the police flatbed trucks whose giant klieg lights bathed the woods in a hot white glare. The lamps were steamed as their heat met the cold night air. Farther along the perimeter, at the beginning of the gravel trail, was an ambulance, its back doors open to the gazebo. A series of smaller lights on individual tripods lit up the gazebo, catching the smooth movement of men as they stepped over the generator cables, moving around what had once been a human body.

Inspector Donnellan rolled down his car window and flipped out his I.D. for the patrolman. The officer nodded and motioned for his men to lift the barrier. Donnellan nosed the sedan in beside the ambulance.

He got out of the car, wrapped his trenchcoat around him, and moved down the path. At the foot of the gazebo he passed a police photographer being sick, his camera lying shattered beside him.

"Dropped it when he started heaving," a voice beside him growled softly. "Now we're waiting for another goddamn camera."

"Hello, Gerry," Donnellan said softly.

Gerry Samulovitch was one of the few Jews on the Boston police force. The only one who worked homicide. A lanky soft-spoken individual, famous for his custom-tailored three-piece suits, Samulovitch's face was said to be a map of Israel, so sharply semitic were his features. But his men—blacks, Irish, and others—loved him because he looked after them. He fought on their behalf in the Commissioner's office, before the Appropriations Committee, in the P.R. Department of the Mayor's office. He went to bat for them whenever there was a less-than-righteous shooting. He remembered their wives' names and the birthdates of their kids. That was why, even though his squad drew the ugliest assignments, his men never quit on him. It was only natural that Samulovitch had landed the Mack the Knife case.

"I expected you ten minutes ago," Samulovitch said conversationally, shielding a match from the wind, relighting a half-smoked Gitane. He had a weakness for things French.

"Traffic."

"Such wit. You want to have a look?"

"That's why I came."

Samulovitch took hold of Donnellan's arm. "Bube, it's bad, very bad."

Samulovitch had fought in two of Israel's wars. He had seen bad. *Very* bad he had spoken of only to Donnellan, a veteran of a different war. No one else could stomach the details much less understand them.

Samulovitch led the way to the body, speaking softly to his people, who moved away. To a man they turned their heads as the detective kneeled and drew back the dark green plastic sheet.

Donnellan flinched. He didn't turn, inadvertently take a step back, or squeeze his eyes shut. He flinched. That was how Samulovitch knew the sight registered. It had to. Even though the corpse was prone it was obvious that its head was all but severed from the torso, clinging to the neck by fragments of cartilage and muscle. The eyes hadn't been closed and stared out in the final terror that had carried the victim to her Maker. The entire chest had been ripped open, the breasts shorn away. Most of the organs had been gouged out, leaving a hideously vacant cavity.

Donnellan was no longer surprised that the photographer had been unable to finish his shooting.

"Enough?" Samulovitch asked.

"Enough."

The homicide detective gently pulled the tarp back over the corpse.

"Positive I.D.?"

Samulovitch passed him a familiar card sheathed in plastic. The color photo showed a girl, no more than twenty, grinning shyly at the camera. She was photogenic. The picture made her look very attractive. Donnellan looked down at the covered body. That lovely face had literally been ripped off the skull.

"Found it in her handbag by the steps. Nothing appears to have been taken. Her wallet's intact. Thirty bucks and change. Ms. Cathy Windsor worked part time in the Business Administration Library. We'll know in a few minutes if that's where she was coming from."

Donnellan handed him back the I.D. "Who called it in?"

"A campus foot patrol. Two greenies, first week on the beat." Samulovitch threw his cigarette butt on the ground in disgust. "One fainted. . . . Francis Xavier, I don't like this at all. For a number of very good reasons. The murder occurred on what are technically university grounds, which means campus security as well as the Cambridge Keystone Cops will be howling for a part in the investigation. Second: the killer is undeniably Mack the Knife. To accomplish such a filleting one would have to be a strong man, skilled in the use of weapons, probably a nice kosher knife. It's his M.O. No copycat killing here."

"You have problems," Donnellan agreed sympathetically.

"I'm not finished," Samulovitch said. "Three: this is a sensational murder. Young co-ed, probably a clean kid from a good family. I'm going to have that yenta Commissioner and the press on my back from the word go."

"If there's anything I can do—"

"I'm not finished. Four: this undoubtedly means I will have to postpone my trip to Israel. I'll lose my deposit."

Samulovitch always finished up with black humor. There weren't enough tears in a human being to weep over everything he had seen in the last fifteen years.

"Forensic's arrived with another paparazzo," Donnellan said, looking across at the light-blue panel truck pulling up the pathway.

"I hate this monster," Samulovitch said suddenly. His whole body stiffened, blood draining from his face. "I wish to God you were with me on this."

"Cathy Windsor makes five?" Donnellan said.

"Five," Samulovitch said hoarsely. "One a week until a few days ago. Two this week. You know what the psychiatrists will tell me: the crazy is revving himself up. The blood lust is catching up to him. He's going to be pulling down three victims next week, maybe four.... As many as we let him have..."

Samulovitch had been handed the case on day one, when the first disembowelled body had been discovered behind the Registrar's Office on the opening day of fall term. The press had a field day with the grisly details. Mack the Knife was born.

He took another girl the following week. Then a third. The Director of Campus Security finally received the Administration's permission to arm his men. Women, students or otherwise, were warned not to walk alone on campus after dark. In spite of the warnings, no one listened. Mack the Knife took down number four, a sophomore from Wyoming, not twenty yards from a passing campus patrol. The next morning the Cambridge Police officially requested Boston Homicide, which until then had only been "assisting," to take over the case.

The terror set in. The same kind of crazed victimized terror Donnellan remembered from the Strangler days, when people passed one another in the street without a word, glanced suspiciously at strangers, locked their doors at night. The kind he imagined haunted the citizens of Manchester and Birmingham when the Ripper was reincarnated. The kind the blacks in Atlanta knew so well when their children had been victimized.

Five killed... how many missing? The official reports said three, all from out of town. Donnellan didn't believe that. There had been more, taken from among the drifters, the runaways, illegal aliens, those not likely to be missed. When he thought of them he imagined a house somewhere, with a cellar, and the girls in that cellar, possibly still alive, until Mack the Knife came downstairs to quench his sick thirst, the knife blades gleaming in his hands....

"Send duplicates of the reports to me—not to the office, to the Museum," Donnellan said quietly.

"Exodus 21:23?" Samulovitch asked.

Donnellan nodded. He understood Samulovitch's sentiment perfectly. More so than usual because the clock in the bell tower across campus began to toll midnight. It was morning, October 17.

Two years ago, October 17th had fallen on a Monday. They had spent the weekend with his Da in County Cork, he, Kathleen, and the two boys, Samuel who was six and Sean a toddler of three. The days on the farm had gone by too quickly. No one wanted to leave. But there were other relatives waiting in Belfast, promises of a long-overdue visit to be kept. They boarded the Belfast Express as scheduled, at Lyme station. The time was half past nine, October 17th.

Francis Xavier Donnellan was forty-four then, his wife twelve years his junior. He had married late, as he jokingly said, because he had never had time earlier. There was some truth to this. Frank Donnellan had been the youngest captain on the Boston police force. But the other half of it was that he had known for a long time what it was he could offer a woman and what he wanted from one. Until Kathleen he had not found her. Ambition, hard work, and promotions alleviated some of his loneliness, but there were those hours when he would suddenly awake and look at his current bedmate, wishing for something more.

The express arrived in Belfast on schedule. Disembarkation was chaos. No sooner had the train pulled into its sidings than throngs of well-wishers descended upon it. A half-dozen relations greeted the Donnellans. Hugs and kisses and assorted exclamations. As they moved off toward the baggage depot, another train was pulling into a parallel siding. Donnellan saw it out of the corner of his eye: Royal Mail freight—a single locomotive, one passenger and three freight cars. The passenger carriage had a fine mesh grille over its windows. Military. The cargo was either one hell of a lot of currency or bullion, or weapons.

Lord God Almighty!

Donnellan raised both arms as though he was about to embrace both Kathleen and Samuel when the first explosion detonated. The charges had been buried in the gravel chips of the railbed between the sidings. As the Mail freight had slowed almost to a crawl, the bomber permitted the first three cars— cargo—to roll by. The remote device had been activated directly underneath the center of the fourth car, the troop carrier.

The force of the explosion snapped the car in two. Two smaller charges ripped through the halves, leaving nothing of the carriage but twisted metal and splintered wood. Had it not been for the high sidings, the blast would have propelled all the wreckage straight into the crowds swarming around the Belfast Express. As it was, the echo of the explosion shattered the glass dome of the station, showering those below with glass and soot that had lain undisturbed for over a hundred years.

"Down!" Donnellan roared, the terror of his voice piercing the screams around him. For a single agonizing instant Kathleen, holding the baby Sean, turned around to face him, her incredulous expression pleading for an explanation. The machine gunners opened up. She jerked toward her husband, falling forward into his arms, knocking him down. All around him Donnellan could see people crumbling to the dirty concrete. His ears were vibrating to the staccato hammer from the Armalite AR-180's, bullets clearing a path toward the Mail train for the killers.

Then silence. He twisted his head so that he could see the freight. Hooded men ran quickly, silently to the doors of the baggage carriages, their backs covered by others who squatted in the midst of the dead and dying, barrels leveled at the entrance gates. Charges were slapped by the door hinges, wires inserted, terminals fixed. Three short explosions blew the doors, a volley of gunfire ended the Quixotic resistance of the guards inside.

He felt blood on the palm of his hand where it rested on Kathleen's back. One part of his consciousness told him she was dead. Another, the professional, was mesmerized by the smooth brutality with which the theft was proceeding. The goal was money after all. Three small armoured vans drew up, one to each gaping carriage door. The dull thud of money bags hitting the reinforced metal floor could be heard. Then the slamming of iron doors, the quick retreat of the sentries, engines being gunned...

Donnellan gently rolled over, placing his hand under Kathleen's head. He rose to his knees, staring down at her. The bullets had passed right through her and into the babe Sean. In death she was still holding her child. Slowly he turned round. Samuel lay a few feet away in a position so grotesque it seemed he had been lifted and thrown bodily to the concrete. The relatives who had come to greet them were also dead, held in one another's clutches, lying under strangers. Donnellan staggered to his feet, surveying the carnage that stretched as far as the exit gates. Then he threw back his head and howled, his grief flying high up toward the shattered dome and out over a stunned, terrified city.

Monday, October 17th, two years ago.

He brought the family home to Boston and after a quiet service buried them in the Catholic cemetery in Marblehead. The following day he resigned his commission on the police force, put the house up for sale, cashed in the bonds and securities that had been meant for his sons' education. Twenty-four hours later he was in London. It took a week to reactivate his friendship with the military attaché at the American Embassy, a man with whom Donnellan had trained in Vietnam. Who owed him his life. He accepted the condolences and quietly called in his markers. Another five days elapsed before a pair of suitably anonymous gentlemen called on him at the Connaught Hotel, settled him and his bags in a Rover saloon, and departed London for the rolling hills of Kent.

In the next six months, Frank Donnellan, the

American "observer" at the Special Air Service compound, ran ten miles a day with a twenty-kilo pack, losing twelve pounds of fat and replacing some of it with muscle in the process. He also scaled walls, traversed precipices, and forded ice-cold steams, dusted off his knowledge of firearms, camouflage techniques, silent killing and demolition, and learned to kill using only the most common household objects. From Kent he moved to West Germany, whose combined BND–Army Intelligence computer banks held the most detailed information on international terrorists. Since the IRA group that had carried out the Belfast Station Massacre had never been positively identified by British intelligence, Donnellan drew up his own list of suspects gleaned from the German files, thanked his hosts, and left for the States.

He figured he had four to six weeks' edge on the killers. The money taken from the Mail freight would be used to buy arms. No question of that. But only four months had elapsed since the bloody theft, too soon to have laundered the funds, too soon for a major arms transaction to have been effected. But he knew where the deal would be coming down: what had been his home—Boston. A coastal port, within easy driving distance of the major American armament factories scattered throughout New England, a city that boasted considerable numbers of IRA supporters and bagmen. His own people. He would be going after his own people. That consideration held no sway over him any longer.

Donnellan did not stay in Boston proper, where his face was too well known, but in Bell's Woods, fifty miles away. By day he put the finishing touches on his operation, piecing together the equipment he would need. At night he took two meticulous hours to transform his face into that of a man ten years older, and headed for Lower Town, into the beer parlours and gambling dens, the Sons of United Ireland clubs and community centers where the newly arrived gathered. Night after night he sipped Bushmills or rich dark Guinness, listened and watched. When challenged he produced his release papers from Belfast's infamous Maze Jail, where the British interrogated, incarcerated, and usually interred their IRA prisoners. No one asked questions after that.

Donnellan called it perfectly. Five months almost to the day of October 17th, the first face from the German computer banks appeared. Two days later, another. By the end of the week, five. He had no fewer than three opportunities to take out the lot of them. But Donnellan waited. He followed, observed, correlated movements to and from Colt, Remington, and the Army bases in between, checking these against the activity in Boston harbor.

On the night of the tenth day after he had spotted the first face, Donnellan, dressed in scuba gear, slipped into the garbage-strewn waters of Boston harbor, swam to the Liberian-registered freighter *Talisman*, and attached eight high-intensity limpet mines set to blow just before dawn. Back on shore at two in the morning, he exchanged the diver's outfit for standard black camouflage gear. A stolen Chevy got him to the condominium tower in the exclusive Hanover Hill section of the city. He negotiated the highly touted security without difficulty, slipped into penthouse suite 3201, and without disturbing those who slept there set two nerve-gas cannisters, primed for release an hour later. Then he headed back to the piers.

At six o'clock, just as first light struggled over the horizon the crew of the *Talisman* began to board the ship. Donnellan stationed himself twenty feet from the gangplank, observing the sailors as they staggered and wheeled themselves on board. The five came, as he knew they would, complete with duffel bags and woollen caps. Donnellan stepped out and called softly to them. Only two words: "October 17th."

Their immediate recognition of the date was betrayed by an attempt to reach for guns. But the five never had a chance. Donnellan leveled the barrel of the Ingram and emptied the clip of .380 subsonic ammunition in two seconds. Walking over to the twisting twitching bodies, he calmly inserted another clip and emptied it as well.

Five minutes later the industrialist who had laundered the blood money and procured the shipment was dying slowly in his bed in Hanover Hill, not understanding what was happening to him. As Donnellan walked off the pier, the *Talisman* shuddered and blew apart, the destruction wreaked by the limpet mines being helped along by sympathetic detonations of over four million dollars' worth of arms and ammunition in crates labelled INDUSTRIAL OILS.

Donnellan looked back once over his shoulder, at the searing wreckage, at the bodies of the five killers who had stolen the love out of his life. And he walked.

Later the same morning, after he had scrubbed his face clean and washed up and donned his favorite Donegal tweed jacket, he presented himself at the Commissioner's office. He asked for his old job back.

They knew. Downtown they knew who had set fire under the IRA. Many were glad the job had been done. The IRA was becoming too influential in the life of the city. Others branded Frank Donnellan a traitor. But no one dared move against him. The fact that there was no evidence did not entirely account for his being left alone. They were afraid of him.

The Commissioner couldn't give him back his old rank. But neither did the department want to lose him. So the Mayor himself created the new title of Inspector for the man no one trusted, an office allocated but seldom used. They called on Donnellan when the job was too delicate for the official hand, too violent for anyone but the hollow man. They gave him the job and turned him loose, never expecting to hear another word about the matter, verbally or on paper.

That was why he had drawn the Bennett Museum

assignment. If anyone was going to hit the exhibit it wouldn't be a nimble cat burglar or alarm-systems team. Terrorists. A fast brutal frontal assault. Putting Donnellan inside with his handpicked team—and advertising the fact—was like sending out a personal message to the outlaws: Don't.

The communicator clipped to the breast pocket of his jacket sounded. Donnellan glanced at the digital clock imbedded in the dash and signalled acknowledgment. That would be Leech wanting access to the fail-safe vault.

Donnellan was tired. He wanted to go home, take a hot bath, sleep a dreamless sleep. Last night, as he walked through the silent exhibit, he paused now and again to look at the pieces. Then he retraced his steps and marvelled. He had never before seen such beauty, a beauty different from the one he found in the quiet of the country. Looking at a painting or statue, he could see the artist striving for that perfect expression of his vision, always believing himself to have fallen short, always taking up the tools for the next attempt. Here were masterpieces upon which men had lavished years of their lives, at the expense of prosperity, responsibility, health, perhaps even life itself. Yet they could do nothing else. Such single-mindedness, such sense of purpose, he understood. What troubled him was the fact that the work of these men would live on, endure, touch countless other lives as it was now touching his. These were the builders, the contributors. He was the protector and the destroyer.

When he walked through the exhibit still another time, Donnellan was filled with an inexplicable sadness. When he had had love he felt close to his God. When he had lost love to the bullet he no longer needed God. Once he too had created, in his own small way, for his family. Now he destroyed in their memory. There was something very wrong in this, very wrong.

Sometimes, when there was a long lapse between assignments, he even believed he might take courage from such creation, return to the land of the living. Such hope was ashes in his mouth now. Cathy Windsor, twenty years old, had been denied her life, denied even a dignified death. Lying there, she was nothing more than a shredded carcass.

Who would want to hurt you so badly, Cathy? What horror did you open that it devoured you?

Donnellan knew he would, inevitably, answer the question she could not. He had not had to look at the body again before agreeing with Samulovitch about Exodus 21:23. He would very likely live by its terms when he was certain he had the maniac.

> Life for a life
> Eye for eye, tooth for tooth, hand for hand, foot for foot
> Burning for burning, wound for wound, stripe for stripe.

Exodus 21:23 was Cathy Windsor's vengeance.

The security command post was on the first basement level along with the laboratories. Three of the four walls were constructed of bulletproof glass. On the left was a series of television screens for the in-house video units. The twelve cameras—Frisco Bay equipment—covered the whole of the Grand Salon, sweeping their designated sectors every seven seconds. The controls were automatic but could be overridden and directed manually. Next to them was a plastic screen with a computer blueprint of the Salon. Superimposed on the screen were the exact locations of every piece of the exhibit, some marked by a green dot surrounded by a red square, indicating the electronic beams. On the right a battery of telephones provided instant communications with the Cambridge and Boston police, the local FBI office. There were direct lines into the offices of the curator, Webber,

Father Edmund Moran, the Vatican liaison, and Percival Leech, Chairman of the Board. A row of switches controlled the electronic locks on all doors leading to the Salon. Beside that panel was a microcomputer which monitored the heat scanners. The scanners told the computer the exact number of warm bodies in the room. If the numbers did not correlate with the computer's information the alarms sounded. The alarms. Connected to the beams, they would blow in the tenth of a second it took a fingernail to break the light. In the next hundredth a horrible distorted claxon would wail, a sound produced by Donnellan's specifications by studio engineers using a Moog synthesizer. The purpose of this alarm was as much to terrify the intruder as to let him know he had failed. Lights came on automatically to maximum intensity. Security materialized within seconds. The intruder might elude the human eye for a moment but never the heat scanners. Capture was inevitable.

In the center of this maze was the swivel highback command chair. The man sitting in it, the Monitor, had easy access to all equipment. He could direct a security operation and watch its results simply by moving his hands. Over this soulless environment there drifted the aroma of fragrant plums. There was always a pot of plum tea brewing.

"Evening, Inspector."

The Monitor's voice echoed off the lime-green cement blocks in the corridor leading from the loading bay to the service elevators. Donnellan waved wearily at the camera. There was no need for him to say anything. The Monitor had been taping off police frequencies since the foot patrol called in the report. The elevator doors opened as Donnellan approached them. The cabin rose slowly toward the Grand Salon.

They were waiting for him, standing in a rough semicircle a few feet from the elevator. Donnellan's eyes flickered across their faces: annoyance in Leech's, concern in Isaiah Webber's; the girl, Lauren, was expectant, the priest impassive.

"I'm sorry to have kept you all waiting."

"What happened out there, Inspector?" Leech asked.

Donnellan stuffed his hands deep into the trench coat pockets. "A girl was murdered."

He did not care for Leech and turned on his heel. He had taken three steps before the imperious voice froze him in his tracks.

"Who was she, how did it happen and when?" Leech demanded succinctly.

When he faced him Donnellan saw Leech hadn't moved an inch.

"Her name was Cathy Windsor. She was a student who worked part time at the Business Administration Library. She was gutted. The coroner estimates the time of death at about half past nine, ten o'clock last night."

"The atrocity took place on our premises?" There was no quiver to the voice, no outrage, no sorrow.

"Yes."

"In that case I will expect a full report as soon as possible."

"You'll have it."

Donnellan led the way into the corridor that ran behind the Salon. As he passed the gents' washroom he heard other footsteps falling in behind him: Leech's firm measured gait; Webber's quick short steps; the staccato clip of the girl's evening heels, the almost soundless tread of the priest.

"Inspector, do you know who did it? Was it Mack the Knife?"

The girl's voice echoed down the corridor. It was underlined with anger, not fear. Donnellan stopped before a door with MAINTENANCE stencilled across its face. "Very probably."

He brought out the communicator. "Let us in."

Above and to the right he heard the faint whir of

the camera adjusting focus. The door, which appeared nothing more than the entrance to a janitor's closet, shuddered as four bolts sprang back.

The room was small, eight feet by fourteen. Stark white walls, no windows. In the center stood a single pedestal. Upon it rested an object covered in chamois. Dust-free air from invisible vents coursed across Donnellan's face. He looked behind him to make certain everyone was in.

"Close up, kill the lights."

The Monitor threw a switch and the door closed. Automatically the cameras in the vault were activated. The bolts drove home. He watched as Donnellan punched a sequence of numbers into the panel insert in the wall. Then Percival Leech crossed over and did the same. The computer verified the combination and agreed on authorized entry. Only then did the electronic beam, creating a cat's cradle around the pedestal, suddenly snap off.

"With your permission, Father," Leech said, his body in motion even before Moran nodded. The Chairman stepped over to the pedestal and deftly lifted the chamois covering. He stepped back, folding the soft leather, his eyes upon his hands. He did not look up until he was back in the group.

The microphones imbedded in the chamber ceiling were so sensitive they registered one collective gasp from those standing beneath. The zoom cameras caught every nuance on their faces: the stunned expression of the two archeologists, the shadow of fear flickering across the priest's face, the hungry eager expression held by Leech. Only Donnellan's visage betrayed nothing. He was the first to look away.

"It's magnificent," Lauren breathed. She moved closer, walking around the pedestal, eyes probing every centimeter. Isaiah Webber was beside her.

"It is a treasure," Father Moran murmured, glancing at the Chairman. Leech's gaze did not move from the cup. His great brows were furrowed in concentration. For an instant it seemed to Father Moran that Leech was being physically drawn to the cup, as an iron filing is inexorably pulled by a magnet.

"Yes, it is the one."

Even the Chairman's whisper was faithfully recorded by the bank of tapes spinning silently to the right of the Monitor.

Percival Leech stepped over and in one swift motion covered the chalice.

"A great deal has happened tonight, pleasant and otherwise. I suggest we retire." He turned to Webber. "Can you begin tomorrow?"

Webber in turn glanced at Lauren Blair. "Percival, if she had her way, we would be taking that cup to the laboratory right now!"

"It's a thought," Lauren hinted. Her head was swimming, the adrenalin coursing through her body. She could not believe how alive and eager she felt.

"Father," Webber sighed. "You're aware that Lauren will be doing all the testing. Tonight was a rare treat for me. I am still undergoing treatment, both at the clinic and at home. It's a rather critical juncture, I'm afraid, so—"

"I understand, Doctor," the priest assured him. "And if there's anything I can do..."

"Just keep a tight rein on her," Webber said with mock severity, eyes dancing. "So tomorrow, Lauren, *you* come in early and see to it that the chalice is brought downstairs. Arrange the necessary—ach! You know what to do better than I."

He looked at his watch and shook his head.

"Father, would you see that she gets safely home?"

"It would be my pleasure."

Webber embraced Lauren, planting the customary kisses upon her cheeks.

Frank Donnellan spoke into the communicator. "We're coming out."

The electronic beam switched on immediately. As he watched the others file out the door, Donnellan tried to determine what it was that made him uneasy. It was the same feeling he had when trying unsuccessfully to center a picture. Somehow the frame would not line up with the floor and walls. Nothing he did could correct that....

"You will have that report for me, Inspector," Leech reiterated.

"I'm going to the coroner's labs now."

"Good night, Inspector."

"Good night, sir."

The door locked behind Donnellan. He followed the echo of the bolts down the corridor.

"...Father?"

He looked up abruptly.

"I'm sorry, Doctor. I was daydreaming."

"Lauren. I assume we'll be working quite closely so let's keep it informal."

They were walking down the Museum steps, the priest holding the umbrella. He looked at her out of the corner of his eye. Her eyes were a sparkling sapphire, the jet hair setting off the ivory curve of her neck. Classical beauty.

"All right. Lauren it is."

"I remember reading your papers on the Near East excavations, near Quatara."

"You and eight others—my loyal fans." His eyes twinkled. "Frankly I don't know how you managed to find time for that obscure volume. Your research in the last two years must have been immense, the time spent—"

"That's one of the redeeming factors about the human brain," Lauren said. "It refuses to remember all the—" She was about to say "shit," but caught herself in time.

"Believe me, blasphemy is not a major sin," Edmund Moran laughed.

"Well, you know what I mean," Lauren blushed. "All the nonsense one has to put up with in the course

107

of a project. But sometimes you look back and ask yourself: how did I even do this? Do you ask yourself that, Father?"

"Priests don't have the monopoly on self-confidence."

A shudder passed through him, the words inadvertently striking too close to home.

"You know, I thought I'd done it all when we made the breakthrough on the process," Lauren said. "I mean, what was left? Now it seems that the discovery was only the beginning."

"It was," he agreed. "Although speaking as a priest, I must confess that if the chalice proves to be the Grail this will be your greatest triumph, no matter what comes afterward."

"Why?"

"Because you hold in your hands the possibility of revitalizing millions of lives, infusing them with a new faith, erasing doubt, giving comfort. I am not speaking only for Catholics but for all men."

"I was never religious, Father," Lauren said. "No one in my family was."

"Not a prerequisite," Father Moran said. "In fact, in a way the agnostic touch is almost preferable in this case. When you present your findings there will be no question of religious prejudice, one way or the other."

"You're assuming I'm neutral," Lauren said, her voice sharpening. "Have you checked?"

"Without asking your permission, no, of course not. I mentioned to His Eminence di Stefano that Doctor Webber's condition might prevent him from conducting the tests, that you would be the one to do them. I added there was no reason to even consider that your religious beliefs, or lack of them, would influence the outcome of the testing."

"I would have thought my being an agnostic would have troubled the Church."

"The Church is not out to convert you," he said

gently. "It's only asking for your considerable professional expertise."

"But the Church wants this cup to be the Grail."

"Could it feel otherwise?"

"And you—do you believe the chalice is the Grail?"

A shadow passed over Father Moran's features, bringing forward that concentrated expression.

What is it I believe?

"I think the chalice is more than a relic," he said carefully, and immediately regretted his words. He shouldn't have allowed doubt or uncertainty to color them. She was too clever not to have picked up on the inflection.

"If you have no objections I would like to come down to your lab tomorrow morning," he said, changing the subject. "I've been intrigued by your procedure. I have no doubt that Rome will be looking over my shoulder as well."

"I'd be happy to see you," Lauren said. "Early though—seven thirty."

"I'll be there."

The wind had picked up, sweeping down Merton Street, flinging the rain against the cobblestones. Father Moran opened the door of her waiting limousine.

"Good night, Lauren."

She looked back at him, the smile generous, warm. "Until tomorrow."

He watched the car move down the rain-slicked street. Suddenly he felt cold and quite alone. The rain was pelting down, the fog drifting past the street lamps. The priest shuddered and hurried to the last limousine.

The drive to the Chestnut Street carriage house took only a few minutes. As the car took the curve around Chapel Hill Road Father Moran saw the police cruiser, lights out, parked at the entrance to the quadrangle.

Her name was Cathy Windsor and she had been gutted.

His lips moved in silent prayer for the dead girl.

"Good night, Father," the driver said.

"Good night and thank you."

He didn't bother with the umbrella but ran up the flagstone steps, fingers fumbling with the key. The door jerked open. Moran was still holding the key as he stumbled inside. When he looked up he barely managed to stifle his scream of alarm. Standing before him was Arturo Cardinal Capellini.

CHAPTER SEVEN

THE CHAIRMAN'S OFFICE was off the main conference room on the top level of the Museum. Percival Leech, having drawn the heavy brocade curtains behind him to block out all light, was sitting behind a Chesterton desk, inlaid with green tooled Moroccan leather. A Piquot lamp provided the only light in the room. The Khoman rugs, French leather sofa, and Japanese sarcophagus were not to be seen. Only the door to the safe, imbedded in the floor like an ancient *oubliette*, glinted in the darkness. The safe was the repository of Percival Leech's trove, the combination known only to him. Installed by a private security firm at his own expense while the Museum was undergoing renovations, the vault was equipped with a destruct mechanism. Any attempt to force it insured instant incineration of the contents.

Percival Leech did not consider the precaution excessive, merely pragmatic. The vault held no state secrets, no formulas for elixirs, no maps to lead one to the cavern of the philosopher's stone. Only provenances. Indisputable testaments to the integrity and worth of objects he possessed. Objects he had in fact stolen from others.

Percival Leech was credited with having the most acute eye of any evaluator alive for historical artifacts, paintings, sculptures, illuminated manuscripts. He had been born with this gift, first exercised it when he was barely twenty. In the ensuing forty years his reputation as an appraiser became worldwide. He served as counsel to kings and presidents, dictators and art thieves, conglomerates and modern-day Croesuses. He told them not only if a piece was genuine but whether it was an exemplary work, what it would fetch on the market, what increment in its value could be expected in the future. A second opinion was seldom asked for, in part because Leech's reputation for destroying the evaluation of other appraisers was equally legendary. The man simply did not make a mistake. And when he wanted a piece himself, he lied, offering to act as intermediary for the sale. The owner of the piece usually consented.

Leech would arrange a sale on behalf of a client to an anonymous third party. That buyer and seller never met was accepted practice. What never came to light was that Leech himself, through that third party, usually a dummy corporation consisting of a Lichtenstein post-office box, was the buyer.

One might have thought that in time the ploy would have been discovered. No matter how careful the thief, he was still human and so prey to the most pernicious of human vices: vanity. The desire of the collector to parade his wares. But vanity did not eat away Leech. He craved only one thing: possession of a desired object. Its possession meant he could enjoy it when he chose. That the piece remained hidden from others, secure in vaults of his secret estate in Monte Carlo, was of no concern to him. Perhaps this was a kind of inverted vanity.

Now Percival Leech admitted to himself that he coveted the chalice. He wanted it from the instant he had set eyes upon it. But for the first time in his career he hesitated on the decision to make it his. The Chairman had dealt with a host of powerful figures, men whose fortunes enabled them to acquire enormous personal collections. Although he knew any one of them could break him with a word or two, Percival Leech never feared cheating these men if they had a piece he desired. He had the utmost confidence in his methods, the meticulous preparations he labored over for months, sometimes years, before the stage for the misrepresentation was set to his satisfaction. Each time he undertook such an act he knew it was his own life he risked on its success. For if it was subsequently discovered, the men he stole from would not raise public hue and cry. Their embarrassment at having been taken for fools would not permit such recourse. The retribution would be direct, personal—an accidental death or, worse, a maiming which would deprive Leech of his unique gift.

Nor was it the Church's involvement that gave him pause. The Chairman had looted the Vatican Museum before. He counted on doing so again. Religious sentiment held no sway over him. But there were other ways to be damned. There was one client he had never dared think of cheating.

Very early in his career, after he had published two articles in an obscure art magazine, Percival Leech was visited by a stranger who said he had read the pieces and been most impressed. He predicted that the young man would, with suitable assistance, rise to great eminence in his chosen field. Percival Leech, son of a penurious New England clergyman, a scholarship student who had come to London to make his mark, took stock of his dismal surroundings—a cold-water flat in Whitechapel—and measured them against the ambition that seethed in his mind. Ambition fueled by the innate certainty that he could overcome his obscure background if only his genius was given that one opportunity to show itself. Not talent. That was for academics. Genius. The original imprint.

The stranger proposed a mutually convenient arrangement. In return for Percival Leech's services in finding a particular object long sought by him, the stranger would see that the young evaluator's talents received their due. There was a single condition: when Leech found the object in question, he was to acquire it for himself and wait until such time as the stranger came to him again. If the piece was already spoken for, either by a private collector or institution, he was to remain in its proximity until he had been contacted.

Did I know then who the stranger was? Of course. But I did not dare even think his name.

The bargain was struck. A short time later, an invitation to review the private collection of a relation of the Royal Family was hand delivered. From that stepping stone Percival Leech saw the whole of his life's road unravel as though by magic. Within five years there was not one great house in England that had not opened its doors to him. His reputation grew in direct proportion to the importance of queries that deluged his office. In short order Percival Leech became *primus inter pares* of the already elite circle of art evaluators. The meteoric rise of his career was crowned by the full professorship Harvard had bestowed upon him.

And he never forgot that initial bargain. Wherever his travels took him—to public museums, private vaults, houses of worship—he always paid particular attention to pieces that approximated the description the stranger had given him. The prized intuition had not responded to a single piece. Until an hour ago, when he had gazed upon the chalice that was said to be the Holy Grail. He had, after thirty years of searching, found that which the stranger desired. In the process he had awakened his own desire for it.

Percival Leech drew another Romeo y Julietta from the humidor, clipped the end with a miniature guillotine whose provenance had, appropriately enough, been traced to Robespierre, and gently brought it to life.

Not once have I thought of cheating him.

Leech understood the concept of limits. Because of the stakes involved he cheated only when he was all but certain he would succeed. Cheating was not a reckless game for him but an art. Yet it had never occurred to him *not* to give the chalice to the stranger.

How will he know you've found it?

He will know.

But you haven't seen him since that first day!

Haven't I? Perhaps not. At least not visually. But I have felt his presence.

Why, of all things you could have, do you want the chalice?

Why do I want anything? Because it is the paragon of a certain artistic expression. The piece is an inexhaustible well of beauty that rekindles the soul. There are very few things a man never tires of, which never fully satiate his fascination.

Is there any way to remove it now—away from Webber and Blair?

There are always means, always.

You could discredit their findings, if in fact they lead to the conclusion that the chalice is the Grail.

Yes, that would be one way. Difficult, very difficult, though.

But from the stranger...?

No.

You know who he is.

Yes.

That you are all that you are because of the bargain with him.

Yes.

Then ask yourself: why does he covet the chalice?

For his purposes.

Then his purpose reflects the worth of the chalice. Does it not follow that whoever possesses the chalice is vested with its powers?

It does.

And if you were successful in possessing it—and hiding it—then what harm could come to you? The stranger would be unable to move against you—if you were the only man who knew where the chalice was.

Dare I do this? If he discovers that I intend to take the chalice for myself he will surely kill me.

Not if you act quickly, decisively, place the chalice beyond his reach!

Insane!

Possible!

To risk everything I have gained up to now?

No, to risk everything for the answer to that question which will haunt you if you do not find it: what is the chalice to him? Why is it so important to him? Can you imagine the power its possession would render unto you, power enough to keep even him at bay?

Yes I can imagine, I can taste it.

The chalice will be your protection. He will not dare to move against you.

That is so.

"That is so," he repeated aloud. He felt himself on the threshold of an incredible discovery, a glimpse into a universe a man could scarcely imagine. After all the years of prudence in his gamble, something had come along that demanded the supreme stake. Percival Leech knew he had no choice. Everyone has a price. His, at last, had been met.

"I tried to call you, several times. There was no way to reach you."

"I knew you would. It doesn't matter. I am here now."

They were in Father Edmund Moran's living room, surrounded by the plants that flourished under his touch. The young priest was seated in a wing chair before the curtained window. The curator had moved himself closer to the crackling fire, palms held out to the flames.

Their reunion had been brief but intense. The two men embraced then drew away, regarding each other at arm's length. It was in the eyes that they learned they had become different men since their last meeting. A change so profound, so unsettling had come over both of them that the need to speak, to explain, was overwhelming.

"No one, not di Stefano, not His Holiness, knows where you are?"

Arturo Capellini shook his head. His skin was flushed from the Geneva sun. The weather had been unseasonably warm and he had spent many hours in the silence of the walled garden adjacent to the Hotel Savoy. But his hands trembled when he lifted them and the usually tranquil eyes could not keep from darting this way and that.

"Thank God that on your last visit to Rome you passed me a spare key," the curator said, a wintry smile creasing his lips.

He had told his pupil where he had gone, the secrecy in which he had fled, whom he had defied. Moran had accepted the narrative without comment. It was clear to Capellini that the young priest's concern was for him, not over how he had acted. He judged Moran ready to receive the explanation for those actions.

"That chalice is here." It was a statement, not a question.

"Yes."

"Di Stefano wanted to have it tested by the Blair-Webber process. Have provisions been made?"

"The testing begins tomorrow."

"Then the chalice could not have been put on display."

"No, in fact, di Stefano made much of the need for secrecy."

"Will you be present when the chalice is tested?"

"I am to be in the laboratories at half past seven. Doctor Blair will explain the procedure. I doubt if either she or Doctor Webber wants to have me looking over their shoulders."

"Have you touched the chalice?" Capellini asked softly.

"Yes, of course," Moran answered, puzzled.

"The actual metal?"

"No, when I brought the chalice to the Museum I did not remove the chamois." Father Edmund Moran did not know where the next words sprang from. "Arturo, did anything unusual happen to you on the morning of October 5th?"

For an instant—only that—he thought he saw fear in Capellini's eyes. But perhaps it was only a reflection of flames in his black pupils.

"Yes."

Arturo Capellini leaned forward and poured out the last of the Montrachet Moran had opened. The wine was cool upon his tongue and he savored its bouquet.

Arturo Capellini said:

"There are things about the Museum of Pagan Antiquities I have never spoken to you of, which have to do with the responsibilities of each successive curator. I did not speak because I was not sure you would eventually succeed me. Now I know that you will. Each curator is permitted to name his successor. Even my actions cannot deny me that right."

Capellini gestured to his student. "Come closer to me. There is a great deal to tell you, but I am tired...very tired."

"Can't we talk tomorrow?" Father Moran suggested. But if Capellini heard him he gave no sign of it. He began to speak.

"You must always remember, Edmund, that the bearers of Christian faith originally came as intruders. It was not their intention to learn about or from the indigenous religions but rather to supplant them. In its essence, conversion is a form of eradication, the destruction of one set of beliefs by another. Too often Christianity ruled by fear. In part, it was responsible for the destruction it reaped in kind.

"You must also heed the fact that simply because a religion is supplanted does not mean its power has waned. Ten years, a hundred, five hundred, is nothing at all to a faith that might have existed *thousands* of years before we ever came to hear of it. Therefore, all artifacts pertaining to that religion must be regarded as still possessing their original meaning, significance, and, above all, power. Just as we invest the cross with power beyond our comprehension, so too the symbols of pagan rites do not lose their authority through disuse or abandonment.

"The vault of our *galleria* contains the most comprehensive collection of pagan ritual objects anywhere. For most, brought to Rome during the Renaissance, we have some provenance in the form of letters, diaries, records of missionaries. But you must remember that these observations were not made by men with scientific training. They are little more than notes outlining the location of the artifacts, the date of discovery, and to what religion or cult they belonged.

"Provenance becomes even more fragmentary before this period. Those who founded the *galleria* in 1767 did little more than put whatever they gathered from other museums under one roof. The actual cataloguing did not begin until fifty years later. Therefore, whatever was brought to Rome prior to 1800 — unless it was a well-known, readily identifiable relic — arrived, as it were, an orphan.

"The result is that we do not know exactly what we have. Since we do not know, we cannot risk exposing these objects. You must never forget what I have told you: the power vested in a relic may be lasting. It will live far beyond its creators, span generations of faithful, retain its power even after its worship has been abandoned.

"All of which brings me to the chalice said to be the Holy Grail."

Arturo Capellini paused, wetting his lips with the wine. Father Edmund Moran rose and threw another log into the fire. The birch bark crackled, caught, and curled back in a sheet of flame.

The curator stared into the dancing inferno.

"I ask you to pay particular attention now," Capellini said, not looking at Moran.

"You're familiar with the Grail legend to be sure. According to it, after the crucifixion, Joseph of Arimathea brought the chalice to Britain. There he founded the Grail keepers, the line of Fisher Kings, at the castle of Corbenic. These custodians became an integral part of the Grail mythology. Allegedly the Grail never left the sanctuary of the Kings. The Arthurian legends only reinforced this conception. However, that is not the whole of the story. The Fisher Kings were not fiction. They existed."

Arturo Capellini looked across at his friend. "I am the latest in their line. When I die, you shall take my place."

"Arturo, what are you saying?" Edmund Moran whispered.

Capellini held up his hand. "Hear me out. In addition to the chalice, the legate brought back what is known as the Palinurus parchment. After studying it, John X was horrified at its implications."

"I've never heard mention of a Palinurus parchment," Father Moran protested. "Di Stefano didn't say—"

"Not di Stefano, not anyone else, knows it exists. Hear me out," Arturo Capellini repeated. "John X and the legate are of two minds. They believe, with all their hearts, that what they hold is the Holy Grail. But there is the Palinurus parchment given the legate by the monk Matthew. There are the legate's own comments concerning the events at St. Gallen prior to his departure."

"I thought this provenance was sketchy at best."

"The provenance is a forgery," Capellini said quietly. "When John X read the Palinurus parchment, along with the writings set down by Matthew from Brideshead's final accounts, he realized the chalice could be more than the Grail. The Palinurus parchment, Matthew's writings, the legate's commentary—everything was consigned to a secret vault. The commentary was rewritten by the legate, eliminating all references to Palinurus as well as Matthew's writings on the knight Brideshead. When a secure place was selected for the chalice, the legate was appointed its guardian. When the legate died, trusteeship of the cup was passed to his appointed successor. What in fact happens is that in the heart of the Church, another line of Fisher Kings emerges, priests who will continue to oversee the safety of the chalice through the coming centuries.

"In the eighteenth century the Museum of Pagan Antiquities is founded. The current Fisher King elects this as the home of the Grail. Upon his demise the cup and its history is bequeathed to the next curator of the Museum, making the Museum the *de facto* curator of the Grail. As David Burney's predecessor passed on the secret to him, so he passed it to me, expecting me to find, before I died, a suitable candidate to carry on the line. You were my choice."

Father Edmund Moran clasped his hands together, elbows on knees, and bowed his head. "Arturo, I don't know what to say. The cup is the Grail but it is not the Grail...." He looked up at his former teacher. "Why Geneva, Arturo?"

"Just before the unification of Italy in 1871 the Fisher Kings realized that civil authority would inevitably eclipse papal rule in Italy. There was no question of moving the cup. It could not leave the consecrated ground of Rome. But the provenances could. Switzerland, with her history of neutrality and discretion, was the logical repository."

"You've brought the provenances with you?"

"As many as I thought necessary. I want you to examine them. Undoubtedly you will have questions. I will do my best to answer them."

"Arturo, why can the chalice never leave Holy ground?" Edmund Moran asked softly.

"We have here, Edmund, what might possibly be the greatest relic in all Christendom," the prelate said slowly. "However, we have no continuity, in terms of records, at a very critical juncture: between the time the chalice returns to Britain in the care of Joseph of Arimathea and its subsequent theft from or loss by the Fisher Kings to the time it reappeared in the abbey of St. Gallen. We do not know in whose hands the chalice lay, what use was made of it. Therefore we dare not bring it into the daylight. Not until this crucial period is accounted for."

Edmund Moran shook his head. "But you have your suspicions, Arturo. Somewhere in those provenances are clues as to where the cup was held after it was taken from the descendants of Joseph of Arimathea."

"Yes, there are clues. But not in the provenances." Capellini paused. "The Fisher Kings managed to collect most of the references concerning the Grail— whether or not these originated in areas supervised or influenced by the Church. Most but not all. We did not obtain the Annals of Joseph of Arimathea. Not for lack of opportunity but ignorance. We had the chance and we failed."

Capellini looked carefully at the young cleric.

"Unlike myself, you *can* gain access to them. You must, Edmund. It is possible that the final clue to the chalice resides within them."

"But the Annals belong to the Church of England," Moran protested. "To ask to see them would mean having to explain why...unless we are prepared to lie about our reasons."

"Believe me, I am prepared to do more than that

if it becomes necessary," Capellini said. "I am willing to share the secret of the Grail with the Archbishop of Canterbury, should matters come to that. Edmund, try to understand: we have no choice!"

"What happened to you in Rome," Edmund Moran asked. "On the fifth of October?"

"What happened that day, Edmund, had its origin much earlier," Capellini said. "A terrible error was committed, a mistake made by Boglidaccio and left uncorrected by his successors, including myself...."

Quickly Capellini outlined the temptation Boglidaccio had succumbed to and how two centuries later, the mistake had reached fruition.

"I was forced to show di Stefano the cup. I had no choice. We entered the vault. I broke the seals. When I touched the chalice my hands burned."

Edmund Moran squeezed his eyes shut until he could feel tears behind them. "Mine also!" he whispered. "Mine also...at the exact same time!"

"There is more," the curator told him. "A young girl was murdered here tonight."

"How could you have known that!"

"I was there, Edmund. In the park. I saw what killed her."

CHAPTER EIGHT

HER SLEEP was deep and for the most part shot through with the excitement of the evening. Collages composed of the Grand Salon, guests moving through the exhibit, the laughter and grandeur, rose and dissolved like some iridescent fountain. But on the fringes of enchantment was the chalice gleaming upon its pedestal within the fail-safe vault. Donnellan was standing beside her, his face very close to her cheek, repeating over and over: "Cathy's dead!" But she could not look at him. She could not take her eyes off the cup...

Lauren had set the alarm for six o'clock. If it went off she never heard it.

By the time she stirred, focused one eye on the clock, groaned, and flung back the covers, Tom Brokaw was repeating the headlines in the final minutes of the *Today* show. She caught something about the capsizing of a ferry in Puget Sound as she headed for the shower. Fifteen minutes later, dressed in her workaday outfit of jeans, sweater, and penny loafers she joined Tim McConnell on the living-room couch.

"You were snoring," he said, kissing her.

"Was not."

"You always snore when it rains." He poured her a cup of Colombian and pushed a basket of croissants across the ceramic coffee table. Lauren looked out the floor-to-ceiling window. The rain was sleeting down at a perfect forty-five-degree angle. Only the sound of ships' horns revealed the existence of the harbor.

"The plum jam's fantastic."

"I wasn't snoring."

"You were, babe. You were beat—whenever it was you came in." The words carried the vaguest hint of reproach.

"Didn't think it was all that late," Lauren mumbled, tearing a croissant and smearing half with jam.

"It was. And this morning you missed yourself on national television."

"Now you've got to be kidding!"

"That little talk you had with Jane Pauley. The cameras were rolling. Got you with Leech and Webber."

"You're joking!"

"No way, babe. Granted, it was only fifteen or twenty seconds, but still, you're a star."

Lauren shook her head. She was about to say something when completely different words came out.

"Was there anything on the news about a murder?"

"Not that I heard. What murder?"

"Last night...near the Museum. A girl was killed."

Tim shrugged. "One death does not a national story make."

She stared at him, incredulous, but he never saw the disbelief, his attention on bringing up a sheen on his Ferragamo boots.

"So what's going on, Lauren?" His voice was quiet now, the banter gone.

Lauren knew what he was referring to. She had never lied to Tim, wouldn't start now. She took another sip of coffee for courage, savoring the strong flavor, and lit the first cigarette of the day.

"The Vatican wants the Museum to run some tests on one of the pieces in the exhibit."

"What for? I thought everything had a provenance."

"Except one piece."

"Which is?"

She hesitated. "I'm sorry. I can't say."

"What d'you mean, you can't say?" he challenged her.

"That's the way the Church has arranged it with Leech," Lauren explained. "At this stage at least, they don't want anyone to know that there is any testing."

"I'm not following. I thought these pieces were the crème de la crème, the best the Church has. You mean there could be a phony or a duplicate they don't know about?"

"No, nothing like that. Just that one piece may be something more than it seems. Honey, I can't say anything more than that. Please, don't push."

To her surprise, he didn't.

"Okay, okay. But it seems this secrecy's a bit much, that's all. The exhibit's overwhelming as it is. The material is fabulous. I doubt if anyone would care that one piece might not be authentic."

"Maybe they're worried about adverse publicity," Lauren said. Suddenly she leaned forward and kissed him. "Thanks for not making an issue out of it."

She paused, still holding him. "You know, I'll be working like hell for the next while. Won't see much of you."

"That I don't have to ask questions about." He grinned and put his arms around her. "Listen, knock yourself out. I'll be doing the same thing."

"What do you mean?"

"I've decided to take your advice: I'm going to appeal the Board decision."

"Oh, Tim!" She squeezed him, burying her lips in his neck. "That's great."

"Gotta do it, babe. I'll talk to Stukley today. See if we can get a joint venture together. Meanwhile I'll get my act together on the lectures. By Christmas we should have a whole new ball game."

"You will, you'll see."

"And you better get your butt in gear. If you were planning to get up early must mean work's starting today."

She drained the last of her coffee.

"Give me a lift?"

"Take the Alfa. I've still got a few things to take care of here."

"That's okay, I'll go by tube. You'll be needing it later on."

Lauren was at the foot of the stairs when she looked back at him.

"I love you, you know."

Then she was gone.

"But I don't love you," the whispered voice said to the empty room.

Tim McConnell was staring into the bottom of his empty cup. He stood up and faced the wall of the staircase between the living room and bedroom. One second the cup was in his hands, the next there was a shattering sound, white porcelain fragments careening around the room, a brown smudge slowly spreading across the ivory paint.

Tim McConnell stared at it, then slowly sat down again. If he hadn't gotten her out of here, if he hadn't thrown the cup, he knew he would have hit her. In the time they had been living together he had struck her only once, a slap across the face, nothing major. But she had warned him: once she could forgive, twice and she would walk.

"Anytime," he muttered, head bowed. "Walk any fucking time you want!"

He had never known love to depart so quickly, so violently, so very completely. Yet that was what had happened last night. The moment Webber had taken Lauren away from him, leading her about to all the celebrities, envy had turned into hatred. He had watched spellbound, helpless, as she became the center of attention and he stood alone, nothing but emptiness in him, a horrible frightening emptiness that not even the coke had been able to break through. In that instant of solitude he had at last realized the truth: that for all his trappings, for as far as he had travelled, he was, in the end, nothing more than the lucky, somewhat talented kid who had broken out of lower-middle-class South Side Philadelphia. The power and influence and glitter of the previous evening were as alien to him as the landscape of the moon. Mesmerized by success, he feared it because in his life he had witnessed only failure—a father who had taken himself and his wife into early graves struggling to keep a small grocery store out of the red. The drudgery, the damned refusal to accept one's lot, the drunken boasts of fortunes to come. Finally the sullen acceptance that life could not be beaten. Acceptance, resignation, remorse. Death.

These were what he fought against. He believed himself so much better than his origins, worthy of so much more, worthy of what was his by right. By right of his beauty, his quick, glib manner, the way in which he stalked success as he did the sleek wealthy girls on the Boston campuses. By right of the sincere effort he applied to his work, to the dreams he dreamed by day, when, lying in the bed of another strange apartment, he saw the golden road to his freedom. Strewn with honors and acclaim, that road would take him to every place he had ever imagined. Every delicacy he had ever imagined, whether an exotic car or an aged wine, would be *his*, to savour, to offer instead of accept, to give rather than to take or to beg for.

Tim had hoped it would be different with Lauren.

But he knew that when she had walked away from him, she was going for good. She hadn't been aware of this, never suspected that a simple action could have such a devastating effect. But it had. She was walking to her fame, the cameras focusing on her. She was walking to embrace her triumph. Without him. And as though Fate had wanted to put in the final twist of the knife there was the job for the Vatican. Christ alone knew what that could be, but when it was over with, she would have even more to crow about.

No, she was gone from him. There was no stopping her. Before the discovery of the Blair-Webber process, they had been equals. At least he had been able to live with that illusion. But not anymore. She was outstripping him, inexorably leaving him in her wake.

He hated her for that.

"But at least I kept my cool," McConnell said out loud, and chuckled. "What bullshit!"

Oh, he planned to see Stukley all right. He would ask Stukley for a joint venture. And as soon as the professor's influence arranged the project he would do everything to get the old son of a bitch off it. The idea had been his from the first. Stukley would be a stepping stone, nothing more. After he did the dig and presented what he *knew* was buried there no one would be able to stand up to him. No one. Not even Lauren.

Tim McConnell sat back on the couch and lit another cigarette. He was feeling good. The depression and anger vanished as quickly as they had come on.

That's what he would do. Undercut the whole fucking lot of them.

Tim McConnell rose and came over to the dining-room table. He reached for the smoker's candle and laid out some lines. Yeah, it would all work out exactly as he had planned.

He did not understand that he had allowed madness to creep in, didn't even realize when it had overtaken him.

Had the mere act of *thinking* brought the man here?

Impossible!

129

Sitting in the morning room of his elegant Beacon Hill townhouse, Percival Leech poured himself another cup of coffee. He had not arrived home until half past three. The fact that his housekeeper was out sick today and breakfast was not prepared did not improve his disposition. But the cold annoyance had disappeared, transformed into a cautious unease when he answered the door and saw who was waiting for him.

The stranger.

At first Leech could not believe it. He recognized the stranger instantly from their first meeting. Thirty years ago. The stranger had not aged. Not a day.

"You have fared well since we last spoke," the stranger said, sitting in a Queen Anne wing chair, his back rigidly straight. The morning's pale light lent a pasty quality to his features.

"Very well," Leech acknowledged.

"Wealth, respect, stature, all of these are yours, in abundance," the stranger mused. "And rightly so."

"I have earned them," Leech said.

"You have *almost* earned them," the stranger amended.

Leech regarded him quizzically.

"You haven't forgotten our agreement?" the stranger asked softly. "After all, you are an honorable man."

"I haven't forgotten."

"Very good. I have come to ask you: when will you bring the chalice to me?"

Leech set down his coffee and sat back in the wicker chair. The rain was streaming down the glass enclosure of the atrium.

"The chalice delivered from the Vatican, which we are about to test?"

"The same," the stranger smiled.

"Under present circumstances it would be quite difficult, impossible to remove it."

"Surely there are means," the stranger suggested.

"I haven't had occasion to give the matter much thought," Leech said. "After all we've only received the cup. What with my staff, that priest liaison, waiting to get at it...Then the security arrangements..."

"I am familiar with the obvious difficulties," the stranger told him, his intonation underlining his impatience.

"Then I ask for a reasonable chance to work out a plan," Leech repeated quietly. "One must proceed cautiously. I don't recall there being anything in our agreement about my having to act imprudently."

"Imprudently, no," the stranger said, rising. "But with dispatch. Your testing will take no more than five days. I will speak to you in three."

Percival Leech did not move from the atrium for the next hour. He sat in the comfortable wicker chair holding his cooling coffee and watched the rain cascade down the curved windows. The scent of plants around him seemed more fragrant now that the stranger had left. Five days. He had three days to decide how to remove the chalice for himself.

The house was smaller than most in that area of Brookline. Its compensation was the two-acre tract upon which it rested, separated from its neighbors by a high stone wall, from the countrylike Post Road by an electronically controlled wrought-iron gate. The Lincoln did not stop at the gates. Cameras mounted on the stone pillars picked up the car as soon as it rounded the final curve of the Post Road and the gates drew open automatically.

The stranger alighted from the car, made his way up the flagstone path, and unlocked the double oak doors. Once inside, he slid the bolts into place.

The house, a perfect example of Federal architecture, appeared barren. Dust lay in a uniform sheet over the floors. There was no furniture in either the living room or dining room. Heavy brocade curtains blocked out all light.

The stranger's footsteps resounded off the boards as he walked down the hallway, the groans of cracked dry wood echoing up the central staircase. He turned left into the study: high frescoed ceiling, dark gleaming hardwood floors, an Adam fireplace freshly cleaned. A single chandelier, very old, gave a brilliant sheen to the oval ebony table. The stranger walked to the head of the table and took his seat.

The stench in the room was overwhelming. The rotting fetid smell of brackish swamp. But it did not trouble the stranger. He was very familiar with it. He craved it as though it were his own.

"Will he do it?"

The voice had a resonance to it that was not human, a rasping hollow quality that made each word echo.

The stranger leaned forward in anticipation. They were there, in the darkness at the end of the room. He heard the slow, seemingly tortured breathing, the scrape of their skin against the floor. Eyes glowed out at him. He was recognized.

"He says he shall do so," the stranger murmured.

"Do you trust him?"

"He has proven himself faithful in the past."

There was a pause. "So he has. But he has been your servant not ours. All that he has he believes he owes to you. He does not know your powers are our powers. But you understand this. You are responsible for him."

"He will obey me," the stranger answered calmly. "Even so, I have other means."

"You are a valued servant," the terror commended him. "After the chalice is returned you too shall pass into our race."

The stranger heard rather than saw the motion, the scraping of knives across wood. He felt the presence closer now. He could almost reach out and touch it. He longed to do this. The voice spoke to him again.

"We are the last of our kind.

"For over a thousand years we have watched as our race has been dying away. Our females have become barren. Our males grow impotent. We have not had issue in a millennium. Because of the theft perpetrated upon our kind by humankind we have been brought to the verge of extinction. It was they who stole from us the font of our life, the chalice which they call the Grail.

"Through the centuries our kind has searched for the chalice. We have gone to every corner of this earth, endured hardships, surrendered our lives, employed the help of humankind in our task. But we did not find the chalice. Without it we continue to perish.

"But the font of our life force is among us once more. Close by. Very close. It is ours to reclaim. With it we shall become strong again. Our numbers will swell. We have already taken females from humankind. Some of them will survive our breeding. We will lay our seed within them and they shall bear our progeny. We will take many of them, for some females will die as soon as our seed is within them. Yet progeny will be brought back. Humankind, which has forgotten us, will once again learn to fear us when we come out amongst them, to reclaim what is our own. We shall grow fruit in their wombs and multiply ourselves while they diminish. When our numbers are many we shall raze the place they call Jerusalem. As it was written by our ancients, this destruction, the third of its kind, will open the gates for our rule. The rule of monster.

"But our font has been corrupted. Although its powers have not diminished it carries the stigma of holiness. It must be cleansed. Those who have watched over it, the priests in their golden tower called Fisher Kings, are accountable. Their blood is to wash our font."

The stranger gazed up in ecstasy and terror as the demonkind shambled forth from the darkness.

"We will get to him whose touch has defiled the host. We shall exact punishment."

"What do you have for me, Robert Redford?"

That was his real name. He was tall, with the physique of a linebacker. But the golden brown hair, crisp blue eyes, and chiselled features made for a striking resemblance to the actor. Donnellan had seen women do triple takes in the street.

Robert Redford, Deputy Chief Medical Officer at the unheard-of age of thirty-six and the department's acknowledged *enfant terrible,* passed the inspector tea in a Limoges cup. Redford was also independently wealthy.

"Ta."

Redford leaned back against the lab stool. "I didn't know they assigned you to this one, Frank. Aren't you on the Museum detail?"

"The killing took place on Museum grounds. That makes me an interested party."

"Right." Redford was familiar with Donnellan's reputation.

Donnellan savored the tea, holding the cup close to his lips. The vapors helped dispel the formaldehyde odor that permeated the air. The lights were harsh in his eyes, fluorescent tubes screaming off white tiles and stainless-steel dissection tables. This was not what he needed at half past seven in the morning, after a sleepless night. But neither did Cathy Windsor.

"Shall we?" Donnellan murmured.

Redford walked over to the "filing cabinet," the temperature-controlled cadaver hold, and pulled back number thirty-two. The platform upon which the remains of the body rested was rolled out onto the trolley, the trolley wheeled under Fuomi surgical lights. Redford drew back the sheet, exposing the entire body, or what was left of it.

"Have you notified her parents?"

"She's from out of state. Illinois. Samulovitch has probably called them by now."

"It will have to be a closed-casket funeral," Redford said quietly. "Gerry brought me pieces of the stomach, liver, and pancreas. He couldn't find the lungs or the heart."

"Cannibalism?"

"I wouldn't care to speculate."

Donnellan looked at him.

"Frank, the uterus is gone as well."

"Christ Almighty...How did she die?"

"You're not going to like this."

"Try me."

"Her chest cavity was gouged out. Literally. As though someone with very strong, long, and exceedingly sharp fingernails did this to her." He stepped back and with the palm open, fingers held taut, made an upward scooping motion. "Death had to be instantaneous. The shock alone would have been enough to kill her."

"Was she raped?"

"There was no indication of penetration."

"The disfigurement of the breasts and face came after she was dead?"

"Most likely."

"Mack the Knife," Donnellan whispered.

Redford nodded, pointing to the torso. "Here, here, and here, where you have the flaps of the skin, that's where the instruments went in. I don't believe the killer could have used a knife so smoothly, so perfectly. The angle of penetration indicates the victim was standing. She wasn't unconscious, Frank. However this happened, it happened in one instant."

"Could the killer have custom-designed an instrument? Used an antique? Something exotic?"

"That's the only reasonable conclusion," Redford agreed. "I've telexed the Smithsonian. A cousin of mine handles historical armament. He'll be sending down material by messenger."

Donnellan picked up a magnifying glass and peered at the minute flaps of skin.

"What about residue? The pelvic bone and rib cage are scratched. You must have gotten something off them."

"I thought we had it made when I saw it. There's residue, all right. But nothing I can identify through the electron microscope."

"What are you telling me!"

"The residue is organic, Frank," the pathologist said quietly. "But I have never come across anything like it. I can't even tell you if it's animal, vegetable, or mineral."

"With all this miraculous equipment you can't tell me what did this to her?"

"Frank, we have the best facilities in the country. You know that. Other labs send their stuff to *us*."

Donnellan squeezed his eyes shut. Slowly he loosened the fingers that were balled into fists. He shook his head and flung the sheet over the remains of Cathy Windsor.

"I'm sorry, Bob. I didn't mean to get on your back."

"I'm glad you're working on this one, Frank," Redford said, his voice dead. "That's one murdering son of a bitch you have out there." The pathologist hesitated. "If it is Mack the Knife, he's a big bastard too. I don't know how you'll take him down."

"Elaborate, will you?"

"The victim weighed a hundred and ten pounds. The force of the thrust would indicate an extremely powerful individual. One hand to rip out everything...Unlikely it's a woman."

"We have a witness who'll confirm that."

Donnellan and Redford turned round to see Samulovitch enter. The detective's eyes were shining.

"A witness, Frank. A guy who says he saw a man running through the quad just before the foot patrol entered."

At a few minutes after eight o'clock, Father Edmund Moran unlocked the terrace doors and pushed them open. The wind coursing through the garden brushed past him, overwhelming the smoke-laden air in the living room. Moran crossed the flagstone patio. He reached out and cupped the heavy sunflowers, ran his fingers over the azaleas, and rhododendrons. He breathed deeply of their scent and, closing his eyes, bade all thoughts dissolve. Impossible. The young priest sat down on the bench hewn of stone and listened to the warble of the robins.

"It is difficult for you to believe."

Arturo Capellini came to his side with two cups of espresso. Moran ran the lemon twist along the porcelain rim and drank. Looking past the open French doors into the living room, he saw the books, manuscripts, and parchments sealed in acryllic, covering the slate coffee table.

"I believe in goodness therefore I must believe in evil. I believe in the manifestation of good so I cannot deny the manifestation of evil. What I cannot comprehend is why you chose me." Moran smiled wanly. "You know I failed all my courses in exorcism."

"This is not a matter of demonic possession or assault," Capellini said. "We are talking about a parallel race, creatures that live side by side with man yet about whom man knows nothing."

A parallel race.

Father Moran closed his eyes, shoulders slumping forward, head bowed. The idea was fantastic, beyond the realm of belief. Had it been expressed by anyone other than Arturo Capellini—a man he trusted and loved beyond all others—he never would have considered it.

In the long hours of dark morning Father Moran

had listened as the curator of the Museum of Pagan Antiquities presented his evidence. Capellini interspersed his monologue with references to the texts he had brought with him. He structured his presentation as an attorney would, and spoke softly, convincingly, leading his pupil along the historical trail and through the wealth of accumulated evidence toward an inescapable conclusion: Demonkind. They existed.

The forgery, on the instruction of John X in the year A.D. 926, was the beginning of an investigation into the origins of the chalice. In a secret memorandum that bore his imprimatur, John X made it clear that if he should predecease the legate Tractus, Tractus was to make no mention of the chalice's existence to the next Vicar of Christ. Until the provenance for the nine centuries between disappearance and discovery of the chalice could be accounted for, even the existence of such a relic was to be firmly denied.

The legate Tractus survived not only John, but his successors, Leo VI and Stephen VII. He devoted the remainder of his life to the pursuit of the provenance, journeying back to Britain and living there until his death in A.D. 948. The search was then continued by his secretary, a monk from the monastic order at Ictus. For the next half-century it proved fruitless. Only with the arrival of William the Conqueror, and the expansion of armed might into the northern reaches of the island, were the first tenuous connections unearthed.

Until this time the Fisher Kings had paid scant attention to the travel diaries and notes presented from the Roman occupation. As the Conqueror's legions moved north reports of a new tribe began to find their way to Londonium. The Fisher King who first investigated these accounts wrote that the soldiers used the word race in referring to this people. An unknown race. Not tribe.

In the following two hundred years the secret

vaults of the Fisher Kings came to hold over fifty documented accounts of a race that bore a common name: demonkind. Returning to the Roman historians, the Fisher Kings painstakingly eliminated all identifiable tribes and clans the legions had come into contact with, including the blue-dyed Druids, whose powers of magic were indisputable. Matching these against the description of the demonkind, the custodians of the chalice were able to begin the resurrection of a history that lay beyond the pale of human experience.

As civilization pushed back the frontier of the unknown, the Fisher Kings followed the soldiers and settlers. They spent centuries studying the configurations at Stonehenge, the catacombs of Bath, and the caves that ran the length of the west coast of Scotland. Every Christian outpost, no matter how small or short-lived, was scrutinized, its foundations laid bare in search of clues that might have been overlooked or purposely hidden away. Clues whose significance their buriers may not have understood but instinctively believed important. Or feared but could not bring themselves to destroy. Most of these troves proved barren. The vaults were empty, the hollow crucifixes broken, their contents looted. But some survived.

"Some...enough for us to understand, to be convinced of the demonkind," Capellini had said.

He brought forth fragments of journals written by traders, holy men, and adventurers. Sketches done in dye on parchment and leather, intricate wood carvings, miniature bronze reliefs. There was even a silver relief of a cup, one glorifying satanic visages.

"They all depict the same face," Father Moran said softly. "Every one of them...hideous. And the written description. There are no discrepancies there, either.

"The demonkind," he continued, his memory spinning back a digest of all he had listened to and read that morning. "They are believed to be human-oid. They walk upright. They have all our attri-butes. They can communicate in human tongues."

"But they are not human!"

"The devil's spawn. Until Darwin, man believed himself to be created in God's image. God was his maker. The devil had no progeny. Nothing in the bible or any other religious source led man to spec-ulate that Lucifer could make creatures in his image.

"But he has. The demonkind are his children. We do not know how or when they came about. We have no parallel story or mythology about their crea-tion.... Yet it must have happened."

"In almost two millennia no one has been able to convince a large part of mankind that such a race exists," Father Moran had argued. "The reports of contact or sighting are fragmentary, isolated, lim-ited to Britain—"

"The rest of the accounts remain in the Grand Banque de Genève. Your proficiency in French and German is excellent. As you will see, the scope of demonkind is at least European. There have been fragmentary reports from Africa. More recently from excavations in the Middle East."

The priest had fallen silent for a few moments. The universe as he had known it, with its immutable, inflexible laws, had shifted. There was nothing he could reach out and grasp to steady himself.

"Very well," he had said at last. "The demonkind have been written about throughout Europe and North Africa. The question remains: why haven't the Fisher Kings unearthed evidence of a single con-certed attempt on the part of man to find them? Even reference to a whole village or fiefdom trying to es-tablish contact would be a start."

"Would *you* believe in a race of monsters? No, of course not. In this day and age you would be thought a madman. Technology and science cannot accept such aberration. There is no place for them in the rational scheme of things. Attitudes were no less rigid and myopic in past centuries. Superstition was most rampant. Religion was a potent force. On the other side of that coin, belief, even suspected belief, in the ungodly, would have been construed as heresy. We burned heretics then. Therefore, the silence.

"There is another possibility, the one David Burney espoused: the demonkind have not been able to procreate. Had they been able to reproduce then inevitably their growing numbers would have brought them into contact with civilization. Confrontation would have been inevitable.

"Hence the cup..."

"That is the central image," Father Moran had said. "It reappears in almost every detailed account. Christianity has Jerusalem as its center. Within the city are holy sites, within the sites, relics and objects attributed to Christ and His apostles. All accounts related to the demonkind place them in the north, particularly in Britain. Was *their* center somewhere in the British Isles?"

"And what was—or is—the cup that appears so regularly in the accounts?" Capellini had finished. "The cup which in all representations is depicted by the same configuration, which bears a resemblance to—no, is an exact image of—the chalice we think is the Grail."

The coffee tasted bitter and cold upon his tongue. Father Edmund Moran set the demitasse upon the stone. He rose, the branches of the apple tree brushing his hair.

"I had never faced evil before until that moment when my hands burned. I cannot express the horror I felt, the coldness of that abyss I was staring into." He regarded Capellini, who remained sitting on the ledge. "You are a material witness to the murder. It is your duty to see the police."

"It is my duty but I cannot fulfill it."

"It is possible—very likely—that a profound evil

141

is growing with the unwitting aid of the Church. It is your duty to alert His Holiness. The Fisher King is no longer the custodian of only the chalice. He must protect the living as well."

"I cannot accept responsibility in addition to that which I have sworn to accept: the safekeeping of the chalice. It must be returned to Rome. Or if that is impossible, then equally holy and consecrated ground: Jerusalem."

"And what about the girl who was murdered? What of Lauren Blair, who will be taking the cup today? Of Webber and Leech? Do you owe them nothing as well? If something were to happen to them, would the conscience of Arturo Capellini not suffer?"

"Nothing will happen to them because they will not have the cup. By tonight it will no longer be in this country." Arturo Capellini came over to the younger man. "The girl in the park . . ." He hesitated. "Yes, Edmund, I saw what did it. And for what purpose? Only one: the chalice. For the first time in a millennium the chalice is not on sacred ground. Already they are here for it. Why? What is it to them? Our duty is to protect that cup. By removing it we preserve those who have inadvertently been permitted to handle it. Can you understand that? This is the only way we can protect them. Unlike Cathy Windsor . . ."

"What if Lauren Blair can prove the chalice belongs to the period of Christ?" Edmund Moran whispered.

Arturo Cardinal Capellini stared at him, incredulous. "That cannot be!"

PART TWO

"There's death in the cup—so beware!"

—ROBERT BURNS
On a Goblet

CHAPTER NINE

THE YELLOW-GRAY MIST swirled about the waters. Standing on the far shore, Capellini strained his eyes to follow the boatman on the punt, working the long-handled tiller from side to side.

Soon he will be out of sight, in the mist.

But the mist parted as the prow of the boat headed into it, and did not close behind it. The soft glare from the water illuminated the craft riding upon the waves. He was able to watch as it approached the shore.

Who is coming?

From the darkness of the opposite shore he saw the figures emerge from the blackness. One by one they came before the boat, standing before it in single file. Only one stepped into the boat.

Why was he chosen? Did the boatman beckon to him? Who is he?

The figure sat in the prow of the punt. The boatman turned his craft round, directing it into the pale-yellow tunnel between the mists. Capellini ventured as close to the waters as he dared, eager to see the face of the new arrival. Would he recognize him? Was he a friend or a stranger? What would he have to tell him?

Silently the boat drew to the shore and the figure lifted his head to see this new land he was coming to.

A little closer...

It was then that Father Arturo Capellini screamed. For the last image he had was of himself, watching in horror as the face of the man in the punt became recognizable. He was himself.

He was just a kid, nineteen, twenty. Beat up Adidas on bare feet, black jeans with studs forming a fleur-de-lys design about the crotch, T-shirt advertising a punk-rock band called the Brown Nosers, a chalk-white pimpled face whose resemblance to a Kabuki mask was made all the more vivid by a thatch of oily black hair perfectly coiffed to duplicate a rooster's comb.

Donnellan looked up at Terence Joseph Campbell's police dossier. Through the one-way mirror he could see Campbell sitting on the hardback chair, smoking Camels. Every few seconds his eyes would flicker toward the door of the interrogation room, focus on the Judas Hole.

"How reliable is he?" asked Donnellan.

"He's not strung out," Samulovitch said, drawing on his Gitane. "The doctor's had a look at him."

"What about the girl friend?"

"She's waiting. There's a policewoman with her for moral support, telling her she did the right thing."

Donnellan closed the file. He wasn't surprised that Campbell wasn't a volunteer witness. Not with three counts of possession and one trafficking charge pending against him. In coke. In the car Samulovitch had told him it was the girl who had called in. Whatever it was Campbell had seen in the park, he could not keep it to himself. The girl had gone off the deep end when she heard the victim was female. Campbell didn't know about her call to the police until Samulovitch was on his doorstep.

"How's he taking it?"

"The kid's not stupid. Wanted to call a lawyer."

"What did you do?"

"Showed him some pictures of Cathy Windsor, asked if he wanted his lady to be found like that.

Assured him on my mother's grave he wasn't being charged, that we just wanted to talk."

"So let's talk."

Terence Joseph Campbell leaped out of the chair as soon as the key rattled the lock. He took a step back when Donnellan's frame blocked the doorway.

"Relax, boyo," Donnellan said softly. "We'll get your statement and take you home."

Donnellan put the tape recorder he had carried in on the table, lifted one foot up onto a chair and pressed the record button.

"Hey, listen, they told me—"

Samulovitch, who had followed Donnellan in, tapped Campbell on the shoulder. "He's not through yet, boychik," he whispered. "Listen."

Donnellan was speaking. "This is a voluntary statement taken from Terence Joseph Campbell, resident at 217 Maplewood Avenue, Apartment 6, in the City of Boston, concerning events witnessed on the evening of October 7th, in the vicinity of the Bennett Museum. The officers present are Francis Xavier Donnellan, Inspector, and Lieutenant Gerald Seymour Samulovitch. Let it be noted that the witness has come forward of his own volition and that his cooperation be made a part of his permanent record."

Donnellan switched off the tape. "That's what you get from us—a marker you may want to cash in one day. Now it's your turn. Do we deal?"

Campbell looked at the machine and shrugged. He hadn't been expecting anything. He was ahead of the game.

"We deal."

Donnellan punched the button. "The witness will now give his version of events as seen on the night of October 7th."

Campbell fished out another Camel from the crumpled packet. Samulovitch had a light ready for him.

"Where do you want me to start?"

"Tell us, in general terms, where you were coming from, going to, at about ten o'clock."

Campbell glanced down at his thigh, at the slight bulge in the pocket. The three thousand in hundreds from the night's deal was still there.

"I was over at a friend's place...in one of the dorms." He was loaded. If a bust *was* coming down, his money would at least bail him out.

"One of the Harvard dormitories?"

"Yeah, that's right."

"There was a little party," Donnellan coached.

"Yeah, a party. You know, couple guys, some chicks..."

"When did you leave?"

"Quarter after ten, I guess. The old lady was waiting for me. I was taking a shortcut across the quad."

"That's the quadrangle at the rear of the Bennett Museum."

"Yeah, I save a couple of blocks that way."

Campbell butted his cigarette. "When I came off Bayview I saw a guy tailing off into the woods. He looked like he was running from that bandstand."

"Did you see or hear anything else?"

"No, just him."

"How far away from the man were you?"

"He was kinda running at me, on an angle."

"Did he see *you?*"

"No, I don't think so. He was totalled...scared. Just the way he ran. He was an old man."

"Why do you say old man? Did you see his face?"

"Not his face. But he had gray hair, cut butch-short. It was the breathing, heavy, wheezing, like he was going to drop at any second."

"Did you notice anything else about him, how he was dressed?"

"Black coat, long...And a red scarf. One of those long things you wrap around your neck a few times."

"A muffler."

"I guess so."

148

"Now the time. When did you see him?"

"Had to be just after ten thirty. Heard the bells ring."

"You're sure of that?"

"Yeah, for sure."

Donnellan gave him a few seconds. "How far away from the gazebo were you?"

"The what?"

"The bandstand."

"Twenty, twenty-five yards."

"You saw no activity around it?"

"Naw. How far can you see in the dark?"

"There are lamps around the bandstand."

"If there was someone he was on the other side."

"You said the man appeared frightened. Was he carrying any kind of weapon?"

"Nothing I saw."

"Was there any blood on his coat, on the hands?"

"The coat was black, man."

Donnellan backed off. "Could you tell us in which direction the man was running."

"Further into the quad. He could have gone anywhere."

"Will you talk to us if you remember anything more?"

"For sure."

"Your cooperation is greatly appreciated."

Samulovitch hustled Campbell out of the interrogation chamber. Donnellan played back the tape, removed the cassette, and walked up to the seventh floor.

His office had a stale air to it, like an attic seldom entered into. The heat had gone on as of October 1: No one had opened the windows. Donnellan jerked both of them up and stuck his head out. Two feet away was the aging brick façade of the police garage. The odor of garbage wafted up from the alley.

"Somewhere in the world it must be cocktail hour."

Donnellan brought his head inside. Samulovitch

had come in and seated himself and put his feet upon the grey metal desk. He proffered a paper cup of Bushmills.

"L'chaim."

"L'chaim," Donnellan murmured.

"Aren't you even tired, Frank?"

"Is it noon yet?"

"Just about."

"Then I'm tired."

"You want a late breakfast? We could go home. Monique will fix omelettes. We have bagels, lox...."

Samulovitch's voice faded as he realized Donnellan wasn't listening.

"An older man, close-cropped hair, black coat...red muffler."

"A prof."

Donnellan looked up at him. "What do you feel, Ger?" he asked softly.

"Like a goose walked over my grave. There's something here that stinks but I can't get close to it."

Donnellan was silent for a moment. He drained the Bushmills and crumpled the wax cup, tossing it into the basket.

"Can I shower at your place?"

"For sure."

"Let's do it."

Not a professor, Donnellan thought as he followed Samulovitch into the stairwell. He recognized the image—black coat, red muffler—but hadn't been able to place it until a few seconds ago. The memory belonged to his boyhood, at school, when in winter the fathers wore black coats and scarves of many colors, predominantly red....

The agent reached out and touched her forearm. "Dr. Blair, Father Moran has arrived."

Lauren stopped, looking up and down the corridor. "Where?"

The agent spoke into the microreceiver tucked into the lapel of his jacket. "He's just cleared external perimeter, ma'am."

"Thank you," Lauren said graciously, and shook her head. This security business would take some getting used to.

Lauren saw the priest approaching from the other end of the corridor. When he came close she was taken aback by his appearance. He was not wearing a collar but a perfectly tailored double-breasted blazer over an ivory white turtleneck. But the lay cloth could not mask the drawn, haunted expression on his face, take away from the falsehood in the smile, the uneasiness that streamed from his eyes.

"Good morning, Lauren."

"Hello, Father. I hope *you* weren't here at half past seven."

"No, I called and asked security if you were about."

I can't allow anything to happen to you, Lauren!

"Lauren, would you mind very much if I observed your tests today?"

"Not at all. I'd enjoy the company." She paused. "Father, is everything all right? You seem a little concerned."

"Apprehensive," the priest said, regarding her steadily.

"I think I understand."

No you don't.... You couldn't! How can you understand that I am lying to you? That I have decided to go against the Church, the pontiff himself...in order to protect you!

The security man unlocked the lab doors for them.

"Before I go, let me show you the alarm triggers," he said. "Two over here on the walls. Two on the floor, here and here. Another two in the next room. Should you need me for anything—*anything*—just hit the button. We'll be right in."

"I'm sure you will be," Lauren murmured. "Thank you."

The guard withdrew, locking the door behind him.

Lauren looked back, shaking her head. "I know the security is necessary, but it makes me feel like a prisoner. Coffee, Father?"

"An impressive arrangement," Father Moran said, looking about himself. "Oh, excuse me, yes, a cup would be nice."

The room was some forty feet by twenty, the walls painted cinder block with a single door on the right-hand side leading into the laboratory. A vast array of technical equipment sat on the counters, lined the walls, interspersed with sinks, burners, and air-circulation ducts.

Lauren Blair noticed the aluminum carrying case first.

"That must be it."

Moran took a step forward then checked himself. *Her hands will not burn. You must not give yourself away.*

Lauren flipped open the lid, removed the cup with both hands, and set it down upon the scarred filler-board counter top. She looked at the priest and lifted the chamois.

The gold vessel seemed to shimmer, casting an intense auric ray at her. The color of the shell inlay ran together, milky white through to the palest red, to oyster gray.

There is more than beauty here, she thought. *It is as though the chalice has an existence, a force, of its own.*

Father Edmund Moran watched as the archeologist scrutinized the cup. She held it in her hands, arms almost straight out, turning it slowly in her fingers.

Her hands do not burn.

"I have never seen anything so beautiful, so...perfect, in my life," she murmured.

What are you? Who fashioned you? For what purpose?

She smiled at him and set the chalice down.

"You're familiar with radiocarbon labs, Father?" Lauren asked. She hung up her jacket and reached into a cupboard, bringing out mugs and condiments.

"I used to be," the priest said. "It's been a while."

"If you like I can give you a brief rundown before we begin," Lauren suggested, spooning coffee into a filter basket. She poured in the water and set the switch.

"A refresher course would be welcome," Moran agreed. He deliberately turned his back on the cup.

"Radiocarbon is a naturally occurring isotope of carbon," Lauren began. "With an atomic weight of 14, half-life of 5,730 years, C14 is continuously produced by cosmic-ray neutrons in the earth's atmosphere, oxydized to CO_2 by atmospheric oxygen. Plants absorb CO_2 from the air; animals feed off the plants; there is also a CO_2 exchange between the air and the ocean and so a constant supply of C14 to every form of marine life. Therefore all living organisms reflect the C14 concentration of the medium from which they draw their carbon.

"When an organism expires, carbon intake ceases. However, the *already incorporated* C14 continues to decay at a fixed rate determined by its decay content. We measure the amount of C14 in a specimen, and by combining this with the C14 concentration in the specimen when it was living together with the decay constant of C14 we can calculate the time elapsed since the organism expired.

"I should add here that radiocarbon dating can only be carried out on what was once a living organism—wood, shell, ash, metals containing some residue of clay or earth.

"Furthermore, radiocarbon dating did not, until the new process, give us an exact date of a sample, within an acceptable plus or minus variable. C14 concentration measurements were found to fluctuate with increasing magnetic-field strength, a decrease in the cosmic-ray flux, and subsequent drops in C14 production rate. However, the deviation is not pronounced on samples younger than two thousand years, such as the one we presume to have here."

Lauren paused. "All right so far?"

"It's beginning to come back," Father Moran said.

"Okay...Over here we have the equipment for Phase One of the operation, the pretreatment of the sample. Let's take the shell inlay for the chalice as our starting point. The sample would be weighed, treated with a 5–30 percent solution of hydrochloric acid to remove contamination, then placed in two liters of water. A vacuum is arranged, phospheric acid added to reduce the shell and release the carbon dioxide, which is collected in a five-liter storage flask. This is then passed over hot copper oxide, generated by using hydrogen to remove water vapor, and finally funnelled through potassium hydroxide to remove radon and other gases.

"Now we move across to the other side of the lab. We have our five-liter counter comprised of a copper plate with quartz insulator and a two-millimeter stainless-steel anode. There is a copper mode guide, gas port, lead washer and weld.

"The counter is placed within the Counter Shield or the 'castle,' which is two feet in width by 41 1/2 inches in length. The castle construction begins with an eight-inch layer of cast iron to protect the sample counter from gamma radiation, followed by four inches of paraffin to absorb neutrons, twenty-three cosmic-ray guard tubes, and one inch of mercury against Y-rays. The castle door is a steel-plate box filled with iron bricks, the horizontal motion being achieved by rack and pinion mechanism.

"Next to the castle is the Sharp Low-Beta Unit, the Baird Atomic #25 pre-amp for the guard counters, Fluke high-voltage supplies, and a ten-pen Esterline-

Angus Operation Events Counter. These record the actual counting of the sample once the counter is inside the castle and the system has been activated. The duration of the count averages 1200 minutes during the week, 4200 during the weekend, the statistical analysis recorded by the Esterline-Angus. Weekend counts, which we favor, are divided into ten-hour intervals and are statistically treated using the 2 of 3 criterion. The number of counts and the counting times of each measurement along with the sample identification are then given over to the computer, an IBM 3820 which calculates the net counting rates, ages, and errors, using predetermined equations.

"And that," Lauren concluded, "is the minilecture on conventional C14 dating. Ready for the next step?"

"I've read the paper you and Dr. Webber prepared. That should help."

She opened the door to the other chamber, revealing an assembly whose major feature was a pair of cylinders, six feet in length, three in diameter, that resembled conventional iron lungs. To one side was the support equipment.

"TRACE," Lauren Blair said. "The acronym for Tandem Rare Atom Counting Equipment conceived by Ted Litherland of the University of Toronto, applied to the archeological field by Isaiah Webber."

"And yourself," Father Moran reminded her.

"I still feel a little guilty about taking credit," Lauren admitted. "So much of the groundwork had already been done. I just came along and rearranged the pieces."

"As did Crick-Watson with the double helix," the priest told her. "Without their rearrangment—for which they received the Nobel Prize—man wouldn't have solved the riddle of the DNA molecule, the key to genetic reproduction."

Lauren laughed. "Okay, I'll take credit where credit's due." She turned her attention to the equipment. "This project began with the following question: could atom-counting improve conventional C-14 dating?

"In the approach initiated by Litherland, the C14 isotope must be segregated from all other atoms and molecules in the sample—a variation of the needle-haystack situation. The critical goal is to eliminate the vast number of these other impurities.

"A mass spectrometer is used to select particles of mass 14, eliminating the common atoms and molecules. An accelerator then breaks up the molecules of C14, leaving only the atoms. Here the mass spectrometer selects the mass 14 again. But a question arises: how can C14 atoms be distinguished from nitrogen 14 and counted? Nitrogen is the most common gas in the atmosphere; C14 occurs only in 100,000,000,000 nitrogen 14 atoms.

"The answer, which was arrived at by the juggling process I mentioned, was to bombard a sample with positive ions, using a tandem accelerator *before* the particles entered the mass spectrometer. The nitrogen 14 does not form negative ions and is left behind. Everything else becomes negatively charged and passes through the machine. Now C14 atoms can be counted and compared to the quantity of C12 and C13 atoms in the sample. Since these isotopic ratios decrease by half every 5,730 years (the half-life of C14) the age of the sample can be calculated.

"TRACE has incredible potential in the fields of geology and nuclear physics, but its importance to archeology is two-fold. Take for instance the shell sample, twenty-eight grams of which is required to be destroyed by using the conventional C14 method. With the accelerator, only a sample the size of a pinhead is needed. Therefore the specimen whose minute quantity made testing prohibitive, can be analyzed. Conversely, a large sample, such as the inlay on the chalice, need not be disfigured. Secondly, TRACE doubles the limit of C14 dating from

50,000 to 100,000 years, although on this sample we won't be working anywhere near these limits. Finally and equally important to this testing is the speed with which we can determine the data. TRACE will do in ten minutes what conventional dating needed three months for."

"Phenomenal," Father Moran murmured. "And the accuracy of the date?"

"With the modification Isaiah and I have implemented in the TRACE unit, we've been able to reduce the plus-minus figure to almost nil."

"How do you plan to proceed?" the priest asked.

"Let's go back into the other section," Lauren said. When they were in the C14 lab she came before the chalice. "Right now all I see is metal and shell. Of the two, shell is organic and suitable for TRACE testing. But there may be some other compositions in the base of the cup. Or they could be just a thin veneer. If there is brass beneath it, I might be able to do something with that, separate some copper, for instance. The other procedures will be as follows: for the identification of raw materials I'll be using a chemical analysis and probably specific-gravity tests. Geographical source of materials will involve chemical analysis as well as isotopic analysis. The fabrication technique will need metallographic microscopy."

"So you won't be satisfied by just determining the age," Moran commented.

"Especially not in this case," Lauren said emphatically. "There can't be any discrepancies between time, raw materials and location of these materials, and manufacturing methods."

"All or nothing."

"Yes." She looked at the priest curiously. "That doesn't worry you, does it, Father?"

"No, not at all," Edmund Moran replied. "If I seem somewhat taken aback it's simply a reaction to this deluge of new analytical methodology. You've worked in the field, I'm sure you appreciate the feeling. You

take something out of the earth that is instantly recognizable. You *feel* the piece is genuine. And if that
object isn't tested soon thereafter, if it's permitted to
languish in some vault building up a mythology, as
in the case of the Shroud of Turin for example, then
it's emotionally difficult to surrender it for scientific
evaluation. The object has become part of the Mystery
of the Church. You wonder sometimes if the Mystery,
the miracle, is not as important as the truth."

"But they can be one and the same, the Mystery
and truth," Lauren said.

"Lauren, I have never heard of, much less witnessed, actual empirical proof of a miracle. A miracle
by definition is inexplicable. It requires a leap of
faith."

"I won't be taking that away from you or the
Church, Father," she said. "The testing will tell us
everything there is to know about the chalice except
for one thing: did Christ's lips actually touch it? So
long as testing does not prove otherwise, you have
the possibility for that leap of faith."

*Here I am speaking about truth yet I cannot look
upon that cup without suspicion, without fear ... and
God help me, loathing.*

"Father ..."

"I'm sorry. I was just thinking of what you said.
You're certain the nuns didn't have you for a while
when you were growing up?"

"A lapsed Episcopalian, I'm afraid," she laughed.
"You'll be needing a lab jacket. Forty-two?"

He nodded and watched as she walked off to the
small linen closet. As soon as she stepped away he
felt the heat of the cup reaching out for him, seeking
him out, wanting to touch him.

CHAPTER TEN

H E COULDN'T GET IN to see Stukley until half past eleven. The professor of archeology had been chairing a conference until then. Tim McConnell had already cancelled his ten o'clock tutorial and now, in order to see Stukley, he was cutting the noon to one class, for the second time that week. There was no other way.

"Don't you have a class at this hour?" Stukley asked benignly, seeming to read Tim's thoughts.

Tim crossed his legs and sat back in the leather wing chair. "They're preparing an oral exposition," he said easily.

Stukley smiled back. A robust man, with a balding freckled scalp, bushy red beard, and sparkling green eyes, Stukley didn't have an enemy in the world. Loved by his students, respected by faculty, he was the sort who worked away quietly on his projects, patiently putting all the pieces in place until he was satisfied with the whole. Overly modest, Stukley sometimes let due credit slip by. It really didn't matter to him. What did was the fact that Tim McConnell was lying to him—about his class. He also knew why the young instructor was here.

"We could have set another time," Stukley said.

"This was convenient."

Stukley chose not to pursue the matter. He reached for his cigars and offered one to the younger man, who declined.

"What's on your mind, Tim?" he said, lighting up and puffing away gently.

McConnell leaned forward, elbows on knees, gazing up at the older man.

"As you probably know, the Finance Committee has refused me the grant for the Bolivian project. Personally I don't think it's a matter of money at all, but rather experience, seniority—in spite of the samples I brought back. You've been working in the same area—hell, you *pioneered* the area—so I propose we join forces. Let's draw up a new presentation, have another go at it."

Stukley nodded, tossed the kitchen match into the tray, and said: "A joint venture?"

"That's it."

Arnold Stukley seldom felt anger. In circumstances where others did so he instead found sorrow, or at worst pity. And he was sorry for Tim McConnell. The boy had a good mind—not exceptional, but worthy of development. Stukley knew that much because McConnell had been an undergraduate student of his. But he was proud and he was greedy. The Lake Titicaca project had been born in this office five years ago. Stukley was still putting the pieces in place. Soon he would go to the Finance Committee. A year ago, he had heard that Tim McConnell was working furiously in the same area. Not without success, either. The child's jawbone he had unearthed in Bolivia had made for interesting theories of south-to-north migration. But the find was only a stepping stone, only another piece of the whole, not the philosopher's stone McConnell believed it to be. He had asked Tim to come by and talk about the find, but McConnell never did. He avoided Stukley in the faculty lounge, even in the street. In that year, Stukley could not remember more than half a dozen words passing between them. Ingratitude.

"Do you have your presentation with you?"

"Just so happens..."

Tim reached inside his briefcase, drew out a thin

folder, and handed it to Stukley. The older man read the salient points quickly.

"A digest really," McConnell explained.

And freshly typed, Stukley noticed, just for him. Nothing new in it. No mention of the recent developments in Brazil, the Venezuelan find.... A rehash of his own work, not plagiarized but not extended, either.

"Why is this project so important to you, Tim?" Stukley asked gently. "Usually one doesn't confront the Finance Committee a second time on the same project, at least not in the same year."

He knew the answer to this too but he prayed the boy wouldn't lie to him.

"There comes a time when a project has to move into the field," Tim said, sitting up, speaking directly to Stukley. "It's my opinion that all the research that can be undertaken here has been done. Theories must be put to the test."

No, boy, Stukley thought. *It's* you *who must be tested. You need a project, a success,* anything, *to forestall what is overtaking you: dismissal from your post. You're grasping at straws. You're aware of this but you refuse to go back, pick up the pieces. This dream of yours has seized you too hard, gone too deep.*

"I know you've been working terribly hard on this project," Stukley said. "I understand how you must feel about the Committee's decision. You also know that I am still not ready with my presentation."

"But if we put our work together—" Tim started to say.

"Do you have more than you've shown me here?" Stukley asked.

Tim McConnell's eyes narrowed. "No."

"You've missed two key developments. Venezuela and Brazil. The Fresca and de Masse expeditions. Their reports were published two months ago."

"An oversight," Tim said, voice faltering. "I guess I was too busy."

"Tim, speaking of oversights, Faculty Committee has been waiting a year and a half now for a publication from you. The deadline is only six months off."

"How can I publish when they refuse to fund the expedition, the source of the work?" McConnell demanded, voice rising.

The older man shook his head but said nothing. The issue was clear: the boy had done no writing since his doctoral thesis. Nothing at all.

"There are two reasons why I can't consider doing a joint venture with you, Tim," Stukley said. "First, I am not ready to undertake any kind of expedition. Two years from now, perhaps as soon as eighteen months, yes. But not now. The second reason has to do with you. Even if I asked the Finance Committee to sponsor the project and included you, the Committee would strike your name. You've neglected your teaching responsibilities far too flagrantly. To the point where several students have complained to the Dean. Faculty would never consent to a leave for you."

A veil of cigar smoke hung between the two men. Then a rasping, ugly voice cut through it, a voice dripping with bitterness.

"What you really mean to say is that you don't want me around. You think I took the project from you, usurped your precious work. To stop me now means you capitalize on everything I've done to date. You'll block me and everyone else until you're damn good and ready to move your ass out into the field!"

Arnold Stukley gave the chair a nudge, pushing it so that it swivelled towards the window, allowing him to see the Yard in the distance.

"I don't believe there's anything more to be said," he murmured. "At least not for the time being. Good day, Tim."

Even the harsh scraping of the chair and the angry slam of the door did not anger the professor. He wished there had been some way he could have reached the boy, helped him. But Tim McConnell had never understood that, as patient as Stukley was, he never really sat still.

The letter was set in his pigeon box at the rear of the porter's cubicle at the Club. The porter had tagged it with a red flag. Urgent. Tim McConnell ripped open the envelope after he had settled himself at the bar and the smell of pungent junipers from the first martini drifted up, promising comfort, solace.

Tim McConnell held the vellum between his fingers, then slowly and deliberately began to crush it in his fist, squeezing it tighter and tighter until a little ball of paper dropped, bounced, and rolled into the trough of the bar. The faint crackle of paper unfolding was thunder in his ears. McConnell reached for his glass and drained half his drink.

The sanctimonious fuckers! "Discuss your progress." There was no fucking progress! They knew it. How could there be when the Finance Committee had stonewalled him? "You are invited to meet..." You are invited to take the first step onto the ladder leading to the guillotine, where we will, with due process and solemnity, behead you for high crimes and misdemeanors against Faculty Regulations! This was the first full martini talking. By the fourth and fifth he had devised and executed exquisite torments for each and every member of the Finance Committee, overcome incredible odds, risen to unknown heights. And he had done this alone. The lounge and the bar became crowded as the chimes struck one o'clock. Business was brisk, the chatter light and easy. The beginning of a new term meant seeing old friends, scouting the new talent. But no one came up to Tim McConnell. Several colleagues recognized him but steered away. Even those who didn't know him sensed the aura of impending defeat over him, the rank, bitter odor of impending disaster that clothed him like an invisible mantle. Success, it is said, has a thousand fathers while failure is the eternal orphan.

"Doctor Leech!"

Percival Leech handed his coat and umbrella to the porter, then bent down to remove his galoshes and passed these over as well. He sniffed disdainfully at the liquor coming off the young man.

"Doctor Leech..."

"Yes." Leech made four syllables out of one, turning round to see Tim McConnell standing over him, face flushed, shining with sweat.

"Doctor McConnell," Leech intoned.

"If I could have a few words with you..."

"I'm sorry but I'm expected upstairs for lunch. Excuse me."

"Doctor Leech." Tim's hand scarcely brushed the older man's sleeve but Leech reacted as though he had been touched by a cattle prod.

"Don't ever do that again!" he hissed. "Never!"

"A few words, sir, please!"

The lobby was thronged. He could allow the young fool to make a spectacle of himself here or he could handle him in private.

"Three minutes, Doctor McConnell."

Leech led the way upstairs, aware that twice McConnell missed a step and stumbled. He turned left into a small smoking room, waited for McConnell to follow.

"You've something to say to me?"

Tim McConnell wet his lips. His throat was burning, phlegm choking. A drink, some water, anything....

"I'm waiting, Doctor McConnell."

"I would like you to reconsider my proposal," Tim said, desperately throwing up the first words that came to mind.

"I don't understand you."

"I would like the Finance Committee to review my grant application upon your recommendation."

Think, Christ, think! Get it together!

"I assume what you are trying to tell me is that you wish me to intervene on your behalf before the Finance Committee with specific reference to the Bolivian project," Leech said succinctly. "Am I correct?"

"Yes...yes, that's it."

There was no hint of understanding or compassion in Leech's eyes. The great brows furrowed and obsidian eyes glittered as though anticipating the thrill, the exaltation, of the kill.

"I will do no such thing."

"But—"

"McConnell, you are becoming a burden to this university, an embarrassment to your colleagues and the department. I will take the liberty of telling you that the Finance Committee considered your proposal a waste of its time. The presentation was amateurish, the budget based on nothing but speculation, the objective egotistical, the benefit of the exercise dubious at best. Instead of cooperating with your colleagues—I refer specifically to Doctor Stukley—you deliberately undercut them, flirted with plagiarism of their work. And why did you do all this? Because you believed the project would somehow atone for your appalling deficiencies in your work at the university.

"I'm afraid it won't. It is highly unlikely you will be given *any* teaching next year in view of the students' complaints about your methods and class attendance. Further, unless you can satisfiy the publishing requirement within the allotted time, your standing in this institution will be reviewed. Given that your personal habits scarcely do you credit, I, for one, would recommend that the university not renew its contract with you."

He listened to the words as only a drunk could: staring at the speaker stupidly, unable to summon a word in his defense, the mind reeling from one accusation after another.

"I trust I have made myself clear," Leech said. "Now, I have an engagement."

Leech's hand was on the doorknob when McConnell seized him by the shoulders. Leech turned round quickly on his heel, his face only inches away from that of his assailant.

"Get a grip on yourself!" he said harshly. "Otherwise the campus police will be called and you will be dragged off in full view of the entire faculty!"

"I'm begging you, for Christ's sake," Tim rasped. "What more can I do—"

"You can end this disgusting exhibition!" Leech thundered. "You are a degenerate and a coward. Now get out of my way!"

What have you to lose, the voice whispered tantalizingly. Beat his face into that door! Rip the sanctimonious expression off his ugly face!

Tim McConnell's hand slid from Leech's shoulder and fell by his side. After the Chairman stepped out, he staggered over to the sofa and flung himself onto it. A shudder passed through his body and he leaned forward and began to cry. In the end he hadn't even been able to strike out at his tormentor. He had permitted himself to be humiliated even though there was nothing to lose. *You are a degenerate and a coward!*

Behind him a sneeze erupted. McConnell whirled around, his face a mask of fury and hatred. Isaiah Webber, half his face covered by an enormous red handkerchief, was shuffling toward him.

"Ah, goodness," he said thickly. "I shouldn't have gotten out of bed. . . . Had to though . . . had to come in."

Isaiah Webber slumped into the chair opposite the younger man.

"I didn't intend to eavesdrop," he said, the words coming out slowly. "I was over by the bookcase when the two of you came in.... I'm sorry."

McConnell said nothing. All the energy was running out of him, like sand through an hourglass.

"Leech can be like that—vicious, thoughtless, a not-so-petty tyrant," Isaiah Webber continued between sniffles. "I know, I've seen him act like that before. It's no good letting him get to you."

Webber paused to blow his nose.

"I shouldn't have come in," he repeated, shaking his head. "Tim, walk back with me. I know a little about your project. Let me hear the rest. Let me think about it. I don't want to see you destroy yourself this way. Waste, needless waste."

"Lauren," Tim muttered, his voice hoarse. "She put you up to this!"

"No, Tim. Lauren didn't ask anything of me. In fact she doesn't even know I'm here. Now come, I need my herbal tea and root essence. And you—what have you to lose by talking to a nosy old man? Come."

Tim rose, wiping the sweat and tears from his face with both palms. He threw his head back and squeezed his eyes shut.

"Close, so close!" he whispered. "So fucking close!"

"I know, I know," Isaiah Webber said, draping a long bony arm over the boy's shoulder. "We'll use the staff elevator, go out the back way...."

CHAPTER ELEVEN

HER CONCENTRATION was so complete that for long periods of time she forgot the priest's presence. But when she looked up and saw him he seemed to be watching not her or the way she worked, but the chalice. It was not interest or anticipation she sensed in him. Rather caution...which was almost fear.

Lauren Blair knew that something had changed within the priest. He was a different man from the one she had been introduced to the previous evening. Try as she might to draw him out, Father Edmund Moran remained taciturn, answering questions about himself, his work at Harvard, and his field experiences with brief, general comments. Nonetheless it was evident he knew his way around a geochronological lab. By one o'clock the chalice had been weighed, photographed, and x-rayed, the step-by-step procedures committed to tape.

"Are you hungry, Father? If you like we can go out. There are several holes-in-the-wall around here."

"Thank you, but I'm not hungry," the cleric answered. He tapped the hardbound notebook. "Rome will be calling this evening. Unless I go home and type up these notes even I won't be able to make sense of anything I've written."

Security escorted them to the corridor that ran behind the Grand Salon.

"I'm told it's been like this since the doors opened," Lauren murmured. From where he stood, Father Moran saw that the chamber was packed. At least two hundred people were wending their way through the roped-off labyrinth. A low gentle murmur, punctuated by sharp exclamations, rose toward the vaulted cupolas.

"We had to bring in additional personnel," security informed them. "They're campus police," he added deprecatingly. "But during the day their presence is enough."

Father Moran was about to ask how the investigation into Cathy Windsor's death was proceeding, but held back. Instead he murmured to Lauren that he would be back in a couple of hours. Skirting the crowds, he made for the front door.

Lauren made her way onto the loading bays and stepped into the quadrangle. Suddenly she stopped. Some twenty yards away was the gazebo. A small panel truck with CAMPUS MAINTENANCE stencilled across its side was parked nearby. Lauren saw two men in white overalls, one on his knees painting the steps, the other pushing a roller across the floor of the gazebo.

Cathy Windsor. She had not forgotten about her. The memory of the killing remained in the back of her mind, persistently infringing on her concentration. The quadrangle was filled with people now, all taking advantage of what the weatherman had said would be the last sunny afternoon before rain came to stay for good. Lauren Blair backed away. She did not see the picnickers or joggers or cyclists. Not the young mothers pushing perambulators or students hurrying toward Haddon Hall for a one o'clock class. Donnellan's sad weathered words rose in her mind.

Her name was Cathy Windsor and she had been gutted.

Lauren Blair moved away from the quadrangle, staying in the shadows cast by the Museum wall. Suddenly she did not want to be alone and hoped that Tim had returned to his office after class.

* * *

Arturo Cardinal Capellini was not downstairs when Moran arrived at the carriage house. The young priest presumed he was still resting up in the guest bedroom. It took him thirty minutes to type up a résumé of the morning's work at the Museum. When he was through the priest brought out a leather-bound address book.

The call to his first cousin, Oleg Baldarese, chief executive of the family concerns in the U.S., was put through to the limousine inching along Fifth Avenue. Moran quickly explained what was needed. In turn, Baldarese assured him that a company Lear would be ready to leave Logan at six that evening. Then a seat would be reserved for an as yet unnamed passenger who would present himself at the Air France desk at Kennedy no later than seven that evening. The Concorde would depart Kennedy at half past the hour, touch down at Charles de Gaulle outside of Paris three hours later. A Baldarese Gulfstream would be waiting for the Paris–Jerusalem leg of the journey. Oleg Baldarese asked no questions concerning the identity of the passenger, nor the reasons for such subterfuge. He trusted his cousin implicitly.

"Everything is arranged?"

Edmund Moran did not turn around. "Yes, it is arranged."

He felt a hand upon his shoulder and looked up. Sleep had restored some of the color to Capellini's features. The eyes were as he remembered them, alert, penetrating. The hand did not tremble.

"You did not sleep at all," the cardinal said.

"No."

"You must not come back here tonight," Capellini told him.

"What else am I to do?"

"Tell me about the arrangements."

"I suggest you come to the Museum at a quarter to four. I will speak to Lauren Blair shortly before then. I need only a few moments to wrap up the cup.

She will try to stop me, argue, but your presence and authority will confuse her. When we leave she will call Leech. But by then we shall be on our way to the airport. An aircraft will be waiting. Once we are airborne no one can stop you."

He finished by explaining what would happen in New York and Paris.

"Your Vatican passport affords you diplomatic immunity but you won't have to use it. The Baldarese offices will have spoken with American and French customs. Your name will not appear on the manifest." The young priest looked at Capellini. "What is in Jerusalem, Arturo?"

"Refuge," Capellini said. "There is a man in Jerusalem who will help me. I have already spoken to him. He is waiting. The cup will be returned to sacred ground until I can determine what is to be done with it."

"What *can* be done with it?"

"I believe the choice is quite simple: we can continue the quest for the true provenance. In time, once the furor dies down, arrangements can be made for testing the chalice. But the tests will be conducted on sacred ground. Believe me, nothing would please me more than to have the testing carried out. But at the present time we cannot permit it." He paused. "One has already died."

"The alternative?"

"If I feel that I or my whereabouts are to be discovered, I will destroy the cup. I will melt it down and pour the gold into the gutter, crush the shell until it is nothing but dust."

"Would you do this even if you weren't certain the cup was the Grail?"

"There would be no choice," Capellini said coldly. "I have permitted the chalice to be removed from consecrated ground. The result has been death. I have the opportunity to retrieve it. I cannot fail."

The curator pulled the ottoman closer to Father Moran's chair and sat down on it.

"Edmund," he said. "I ask you to listen very carefully to me. You must endure and survive the ordeal that lies ahead of you. The entire force of the Church will bear down upon you, even before I have landed in Jerusalem. To give yourself time to prepare for the onslaught you will come to New York with me. Take a hotel room for a night or two. You will be found eventually, possibly even before you contact di Stefano yourself. But you must give yourself time to prepare.

"When they demand to know what happened, you are to blame everything on me—"

"How can I do such a thing?" Edmund Moran cried.

Capellini waved his hand impatiently. "Listen to me. You are to say I coerced you, forced you into giving up the cup, used my authority and position to hold you to silence."

"I can't!" the priest whispered. "I can't turn against you."

"You must! And you will!" Capellini said with icy calm. "I am destroying you, Edmund. Because of me, the esteem you have in the eyes of the Church will be severely compromised. I will have come close to ruining you. But you must not let them complete what I have begun. Use me to shield yourself, which is only just. Trade on the power and influence of your name. In the modern world the Church can ill afford to lose allies of Baldarese stature. If you meet di Stefano's rage with your own, show him how you had no choice but to obey me, neither he nor the Holy Father will be able to fault you.

"You must fight this way, Edmund. Not only for yourself but because you are the next Fisher King. With the grace of God I will live to learn the truth about the cup. But if not, it is you who must continue the quest. I have left you the name of the man in

Jerusalem. If anything untoward should befall me he will be expecting you. Similarly, provisions have been made with the Grande Banque de Genève. Its director is an old friend of mine. I have spoken with him about you. He knows that if you come, it will mean that I could not.

"Finally, if nothing changes by the time you become the chalice's custodian then you will have to decide what is to be done with it. Neither di Stefano nor His Holiness will live forever. There is a chance that after their demise you will be able to return the cup to the Church. There you will be able to carry out the final tests, if these are still necessary."

The curator leaned forward and gripped Father Moran by the shoulder.

"I love you as though you were my own flesh and blood," he whispered, tears streaming down his cheeks. "You can deny me and still fulfill the promise within yourself. I have asked you—demanded—that you forsake your talents and ambitions for this cause. I must now beg of you to forgive!"

Edmund Moran rose, bringing the older man with him.

"There is nothing to forgive," he said, his voice calm, resolute. "I will stand by you. I ask only that you hear my confession, bless me, and pray with me."

She was back in the lab in less than an hour. Tim had not answered when she called his office. The porter at the Faculty Club informed her that Doctor McConnell had lunched there but left. There was no message waiting for her back at the Museum. To take her mind off Tim, Lauren did not wait for Father Moran but set to work on the chalice. By the time he arrived she had removed an infinitesimal piece of shell and was preparing it for the TRACE.

Father Edmund Moran timed his entry perfectly. The hour was half past three when security admitted him to the lab.

"Lauren!" he called out.

"In here." Her voice carried clearly from the inner room that housed the TRACE equipment. "Be with you in a minute."

Moran did not wait. The chalice remained on the lab table, the wooden crate and aluminum carrying case tucked on the shelf underneath. He brought these out, fumbling with the chamois cover. Without pausing to think he slipped the leather over the chalice.

"Father, what are you doing?"

His eyes darted up to the clock. The limousine he had ordered should have picked up Capellini by now and started for the Museum. His hands lifted the chalice into the crate.

"There has been a change of plan," he said, not daring to look at her yet. He pressed the cover onto the crate, feeling the small finishing nails slide into the original grooves.

He turned to face her. "The chalice is being returned to Rome."

"But why? On whose authority?" She was standing before him, black hair shining in the lights, blue eyes refusing to let him go, mouth taut in anger.

Forgive me, Lauren, that I must do this to you!

"The instruction comes from the curator of the Museum of Pagan Antiquities," Moran said. "He will be here in a few minutes."

"Why?" The demand was harsh, unyielding.

"That is a matter of confidence. I'm sorry."

For an instant he thought she would relent. But no.

"I had better call Doctor Leech and ask him what this is all about."

"No, Lauren!"

His hand flashed out, seizing hers by the wrist before it was anywhere near the wall phone.

"What are you doing?" she cried, snatching her hand away, incredulous.

174

"Leech does not know yet," Moran said desperately. "If he is to be told, Capellini will—"

"*If* he is to be told?"

"The chalice belongs to the Church, Lauren. I am not obligated to explain anything to you or anyone else!"

"The chalice has been entrusted to the care of this Museum!"

"Lauren, please..." Moran pleaded. "Please don't force me to turn on you. For God's sake, trust me! We know what we're doing!"

The priest looked up at the clock. A few more minutes, no more. He lifted the crate into the carrier.

"I don't understand, Father," Lauren said, staring at him. "What's happened to you? Ever since this morning you've been acting as though there's someone looking over your shoulder. What is it you're afraid of?" She paused. "What is it about the chalice you've been keeping from us?"

Moran looked up at her just as the telephone rang. He snatched at the receiver.

"Father Moran speaking."

The caller was the chauffeur. He was still waiting for his passenger. There had been no answer at the door nor to his phone call.

"I'll be right there."

Edmund Moran stared at the carrier with loathing. What had happened? Where was Capellini?

"I want you to get out of there," he said, punching "O" for security. "This is Father Moran, would you unlock the doors for us, please?"

"But why?"

"Just do as I say. Extend me that last bit of trust. Promise me, Lauren, for the love of God, promise me, silence for another thirty minutes."

She looked at him steadily, weighing the desperation in his voice against what reason told her to do.

"Thirty minutes," she said softly. "But no more."

* * *

He was in the garden, standing under the apple tree, listening to the soft warble of the birds. A last moment of solitude to gird his courage.

He did not hear so much as feel the presence of something behind him. But he did not turn around.

"Priest!"

The voice was not human. If a snake were able to speak that is how its voice would have sounded. Last evening in the park, the voice calling after him: "We have been waiting, waiting for you..."

"Ah, priest, you were so clever," the voice rasped at him. "So clever even your kind did not believe you. But you know better, priest. You knew enough to try and take the chalice back!"

Slowly Arturo Capellini began to turn around. He could feel hot breath on the back of his neck, the foul, foul stench that was enveloping him.

"You have defiled our font, priest. You have touched it and it has scarred you. Now the font must be washed clean, made pure once more. We shall wash it, priest, in your blood."

Arturo Capellini twisted his head around. In that split second he realized he was going to die. He had the image of the stranger who was himself, who had at last arrived on that distant shore. But that was not the image he carried to his death. A hand, scaled and peeling, black and rotted green, shot out at him. Fingers with talons like scythes cut into his throat. The head of Arturo Capellini teetered for a single horrible instant on the stump of his neck, then dropped on the flagstones, rolling face up, the eyes open in stark terror, the lips curled back in a scream that would last on into eternity.

He was running in the long loping strides he'd developed on the athletic field. He had flung his jacket off just outside the Museum. The wind felt cold against his chest, the air chilling the lungs. But he ran on, strides lengthening, knees pumping until he was almost sprinting.

What's happened to him?

Father Edmund Moran could have saved himself a minute, perhaps ninety seconds, by cutting diagonally through the quadrangle. Instead he stayed on River Street. If the limousine was en route, that was the direction the driver would follow. He didn't see it. Only bewildered looks cast at him by passersby, the curses flung at him by motorists as he darted out into traffic, crossing over to Chestnut Street.

The stretch Cadillac was parked at the foot of the path leading to the coach house. The driver saw Moran run up and made to get out of the car. He shouted something but the priest already had his key out. The next instant he was inside the house, the door closed behind him.

"Arturo!"

Father Moran pressed his back against the door. For a moment he did not move, taking deep breaths, trying to calm himself.

"Arturo!"

The rank vile smell assailed him, inundating him like some giant wave. The priest moved forward into the living room. The odor was overwhelming here. Suddenly he whirled around. Nothing.

He acted on bedrock instinct, crashing through the French doors into the garden. The eye registered the decapitated corpse of Arturo Capellini but Moran did not stop. His peripheral vision captured a sight that propelled him forward. It was coming after him. It wanted him.

One leap brought him up to the stone bench. In the same motion he flung himself at the garden wall, scraping his palms against the rough ledge. His shoulder muscles screamed in pain as he hoisted his body to the left, heel catching the top of the wall. One more twist and he was over, dropping onto the sidewalk below. As he staggered back, he saw what was waiting for him standing on the ledge, its legs apart, grinning in bloody anticipation.

"Ah, priest!"

His feet came out from under him. He felt himself falling very slowly toward the ground. The sidewalk loomed up, catching him on the temple. There was the warm rush of blood, a gasp, then oblivion.

CHAPTER TWELVE

GERRY MUST HAVE CALLED HER from the office. When they arrived at his Brookline apartment Monique Samulovitch was placing breakfast on the table: fresh hot bagels, cream cheese with bits of lox mixed in, omelettes filled with French bacon, mushrooms, and sauteed onions. Donnellan groaned. Once he started eating he could not stop. Samulovitch refused to let him drink coffee.

"Mineral water," he advised solemnly. "Coffee will only keep you up. Now you'll get upstairs, shower, and sack out for a few hours."

"The Museum—"

"I've already called them. They know where you are." Samulovitch gripped his forearm. "You need the rest, Frank. Take it when you can."

Donnellan made his way upstairs, feeling every one of his forty-six years. He stood under a hot shower for ten minutes then climbed gratefully in between cool sheets. He lay there, hands folded behind his neck, staring at the ceiling.

Black coat, red scarf. An older man. Why do I automatically think of a priest?

What Donnellan saw in his mind's eye reminded him of a sketch in the overleaf of an H.G. Wells novel, *The Invisible Man*: a fully clothed figure without a head or a face, and a hat that remained suspended above the coat collar. That was the image he fell asleep with. Later, in his dreams, the face came to him. It belonged to Lauren Blair.

* * *

"Get up, Frank!"

He responded to the touch on his shoulder even before the words registered. Automatically his head turned toward the clock radio. 4:01 flipped over to 4:02.

"The Museum..."

"Negative." Samulovitch handed him his trousers. "Homicide on Chestnut Street." The detective paused. "Very bad."

"Who lives on Chestnut Street?" Donnellan asked, clearing his throat. He stuffed his shirt in the trousers, slipped on the camel's hair vest, and strapped the supple leather holster across his back. The .41 Magnum slapped hard against his ribs. Donnellan reached for his tweed jacket.

"A Father Edmund Moran. But he's not the victim."

"Lauren..." Donnellan whispered and began to move.

They made Chestnut Street in twenty minutes, Donnellan driving. The area was sealed off by black-and-whites. An ambulance was being loaded. The coroner's black station wagon with its frosted rear windows was backed up almost to the front doors. As Donnellan saw the ambulance begin to coast down the drive he swerved in front of it. Ignoring the protests from the driver, he ran to the rear and wrenched open the doors.

"Jesus Christ, mister!" the paramedic shouted at him.

"Is he alive?" Donnellan asked softly.

There were abrasions on the priest's left cheek, a faint trail of blood along the right temple. The eyelids fluttered. The face was the color of old ash.

"Mild concussion. But he's in shock. Now, what the hell—"

Donnellan brushed past him. He slipped one hand beneath the priest's head and gently lifted it up.

"Father Moran...Father...Can you hear me?"

The eyelids lifted slowly, revealing bloodshot eyes, the terror imbedded in them making Donnellan wince.

"Father..."

"Lauren..." the priest whispered. "Lauren must know...she must be told." The sentence trailed off into a guttural moan. The next instant the thrashing began.

"Hold him down!"

The paramedic scrambled up behind Donnellan, syringe out. Donnellan shielded him from the priest's clawing hands long enough for the needle to penetrate. Donnellan cried out as Moran's grip tightened about his throat in a final spasm. He pried the fingers loose.

"Something goes wrong with him, it's your ass!" the medic ranted. "Now get the hell out of here!" He thumped twice on the driver's partition.

Donnellan slammed the rear doors shut and the ambulance took off. He reached for his communicator and depressed the switch that sent out an automatic signal. Instantly the reply came in.

"This is the Monitor."

"This is Charger One. Overlord. Repeat Overlord. I'm coming in."

"Frank...Frank!"

Samulovitch was standing by the open front door of the carriage house. He was shaking his head as though in disbelief.

"Same fucking thing, Frank!" he whispered. "Same as Cathy Windsor."

"A woman..."

"An old man."

Donnellan ran past him into the garden where the forensic team was setting up its equipment.

"Back off!"

He lifted the tarp from the body and stared keenly at the corpse. The horror did not register. He did not see it because in a way he had known what to expect.

He was looking for something else...and found it.
The black coat, shredded and matted with blood. The
red scarf trailing out of the right-hand pocket...

"Where's the head?"

The forensic man's jaw dropped.

"His goddam head, I want to see it!"

"In the car..."

"Did you see it?"

"Yeah..."

"Did he have a crewcut?"

The technician looked at Donnellan in disgust and
backed away.

"Yeah," he hissed. "He had a fucking crewcut!"

The wall clock in the Museum's Terrace Café
chimed quarter past four. Lauren ground out her
cigarette and glanced around her. The ever popular
tea hour at the Bennett was in full swing. Boston
matrons sat primly on French wrought-iron chairs,
sipping Twinings and nibbling on petit-fours. Students mixed with the younger faculty; the talk
ranged from the subjects of where to winter this year
to esoteric commentaries on the Vatican exhibit. The
hanging plants, gay red-and-white-checkered table-
cloths, and solarium ceiling put a Continental patina
over the setting.

Lauren was oblivious to it all. In five minutes
Father Moran's thirty minutes would be up.

And what will I do then?

She would return to the lab. If Moran hadn't returned she would—damn, what had gotten into him!
What was it about the chalice that frightened him
so badly?

Lauren decided. If Father Moran wasn't there
when she got back, she would have security put the
cup back into the fail-safe vault. She would keep her
silence as he had asked, but only if he had told her
the truth. Otherwise she would go to Leech.

A soft but incessant beep filled the terrace. Almost

in unison heads looked up and around. It was the signal that the Museum was closing—more than ninety minutes ahead of schedule.

Lauren saw two things simultaneously: the first was the entry of two well-dressed but definitely out-of-place men who stationed themselves on either side of the double French doors. They were looking directly at her. The Muzak ceased. The familiar tape-recorded message wafted out over the speakers.

"Ladies and gentlemen, the Terrace Café will be closing in five minutes. Thank you."

The babble of curiosity had barely started when it ceased. Frank Donnellan entered the café, making for her table.

"Inspector—"

"Lauren, would you come with me, please." The concern in his soft brown eyes was obvious. It dissolved the protest forming on her lips.

Lauren rose and moved ahead of him, conscious of the arm on her elbow. Security fell in behind them. Coming out of the rear stairwells into the corridor that ran behind the Grand Salon, Lauren saw the Museum emptying, campus police shepherding out the public. She caught a glimpse of Donnellan's men observing the exodus from the second-level balcony.

"Another accident, Inspector?" she murmured.

He looked at her sharply. "Another one," he nodded.

"Not Father Moran!"

He stopped dead. "Why him?" The intensity in his voice shocked her.

"Inspector!"

Percival Leech was standing in the elevator car, glaring at Donnellan. He stepped out, the doors sighing to a close behind him and his escort.

"Would you be so kind as to tell me what is going on?"

"The Museum is being sealed. Including the labs.

183

It will remain off limits to all personnel except my staff until further notice."

"Inspector, I fear you are overstepping the bounds of your authority," Leech said frostily. "Unless you offer me convincing reason why the facilities should be so quarantined, I will countermand your directive."

"A priest has been murdered," Donnellan said softly.

"But you said Father Moran..." Lauren cried.

"It wasn't him. Father Moran was in the area of the killing. He could have been the second victim."

"Then who was it?" Leech demanded.

"We don't have an ID yet."

"And did this outrage take place on Museum grounds?"

"No, at Father Moran's home."

"Oh, my God!" Lauren whispered.

"Then I fail to see why you're closing—"

"My jurisdiction is security," Donnellan cut him off. "Father Moran is the Vatican liaison for this exhibit. A threat against him is a threat against all of us. Therefore, I *can* authorize a quarantine. Please do not misunderstand me, Doctor Leech: until I find out what the hell is going on the exhibit stays closed!"

"How was he killed?"

The two men stared at Lauren Blair.

"How was he killed?" she repeated. "Like Cathy Windsor?"

Donnellan nodded. "Like her."

"Donnellan, unless you can prove that the two killings are a direct threat, as you put it, to the exhibit, the doors to this Museum will open punctually at nine o'clock tomorrow morning. Further, I am still awaiting the report you promised me on last night's events." Leech did not falter under Donnellan's enraged stare. "I mean that, Inspector, believe me." He turned to Lauren. "And the testing will proceed as well. I'm certain the Inspector can make more than adequate provisions for your safety."

Donnellan studied him for what seemed a very long time. "Yes, that I can promise you," he said softly, and led Lauren away.

"You still haven't told me where we're going."
"Mass General."

Donnellan swerved around a UPS truck that tried to pull in between him and his escort of outriders. "Lunatic," he muttered, glancing at the girl. Lauren was sitting back, looking straight ahead with a steady gaze which told him she was seeing nothing of what was happening on the road ahead of her.

"Why are we going there—"

The rest of her words were drowned out by the roar of engines reverberating within the Brookline Parkway Tunnel.

"I thought you might know that."

She swivelled around to face him, bracing herself with one arm against the dash.

"Why do you say that?"

"I managed to get to Father Moran before he lost consciousness. He was very concerned for you. More than for himself." Donnellan paused. "Do you know why he should feel that way?"

Lauren looked away. "No, I don't."

"Why did he leave in such a hurry, Lauren?"

"I don't know, Inspector."

"Would you call me Frank?"

Out of the corner of her eye she saw he wasn't smiling and that his eyes remained on the road. There was a shyness to his question.

"All right."

Donnellan followed the motorcycles up to the emergency exit and killed the engine.

"You're not lying to me, Lauren," he said. "I can tell that. But neither are you sharing what you know. Perhaps there is some understanding between you and Father Moran, a matter of trust. The question I put to you is the same one I will ask him: is that trust worth a human life?"

Mass General was one of the few hospitals in the country with a special section reserved exclusively for police suspects. Located in the west end of Holloway Tower, the three-room unit was separated from the rest of the ward by electronically operated doors. The windows were bulletproof, the rooms bare except for essentials. Any object that could conceivably be adapted for use as a weapon or means of suicide had been removed.

Lauren Blair and Frank Donnellan were escorted to Holloway West by the attending physician.

"There's been a rather peculiar development," the doctor was saying in a pronounced English accent. "It would appear that the good Father is suffering from amnesia."

Donnellan placed himself between the physician and the door to Moran's room. "What are you saying?"

"Only that he appears to have no recollection of the events that led to his coming here," the Englishman replied calmly. "Your men seem quite proficient in their interrogation techniques. They're convinced the loss of memory is genuine. As is Doctor Weingert, our chief of psychiatry."

"Ask Lieutenant Samulovitch to meet us in there," Donnellan said, gesturing at the next room. "What is Moran's physical condition?"

"Aside from a very mild concussion, he's perfectly all right. If it weren't for the other factor I would say there is no reason for him not to be discharged." The physician paused. "Would you like me to call your man in now?"

"Please."

Samulovitch was in the room a minute later.

"Ger, this is Doctor Lauren Blair. She's working on the chalice."

The detective regarded Lauren coolly. "You were with him in the lab—"

"We'll get to that later," Donnellan interrupted him. "What do you have?"

"Bupkas." Samulovitch pulled out a crumpled pack of Gauloise Disque Bleu. "The last thing he remembers is entering his house. After that we draw a blank."

Samulovitch turned his gaze on Lauren Blair. "He won't say why he left the Museum, why he *ran* all the way to Chestnut Street...."

"Have you told him there's a victim?"

"We have a positive I.D., Frank," Samulovitch said gently. His eyes darted again to Lauren.

"It's all right. She's involved."

"He's a priest, Frank. No, actually he's a goddam cardinal."

"What!"

"Arturo Cardinal Capellini, late director of the Museum of Pagan Antiquities."

"That's where the chalice came from," Lauren whispered. "Pagan Antiquities."

"We talked to the driver," Samulovitch continued. "He was to take Capellini to the Museum then out to Logan. Word is that there was a private jet laid on for New York. We checked the seven to eight departures out of Kennedy. Capellini's name doesn't appear on any of the manifests. But...there's a seat on the seven o'clock Concorde unaccounted for."

"What about his entry into the country?"

"Came in yesterday afternoon. Swissair, direct from Geneva."

"Have you called anyone?"

Samulovitch shook his head. "The body's a John Doe at the morgue. I called Bobby Redford. But you know what he'll tell us."

"The pattern is the same."

"Frank, we won't be able to keep this one to ourselves. A foreign national is involved. A biggie at that. We'll have to bring in the Feds."

Donnellan held up his hand. "Do you know who arranged for the Lear?"

"The Baldarese Company out of New York."

"Baldarese?"

"Frank," Lauren touched his arm. "Father Moran is of the Baldarese family."

"It's all falling into place but I can't see it," Donnellan muttered. "Ger, try and keep the FBI out of this for as long as you can—"

"There's another problem. The press. The girl in the park, that's one thing. But a second murder, the next day, same style..."

"Buy me some time," Donnellan told him. "Keep them away from me until I've had a chance to talk to Moran. Say the amnesia is genuine. What that adds up to is that Moran is very probably a witness. What he saw in that house almost got to him. Now we have to get it out of him."

When he awoke he was conscious of a dull throbbing pain on the left side of his head. Father Edmund Moran raised his hand and felt the bandages wrapped around his forehead. He opened his eyes and saw two men standing over him. They told him he was at Mass General. They asked him a number of questions he couldn't answer and presently a doctor came in and pronounced him physically fit but suffering from traumatic amnesia. Still, the men who identified themselves as Boston detectives kept hammering away at him. The more questions they put to him the more confused he became.

When one of the detectives abruptly left the room, leaving his partner inside, the priest thought it was only a routine pause. He did not expect to see Frank Donnellan come in...or Lauren Blair.

"Father," Lauren called out.

"Lauren..."

Did I ask to see her? I must have. Yes, I wanted to tell her something....

Donnellan motioned for the remaining detective to leave. When the door was closed he came over and stood alongside the bed.

"Arturo Cardinal Capellini is dead, Father."

"Frank!"

"He was killed in your home, in the garden," Donnellan continued, his voice soft, pitiless. "We know about the Baldarese Lear, the seat reserved on the Paris Concorde. Would you tell us the rest of it now?"

Edmund Moran looked away. He felt very serene, as though what Donnellan was saying was already known to him. He thought of Capellini as an old friend who had died a long time ago, a fond memory, tinged with sadness.

"Capellini is dead, Father. Do you understand that?"

"Yes, of course."

"Do you know how he died?"

Moran frowned. "No, I can't....Strange, that I can't remember. I should be able to."

"Why did you leave the Museum, Father?"

Moran looked over at Lauren. His eyes lit up in a vacant smile, as though he were thanking her, but he said nothing.

For an instant it appeared to Lauren that Donnellan would reach out and seize the priest. But the great fists slowly uncurled and the voice was as soft as that of a mother with her child.

"Why did you want me to warn Lauren? Is she in any danger?"

The blank helpless expression remained. "I don't know, Inspector. I can't remember." He looked askance at Lauren. "Has something happened? *Will you please tell me what's happened!*"

"Father, will you excuse us for a moment?"

Donnellan guided Lauren into the hall.

"Genuine amnesia," he said. "He must have seen

the killing. But the memory is so painful, so vivid, that his mind refuses to call it back. But he knows the killer. He's seen him."

"What will you do?"

"I have to try and get the picture out of him," Donnellan said. He saw the flash of concern. "I promise you, I will not hurt him. One of my people will take you home."

"No, Frank. I want to go back to the Museum."

"Lauren—"

"Hear me out. First I will stop by Isaiah's house and tell him what's happened. Arturo Cardinal Capellini was head of the Museum of Pagan Antiquities. You will have to inform the Vatican at some point, probably very soon. If the Church wants to take back the chalice, Isaiah and Leech should be forewarned."

"Is that what Moran came for, the chalice?"

Lauren bit her lip.

"It's all right, colleen," Donnellan said gently. "I would have learned soon enough. There aren't any secrets when murder's involved. Why do you want to go back to the Museum now?"

"To finish the testing. I don't want that cup taken away until I know what it is."

"What can it be, Lauren?"

"I don't know."

Donnellan looked at her and nodded. "All right. Give Webber the details but ask him to stay quiet. I'll call the Museum and have the chalice brought out. But the alert status remains. Two of my people will be with you in the lab."

Without knowing why, Lauren reached out and cupped Donnellan's cheek.

"Thank you."

CHAPTER THIRTEEN

O VERLORD WAS STILL IN EFFECT.
  When the gray sedan drew up before Isaiah
Webber's home, the two agents Donnellan had assigned to Lauren alighted first. Flanking the archeologist, they escorted her up the steps. While
she waited for the buzzer to be answered, one of the
agents turned his back to her, eyes scanning the
twilight that was falling over the city.

"Tim!" she cried as her lover answered the door.

"Babe...Where the hell have you been?"

She knew at once he had been drinking. His face
had the telltale sweaty pasty quality to it. Even
though his breath was leavened with coffee, the hands
were frigid and trembled when he reached for her.
Lauren drew away from his grasp and stepped past
him.

"Lauren, who are these guys?"

"Museum security. Tim, what are you doing
here?"

He stepped back, eyeing the agents who had quietly slipped in and closed the door behind themselves.

"I called you at the lab, at home. There was no answer. Then I met up with Isaiah at the Club. We came
back here. That's when we learned about the killing
at the priest's place...what's his name, Moran. I figured I might as well stay put. You were probably with
the police. I knew you'd call Isaiah sooner or later." A
veiled recrimination.

"Laurennnn...Laurennn, is that you?"

The voice coming from the den off to the right of the hall was broken by a hacking cough. Isaiah Webber, a frayed but elegant housecoat wrapped tightly around his thin body, shuffled out, holding an enormous purple handkerchief to his nose.

"Ah, my dear, it is good to see you." He blinked and looked past her. "Who are these gentlemen, Lauren?"

"Frank—Inspector Donnellan's personnel."

"Yes, I see, of course," Webber murmured hoarsely. "You must all come into the parlor. Unfortunately Mrs. McTaggart has left for the day, but I can make tea...."

"Isaiah, please, don't go to any trouble. We won't be staying."

The parlor was in keeping with the Victorian architecture: wing chairs of soft pastels, potted ferns and rubber plants in front of the fireplace, and in the corners a sideboard that was three times as old as its owner. A frayed Oriental rug with cavorting mythical beasts glowed in the rays of the Revere lamps Webber turned on.

"A man has been murdered," Webber stated, sitting back in his recliner, bony ankles showing between housecoat and slippers. "Was it—"

"No, Father Moran is all right."

"I am grateful for at least that much."

Lauren looked at Tim. "What I have to say must be kept in confidence."

"You've got it."

Without mentioning Father Moran's condition or the strange turn of events at the Museum, Lauren Blair explained who it was that had been killed and the implications the murder was sure to have.

"That's why I'm returning to the lab now," she finished. "The Inspector will be speaking to Leech if he hasn't already done so. I wanted you to know before Leech called."

"This is an outrage," Webber said softly. "A man

PHILIP MICHAELS

of God, an innocent girl. What in heaven's name is out there?"

Silence hung in the air.

"You will call me when you're finished for the night."

"I may be there *through* the night."

Isaiah Webber nodded sadly. "I thought as much. I feel so helpless, Lauren. This old body of mine—"

"Isaiah, don't."

"Perhaps Tim can help. He and I have been getting to know one another quite well, I think."

Lauren glanced at her lover. He spread his hands. "I'm yours if you want me."

"No, I will do this alone."

"Then at least let me buy you some dinner," Tim said. "You don't look as though you've eaten, and if you plan to make it an all-nighter..."

His voice was soft and gentle the way she remembered it at the beginning.

"All right, dinner."

Suddenly Isaiah almost leaped from his chair, moving over to the two security personnel.

"You will see to it that nothing happens to her!" he demanded fiercely. Then his voice dropped to a whisper. "You will promise me this!"

The Partridge was the most popular tavern in Cambridge. Sandblasted brick walls, four dart boards, refectory tables, fried clams, chowder, pizza, and seventeen imported beers. Tonight, as every night, it was filled with students from Harvard, Boston U., and M.I.T. Tim McConnell managed to get them a couple of seats at the end of a table. While he ordered clams, a shrimp cocktail, and drinks, the security flipped open their I.D.'s for the manager, who made space for them at the bar only a few feet away.

"I was worried about you," Tim said once their food and drinks arrived.

She looked up at him, studying his features. His

193

face appeared blurry, as though it was a photograph yellowing and dimming with age.

"I'm all right."

"I still think I should be with you tonight."

"I said I'll be all right!"

She did not raise her voice but the force of the words made him recoil. She reached across and covered his hand.

"I'm sorry."

Tim McConnell shrugged and said nothing. He dug into his fried clams with gusto. She watched him eat, picking at her shrimp cocktail. Her food was barely touched when he was done.

"I needed that," Tim said, draining the last of his Tuborg.

"Didn't you eat at lunch?"

"Didn't have much of an appetite then."

"What happened with Stukley, hon?"

Tim lit a cigarette. "He turned me down flat." The smoke billowed forth from his nostrils. "I also ran into Leech, literally. That was the kind of encounter Spielberg could have filmed."

"Were you drunk?"

He looked at her coolly. "I was *very* drunk."

She looked away, fighting tears.

"It was Webber who bailed me out."

"Isaiah?"

He nodded. "He took me home, sobered me up, read the proposal, and says he's willing to back it. If not through the university, then another foundation."

"Tim, that's great," she stammered.

"Surprised?"

"Of course!"

"Well I'm not. I think it's about time someone saw the potential in the project."

"God, if you had told me sooner—"

"Hey, you have enough on your plate." Tim rose. "If you're going to work you had better move."

"Tim—"

He cupped her face and kissed her gently. "Call me tonight when you have a minute."

Then he was gone, leaving confusion in his wake.

Either way he looked at it, he was taking a chance. Weingert, the chief psychiatrist at Mass General, had been surprisingly forceful in his arguments against Father Moran's leaving the hospital. More tests were needed. Next of kin should be notified if the priest's condition suddenly worsened. The attending physician also pointed out that if anything untoward happened to Moran, it would be the police not the hospital that would be liable. Matters did not improve when Donnellan refused to tell either doctor where Moran was being taken.

It was the priest who swung the balance in his favor.

"Doctor, there is nothing physically wrong with me, is there?"

"Not really, no."

"Then I will come with you," Moran said to Donnellan. "I don't remember anything of what you've told me. Yet how can I *not* believe you, a man I trust? I have to know the truth, perhaps even more than you."

They had been inching along Boylston for ten minutes before they got around the New England Telephone repair truck. Donnellan glanced at the priest. Moran was dressed in the same clothes, dusted off, he had worn earlier in the day. There was a small tear in the elbow of the blazer. He was quiet and appeared oblivious to the din of the traffic. Although Donnellan had no patience for rush-hour madness, he refrained from using the flashers and the siren. These would get him to the Hancock Building sooner, but they might also attract the attention of other units. Donnellan did not want an escort to where he was going. It was also possible that Mass General had contacted the Commissioner's office, to cover their ass completely. Samulovitch's nemesis would want to know what in the hell Donnellan was doing spiriting around town with a material witness who still required medical attention. Especially when he wasn't officially tied into the case.

Donnellan turned off the ramp for the underground parking garage and slid the vehicle into a space marked PRIVATE, next to a single elevator. He looked squarely up at the camera mounted on the pillar and asked Father Moran to do the same. The doors opened. As soon as they were inside, the lift began to move swiftly, not stopping until the car had arrived at the thirty-seventh and topmost floor, directly under the helipad on the roof.

"Hello, Frank," a voice purred as the elevator door opened and Father Moran followed Donnellan out.

"Hello, Phil."

Phil was twenty-nine, tall and comely, with a peaches-and-cream complexion that belonged on a glossy page of *English Country Life*. Her hair hung halfway down her back, her milky blue eyes smiled at Donnellan. Philippa Simmons was a divisional psychoanalyst, late of Langley where she had worked on defectors, separating infiltrators from the real article.

Phil had also stayed with him after Kathleen's death ... after he had finished what the C.I.A. tagged as Donnellan's Donnybrook. Kathleen's maid of honor, Phil had moved in without asking him. She stayed for almost six months until she had sweated the poison out of him, his fury and madness cushioned by her embrace, her care and loving. When he was whole again she had gone away, back to her life. Donnellan owed her more than he would ever be able to repay.

"Phil, this is Father Moran."

"Father." Phil took Moran's hand, feeling the trembling. "This way, gentlemen."

Phil tagged them both with blue plastic badges. At the receptionist's desk they turned right into a white tunnel: white spotless floor, white walls, ceiling. The sound of their footsteps was completely absorbed by the special tiles. There might have been a firing range next door and no one would have been the wiser.

The cubicle was barren except for two comfortable executive-style chairs beside which stood the lie-detector unit: four feet long, twenty inches wide, three styli and a large roll of pale-green graph paper. On the left wall was a large rectangular mirror, a one-way glass for the observation room.

"Father Moran, if you'd like to sit here... Please make yourself comfortable. There's a reclining control by your right hand."

The priest sat down, cushion sinking gently beneath his weight.

"I might even fall asleep," he said, smiling.

"Has the procedure been explained to you?"

"No."

Gently Phil pulled up his sleeves and began taping the electrodes to the priest's bare arms. "Have you ever undergone hypnosis, Father?"

"No."

"Inspector Donnellan tells me it is likely you were a witness to a violent crime, that you have no recollection of seeing it."

"If he says so, then it must be true."

"Do you have any feelings, even the vaguest suspicion or hints about what you might have witnessed, anything at all?"

"No, I'm sorry."

"That's fine, Father. Not to worry."

She's so good, Donnellan thought. The modulation in her voice, the sure unobtrusive movements of her hands as she hooked up the machine to Moran's arm. She kept her eyes on the priest, never permitting his gaze to waver, forcing him to concentrate on her, on what she was saying.

"We're assuming, Father, that your witnessing the commission of a crime has caused your condition. In self-defense your mind refuses to allow your memory to retrieve those moments, possibly even seconds. But they do exist. Somewhere in your subconscious they remain. If you allow them to remain buried then they will manifest themselves as nightmares or hallucinations. However, if we can bring them to the surface—confront them—we'll have them neutralized."

Phil paused. "It's going to be painful, Father. I can't tell you that it won't. But please, please understand that whatever you see has already taken place. It is in the past. It can't hurt you here, now, among us."

"What is the purpose of this machine?" Father Moran asked quietly.

"The lie detector will monitor your blood pressure. This unit is the most advanced to date. It can differentiate between states of extreme anxiety and those of mendacity. We will be able to determine if what you saw actually existed or whether in those seconds something quite different occurred."

The priest looked up at Donnellan. "I have not harmed anyone, have I, Inspector?"

"No, you have not."

"Just for the record."

"For the record," Donnellan smiled.

From her pocket Phil brought out a small metronome and set it at eye level on the standup tray. The pike was gold-plated, brilliant, the adjustable weight missing.

"If you're ready, Father, we'll begin."

Father Moran closed his eyes.

God, please stand by me in this hour of need. For upon this Rock I have built my faith and the gates of Hell shall not prevail against it.

He opened his eyes. "I am ready."

The metronome pike began to swing silently back and forth. The light in the cubicle dimmed until only the shadows of Simmons and Donnellan could be seen, floating along the walls. The overhead beam on Father Moran brightened, glancing off the shiny graph paper, moving down the machine, illuminating the jagged peaks and plunging valleys formed by the fine stylus recording the electrical probes flowing into his body. A picture of the inner workings of a man...

"Are you watching the pike, Father?" Phil asked softly.

"Yes."

"It is a bright, golden pike."

"Yes."

"And it is difficult for your eyes to focus on it.... They are closing.... Slowly they are closing. ...The brightness is coming inside you...into your mind...the brightness is a lamp for your thoughts.... You are now beyond us.... You are with your thoughts...memories..."

The priest's eyes fluttered and closed.

"Deeper and deeper... The lamp is moving with your thoughts.... You are leaving us, listening only to my words.... And you are sinking further and further away from us...."

Father Moran's body relaxed, the head sliding gently to one side, mouth open just enough to show he was using it to breathe.

"He's gone," Phil murmured.

"Quick."

"The aftereffect of the sedative. Fatigue. You. He trusts you."

Phil leaned forward. "Father, can you hear me?"

"Yes." Even the voice was relaxed, the words soft, free of that nervous edge.

"Are you comfortable?"

"Yes."

"What is your other name, Father?"

"Baldarese. I am a Baldarese."

Phil looked at Donnellan. "Now we go in. Ready?"

"You're thinking violence?"

199

"If what you said is true, his reaction could be quite dramatic."

"But you can bring him back."

"Yes, eventually. But maybe not quickly enough."

"Let's do it. It's the only chance we'll have."

"Go easy on him, Frank."

"Father, I want you to guide the lamp to late afternoon, today."

"Late afternoon."

"Arturo Cardinal Capellini. Did he come to visit you?"

"Yes."

"Did his visit have something to do with the exhibit?"

"Yes."

"The chalice?"

"Yes."

"Did Capellini have something to tell you about the chalice?"

"Yes."

"Did he tell you?"

"Yes."

"Were you going to meet at the Museum this afternoon?"

"Yes."

"Were you going to show him the chalice?"

"Yes."

"Had Capellini come for the chalice?"

"Yes."

The readout was stable, the stylus moving well within the two red lines that indicated truthful responses.

"Did you make arrangements for Capellini to leave the country with the chalice?"

"Yes."

"When Capellini did not appear at the Museum you returned home, where you knew he had to be?"

"Yes."

"Did you think he was in any danger?"

The first hesitation. "Yes."

"Was the danger related to the cup?"

"Yes."

"Because of what you learned from Lauren Blair?"

"No."

"What Capellini had told you?"

"Yes."

What in God's name is going on?

Phil placed her hand on his forearm. "The readings are becoming erratic. You're probing close to the actual memory. If you want more general details get them now. There's no telling how much control you'll have later on."

He could do it, Donnellan thought fiercely. He could take him apart like a stalk of celery. He could get into his mind and unearth every last detail.

He thought of Cathy Windsor... and Arturo Cardinal Capellini. A cardinal! One part of him whispered that that was all the right he needed to intrude on the privacy of priestly communications.

But he had already violated that privacy. He had the papers, notes, and ledgers Samulovitch found in Moran's house. They would tell him everything he needed to know about the chalice.

"Father, do you remember entering your house this afternoon?"

"Yes."

The word trembled on the tongue. A soft sheen of sweat broke over Moran's face.

"Was he waiting for you?"

"No."

"Where did you see him?"

"In the garden."

"Was there anyone else there?"

"Yes."

"A man?"

"No."

"Woman?"

"No."

Phil's eyes darted to the readout. The priest was telling the truth.

"An animal?" Donnellan murmured.

Father Moran was silent.

"He doesn't understand the reference," Phil murmured. "Whatever he saw was neither man nor woman, but not an animal either." She looked up at Donnellan.

"A heavy disguise?"

"Maybe." Phil considered. "Shit, you're onto something very odd here."

"Father, what you saw, was this figure close to Capellini?"

"Yes."

"Was it standing over him, holding him, touching him...?"

"Holding him up..."

"Did you see the figure's face?"

Father Moran's eyes snapped open, wide in stark terror, oblivious to the light.

"Yes!" he screamed.

Donnellan was around him in an instant, ready to hold him down by the shoulders.

"Don't!" Phil hissed. She swung back to the priest. "Describe it, Father! Now. The lamp is on the figure. You can see it. *What does it look like!*"

"It...it's horrible." Moran was shaking, his head rotating furiously around the axis of his neck. "Bleeding claws...Oh God, it's not human. Not human! Monster...face...but not a face. Like Capellini said. Evil...not of this world...Reptile. Tearing Arturo! Killing him. He has no head. It sees me....God, it's coming after me. It wants me. It will have me! Talons! Teeth!"

With a strength Donnellan had encountered only in drug-crazed men Father Edmund Moran leaped out of the chair. The wires snapped away from the lie detector as the force of his motion carried him against the wall. For an instant he hung there, splayed, then, incredibly, he began to try to force his way into the wall, clawing and pummelling at the hard plaster.

"Bring him back!" Donnellan roared. He managed to get one arm around the priest's neck before Father Moran bellowed and set upon him like one possessed. The blows hammered down upon Donnellan's face and chest, fingers seeking to rip his face open.

"Monster...monster..." the priest shrieked, drooling, his feral expression mindless, filled with hatred and terror, as though his face were taking on the visage of what was screaming to be released from within him.

Suddenly Father Moran shuddered and fell to one side. Donnellan caught him just before he hit the ground.

"Frank, it's finished. It's finished, over with!"

He glanced up at Phil, standing a few feet away, a .22-caliber pistol in her hand. Slowly he staggered to his feet.

"What the hell—"

"Thorazine. Superconcentrated. Enough to knock out half a dozen offensive linemen. But look at him..."

On the floor, Father Edmund Moran continued to twitch, his body writhing, as though in some macabre prone dance, arms raised high, fingers curled.

"The question is, is he defending himself or imitating whatever it was he saw, whatever almost got to him?"

Phil replaced the gun on the chair and punched the red emergency button. She cupped Donnellan's face, running cool fingers over brutal red welts.

"There's something out there, Frank," she whispered. "Something that makes me feel very very cold. It's part of him now. He is your memory."

CHAPTER FOURTEEN

SITTING ON THE STOOL in the front lab, Lauren Blair was the picture of total calm. Bringing the cigarette to her lips, drawing in its smoke, and parting her lips minutely to release it in a steady stream were her only movements. She was slowly emptying her mind of all thoughts except those related to the task ahead of her. All questions, concerns, speculations, daydreams slipped away until the only thing of which she was aware was the subject at hand. After three minutes there was only her, the chalice, and the silence of the lab. The two security agents with her had become invisible. Letting the cigarette fall into the ashtray, she set to work.

Lauren had decided to break her work down into four specific steps. First, she would deal with the shell inlay. Only a fragment was required for the TRACE process. If her assumption was correct, the date of the inlay would correspond with what she would learn from the second and simultaneous step: the chemical analysis of the actual bowl. Third, she would also run an isotopic analysis for the geographical location of the metal and, last, a metallographic exam to determine the fabrication technique.

She set the chalice under a Faome lamp and with a fine scalpel made a curved incision at the precise point where the inlay met with the bottom layer of metal. After transferring the sample to a glass slide, she began to implement the procedure she had described to Father Edmund Moran.

Lauren had several techniques available to her

for the chemical analysis: optical-emission spectrometry; atomic-absorption spectrometry, x-ray fluorescence, or neutron-activation analysis. Of the four she chose the last. Because the nuclear reactor had been specifically constructed for the Bennett Museum, it could accommodate objects twice as large as the chalice. At that moment she wished Isaiah were with her. Five years ago he had literally begged the Board for funds to build such a custom unit. The reactor had earned its investment back many times over. Today it was critical.

Neutron-activation analysis was ideal for the testing, not only because it was nondestructive in terms of the sample but because it analyzed the whole of the body surface, had a concentration range of 100 percent, could deal with forty to fifty elements, and had an accuracy range of plus/minus 2 percent.

Lauren brought out a metal can the size of a small kettle and placed the chalice inside, sealing the cover. Once inside the reactor, the atomic nuclei of the specimen would be excited by the bombardment of slow neutrons interacting with the atomic nuclei of the constituent elements. The process would then transform the nuclei into unstable radioactive isotopes. These would then decay into stable isotopes, the half-life for the decay process varying from a fraction of a second to a thousand years. The decay of radioactive isotopes would invite the emission of gamma rays. The energy level of the rays would provide for identification of the specimen's constituent elements while their intensity would result in an estimate of concentration of a particular element.

Lauren placed the sample into the reactor and set the time for three hours at a neutron flux of 10^{12}-10^{13} neutrons $cm^{-2}s^{-1}$. In the case of gold, the stable isotopes would become radioactive under the bombardment, decay to an excited state of the stable mercury isotope with the emission of the beta particle. The required gamma ray would be emitted when the mercury nucleus assumed its unexcited state, the process simultaneous with emission.

She set the semiconductor counter, a lithium-drifted germanium crystal which would give her a better reading at lower concentrations of extraneous metals, and left the reactor room. Back in the lab, behind the shield, she activated the reactor.

Lauren went into a small cubicle that housed the Krebs laser, a variation of the surgical laser developed by Shiner.

The initial step in metallographic microscopy was to cut a thin slice off the specimen, thus providing a complete cross section. In practice, either a small core through the body of the artifact would be removed, or a tapered slice cut from the edge. However, in the case of the chalice these last two options would noticeably disfigure the cup's smooth rim. Therefore Lauren elected to use a laser that would literally shave off a minute strip from the rim, so thin and in keeping with the contours of the cup that it would go unnoticed by the naked eye. The surface of the strip would be polished by a fine grade of emery paper and, finally, diamond paste. The sample would then be etched by feric chloride, acidified with hydrochloric acid. Thus polished and etched, it would be placed under a reflected light of the metallurgical microscope, the magnification adjusted for X350 to X400. The intense magnifications would detail the internal structure of the metal which would in turn provide specific information on the thermal and mechanical treatments the metal had been subjected to. These would then be correlated with available data on metal fabrication in the period A.D. 0 to 50. If all went as Lauren expected, the details of the fabrication techniques would match up exactly with the Table of Manufacturing and Design provided in Libby's comprehensive work on the subject.

She brought the cup into the laser cubicle and set it twenty inches from a gun on a raised round surface that resembled a revolving cocktail tray. Once the chalice was fixed to the surface, the plate would move automatically, the rotation speed correlated with the intensity and cutting speed of the beam. This, plus the fact that the laser was fixed to cut at .05mm, would insure a smooth uniform sample.

Lauren secured the chalice to the plate by suction cups, adjusted the rotation speed, then stepped behind the laser gun. She set the cutting rate and fed power into the unit. The plate rotation synchronized perfectly with the laser emission. In twelve seconds she had her sample.

It happened by accident at four o'clock in the morning.

Lauren had decided to supplement the radiocarbon testing of the shell with an isotope analysis. But its result would insure that if a question of the shell's geographic location was raised by Isaiah, an answer would be at hand.

Lauren took another half-milligram of sample, from the sample incision made to remove the radiocarbon sample, and treated it with phospheric acid, thus releasing the carbon dioxide from the calcium carbonate. This gas would be ionized and the oxygen/carbon isotopic ratio determined. This would give her an exact (.01% error margin) reading of the aquatic environment of the shell. The reading would also prove conclusively whether the shell was Mediterranean or Black Sea in origin, or if it had come from farther south, perhaps the Indian Ocean.

Lauren positioned the chalice under the Abbey microscope, moving it around until she spotted the minute niche in the shell where the previous sample had been removed. She increased magnification to X200 and moved the scalpel into position. That was when she saw it: a stain. A thin streak of brown that lay between the metal and the shell inlay, in a groove so small she had to increase magnification to X250 to see it clearly.

Frowning, Lauren lifted her head from the microscope. Six months ago the Museum had received a Minoan dagger. While testing it she had discovered a similar stain between the silver inlay and the bone handle. An electron microscope revealed the substance to be blood. Very, very old blood. The geochronological date of the blood had been the final proof that the dagger did in fact belong to a particular period. Because blood was organic. It could be tested through TRACE....

Dating the blood...

Lauren turned back to the microscope, moving the lens one hundredth of an inch. The brown stain disappeared into the crack within the shell inlay itself.

Could it be...?

Reaching for a slide, Lauren scraped off a few grains of the dried pigment onto the glass, covering that with another slide. She left the lab and walked upstairs to the physics lab on the next level. The doors parted when she inserted her card. The light came on automatically. Even before she sat down at the console Lauren was punching in the appropriate program on the keyboard of the mass spectrometry unit.

Built by Sharpe Precision Instruments of Hartford, the spectrometry unit was the most advanced scanning device in existence. Given a single grain of sand, its infrared rays could identify the chemical and structural composition, and at the same time render up a three-dimensional picture on the monitor. All in under two minutes.

The computer replied that it was ready. Lauren fed the slide into the slot and asked for the substance's biological identification. Within seconds the infrared rays were bombarding the sample, sending streams of information back to the computer's storage banks, which in turn were correlating it with the data held there. The monitor glowed and the printer started up. Without question the substance was, in chemical composition, blood. The three-line analysis was curt to the point where Lauren thought the computer had been bored by so simple a task. She tore off the printout sheet and headed downstairs.

Ten minutes later she organized the TRACE procedure and returned to the chalice. Carefully she scraped away a few more grains of blood, cleaned them and placed them within the TRACE unit counter.

Lauren moved over to the data recorder. A digital unit, it resembled a clock lying face up. To the right were bars, each representing a given geochronological period ranging from the year A.D. 1500 to 100,000 B.C., the limit of the TRACE unit. As TRACE analyzed the fossilized remains, extracting the secrets of the blood's "death," the digital counter began to roll back time.

"A long shot," Lauren muttered to herself. "Too much of one."

She made a sour face as the timer's pace slowed at the year A.D. 400.

"That's it."

She fully expected the counter to stop between A.D. 20 and 25, readjust, then settle on an exact year in between.

The counter flipped over into the B.C. sector.

"Oh Jesus."

Her fingers danced over the console, punching in a confirmation program, followed by a backup systems scan. Everything was operating normally. There was nothing at fault with TRACE.

The counter passed 1000 B.C. and speeded up.

No, this can't be happening, Lauren thought to herself, then said aloud: "The goddam chalice isn't that old. I *know* it isn't!"

The centuries slipped by, 2000 years becoming

20,000. Lauren watched, unable to understand what was happening. All the while the red malfunction light remained inert. There was nothing wrong with the system!

"No, no way!" she whispered as the counter slipped past 50,000 B.C. "It's got to stop."

The digital readout was nothing more than a blur when suddenly the malfunction alarm sounded, a persistent high-pitched beep punctuating the flashing light. Lauren asked the computer to define the cause of the malfunction. She didn't know it but all she had to do was look over to the clock for an answer. The geochronological face was completely colored, the needle wavering just past the 100,000 year limit. The substance within TRACE, the blood upon the cup, could not be dated within the range of the machine. That blood was older than one thousand centuries....

He awoke in total darkness. His eyes opened, blinking rapidly, trying to focus, but saw nothing. Father Moran uttered a low guttural moan and jerked his body forward. The padded restraining straps on his wrists bit into his flesh.

"No...God help me, no!"

Then the lights came on, soft blue orbs that seemed to swim over the room.

"Father Moran..."

"Donnellan!" His throat was parched, the single word almost choking him.

"It's me, Father...on the right."

Edmund Moran had never been so glad to see a human face. Again, on instinct, he reached forward, straining to touch the detective who was standing by the bed. Again the straps held him back. Donnellan bent over, fingers working quickly to remove the restraints.

"I'm sorry about these," Donnellan said. "But we

couldn't control you . . . you might have injured yourself."

"Some water . . ."

Donnellan undid the last knot and reached across
for the Tempra-cool pitcher and paper cup.

"No, let me hold it for you," he said, bringing the
cup to the priest's lips. "Rub your hands together,
as if you're drying them. . . . That's right."

Father Moran sipped greedily at the water. It was
cold, sweet, and delicious.

"Keep rubbing your hands. Is the feeling coming
back?"

"Yes . . . yes, it is."

"All right, let me help you to sit up."

Father Moran pushed himself up and Donnellan
adjusted the pillows behind him. He looked around
himself, squinting, trying to make out what lay in
the dark corners of the room.

"How long have I been here?"

"Five hours. It's almost four o'clock in the morning."

"Five hours . . ."

Father Moran swung back the covers and made
to stand. He faltered, clutching at Donnellan's shoulder.

"No, I have to return home—"

Donnellan pressed him back into the bed. "Do you
remember where you are?"

"Yes, of course. The Hancock Building."

"Do you know why?"

The priest stared at him, terror mingling with an
awful realization. "Arturo . . ." he whispered.

"You remember everything now, don't you?"

"Yes," Edmund Moran said in a dead voice. "I
remember everything."

"Tell me what you remember," Donnellan said
softly.

"Arturo is dead," he said flatly, looking past Donnellan into the recesses, as though he expected to

see something there, waiting for him. "He is dead, murdered, eaten, by the demonkind." He looked up at Donnellan. "You know this."

"I know he was murdered."

"Then you have been in my house. You must have taken the papers and documents that were there. You understand what Arturo came to warn me about."

"I know about the papers," Donnellan said. "But I need you to help me interpret them."

"We must go at once," Moran said. "They are out there. Lauren—"

"She is safe. My people are with her."

"People, Inspector," the priest smiled. "You saw what those things did to Arturo...the girl. *They eat people!* We must leave here," Moran muttered, and swung off the bed.

Donnellan heard the door open behind him and saw Phil enter with an orderly at her side.

"There is a shower stall in there, Father," she said kindly. "The orderly will be there to make sure you don't fall. You're still weak."

But Edmund Moran made his own way to the bathroom. As soon as she heard the sound of streaming water Phil came over to Donnellan.

"Give him these," she said, reaching inside her jacket and handing Donnellan a vial of pills. "It doesn't appear that the aftereffects of the tranquilizer will help him sleep. These will."

"Are you going to be here for the next while?" Donnellan asked, pocketing the vial.

"May be in Washington the day after tomorrow. Why?"

"For long?"

Phil spread her hands. "Who knows? No one ever tells me anything until I get there."

"I would have wanted you here, just in case."

Phil shook her head. "What is happening out there, Frank?" she asked softly.

"I wish I knew. Demonkind...what the hell is that? I take it you haven't come up with any ideas?"

"I've been over the tapes of Moran's session three times now. What can I say? He's telling the truth."

"But that isn't possible! Can't he *believe* so deeply that what he *thinks* he saw was able to fool the machine?"

"No one can believe that much," Phil told him flatly. "The computer analyzing the readout was completely satisfied he was telling the truth. And believe me, the machine does not like to admit that. I've gone over all the readouts. No fault lines. Even if he had hypnotized himself to say what he had said, the machine would have picked up the lie. Moreover, Frank, the *way* he gave that description—fragments, built on such terror, terror that continued even after I pulled him back—mitigates against his having set up this little spectacle."

"Incredible," Donnellan murmured. "An eyewitness account by a supposedly sane, rational man that doesn't do me the least good."

"Doesn't it?" she challenged him. "I think what you mean is that you can't tell the Commissioner what you have. No one would believe you. But think, Frank! Moran's description of the creature tallies with the way the bodies were dismembered, the strength it would have taken to do that in such a short period of time, the lack of apparent connection between the victims...."

"All of which point to what conclusion: that Arturo Cardinal Capellini and Cathy Windsor were victims of a monster? A demon? Something inhuman? Mack the Knife, yes, but—"

"That would appear to be the conclusion," Phil interrupted. "Not logical, not rational. But true for all that."

"*You* think it reasonable?"

"Reasonable or not, it is the *only* conclusion you have."

Donnellan moved very close to her, his eyes holding hers. "Tell me," he said softly. "Do you believe there would be something like this out there? I mean, can a creature such as he described exist!"

Phil curled a stray lock of hair behind one ear.

"I've had occasion to talk to some Russians who were heavily involved in the Soviet parapsychology program. What they had to say frightened me, Frank. Can you imagine a battalion of zombies moving at you, specially bred men—bred the way we now breed dogs—whose brains have been so developed that they can deflect a bullet by willpower alone? Sounds bizarre? Sure. Beyond the realm of possibility? For the time being. But not for very long. Now, is one to consider such a man truly a human being, as we've defined the word for thousands of years, or is it something—not someone—but something else?"

"Phil, I can buy that—up to a point, as you said. But we're not talking—or rather, Moran isn't talking—about zombies. He's describing monsters!"

"I wish I could give you something more," she said. "But from here on in you have to go at it on faith—in what he tells you, on the faith of the computer that cleared him. Don't close your mind to possibilities, Frank. Not in this case. Even thinking of the tapes we made of his session makes my skin crawl."

She cupped his cheek with her hand. "If you need me, you know where to find me. I'll have copies of the tapes sent over to the Museum. The originals will remain here. You know I can't destroy them."

"I know. But this isn't an Agency matter."

"Who knows whose matter it is?" She paused. "Whatever's out there, Frank, please get rid of it," she said with unexpected intensity. "I don't like the feeling of geese treading over my grave."

The sound of water in the bathroom ended abruptly. The high-pitched squeal of the communicator startled both of them.

"Donnellan."

"This is the Monitor. You are wanted here ASAP. This is not, repeat *not,* a Code Three or a Code Four. Acknowledge, please."

"Acknowledged."

Code Three was physical assault upon the premises. Code Four was murder. Thank God for small mercies.

"You must be very hungry. We can stop for some food. It will only take a minute."

Donnellan looked over at the priest in the passenger seat. Father Moran shook his head.

"I would prefer we return to the Museum. Obviously Lauren has something for you, perhaps for both of us."

"Do you want to talk?"

"Inspector, would you have a cigarette?"

Donnellan reached into his trench coat and offered a pack of Players. Moran punched the dash lighter, waited, then held the glowing tip to the tobacco.

"That's very good," he murmured.

"Father..."

"There is nothing to hide anymore, Inspector," the priest said slowly. "Arturo's death absolves me of the secrecy he imposed upon me. But we must talk together, the three of us. The chalice concerns us all now."

"Not only us, Father," Donnellan said. He pulled up to the corner of Brookline and Erie. There under a bright orange lamp post was a newspaper booth. An old woman was lugging sacks of papers, the morning edition of the *Globe,* toward the stall. He could not make out the print for the plastic that shielded the papers from the clammy fog, but the headline on the cardboard stapled to the booth was all too clear:

CAMBRIDGE HORROR! SECOND VICTIM CLAIMED!

"The word is out," Donnellan murmured. "We

haven't much time, perhaps none at all, before this thing goes *very* public." He looked across at the priest. "Before you're brought in on the investigation of the cardinal's death."

"You must prevent that, Inspector," Moran said softly. "There is nothing the police can do. Believe me, nothing. We will have to do it ourselves. I will tell you how."

Donnellan drove slowly through the deserted streets of Cambridge. Aside from the campus patrols and the prowl cars that sniffed at the edge of the campus, there was no one else about. Light came late on a morning such as this. Perhaps it would never come at all. He turned off into Merton Street, the sedan rocking gently along the cobblestones, the tires veering from left to right on the slippery incline.

"A redundant question, Father, but how do you feel?"

Moran smiled faintly. "Better than I must appear. Don't worry about me, Inspector, please. I will carry on. I must."

Lauren Blair was waiting for them in the employees' alcove, where two small tables, several plastic chairs, vied for space with the coffee and cigarette vending machines. One glance told Donnellan that in spite of the all-night session something had happened that kept her fatigue at bay. He was grateful for the smile that reached out for him, the touch of her hand upon his.

"Father Moran..." Lauren said.

"Lauren—"

She looked at Donnellan, who shook his head. "It's all right. We'll talk later."

"You've continued the testing," Moran said.

"Yes, Father."

"Where is the chalice now?"

"In the laboratory."

"It must be taken out of there at once. We must remove it to consecrated ground."

"I think you had better listen to my findings, Father."

"Findings..." The apprehension in the priest's voice was all too clear.

"I tested some of the shell inlay," Lauren said, crushing out her cigarette and standing up. She took a few steps then turned and faced the two men. "Its date jibed with the other factors. As I was preparing it for testing I noticed a brown stain between it and the metal. A brown stain. It was blood, Father, very old, dried blood."

"Go on, Lauren," Moran said.

"You know that TRACE has the capacity to give us dates as far back as a hundred thousand years. In this case the recorder simply went off the scale. *That blood, Father...is older than a hundred thousand years!*"

"Oh, my God!"

"I ran the test three times. I've correlated two samples of the blood to make certain. The results were identical. There is no mistake, no malfunction of the equipment...."

Lauren fumbled with another cigarette, cupping Donnellan's hand around the flame.

"I don't know of any test currently in use or under development that would give us a firm reading on that substance," she said, running her fingers through her hair. "Even if we had instruments that could accurately gauge up to a million years, I doubt that would make the slightest difference."

Lauren paused. "Do you understand what I'm getting at, Father?"

"There's no doubt that the substance is human blood?"

"None. I've checked the cell structure....But it can't be human blood."

"Yes, it can, Lauren," the priest said softly. "There was one man in the history of the world who had such blood. Christ."

No sooner were the words out of his mouth than Father Moran realized what he had said. *It couldn't be! God help him, it couldn't be!*

"That's the only conclusion I could come to," Lauren said. "There just isn't any other explanation. But one question: the chalice was used by Christ at the Last Supper. How could His blood have gotten on the inside of the cup?"

"The chalice was also present at the Crucifixion," Father Moran told her gently. "According to legend it was held up to catch His blood after the Longinus spear pierced His side. The known fits with the unknown...."

The priest rose and came to her. "You haven't told anyone else about your findings."

"No, of course not. I wanted to call Frank to see about you—"

"I think we should talk," Father Moran said softly, turning to Donnellan. "I need both of you now. I think you will believe me now. Is there somewhere else?"

"I have a small office," Donnellan said.

"Yes, that will do quite well," the priest murmured. "And, Inspector, would you be good enough to bring over all the papers and notes from ...my home."

As he turned and began to walk down the silent corridor, Father Edmund Moran was thinking of what he would say to them. He would begin at the beginning. He would tell them how hands had burned...how Arturo's hands had burned. That was where it had all started.

CHAPTER FIFTEEN

L IGHT DID NOT COME into the morning. It was rain that broke the silence and the darkness. Starting out as a faint patter, gentle and seemingly without consequence, by seven it was slicing down in hard even sheets. Blackness relented only to become mist.

The real estate agent on his way to the city pulled over on the shoulder of Post Road. He lowered the Mercedes' electronically operated window and peered through the fog, straining to glimpse the Federal-style house. He had been stopping here at least once a week for the past several months, trying to decide what was going on with the property he had sold almost two years ago to the day. His conclusion: Nothing. At the time of final sale he hadn't cared that the buyers had stayed away, preferring representation by a Boston lawyer. Now he did. Because property values had skyrocketed. He wanted to repurchase the house, knowing that he could turn it around in less than thirty days for a scandalous profit. But the buyers eluded him. Their lawyer had been no help. His fee had been paid up front. Title searches took him through several religious foundations and eventually to a post-office box in Luxembourg. Nothing from the telephone company or the local fuel merchant, utilities or post office. The car was his last hope. Every morning on his way to work the agent slowed before the house and looked up at it. Sometimes he stopped and had a cigarette with his thermos coffee. The car continued to elude him.

He felt raindrops on his knuckles and was drawing up the window when he saw it: the gleaming stretch Lincoln with only its fog lamps on, rounded the corner, slowing before the parting gates. Coffee spilled into the agent's lap as he shifted gears. He made it to the gates just as the Lincoln swept through them, the oversized tailpipe disgorging billows of fumes. The agent slammed his hand against the Mercedes' large padded steering wheel as the gates drew abreast. He had had a clear view of the limousine's plates: one-half of the green renewal sticker. The rest of the plate was covered in mud.

We haven't long here, the stranger thought as he alighted from the car. He reached back and helped the other passenger out. The man lifted his face, oblivious to the rain, to gaze at the elegant façade before him. The stranger knew he saw nothing, would remember nothing of this when he returned to the world of the humankind. The stranger opened the oak doors and beckoned the man to enter. When they were inside he closed the portals and, as always, barred them.

The stranger led the way to the library. It remained exactly as he remembered it. He bade the man to sit on his right and took his place at the head of the shining oval table. As always he neither saw nor heard anything at first. There was only the stench. He breathed deeply of it, hungering for it.

"I have brought you a novice," he said, unable to keep the excitement from his voice. "Not only can he be of service to you now but he covets the wisdom and power of your realm. He is—"

"We know who he is."

It was the serpent speaking. The scaly lids drew apart and eight pairs of eyes, coal red, glowed in the dark. The scraping of nails across wood reached the stranger's ears. Hot fetid breath wafted across the table, overwhelming him.

"He is the one you will send if the other fails," the demon rasped.

"Yes, he is the one," the stranger whispered.

Out of the darkness the horror shambled forth. The stranger gazed upon his deity in stark terror that was a kind of ecstasy.

Accept the offering, he begged silently. *Accept him into your race and I swear he will not fail you. Accept him so that when he succeeds you will at last deem me worthy of conversion also.*

"When you succeed, whether through him or the other, then you shall be worthy," the demon spoke. It was standing directly behind the stranger, the hands just above the shoulders, the talons grazing the cheeks. Then at once it covered the man's face with them.

"We have looked into your heart and saw in it pride. Thwarted ambition. Avarice. Lust. Gluttony. These are what humankind call the deadly sins. To us they are virtues.

"You know not what is happening to you now because the potion will not allow it. You do not feel your soul being sucked from your body. Your soul slakes our thirst, just as the flesh and blood of the humankind satisfies our need to feed. We lust for you because you are sustenance for us. But you are also young and strong and have surrendered to us. We have need of males such as you."

Out of the corner of his eyes the stranger saw the man's head jerk back. A muffled grunt passed through the demon's scaly fingers. Blood appeared in a dozen rivulets across the man's face.

"We drain the life force from you so that you may lose yourself to humankind forever. With the passage of this blood you renounce all allegiances to what humankind deems holy. To us—to you, what you shall become—it is apostasy...."

The claws came together and entwined before the man's face. The stranger feared for him, for the man's skin was drenched in blood. The shaking began. The man's legs started pummelling the floor, his torso straining to rise from the chair.

"We are freeing you of the last vestiges that bind you to humankind. We are purging your memory of all the filth that has gone before. Now as you listen to me you will learn of the true heritage....

"Each evolution has had its overlord. What the humankind calls God has guided them from the primordial slime of their origin. Our light is Lucifer, the rebellious angel who dared, and who, for his courage, was banished....Just as we have been.

"But Lucifer did not forfeit his claim upon creation. There were creatures who belonged only to him: the viper, the scorpion, the crocodile, and the spider. Of all his domain he chose us, when we were feeble and struggling like the first man. He nurtured and watched over us, guiding us through the eons of evolution, shearing us of the weak, propagating the strong, watching us multiply and grow strong.

"Since time immemorial we have preyed upon humankind. We hunted them in the swamps and the forests, along the savannahs and fringes of the deserts. We burned ourselves into man's memory. His fear of us became part of his psyche. Our fearsome images adorned the walls of his caves and, later, the first temples he erected to his God. But we continued to hunt and devour him. We destroyed and ate what we destroyed in the name of our lord. In time it was revealed to us that we were the instruments of Lucifer's vengeance. Himself an outcast, he conceived us to rid the earth of the Lord's creations. We were the teeth that shredded his work, the jaws that consumed his progeny.

"Yet man continued to multiply. No matter how quickly we killed, how much fear we instilled in him, man continued to bring forth issue. Even our attacks upon his females, when we ripped out and gorged upon their wombs, proved worthless. Man retreated into the mountains and the deserts. He fled under the earth and from there continued to plant his seed within woman. We sought and we killed. But we did not find enough of them, not enough and not in time to extinguish the hated species.

"Still, we ruled this earth. We walked side by side with our brothers the reptiles and monsters, and rejoiced in man's inevitable extinction. For it was to be. Our females bore many litters. Our kind wandered to every part of the earth, stalking man as he migrated. We never gave him peace, we took his domain and made it ours. We paid tribute to Lucifer and basked in the glory of his pleasure. To reward us, he fashioned a cup, a chalice, in the forges of our Hell. It was our font, the wellspring of our existence. We cherished the cup. Over and over again we filled it with human blood and drank from it. We quenched our thirst off what gave them life. We emptied their bodies of souls and brought them as tribute to Lucifer.

"Yet all was not as it should have been. We erred in our presumption that man had ceased to be a threat. Our hunts grew shorter. We preyed upon animals and our instincts to hunt man waned for the mindless creatures of creation were too easy to track, kill. In time, which we had no concept of, we forgot about man.... Until man came down from the mountains, emerged from the deserts and caves.... He came with weapons fashioned from bone and wood and gut. He sought us out by day and struck at night when we were sated and weary. Our fury was terrible but we discovered that man was not the same as he had been. He had risen above the beasts. He was no longer the easy prey, but the predator.

"We begged Lucifer for instruction. His word was to go forth and kill all men so that his domain might be complete and perfect. It was our great joy to do this for him. But we could not. In what came to be called millennia, man had learned cunning and reason. Although our savagery terrified him, he would not retreat. Oftentimes his ferocity matched our own. He had learned of fire and fashioned tools of iron against us. Yet we could have triumphed, *should* have triumphed but for a single tragedy.

"The cup of Lucifer, our font, was lost to us.

"How this came about was never known to us. We understood that no one of our race would covet the cup for himself. It was unthinkable that there was a thief among us. For in stealing from us he diminished himself. The fury of Lucifer would be far greater punishment than we could ever exact.

"Yet we were culpable nonetheless. There could be but one conclusion: somehow, in spite of our protection, the humankind had gained entry into our shrine and stolen the cup.

"Lucifer was not to be appeased. We begged him for the opportunity to redeem ourselves. We promised we would ravage the humankind until we learned where the cup was hidden. No matter how many of us perished we were willing to sacrifice everything.

"But Lucifer was not to be appeased. In spite of our efforts and trials, he turned away from us, placing us beyond the pale of his light. Our young died first. Our females became diseased and barren. The males grew impotent. The race that was to have ruled the earth became the quarry instead. Without our font, without Lucifer's help to guide us, we wavered. Some of us kept up the hunt for the chalice. Others did what they could to protect the tribes from the ever-increasing encroachment of man. Soon man came to roam our territory at will, plundering our lives. Soon it was we who had to take refuge, move into the mountains by the sea, into caves where man did not follow.

"So it was for time eternal. Our race withered and died until it became only a dim memory in the mind of man. Defeated and forgotten, we were relegated to those creatures we had seen perish before us: the dinosaurs, the giant reptiles, and the winged birds of prey. We watched as man gathered together in his tribes, as he built great cities, monuments and citadels to himself and his gods. We witnessed the triumph of the true God in the wilderness of Judea. We watched as the promised Messiah came to his people. Helpless, enraged, we watched as man inherited our domain. We had only one hope: that our longevity, the one gift which Lucifer saw fit to leave us, would sustain us. Man measured existence in decades, we in centuries....

"It was time that saved us. Our tribe, which dedicated its life to retrieving the chalice, heard of a magical cup that was being brought to Britain by a man called Joseph, of a place known as Arimathea. We yearned to glance at the cup. From all that was whispered of it, the cup could have been none other than our font. But before we could reach him, Joseph died. We pillaged his house and lands but found nothing.

"In the centuries that passed we once again revealed ourselves to humankind. Desperate to unearth the chalice, we raided their houses of worship, tortured their priests so that they might tell us where the font was to be found. Humankind came to know us again. Its scribes wrote of our ferocity and its painters depicted our features from accounts man himself could scarcely believe...did not want to believe.

"Then came the Quests, led by the human King Arthur and the one knight who prevailed, Brideshead."

The stranger closed his eyes and savored what he had heard. The story of the cup, with the entry of Brideshead into the story, was familiar to him. What had gone before intoxicated him. The race of Lucifer...the tribes of the Fallen Angel. They were not myth or dream or fiction. They existed. Soon they would grow and multiply. Soon they would come forth once again to claim their birthright. And he would be among them....

He did know how much time went by before the demon ceased to speak. He felt himself afloat in another dimension, a part of a parallel but different universe. He longed so much to remain there.

"You have done well to bring him to us," the demon addressed the stranger. "Now gaze upon the transformation that has come over him."

The demon removed its hands from the face and the stranger gazed upon the horror beneath. The man was no longer a man. In place of human features was a reptile's face, oily, scaly skin covering a skull swollen to monstrous proportions. The hideous mouth opened, saliva dripping from the teeth. Then the scales over the eyes drew back and two red coals sank into the stranger's eyes.

"Look up and see what you too shall become," the demon spoke. "Take him and return to the humankind. He is to do our service." The demon paused, raising its head. "Service against the priest who even now tells the little he knows of us to the woman and the man who would protect her...."

Inhuman laughter resounded within the study, piercing the soft wood panelling, pulsating into the very walls. If someone had chanced to pass the house at that moment they would have sworn that the very foundation quivered.

"That is the whole of it. Now you know as much as I do."

Father Edmund Moran rose from the ancient oak swivel chair and thrust his arms back, then rolled his shoulders forward. He clasped his hands together, regarding Lauren Blair and Frank Donnellan.

"Fantastic..." Donnellan muttered. He stood up

and came over to the window, separating the Venetian blinds, staring out at the cold ceaseless rain.

The office was little more than a cubicle with a small desk, a battered couch, and a battery of telephones. Along the couch in haphazard piles were the notebooks and papers Donnellan had had Samulovitch bring over from the priest's house.

"A secret society of Fisher Kings within the Church, unknown to any pontiff. A chalice that has lain under their protection for centuries ...Something that might once have been used for devil worship but which may also be the Holy Grail." He turned to face Moran. "And the demonkind," he finished softly. "How in the name of God am I to believe *that?*"

"The provenance, Frank," Lauren spoke up quietly. She lit a cigarette in sharp nervous gestures. "There is a written history."

"Do *you* believe it?"

She looked at him. "Yes, I do."

For an instant he seemed to sag, as though whatever he had been straining to prevent had at last overtaken him.

"Yes, I believe it," he whispered through clenched teeth. Savagery sparkled within his eyes, the lips drawing back, skin tightening over his cheeks. "That is why I'm going to do what Capellini should have done—destroy the cup!"

"No, Frank!"

She was beside him in an instant, hand on his arm, feeling the hard outline of the gun against her. "The blood I found... You admit that only one man could have had such blood!"

"Maybe I was wrong....Maybe you were wrong too. It could belong to...them."

Lauren shook her head. "No, Frank, that's not true. You know that."

"Father, what do you say?"

"I say first that I beg both of you to forgive me.

227

By force of circumstance my burden has touched you. My danger has become your own." The priest paused. "One part of me agrees with you: the cup should be destroyed. But I would sooner destroy myself than it. For I believe the cup to be the Holy Grail, whatever its origins. I believe Lauren has brought forth proof that makes such a conclusion inescapable. Therefore no matter the evil contained within it, there is also goodness and divinity."

"Of which we have seen precious little," Donnellan retorted.

"Bear with me, Frank," the priest pleaded. He turned to Lauren. "Knowing what you do of the cup, is there anything more you can do?"

Lauren had anticipated the question.

"The final test of the inlay, to determine the geographic origin of the shell...And one other possibility. If the gold *is* a veneer, if the chalice is actually fashioned on the corpus of another cup, then I would have to do a complete cross section to get at the original cup."

"But haven't you already done this?"

"No, Frank, I shaved off a very thin strip of gold. I would need a probe to tell me how thick that outer layer is."

"How long would that take you?" Edmund Moran asked her.

"No more than a few hours."

"Would you do this?"

Lauren looked at Donnellan. "Would you be there?"

"Yes."

She nodded.

"And you, Father?"

"There is a definitive answer to the identity of the cup," the priest said.

"In the Geneva provenances?" the Inspector asked him.

"Not there. In Canterbury, England."

"Canterbury!"

"I know where the last writings of Joseph of Arimathea are stored."

"But wouldn't past Fisher Kings have already examined them?" Lauren asked.

"The *known* writings have been examined, those that are in Rome."

"There are others?"

Edmund Moran nodded. "Yes."

"You are a material witness to a killing," Frank Donnellan murmured. "We have your evidence on tape."

"Frank—" Lauren started to say, but the priest held up his hand.

"I am fully aware of this. It is not I but you who must decide what can be done. What do you say?"

Donnellan considered. He thought of all that he had to lose. Then he made his decision.

"I say we had better get you started."

CHAPTER SIXTEEN

TWO O'CLOCK in the afternoon. Rome was silent, the city breathing slowly, quietly, during the midday break that reduced its frenzy and chaos to a monotonous hum.

The pause was observed in the Vatican also. Activity ceased in all palaces, offices, and departments. All save the papal quarters.

Unlike his Roman spiritual subjects, Urban preferred a light meal at midday. On this day, his table was set for two. Knowing the pontiff's preferences, the kitchen had produced a clear beef broth, grilled trout netted that morning in the ponds at Castel Gondolfo, cold asparagus with fresh mayonnaise, a cucumber salad, and gelatin for dessert. Uncharacteristically, Urban dismissed the servant as soon as the food was brought. Further, he asked Dominic Cardinal di Stefano not to speak of the issue he had raised an hour earlier. The conversation, what there was of it, dealt with generalities.

"You are impatient, Dominic," Urban said, sipping camomile tea.

"I must confess that is a weakness in my character. I trust His Holiness will forgive me."

"Your mood is understandable. But you must appreciate that our minds do not work in the same way. Yours is a remarkable computer that correlates facts and figures, pros and cons, actions and reactions, resulting in models of action. Mine is, alas, slower, perhaps more contemplative. For example, Dominic, I am trying to understand why such an astonishing revelation is bounded by tragedy of equal magnitude."

The question was not rhetorical.

"An unfortunate coincidence," di Stefano said at once, taking advantage of the opening. "One whose constituent parts should not necessarily be presumed to be equal. We know that Arturo Capellini was not a well man, even if the manifestation of his illness was sudden and its symptoms hitherto undetected. The illness made him irrational. One might go so far as to say it induced paranoia where the chalice was concerned. It led him to reject medical help, leave the Vatican, and ultimately reappear in Boston for reasons unknown to us. Unless he shared these with the young Baldarese—Father Edmund Moran as he calls himself—we will probably never be privy to his motives."

"What of Baldarese?" Urban interrupted.

"Calls to his residence have gone unanswered. The diocese prelate, Connelly, does not know where he is."

"He was very close to Capellini," Urban mused. "In view of what has happened he mightn't have thought to contact us. He has tremendous responsibilities for one so young. Perhaps Capellini went to Boston because Baldarese is there and— Ach! It is all rank speculation. Perhaps Baldarese didn't even know Capellini was in the same city."

"I concur with your Holiness," di Stefano said. "It is strange we should have been informed of Capellini's death by the United States federal authorities and, until now, not received any word from Baldarese."

"Nor have we heard from him about the chalice," Urban said softly. He sat up and looked keenly at his secretary. "Truly you have brought us a miracle, Dominic."

"Not I," di Stefano shook his head. "The Lord made me His instrument, that is all."

"Blood that is older than a hundred thousand years...blood that cannot be dated," Urban murmured. "According to Percival Leech there is no question but that the substance is human issue. Dare we believe, Dominic, that this is the final proof? I confess before you that I stand in awe of it....I am almost afraid to believe in what Leech has told us is the truth."

"How can you feel otherwise, Holiness?" di Stefano asked. "The chalice from which Christ drank...the discovery has implications we may not have foreseen."

"It is one thing to dream, to pray for a miracle," Urban said. "At that point one is so confident one has taken stock of all possibilities relating to it. Yet when that miracle comes to pass one is humbled by it. One is almost—no, let us be truthful—one *is* afraid to accept it."

A silence came between the two men.

"How may I serve you, Holiness?" di Stefano asked quietly.

"I want to have word from Baldarese this time tomorrow. If it is not forthcoming then you will go to Boston and take personal charge of the chalice. Let the Tour continue, but bring back all of Leech's reports. Ready our own experts to verify them."

"And the chalice?"

Urban hesitated. "I have yet to decide whether that shall remain or if it should return with you. There is something wrong here, Dominic. I can feel that. Something that has to do with the cup....We must protect it at all costs!"

It was half past six by the time Donnellan turned into the curved drive of the Harbor Square complex. Lauren remained in the car, conscious of the engine running, of the silence, of the harshness of the cigarette smoke at the back of her throat. She leaned forward and ground out the stub.

Donnellan looked in the rear view. Another sedan pulled up behind them, dousing its lights, only the wipers moving.

"They'll be coming up with me?" Lauren asked. "Inside the apartment?"

"If you've no objection. Otherwise they can wait in the hall."

"I think they'd be more comfortable inside."

"You're very kind, colleen."

Lauren hesitated. "What can I tell Tim?"

"That you will have protection until this thing is broken," Donnellan said quietly. "Nothing else."

She turned to face him. "Frank do you believe, really believe, what Father Moran told us?"

He brushed impatiently at the brown forelock that had tumbled across his brow.

"What do I believe?" Donnellan muttered, staring at the mesmerizing strokes of the windshield wipers. "I believe that I must help Father Moran however I can, even if it means aiding and abetting a material witness to leave the scene of a homicide. I believe I must withhold this tape even though it provides a description of Capellini's killers. I believe—I *sense* that you are in danger and so I will render you any protection necessary. But if you were to ask me: do you believe in trolls, goblins, or witches, I should laugh in your face...." Donnellan looked at her. "I should laugh, colleen, but I cannot. Therefore I must believe, mustn't I?"

"How much time do we have?"

"Almost none," Donnellan said flatly. "Gerry won't be able to keep the Commissioner at bay much longer. I would venture to say Capellini's identity has come out by now, which means the *Federales* are about to be called in, the proper Church authorities informed...the hunt taken up for the good father." He moved a little closer to her. "I have to go, Lauren. He's waiting for me."

"Can I reach you?"

"Instantly."

Her eyes held his then dropped, staring at the large strong hands. "Would you tell your men I'll need a half-hour, no more. Then we go back to the Museum."

Donnellan was about to protest but thought better of it. He needed this girl, badly. As much as anyone, he needed to know what that cup was.

"I'm sorry, colleen, that you ever laid eyes upon that heathen chalice!"

The ferocity of his words stunned her. The care and compassion within them went out and enveloped her heart.

"You'll come to the Museum after...after Father Moran has left?"

"Yes, I'll be there. As soon as I can."

"Bring me a bone sample that has been... scarred by them," Lauren said tightly. "A bone from Cathy Windsor's body."

He stared at her, uncomprehending.

"Lauren—"

"There is one way to prove whether Father Moran is right about the creatures. I can run the residue of their...their nails under the TRACE. Then we'll know for certain how old they are. If the machine can date them...."

"My God, yes," Donnellan started. "Yes, we can do that!" He looked at her. "Lauren, I'm sorry."

She smiled briefly. "We have to know."

Without another word Lauren opened the door and slipped into the downpour, running for the front door. She dared not stay another moment in his warmth.

They had the elevator car to themselves. The halls were empty. Those tenants who started work early had already left. Others were just getting out of bed. Lauren unlocked the door to her apartment and led the way to the first landing. The security moved swiftly through the apartment, checking all rooms and closets, moving so silently that Tim McConnell, sleeping in the bedroom, never stirred. By the time they finished the coffeepot was filling.

"Please help yourselves," Lauren told them. "I'll take a shower, change, and be with you as quickly as I can."

She went into the bedroom and in the pale gray light began to undress, all the while looking at Tim. He lay sprawled on his belly, one leg bent at the knee, thrust upward, the strong shoulders tapering off into fine lean arms, long supple fingers. His hair curled down to the back of his neck. His breathing was soft, even. The smell of him made her pause and lean forward. Suddenly she wanted nothing more than his warmth and strength, to slide beneath him, her legs parting to let him come into her. She wanted to lose herself within him, to forget the cold, the blood, the unknown terror. She wanted everything to be as it had once been.

A mirage, Lauren thought. A beautiful shining mirage.

She turned on her heel and walked quickly to the bathroom. In the billows of steam she fiercely scrubbed the sweat and fear from her body. She took care to comb her hair and carefully apply makeup and daub on her favorite scent. The little things. When Lauren came downstairs, one of the agents handed her a mug of coffee.

"There's a call for you, Doctor Blair," he said.

"Frank—"

"No, Doctor Leech from the Museum. He said it was urgent. He would like to see you right away."

Percival Leech was seated behind his desk, reading the last of thirteen legal-sized pages, transcripts of the tape he had removed from the TRACE laboratory. Lauren Blair's tapes, which had recorded her discovery that the blood could not be dated.

His secretary's typescript was perfect. Leech initialled the bottom of the final page and buzzed his secretary to reserve time on the Panaflex MV1200 Facsimile. He would take the transcript over to the University Administration Building within the hour. The MV1200 would reproduce the transcript, feeding it page by page via satellite to the Vatican. In the office of Dominic Cardinal di Stefano, its twin would instantly reproduce the pages. Urban IX would have the follow-up confirmation that the cup entrusted to the Bennett Museum was in fact the Holy Grail.

Percival Leech drew out the timer from his vest pocket and flipped the cover. The Patek Philippe read ten after eight. He had had Donnellan paged an hour earlier. Still no response. No matter. Leech pressed the automatic dial and waited for the connection to be put through to Lauren Blair's home number.

"You did what?"

Lauren Blair could scarcely control the fury in her voice.

"There is no need to take that tone with me," Percival Leech said levelly. "Please, sit down. Perhaps you would care for some coffee."

He lifted the Georgian silver set and without bothering to wait for her answer poured a cup, rising to hand it to her.

"Doctor Leech, I submit you had no right to remove the work tape from the laboratory without consulting me," she said tightly. "Much less make a transcript and send it to Rome."

"I beg to differ," Leech countered, sitting back. As he sipped the coffee he handed her a yellow Telex. "The Vatican has been apprised of the unfortunate incident at Father Moran's house. How I have no idea. But when I called His Eminence di Stefano with the news of your discovery he mentioned that until such time as the authorities have given him further word of the tragedy, I was to be the custodian of the chalice. An interim measure, you understand."

Leech paused. "And since this chalice belongs to the Church this written document supersedes anything that Inspector Donnellan might object to."

"What about Father Moran?" Lauren challenged him. "He's the Vatican liaison."

"I was surprised," Leech admitted. "The directive applies equally to Father Moran until such time as I hear from di Stefano to the contrary. Apparently the Vatican has been unable to contact him." His eyes bored into hers. "*You* wouldn't happen to know where he is?"

"No," Lauren said without hesitation. It was true: she didn't.

"There is still one test to be done on that cup," she continued.

"And that is..."

"On the shell inlay. For geographic location."

"A trifling matter, surely."

"Perhaps, but it must be done," Lauren insisted.

"Really, Lauren—"

"I will not sign any authentication papers without it," Lauren said coldly. "Not without every test completed."

"Why are you making matters so difficult?" Leech asked softly, his voice a stiletto. "Surely you see that your cooperation would be to our mutual benefit."

Lauren rose, her coffee untouched. "Doctor Leech, I submit you have undermined the fundamental premise of any research endeavor: you have drawn conclusions before all the facts are in. In so doing you have placed my reputation and Isaiah's in jeopardy. Yes, I understand that there is a 99.9 percent chance that the chalice is the Grail. But *all* tests must be in. All tests must be *verified!* References checked and cross-checked. Without prejudice. You have prejudiced the research. The Church wanted to believe the cup was the Grail when the cup was first brought to the Museum. Now it has your assurance it is exactly that. But it is I, not you, who will have to answer if there are any discrepancies."

Lauren looked hard at him. "Since you are now responsible for the cup, do I have your permission to run the final test?"

"By all means," Leech said almost cordially. "I assume you will not need more than a few hours. After that I want all your papers and notes in this office. You will have security take the cup back to the fail-safe vault. Your work will be finished. I will look after the final report. I'm sure you will be able to sign it without any professional reservations."

Leech turned in his chair and picked up a file. "That is all. You may leave now."

The force with which the door closed behind her told Leech he had succeeded. He had made her angry and anger caused mistakes. How big an error would Lauren Blair make? Would it be large enough for him to exploit? Large enough for him to devise a means to take the cup? For time was almost gone and still the moment was not at hand.

The remnants of fatigue clinging to her were rent by her anger, evidenced by the staccato click of bootheels on terazzo.

He had no right! she seethed. No right whatsoever! Yet in the back of her mind a small voice reminded her that all Percival Leech had done was to violate implied professional ethics. The Vatican had entrusted the cup into the Museum's care. Leech was the Bennett Chairman. Technically he could make any inquiries regarding the chalice he saw fit. When push came to shove all he had really done was to violate an unspoken trust.

Admit it: If it weren't for the killings, for what Father Moran told you, you probably wouldn't have reacted so violently.

True.

Lauren descended the staircase leading into the Grand Salon. Through the rain-streaked windows she caught a glimpse of the crowds waiting to enter.

"Will you open the Museum?"

"Right on schedule."

The yellow Telex gave Leech all the authority he needed. It also gave him the chalice. Without understanding what the cup could be.

"Can you reach Inspector Donnellan?" she asked at once.

The agent unhooked his communicator and spoke to the Monitor.

"He should be on the line by the time we're downstairs."

"Thank you," Lauren murmured.

Her mind was working furiously, fashioning, molding an idea that had suddenly leaped into it. Its implications would mean defying Leech, going against the instructions he had just issued. If she was wrong then no amount of explanation or apology would suffice. Leech would see that her name was blackened with the scientific community. Not immediately, for her credits were too strong for that. But the innuendo would begin—about her arrogance, disrespect for authority, taking matters into her own hands on the flimsiest pretext....

There was also Isaiah Webber. She would have to act without consulting him, asking his advice, sharing what she knew. That alone would pain him. And if she were wrong his name would suffer as well, for technically they were a team. He would stand by her, but even so, what could she say to him? That would be the worst of it.

But what of Father Moran? What had he already committed himself to? And Frank. Could she stand by and do less? She was the only one who had the means and expertise to provide the proof that was needed.

The agent opened the door into the communications chamber. The Monitor in his booth looked round, returned to his caller, then held up the receiver. The Plexiglas door opened for her.

"It's the Inspector. He's out at Logan."

Lauren took the receiver and pressed it hard against her ear. A shiver coursed through her body. Then she drew the door shut.

"Frank," she said softly. "Something's come up. I need your help...."

CHAPTER SEVENTEEN

FATHER EDMUND MORAN boarded the seven-forty Eastern flight without incident. Donnellan had stayed with him until the last minute, using his police pass to accompany him through the security checkpoints to the flight deck.

Just before the hatch closed the priest turned to Donnellan and gripped his hand.

"Don't let the chalice be moved," he said. "I'll be calling as soon as I have finished at Canterbury." Moran hesitated. "Please, look after yourself... and Lauren."

"I shall," Donnellan promised him. "Good luck and Godspeed!"

Edmund Moran refused breakfast and slept through the seventy-five-minute journey. He cleared customs smoothly at Toronto International Airport and proceeded to the British Airways lounge. The Concorde ticket was ready for him. Boarding was already underway. He breakfasted as the elegant jet climbed to its cruising altitude over Nova Scotia, then drifted back to sleep, oblivious to the beauty of the turquoise stratosphere beyond the windows.

In London the debarkation proceeded rapidly and with the minimum of fuss accorded Concorde travellers. The customs inspector took one glance at the red Vatican passport and waved Moran through. The priest ducked into the lounge and from there telephoned the director of the Baldarese concerns in the U.K., his great aunt's husband. Even before their conversation was completed, a limousine was on its

way to Heathrow. Father Moran remained within
the lounge, mentally gauging the time it would take
the car to arrive. Then he plunged into the melée of
the main terminal, pushing through the throngs of
Europeans, West Indians, and Pakistanis who jammed
the concourse. Ignoring the persistent cries of cab-
bies, he made for the private-car loading zone. In the
midst of a row of vehicles bearing the diplomatic
plates he saw the Rolls Royce with the Baldarese
coat of arms emblazoned on the door. Now, if the
archbishop had received his telegram...

The drive to Canterbury lasted a little more than
an hour, the car making excellent time on the new
M7 motorway. Gravesend, Sittingbourne, Faver-
sham materialized against the leaden sky, then just
as quickly disappeared into the swirling rain-laden
mists. The spirit of this part of England, in some
ways the most ancient in the land, settled over
Father Moran. He felt the centuries peeling back to
an earlier, harsher time.

It was here that the Romans had founded Durov-
ernum, a trading station at the hub of three military
roads that crisscrossed southeastern Britain. Seven
hundred years later, under Ethelbert, the site was
named Cantwarabyrig, the borough of Kentish men.
Holiness was conferred upon the city when Augustine founded the Benedictine Monastery there, to be
enhanced by Lefranc who built the priory of Christ
Church, later bloodied by Henry's knights who cut
down Thomas à Beckett in the shrine. Edmund
Moran had spent two years in Canterbury, among
the ongoing excavations. There had been other digs,
more prestigious, with the promise of greater treasures. But the very air here was imbued with something that drew him. It may have been Canterbury's
aura of ancient sanctity or its appeal to the romantic
imagination. It could not be denied. But in his digs,
Father Moran had found neither holiness nor the
remnants of past chivalry. Within the foundations

of the Augustine temple he had helped unearth the remnants of an earlier temple, decorated with beasts and creatures that held no meaning for modern man. He had been fascinated and repelled but also at a loss to explain them. Now he had seen the face of one such beast... and it had been alive.

The car drew smoothly into the city, slowing down at New Dover Road where it became George Street, gliding past the old city walls. He glanced at the City War Memorial, then lifted his eyes as the magnificent Cathedral came into view. The imagination and toil men had grafted together to pay homage to their God never failed to leave him spellbound. These stones, set one upon the other over a period of two centuries, became soaring arches, trefoils, finials, and traceries. It all seemed so timeless, so indestructible and enduring....

The car drew to a halt before the North Gates. Across Palace Street, on the northwest corner, was the stone cottage of the archbishop, resembling a headmaster's quarters. Father Moran knew the façade was deceptive. The interior spread out on both sides and ran well back into a large lot. The architect who had designed the residence at the turn of the century had in fact constructed a miniature palace.

Edmund Moran depressed the intercom button and spoke with the driver.

"Would you call on the archbishop, please?"

He watched as the driver entered the black wrought-iron gates and came to a gleaming black door. An instant later the archbishop's servant appeared. The conversation was brief. The driver, holding an umbrella, returned to open Moran's door.

"It's good to see you again, Master Edmund."

"And you, Playter."

Edmund Moran smiled at the old servant. Playter, who had served two archbishops and remembered the names and faces of all who crossed this threshold, grasped Edmund's hand in both of his.

"It's been a long time, sir," he murmured, ever-alert eyes scanning the priest. "You've filled out nicely, if I may say so. But a bit peaked, aren't you?"

During the Christ Church excavations Playter had become fond of the young priest.

"There are difficulties," Edmund Moran conceded, stepping into the fruitwood-panelled vestibule.

Playter nodded sagely. Another man would have said the journey had tired him. But from Edmund Moran he expected only the truth.

"His Lordship is waiting for you in the Green Room. Come, wash up. After all that travelling I expect you wouldn't mind a nice cup of tea."

Edmund Moran gently embraced the old man and proceeded to the guest bathroom. He thoroughly scrubbed his face and hands, washing away the inevitable grit of travel. When he emerged Playter was waiting.

The Green Room was a large solarium. No less than forty different varieties of plants and flowers flourished there. In one corner, near the hot-air vents, was a comfortable sofa, several rattan chairs, and a coffee table. Edmund Moran's heels clicked across the Spanish tile floor.

"We are here."

From between a row of blossoming orange trees the archbishop of Canterbury appeared, a gardener's smock over his cassock, hands encased in white gloves holding a pick and trowel.

"Edmund Moran!"

"Your Lordship," the priest replied, bowing from the waist.

"My boy, it is good to see you!"

Richard Arthur Clarence set down his tools and removed his gloves.

"Such a surprise. And a most welcome one."

Edmund Moran felt his bones crack as the archbishop embraced him. His Lordship was a bear of a man, tall and generous of girth. His walk was reminiscent of a proud ship moving effortlessly through a yielding ocean.

"You do not appear well; come over here and sit by me," Clarence said imperatively.

"I am indebted to Your Lordship for seeing me," Edmund Moran said, sleeve brushing against a Wandering Jew.

The archbishop settled himself in an alarmingly frail wicker chair.

"There is a joint in the oven that should be ready within the hour. You couldn't have partaken of that mealy air fare, Concorde or not."

At the mention of supper Father Moran realized that he hadn't eaten since last night. "Thank you, Your Lordship," he said.

"Ah, and here is Playter with your tea," Clarence murmured, indicating the servant who had just entered pushing a trolley. There was a large pot of tea and a chafing dish from under whose lid there drifted the smell of freshly baked buns and biscuits.

"We shall pour ourselves, Playter, thank you."

The servant withdrew.

"You still take your tea clear?"

"Yes, my lord."

"Your communiqué was rather breathless, Edmund," the archbishop said, handing his visitor a cup. "A sense of urgency was conveyed, to be sure, but also panic, fear.... Or am I inferring too much?"

"You are entirely correct."

"Then how may I assist you?"

Edmund Moran set the saucer down on his lap. "I need to read the Annals of Joseph of Arimathea."

"And what does Rome want with the Annals?"

The voice, proud, resonant, underlined with angry challenge, startled Moran. He twisted around to see a figure in a monk's habit standing behind and to the right of him. He recognized him as the Abbot Athelstan, leader of the Blackfriars, the largest and most powerful monastic order within the Church of England.

The priest rose and paid homage to the man who held all things Roman in undisguised contempt. Athelstan, a diminutive man disfigured by a plum-colored birthmark that covered the entire left side of his face, withdrew his hand as soon as Moran's lips touched it. He turned and, leaning heavily on his cane, hobbled to the side of his archbishop.

"What is it that Rome wants with the Annals?" he repeated harshly.

"I do not come on behalf of Rome, Athelstan," Moran said.

"No?" The abbot's eyebrows, thick and arched like wings, rose majestically over agate eyes. "Then how are we to interpret such an *urgent* matter?"

"Perhaps if Edmund is given the opportunity he will tell us," the archbishop said mildly. The restraint in his voice was a familiar warning to the Blackfriar. "Indeed," Clarence continued, "I too was surprised when you asked that Athelstan be present when you arrived. The reason you asked for him is now clear. But the reason behind that?"

"My lord," Edmund Moran began. "It is known that the Church of England, more specifically the order of the Blackfriars, has what both contend to be the Annals of Joseph of Arimathea. In recent years the Holy Roman Church has made several requests to be allowed to examine the same. All have been turned down."

"Perhaps you have forgotten it was your own Church that deemed the writings apocryphal," Athelstan rebuked him. "Your masters denounced the matter as heretical, a work of fiction, a fraud."

"That was almost a century ago," Moran reminded him quietly. "I grant you that a terrible mistake was made then, by men more aware of the theological and ideological differences between our churches than our common heritage. It was done when rivalry between our faiths was at its worst. Moreover, the Annals were read by ecclesiastical scholars, not historians or scientists. The physical aspect of the Annals was not taken into account. There was no scientific evidence to bolster your contentions."

"They are not contentions anymore," Athelstan retorted. "The most modern scientific methods have proven—at least to our satisfaction—that the writing can be attributed to Joseph of Arimathea."

"Yet you have never permitted them to be examined by laymen," Moran said. "In spite of repeated inquiries from universities and museums, not to mention the Vatican, the Annals have never left Canterbury."

"Nor shall they!"

"I hope very much to change your mind about that."

"What is it that Rome wants to know?" Athelstan demanded. "What is it about the Annals that has suddenly chafed the Roman skin?"

"My inquiry does not concern the Church, at least not directly." Desperately Moran turned to the archbishop. "My lord, perhaps more than the abbot appreciates I understand his sentiments concerning the attitude of Rome toward the Annals. But I beg your indulgence. There is a great deal I have to tell you and very little time."

"Considering your hasty travel arrangements I wouldn't have thought otherwise," Clarence murmured. Turning to the abbot, he said, "Let's hear him out, shall we, without interruption."

"As your lordship desires," Athelstan said dryly.

"You have our attention, Edmund. Please..."

"Thank you, my lord. But before I begin I must point out that what I have to tell you is extremely privileged information. No one in the Church is aware of it. *No one.* Including His Holiness Urban—"

"You are already straining credulity, Baldarese!"

Athelstan interrupted. The archbishop silenced him with a raised hand.

"You are asking us to respect a confidence," Clarence said. "You are not a man given to melodrama or frivolous requests. Therefore I give you my solemn assurance that what you say shall not go beyond the wall of this house. You have *both* our pledges."

"I thank Your Lordship," Moran said. "As you are aware, the Vatican Tour opened in Boston several days ago. Included in the Tour but not placed on exhibit was a certain chalice, removed by Cardinal di Stefano from the Museum of Pagan Antiquities. This was done against the express wishes and warnings of Cardinal Capellini. The chalice in question, my lord, is very likely the Holy Grail...."

For the next hour, Father Edmund Moran recounted every detail of what had happened since the cup had left the Museum of Pagan Antiquities. He held back nothing, not the burning of the hands, not a single grisly detail about the murders that accompanied the cup's arrival in Boston. He spoke of the Fisher Kings and the duties that had been bequeathed to him. He laid out the research conducted by the Bennett Museum and finished by explaining the irrefutable proof of the chalice's authenticity: the blood which could not be dated.

When he finished, Edmund Moran felt fatigue sweep over him in battering waves.

"The archaeologist, Doctor Blair, and Inspector Donnellan, they're the only ones, besides ourselves, who know the entire story?" asked Clarence.

"Yes."

"The archeologist, Doctor Blair, and Inspector

Edmund Moran accepted it gratefully. "I thank you for your attention. And yours, abbot. But do you believe me?"

"How can I not believe you?" Clarence murmured.

"Then it is true," Athelstan murmured. "Everything Joseph wrote about is true." He turned to

Moran. "It's confirmation you want, isn't it? Of the demonkind's existence. From an unimpeachable source..."

"Yes," Father Moran whispered.

The abbot regarded his archbishop. "The cup in their possession is almost certainly the Grail, my lord. The description tallies. The reference to the demonkind...It is all in Joseph's writings."

The archbishop rose and came over to a planter that held dazzling sunflowers. He reached out and gently cupped a bulb, stroking the grainy face.

"The Annals of Joseph of Arimathea," he murmured. Then he faced Edmund Moran. "They are his final testament. A warning in which he spoke of a cup that was taken to the Holy Land. A cup presented to Christ, touched by him. A chalice whose true origins Joseph became aware of only much later. He doesn't say how this came about. Only that it had. He became certain the chalice was evil so he returned it to Britain and buried it. The cup was never meant to be found, Edmund. Never."

"But the Annals—" the priest started to say.

"Were found in a different location. You see, we thought the same thing: logically the cup and the Annals should have been buried together, since the writings were a warning against the cup. Without the chalice what could we make of the Annals? Even if we were convinced Joseph had written them, their contents were so incredible we *couldn't* believe them!"

Father Moran rose. "Will you permit me to read the Annals?"

Clarence looked at his abbot. "Under the circumstances, can we deny him?"

"No, we cannot," Athelstan replied. "The Roman Church laughed at us when they read the Annals. How could such a race exist? they asked jeeringly. The Grail does not exist, at least not in the physical universe, they maintained. Now one of their own has learned differently. Joseph knew, possibly firsthand, of what he spoke. The demonkind existed then. Perhaps they have survived to this day. Not only survived but are on the offensive."

He gripped Moran's hand. "I will give you the Annals but you may not discuss their contents with anyone, not even those who already know. Your word will have to be good enough."

Edmund Moran shook his head. "You don't understand. It's not them that I must convince. *They know.* I must have the Annals to corroborate Capellini's story when I speak with Cardinal di Stefano. It is he who must understand that the cup has to be returned to the Church."

"You will not convince di Stefano of anything!" Athelstan spat out. "It has been his avarice that has unleashed what should never have been found. At least Capellini and his predecessors understood enough to hide the chalice, for their own sakes, to say nothing until they knew what it was they had. To keep it from the likes of di Stefano must have been quite a feat. But as you yourself said, he has made the cup's authentication his personal passion. When he learns of the test results he won't be listening to you or anyone else. Certainly not when you tell him the Annals have already been condemned by the Holy See!

"God in Heaven, the cup should never have been found! Never! Joseph himself intended it that way. He buried it for that very reason. But man persisted and prevailed. Stupid. . . . Why in the name of all that is holy didn't Joseph destroy it!"

"That is enough!" Clarence commanded. He rose between the two men. "Do you agree to show Edmund the Annals?"

"Of course, but subject to my conditions."

"The Annals belong to your order," Clarence acknowledged. "But if there is no other way to convince di Stefano of the chalice's danger then perhaps you will reconsider. Because if what Edmund says is true, if what we know about the Annals is true, then the danger is not limited to Catholicism. It concerns us all."

"Let him read first," Athelstan replied. "Then he will see how much of a chance he will stand of having Rome believe him!"

"I really don't see where we have much choice," Lauren Blair said. She paused and looked at Frank Donnellan. "No choice..."

They were the only two people in the Terrace Café. Though the place was still closed to the public, Donnellan had persuaded one of the waiters to bring them coffee. Now he leaned across and covered her hand, gently pulling her fingers away from the few strands of hair she had been curling. Her skin was cold to his touch, the face pale, eyes larger than he had ever seen them before.

"Leech wants the cup today," he murmured.

"As soon as I've finished the last tests."

"And he doesn't know—doesn't even suspect—anything of what Father Moran told us?"

"Of course not!" Lauren shook her head. "Christ, I'm sorry," she whispered, fingers tightening on his. "I'm so sorry."

"I think you're right," he said softly. "Short of removing the chalice from here there's nothing we can do. We might as well hand it to him right now."

"No!"

He reached across and cupped her cheek in his palm.

"Are you certain, colleen? I'll help you, you know that. But are you willing to take that risk?"

"Not I, Frank," Lauren said, slipping her fingers through his, nails digging into his flesh. "What can Leech do to me? Accuse me of trying to steal the cup? That would be too absurd." She paused. "But what about you, Frank? I can't take the chalice out of here without you. You're the one who's really responsible for it...."

Donnellan reached for a cigarette, lit one for her and one for himself. He had been lucky so far. There hadn't been any clamoring from downtown about the Capellini killing. He had managed to get Father Moran out of the country. But when Rome failed to get in touch with the priest, they would request that the FBI find Moran. In turn, the Feds would lean on the Commissioner who would in turn call Donnellan who would have to tell them...What?

Donnellan sat back and laughed bitterly. "Here we are, two reasonably intelligent people, sitting on something no one else could possibly believe." He shook his head. "We're committed, Lauren. We might as well play it out. In the little time we do have."

Lauren was about to speak but thought better of it. She wanted to tell him the risk *was* worth taking. That it *had* to be taken. She wanted him to know she would stand by him when all hell broke loose. Somehow it all seemed very little alongside what he was offering.

"Maybe we'll get lucky," she smiled wanly. "Finish the testing before Leech comes looking for me. Maybe the shell inlay will correspond perfectly with the rest of the information...."

Donnellan rose. "I pray that you're right, colleen. With all my heart I pray. But I don't believe that what you will find will make matters easier for us."

They returned to the lab together, Donnellan to crate the chalice, Lauren to use the outside line for a phone call. Donnellan was joined by the Monitor and the two security agents he had assigned to Lauren. Quickly he explained where the cup was being moved but did not elaborate as to why.

"All you need to know is that I am acting in direct contravention of my instructions," he told them. "I am removing the chalice without the authority of

either Father Moran, who is absent, or Percival
Leech. There is an outside chance I will have it back
here before Leech comes for it. But it's very slim.
When he does appear you are to tell him only that
I have taken the cup. You don't know where or for
what purpose. You are not to be involved in any
way."

"What about the rest of the men, Frank?" the
Monitor asked.

"Tell them only after Leech comes down."

The Monitor looked at the other agents. "We don't
like the idea of your walking around with that thing
without someone covering your flank," he said. "If
nothing else, it's lousy security."

"I appreciate the consideration," Donnellan said
quietly. "More than you may know. But if I'm wrong
and this thing blows I don't want any fallout on you.
You're all too good for that."

There was a moment's silence. "In for the penny,
in for the pound," the Monitor shrugged. "We'll be
waiting for your call, Frank. Remember, if there's
anything you need—"

"I'll remember."

Five minutes later Lauren Blair and Donnellan
were standing under the awning that covered the
loading bay, watching as one of the agents backed
up the car.

"Everything set?"

Lauren nodded. Gripping the aluminum carrier,
Donnellan stepped off the bay. Crouching they ran
for the car.

"Where to?"

"The Geochron Laboratories on Sheridan Street
in West Cambridge."

Geochron Laboratories was a one-man show. Specifically Matthew Tyler's show. Located in a series of
refurbished, revitalized warehouses in Cambridge's
West end, the Geochron facilities rivalled those of the

Bennett Museum. To anyone who knew the lab's history, this came as no surprise. There had been a time when Matthew Tyler had been heir apparent to Percival Leech for the chairmanship of the Museum. A respected scientist and evaluator in his own right, Tyler had begun his fall from grace when he had first, privately, questioned Leech's evaluation of a series of paintings belonging to Chicago's Hirshorn Foundation. Leech refused to consider his subordinates' claim and Tyler went public. Before a definitive evaluation was made Percival Leech had withdrawn his services. No one had ever learned whether Leech or Tyler had come closest to the evaluation the foundation eventually arrived at independently.

In the aftermath, Matthew Tyler set up shop across town from the Bennett. It had taken ten long hard years before Geochron gained a reputation as one of the premier commercial dating facilities in the country, a decade during which Tyler had survived every attempt on Leech's part to drive him into the ground. From discreet professional slander to deliberate underbidding for contracts whose overrun Leech made up from his own pocket, Tyler survived the gamut. Not without a little help from his friends, the most trusted of whom was Lauren Blair.

Sitting back behind his desk, Tyler, a slim athletic man with a generous smile and a penchant for three-piece dove-gray suits, regarded the girl to whom he owed so much.

"Lauren, you know there's no problem in your using the facilities. In fact, Lab One, with the experimental TRACE unit I bought from the university, is free at the moment. I'm having difficulty with the two other factors: the secrecy and Inspector Donnellan's role in all this."

"Doctor Tyler, I am here because the piece is from the Vatican museums," Donnellan answered quickly. "As my credentials prove, I am the director of security at least as long as it is in the city."

"All well and good," Tyler said quietly. "In the past a number of priceless artifacts have been entrusted to us. I'm sure Lauren can vouch for that."

"It isn't a matter of trust, Matt," Lauren said. "We can't identify the piece because we don't want Leech to know where it is or what we're doing to it."

Tyler's only reaction was a faint smile.

"Are you suggesting that there might be a disagreement between him and you as to the authenticity of this piece?"

"There could well be a dispute," Lauren said quietly.

"On a piece belonging to the *Church?*" Tyler asked, incredulous.

"Yes."

"And you wouldn't have come if he hadn't denied—or wasn't about to deny—you testing facilities."

"That's why we're here, Matt." Lauren was aware of the bitterness Tyler felt toward Leech. But if Tyler was going to help her, it wouldn't be to get back at the Chairman. He was a bigger man than that. It would be to help her. "I know what I'm asking of you, Matt," she said. "I'll understand if you pass."

Tyler opened his desk drawer and drew out Geochron's standard testing application form. "My interpretation of what has transpired," he smiled, "is as follows: You, both a friend and an eminent archeologist, came to me with a request to use Geochron's facilities. But alas I was rushing out to an important meeting and couldn't stay to hear all the details of what you wanted to test. However, knowing you as I do, I scribbled down my authorization"—Tyler signed with a flourish at the bottom of the page— "marked down the facility made available to you, which is Lab One, and, just to keep everything above board, a nominal charge." With a twinkle in his eye Tyler wrote "Bennett Museum" in the space reserved for "Credit to."

"And before you could say Jack Sprat, I was gone."

Tyler rose, retrieved his coat and umbrella from the rack in the corner, and headed out.

"Thank you, Matt," Lauren called after him.

"Jesus, that was a quick change of heart," Donnellan muttered when Tyler was out of earshot.

"No, it wasn't," Lauren said. "All he needed was a way to cover himself. Even so, if Leech finds out the cup is gone, he'll deduce very quickly where to look. Matt could still take a beating."

"Then we should move, colleen," Donnellan suggested.

CHAPTER EIGHTEEN

"HIS LORDSHIP desires to know if you would join him in the drawing room for coffee?"

Playter looked at the young priest, sitting sprawled in the hard straight-back leather chair, staring at the 5 x 7 Plexiglas slabs that littered the Queen Anne desk. It was half past twelve in the morning. In spite of the gargantuan meal the archbishop had pressed upon him, and the bone-numbing fatigue of his journey, Edmund Moran's concentration had not faltered. The Annals mesmerized him, the horror he was slowly unfolding consumed him like the fever.

Father Edmund Moran leaned forward and carefully stacked the slabs until they formed a pile some sixteen inches high. The Annals of Joseph of Arimathea, written in his own hand almost two thousand years ago. Discovered by the Blackfriars on the original site of Christ Church Cathedral, the parchment had been carefully cleaned, treated to preserve the dye of the script and pressed between Plexiglas sheets. Preserved as a fly or beetle in amber.

The Annals of Joseph of Arimathea. Authentic beyond question. Complete with drawings that depicted two cups, the first readily recognizable to Moran, the second a chalice of identical proportions but smaller dimensions that mesmerized him like a snake.

Whoever the artist had been, he had taken pains to detail the figures and landscapes on the smaller vessel. The terrain was hellish, replete with scenes of chaos and destruction, of monsters feeding upon

people, vipers preying upon children, demons strid-
ing unopposed through fields of corpses. The reliefs
on the cup were equally vivid. Although the features
varied, all the figures combined human and reptilian
characteristics. As did the beast who had stood over
him on the garden wall. And at the very top, just
below the rim, were the faces of Lucifer: the goat,
the viper, the raven.

"Edmund..."

"I'm sorry, Playter. Yes, wait for me—I'll walk
down with you."

The demonkind lived. They had endured. Now
they had returned.

The archbishop of Canterbury was in the pan-
elled drawing room. Sitting at the other end of the
French leather couch was Athelstan, the abbot of the
Blackfriars. In front of him, on a green-veined mar-
ble table, were the notebooks and ledgers Arturo
Cardinal Capellini had bequeathed Edmund Moran.

"Good evening, Edmund," the archbishop said. He
poured a cup of tea and handed it to the young cleric.
"Or is it?"

"I think not, my lord."

Clarence returned to his seat. "Nor do I. I have
been perusing these writings as Athelstan finishes
with them. It seems to me they and the Annals are
complementary."

"Yes, they are," Edmund Moran answered in a
hollow voice. "The Annals are the final proof." He
looked at the abbot. "There can be no question now,
can there?"

The abbot closed the ledger he had been reading.
"None."

"So I must ask you again: will you permit me to
present the Annals to Dominic Cardinal di Stefano
in support of the evidence gathered by the Fisher
Kings?"

The clock in the corner pealed three times. Athelstan waited as its resonance faded. "I am still re-

luctant to accede to your request," he said. "Don't misunderstand me: it is not that I can't bring myself to trust you. Having read this, knowing now who you are, I cannot help but believe everything you've told us. But I cannot say the same for di Stefano. Can *you* assure us that even if he deigns to read the Annals he will believe them? Can you assure us that they will not be 'lost' or misplaced while in his possession? Under the circumstances surrounding the chalice, the stakes involved on the part of the Roman Church, this may not be a convenient time to deal with the truth."

For a moment Edmund Moran said nothing. Athelstan's words, his suspicions about di Stefano's integrity, did not anger him. He had entertained the same thoughts as soon as he'd finished reading the Annals.

Did di Stefano want to know the truth? He had refused to listen to Capellini because the curator stood in the path to his end. Would di Stefano listen to him? Like Capellini, he had gone outside the Church. He had permitted strangers, some outside the faith, to become privy to secrets not even the pope was aware of....

No, he will not listen!

But he said: "I must try. I don't believe we have any choice. The Church must be convinced that the cup has to be returned to consecrated ground. It must be buried deep within the Vatican and its place sealed so that no man can ever look upon it again. That is what must be done. If Joseph is correct and the cup is the demonic font, a life force for these creatures, then the only way we will be able to destroy them is by denying them the chalice. We still have a chance to do that. I ask you: in view of what is at stake, are we not obligated to at least try? It is not necessarily our lives we must consider. Innocent people have already died. Even if, with God's will, we prevent more slaughter, we owe it to the victims."

The archbishop glanced at his abbot. "I don't believe Edmund overstates his case," he said quietly.

"Nor do I," the abbot replied. "But my objection still stands: I cannot trust Rome with the Annals. Di Stefano will check. He will learn that his own people were not convinced of their authenticity. Even if he is convinced otherwise there is nothing to prevent him from 'losing' or destroying the papers, if it so suits his purpose."

"I believe we have a way of insuring that doesn't happen," the archbishop said. "The Annals will be passed under my imprimatur."

There was a knock on the door and Playter entered. "Father Moran, there's a trunk call for you. From America."

"God, no!" the priest whispered. "Playter, I'll take it in here."

"Edmund, if you want privacy—" the archbishop started to say.

"No, my lord," Moran said, crossing over to the great barrister desk that dominated the drawing room. "There aren't any secrets anymore."

The transatlantic connection was bad, static crackling through the line. Far far away a voice was calling his name.

"Lauren! Lauren, is that you?"

"Father Moran—"

"Lauren, you'll have to speak up."

There was a second's pause. "Is that better?"

"Yes, much. Lauren, what is it?"

"The tests on the chalice are complete," Lauren was saying. "Father Moran, the shell inlay, it could not have originated in the waters of the Middle East."

"Not—Lauren, are you certain?"

"Absolutely."

"But where—"

"Off the coast of Britain. The shell used in the chalice is particular—no, *exclusive*—to the North and Irish Seas."

"The North Sea!"

"There's no mistake, Father. I doublechecked before calling you."

"But how—"

"Father, there's something else. The weight of the chalice."

"Go on, Lauren, what about the weight?"

"That's bothered me from the beginning. The cup is too heavy. If it were solid gold it would weigh less. It would have to. Its dimensions demand it. I've run the figures through the computers. The cup is three pounds too heavy. But the real problem is that there is no question as to the purity of the gold. It's as though there is something within the cup, some sort of skeleton around which the gold has been plated—"

"Lauren...Lauren, can you hold on for just a minute?"

"Sure, what—"

"Just a minute, Lauren!" Moran turned to the abbot. "The plate with the two drawings of the chalice—pass them to me, please!"

He snatched the Plexiglas from Athelstan's outstretched hand and held it to the light, studying the twin chalices. It was possible, all too possible.

"Lauren, are you there?"

"Yes, Father."

"Have you drilled the cup with the laser?"

"No, I wanted to talk to you first."

"All right, please listen very carefully. Turn the cup over and drill into the inside curve of the base. In four places, the central points of the compass, about three quarters of an inch in. I think you will find another metal—the base of a cup within the cup."

"Father, I'm not certain I understand."

261

"Lauren, please, the gold may just be a plating. Thick, but a plating nonetheless."

"Have you spoken with the Vatican, Father? Do we have permission to drill?"

Edmund Moran closed his eyes. "No, we do not," he said. "But I found what I came for, Lauren. It is likely, very likely, that the original cup, the demonic font, is sitting right inside the chalice we think is the Grail. You must drill! Do you understand? We have to try...Lauren!"

"All right, Father. I can use the laser. What if I find another metal?"

"I shall be in Rome first thing in the morning. I'll call you from there."

Static rippled across the line.

"—sure you want me to proceed, Father?"

"Yes!" Moran shouted. "Do whatever you must to get through to that second layer of metal."

"Good luck, Father."

"Lauren, is Inspector Donnellan with you?"

"Yes, do you want to speak to him?"

"No, I just wanted to make certain you're all right."

"I am, Father. Good luck to you and Godspeed!"

"What did she tell you, Edmund?" the archbishop demanded as soon as Moran hung up the phone. Quickly the priest explained Lauren's suspicions and the conclusion he had drawn from them.

"It's not unreasonable," Athelstan commented. "The plating could be that thick. Certainly the technique was being used then."

"But how did the cup come to Joseph in the first instance?" Edmund Moran demanded. "You've seen the drawings. He never would have permitted such an obscenity to be plated and subsequently presented to Jesus. That's unthinkable!"

"It is possible that Joseph commissioned a special work to take back to Galilee," the archbishop suggested. "Could it not have been the actual craftsman who, unknown to us, chose to fashion that cup on the frame of the font. Obviously it was later, much later that Joseph learned what it was that had graced our Lord's presence. That was why he returned the cup to Britain instead of leaving it in the Holy Land. The cup was never 'lost' as the Arthurian legends suggest. It was buried."

Edmund Moran glanced at the clock. "I don't think there is any question: in a few hours I must call the papal secretary. The evidence is overwhelming now: the Fisher King records, the Annals, the likelihood of another cup within the chalice. It's not possible for His Holiness to refuse to act."

The archbishop regarded his abbot. "Would you agree to parting with the Annals protected as they would be by my signature?"

Athelstan rose. He came over and lifted the Plexiglas sheet.

"Call Rome."

He did not take his eyes off the macabre detail in the second drawing of the ancient font.

"You have allowed her to make a fool of you, steal the chalice from under your very nose," the stranger said contemptuously. "I am disappointed in you, Percival Leech. I thought you better prepared than that!"

The Chairman of the Bennett Museum regarded the stranger's reflection in the rain-streaked window. He swivelled around behind his desk and reached for the phone.

"Get me Lauren Blair in the laboratory," he instructed his secretary.

"She won't be there," the voice intoned.

Percival Leech tightened his lips but said nothing. When the phone rang it was not his secretary but the Monitor who spoke to him.

"Where is Lauren Blair?" Leech demanded crisply.

"I'm sorry, sir, I don't know. She's not in the lab. Your call was rerouted to me."

"Then I shall speak with Donnellan."

"He's not in the building at present."

Leech paused. "I see. I assume that if Doctor Blair isn't there she must have completed the testing. She was to have brought the cup to me but failed to do so. I would like it sent up now."

"Again, sir, I'm sorry, but the chalice was removed from the premises by Inspector Donnellan."

"The chalice was removed! On whose authority?"

"Inspector Donnellan's, sir."

Leech swivelled around toward the stranger, who remained facing the windows. He thought he saw a ghost of a smile in the opaque reflection.

"I want you to find Donnellan for me at once," Leech said, his voice level.

"I will do my best. Is there anything else, sir?"

"No, nothing."

Leech broke the connection.

"She anticipated you," the stranger said. "She has found something within the chalice."

"What could she find?" Leech snapped impatiently. "Besides the blood?"

"Of which you so faithfully informed the Vatican," the stranger finished softly.

"Better that di Stefano learn that from me than her or Moran," Leech retorted. "I told you: the chalice is now under my personal supervision."

"In theory, perhaps," the stranger demurred. "Certainly not in practice."

"I will find it," Leech said, rising.

"You are a clever man," the stranger said. "You see that by removing the chalice Lauren Blair has given you the opening you've been waiting for."

"Indeed she has," Leech murmured. There was nothing he could hide from this man.

"Then permit me to assist you. The cup has been

taken to Geochron Laboratories." The stranger smiled. "There's a certain irony in that, don't you think?"

Alitalia Flight 404, London–Rome, departed on schedule, at six-twenty in the morning. Airline officials did not think it prudent to mention the strike simmering in the control towers of the Roman capital. No sooner was Father Moran on board than the hatch was closed and the aircraft backing away from the gate. The priest placed two tote bags underneath the empty seats beside him, then leaned back and gently closed his eyes, his mind fixed on the soft drone of the engine. Before he knew it he was asleep.

A Vatican limousine was waiting for him on the tarmac. It whisked Father Moran out of the airport and through the already teaming streets of the city to the Via Della Conciliazione gates. Flanked by two Swiss guards, Father Moran was escorted to the offices of Dominic Cardinal di Stefano.

"You are not looking at all well," di Stefano commented. "I could have some coffee brought in, perhaps some breakfast."

"Thank you, Eminence. But that is not necessary."

"Of course the Holy See has been informed of Arturo Capellini's tragic death," the papal secretary said. "Appalling, what goes on in America... a man of the cloth, murdered. I'm certain his death came as a great shock to you."

"I was there when he was murdered, Eminence."

The secretary's eyebrows shot up. "Indeed, and did you see the killer?"

"I did, Eminence."

"Surely that must have been a great help to the authorities' investigation."

"Eminence, I would not have asked to see you at this hour unless the matter was urgent," Moran said, desperately trying to change the subject. "Extremely so."

"That much I have gathered," di Stefano said quietly. "It also seems that you might have better prepared yourself. You are the Vatican liaison for the Tour. I expected *you* to have informed the Holy See of the latest test results: the blood in the chalice."

"My being here is directly related to the chalice, Eminence."

Di Stefano's eyes narrowed. "Perhaps you would first explain to me what Cardinal Capellini was doing in Boston."

"If I may, Eminence, I should like to begin at the point when Cardinal Capellini first showed you the cup...."

For the second time within the space of twenty-four hours, Father Edmund Moran related the twisted narrative the story of the chalice had become, this time adding the discussions he had had with the archbishop of Canterbury and Athelstan, the abbot of the Blackfriars. As he spoke he produced the documents that supported his words, bringing out the Annals of Joseph of Arimathea last.

Dominic Cardinal di Stefano listened in silence. When Moran was done, the prelate rose and poured himself a cup of coffee from the silver urn.

"Father Moran," he said slowly. "You have betrayed the trust His Holiness has shown you. I am appalled by your actions, disheartened and appalled."

Edmund Moran paled. "Eminence—"

"No! I have heard you out. Now you shall extend that same privilege to me. You have been derelict in your duties, Father. First and foremost, after Capellini told you of his attempt to prevent the chalice from leaving the Museum of Pagan Antiquities, after he had confided in you that he literally fled the Holy See and was again undermining the efforts of the Holy Father in regards to the Tour, it was your responsibility to inform me at once. This you did not do.

"Instead you permitted yourself to be swayed by

his words. His delirium infected you. Though I do not wish to speak ill of the dead, there is no question in my mind that Capellini was suffering from some psychological malady. There was no rhyme or reason to his actions. Nonetheless you became his willing collaborator.

"If that weren't enough, you did not even see fit to inform His Holiness of his death. Instead you took it upon yourself to pursue Capellini's dubious inquiries. Even though the discovery of the blood proved conclusively that Christ had touched the cup, you persisted. And where did such stubbornness lead? To your greatest error.

"If your narrative is accurate, then without even informing the Holy Father or myself you broke the trust of secrecy, confiding the discovery of the chalice to a rival church. The English church, no less, which, as you well know, has been far from amicable to the Holy See. You, Father Moran, have sowed the seeds for gossip and slander against the cup."

Di Stefano paused and looked keenly at the younger man.

"How could you have done such a thing?"

"Eminence, I speak with all respect," Edmund Moran said. He would not permit di Stefano to intimidate him! He had to make him see! "But I must ask you: if I had come to you with the evidence Arturo Capellini passed on to you, before I had a chance to corroborate it, would you have accorded me any more attention than you did him when he tried to warn you about the chalice?"

"No!" di Stefano thundered. "I would not have. Instead I would have revoked your standing as the Vatican liaison of the Tour, something I do at this very moment!"

"Even if you dispute the Fisher Kings' writings, Eminence, you cannot discount the Annals!" Moran cried desperately.

"I can and I do!" the papal secretary replied immediately. "You speak to me of Fisher Kings. What are they but some surreptitious group within the Church. Outlaws! According to you—*and* Capellini *and* whoever came before him—they have been responsible for hiding a priceless relic from the Church for over a thousand years! I find that incredible! Bad enough that this should happen in our house. Worse that you have seen fit to make our embarrassment public!

"As for the Annals, as you call them, surely you're aware that I have given a great deal of attention to the documentation surrounding the Grail. I am familiar with the 1864 report of the Religious Doctrine Committee, which studied the Annals. Nothing you have told me leads me to re-evaluate their conclusions."

"But the conclusions were based on doctrinal disputes," Edmund Moran shot back. "Since then the Annals have been proved to be those of Joseph of Arimathea. The evidence is overwhelming. The archbishop himself gave them his imprimatur."

"I'm afraid I beg to differ with the archbishop," di Stefano replied coldly. "In fact I don't believe Joseph is the author of the Annals. Furthermore the fact of the blood—"

"But I have explained to you, Eminence, there is a doubt as to the chalice's integrity. I believe the gold is only a plating, thick but plating nevertheless. Doctor Blair suggests there is a marked discrepancy in the weight—"

"I am not interested in what Doctor Blair might consider a discrepancy," di Stefano cut him off. "In my opinion her work is complete. She has helped prove that the chalice is the Grail."

"And the burning of Capellini's hands," Father Moran said, his voice going cold, dead. "My own...the murder of the student and Arturo. What of *them*, Eminence?"

"Tragic, very tragic. But having no connection with the cup."

"An evil has been unleashed," the young priest said. "An evil for which the Church is responsible. I beg of you in the name of all that is holy, give me leave to return the cup to the Vatican, to this most consecrated ground. While there is still time..."

"No, Father Moran, I shall not do that," di Stefano said. "But I command you thusly: you are hereby withdrawn as the Vatican liaison for the Tour. You will remain within the Holy See until I or the Holy Father sees fit to give you new duties. Now it is late—"

"Eminence, I have promised to return the Annals to the archbishop."

"They shall be returned."

"And the legacies of the Fisher Kings?"

"These belong to the Church. They will rest with me until I have made provisions for them."

"I'm afraid such an arrangement is not satisfactory," Edmund Moran said.

Di Stefano's eyes bored into his own. "Did I hear you correctly, Father?"

"I said the arrangement your Eminence proposes is not satisfactory."

"You have proven obstinate and disobedient," di Stefano said softly. "I suggest you curb yourself."

Edmund Moran rose and started to gather up the material off di Stefano's desk.

"Leave that!"

"No, Eminence, I cannot," the priest replied, not looking up.

"I command you!"

"You know the Annals are correct," Edmund Moran murmured.

"I know no such thing! You presume to place such thoughts in my mind!"

"You're afraid, aren't you, Eminence?" Father Moran said softly. He faced the Cardinal and his gaze refused to let go that of the older man. He was no longer Father Moran but a Baldarese, a nobleman equal in every way to this prince of the Church.

"You are afraid, Eminence, that Arturo Capellini was right in his fears. You are afraid because you *know* in your heart the blood of two innocent people rests upon your vanity! The vanity of having found the centerpiece of the exhibit, the miracle of the Grail in our time—"

"Blasphemy!"

"I love my Church, Eminence, and I will continue to serve her. Even if in doing so I must stand against you."

"I will censure you—excommunicate you if need be!" di Stefano shouted. "As God is my witness you will do nothing! Do you hear, nothing!"

"Wrong, Eminence. I will move against you. You have not had to confront the horror you've unleashed. I will force you to look upon his face. As I have!"

Father Moran gazed into the seething eyes so lacking in understanding, so devoid of compassion. He realized that he was standing on the brink. To defy di Stefano meant to defy the Church as represented by the Cardinal. There was only one punishment for such disobedience—he would be stripped of his priestly robes. Everything he had labored for would come to nothing. He would become a leper, ostracized from his home. He looked away and saw the smiling face of Arturo Capellini. He saw Lauren and the Inspector and the grotesquely contorted features of the creatures that wished so much to devour him.

"I am the next Fisher King, Eminence," he said softly. "It is not within your power to take away that which God alone has placed in my hands."

"You are not to remove the Fisher Kings' dossier or the Annals from this office!" di Stefano shouted at him, stepping toward him.

Edmund Moran zipped up the leather cases. "These do not belong to the Church, Eminence. They have been entrusted into my care, the care of the Baldarese. If you wish to stop me consider that the resources of my family stand behind me. In seven hundred years, not one cleric, not even a pope has gone against the Baldarese. Now is not a good time for allies to become enemies, to break with tradition."

Father Edmund Moran walked to the door. His were the only footsteps. Gently he walked through the door and shut it after himself. As he had feared, his church would not help him. He, Lauren Blair and Frank Donnellan now stood alone. He wondered if they would understand when he called to tell them Rome had abandoned them.

CHAPTER NINETEEN

T HE STRANGER and the young man were sitting together in the darkness. The rain had tapered off to a light drizzle. With the night came the thick unyielding fog that slithered over the city and then rested, like a snake returning to its nest.

"Do you feel them?" the stranger asked. His eyes were lightly closed.

"Yes," the young man replied. "They are leaving together. The young woman and the man, Donnellan. She is tired...very tired. He has convinced her to stop work so that they might both eat."

"What else?"

"The telephone is ringing. It is the priest. He is trying to reach them."

"And Leech, what of him?"

The young man's voice hardened. "He is almost there. He will try to betray us."

Percival Leech had taken the only precaution he could: his call to Geochron was answered by the night watchman who confirmed that the company offices were closed. When asked about Lauren Blair, the watchman replied that she was working at Geochron but had gone out for a bite of supper. She was expected back within the hour.

Percival Leech left the Bennett at once. He drove slowly through Cambridge, as much because of the fog as to review one last time the plan he had devised.

The stranger was right. The opportunity to seize the chalice had at last presented itself. But for himself. Lauren Blair had made the cardinal error of removing the cup from the Museum. By helping her Donnellan had compromised himself. Given the secrecy of their actions, it was highly unlikely that Donnellan could have secured protection other than his own for the chalice. So if the cup were to disappear there would be only two people to blame. Two people, who, when the chalice could not be found, would be accused of attempting to steal it. Donnellan would try to protect the girl. Lauren Blair's reputation would work in her favor. But the fact remained that Lauren and Donnellan had taken the cup; nothing could change that.

Leech took satisfaction in parking in Matthew Tyler's bay. Without bothering to unfurl his umbrella he ran across the lot to Geochron's rear door and pressed the bell. Two full minutes elapsed before the door opened just a crack, enough for Leech to see the night watchman was a young man, probably a student making extra money.

"I am Percival Leech, Chairman of the Bennett Museum. My credentials."

The student scarcely glanced at the Faculty I.D. He recognized Leech.

"Sorry, sir, didn't mean to keep you waiting."

Once inside, Leech immediately started down the corridor. The young man had to run to catch up to him.

"Doctor Blair is in Lab One, I presume?"

"Yes, sir. She was. She's gone out for supper. I didn't know—"

"She was expecting me," Leech interjected. "I'll wait for her in the lab. If you would be so kind." Leech gestured at the door.

The student hesitated. The man called Donnellan had told him in no uncertain terms not to open the lab until he and Lauren returned. But to say no to Leech.... The student, an archeology major, figured Leech would be helpful where he wanted to go. No use making enemies.

He fumbled with the key and unlocked the door, stepping before Leech to push it open.

The first blow stunned the student, catching him on the back of the neck. Then, gripping his hair with both hands, Leech smashed his head against the cinder-block walls. The cracking of cartilage and bone resounded in the lab until Leech, with one last vicious twist, snapped the boy's neck.

He thrust the body away from him, backing away as it crumpled to the floor. When he looked down he saw blood on his fine kid gloves.

"Burn them!" he muttered to himself. "I'll have to burn them!"

Stepping over the corpse, Leech moved into the lab, past the tables laden with conventional burners, counters, and beakers. The professional in him was offended. For all his success, Tyler was still in the dark ages of geochronological technology. What had Lauren Blair hoped to accomplish here?

Then he saw it. At the far end of the laboratory was the Rogers microscope. Beside that, the laser, ready for cutting. The chalice rested on the ledge beneath the diamond-polished lens. Its auric magic beckoned to him, drew him irresistibly toward it. The Holy Grail, proven as such beyond all doubt, evidence of the kind neither science nor the Church could dispute. Even if they did, its worth to the stranger was all the authentication Leech needed.

Percival Leech moved up to the microscope and adjusted the lens for X50, allowing him a sharp definition of the metal. At this magnification he could barely discern the triangular incision Lauren Blair had made to test the sample.

"Unbelievably perfect!" Leech breathed. "So exquisitely beautiful..."

The more he studied it the more his fascination began to overtake him. A fascination based on the understanding that as soon as the cup was his, neither the Church nor the stranger would dare move against him. Especially not the stranger. He would permit Leech to live out the course of his natural life in the secure knowledge that at last he owed nothing to anyone. And when he died, the stranger would be told where to find the cup. Leech would possess it for a time. It would be his greatest triumph. After he was gone he didn't care what the stranger made of it.

Percival Leech adjusted the magnification to X200, working the zoom lens so that it was directly over the center of the cup, staring down into the fine-grained basin. The metal swirled, solidified as the zoom braked at its appointed matrix. Perfect, so very perfect. An excellence to be found only within Nature...

Suddenly he drew back. He blinked rapidly, then pressed his eyes against the viewer. He thought he had seen something move in the basin of the chalice, among the fine grains. Impossible, of course. Percival Leech increased the magnification to X400.

It *couldn't* be!

Under the intense magnification the whorls were fragmenting, drifting apart like cells or amoebas, splitting up....Splitting up then reforming in some sort of pattern.

He increased magnification to the maximum. The whorls dissolved completely, leaving a golden aura. And in that aura something was taking form. He could see, clearly, two red dots, glittering like rubies against velvet, and a slit that opened and closed, like some obscene mouth....

"God, no!" Leech whispered. Yet he dared not take his eyes away. The horror that was staring up at him was hypnotic, its twisted mouth now bristling with teeth, grinning obscenely, taking form so that what could be called a face, a mask of horror, was now discernible...and alive.

Percival Leech wasn't even aware of the thin moan that escaped his lips. All he could see was an arm—if it could be called that—a scaly limb with incredible talons weaving beside the feral face. But that was impossible.

Suddenly it struck. Percival Leech's head snapped back. In the last seconds of his life he did not believe he could be dying. He tried to open his eyes but only the left one obeyed. And from the corner of that eye he saw a talon planted within the other one, digging deeper and deeper, curving up like a fish hook until his brain exploded.

For a hellish instant he hung there, impaled on the talon. Then in one swift motion the talon retracted from whence it had come. As Percival Leech fell to the floor, a rounded bloodied object fell with him, rolling away from the corpse. It was his right eye, perfectly plucked out from its socket, the muscles and tendons cleanly severed.

At high noon, Rome was plunged into chaos. Not even the elegant Bernini Bristol Hotel escaped the travelers' hysteria. As the traffic controllers at Leonardo da Vinci Airport began to walk off for their six hour sympathy strike, departing guests pleaded with the management to keep their rooms while new arrivals fumed at the front desk. But the Balderese name had not lost it's magic. One of the assistant managers drew Father Edmund Moran away from the melée of the lobby and ushered him up to the fourth floor suite which the Baldarese rented by the year.

From the fridge Father Moran removed two bottles of Perrier water, brought them over to the writing desk in the living room and pulled the telephone forward. Within a half hour he knew that there was no conventional way he would be able to leave the city. The conditions at Leonardo da Vinci, chaotic on the best of days, were now hopeless. A recorded message courtesy of Alitalia informed him that the facilities would remain inoperative until at least midnight. Calls to the major car rental agencies yielded nothing: every available vehicle was either on the road or already reserved. The situation was no better at the train station where the dispatch clerk informed him that no reservations were being taken. Anyone who wanted to get on a train had to come down to the station in person and take his chances when the gates opened.

Father Moran stepped out on the balcony of his suite and listened to the din of the city. Even getting out of Rome would be difficult enough. To try and get to another metropolitan center—Turin, Parma, or even Venice—from where he could take a flight to Paris or London was almost impossible. Yet there had to be a way...there had to be! He could not permit such idiocy to delay his return to the States.

Think! He tried to shut out the cacophony of a thousand horns and claxons that seemed to be blaring directly at him. There has to be a way. Father Moran went back into the living room, locking the double-glazed doors behind him. Once again he thought of the prodigious resources of his family. Somewhere in them was the key to his predicament. He needed a little time, a little patience...but he would find it. Father Moran returned to the desk and began making notes. Twenty minutes later he had managed to cajole the operator into connecting him with Ostia, lying some thirty miles to the west. The operator of the small seaplane charter service at first demanded three times the usual fare to fly him to Geneva. Father Moran offered him half that figure, to be paid in cash. The operator agreed but only if Moran arrived within two hours. The plane would be held until the party that had reserved it arrived.

Father Moran left his suite and downstairs elbowed his way through the crush in the lobby towards the front desk. He drew the concierge aside, slipped him ten thousand lira and explained what he wanted done. The Baldarese suite would be available to the first person who was willing to exchange the use of a car for the use of the suite. Moran made it clear he didn't care if the concierge double or triple charged the other party. All he wanted was that car. The concierge assured him the matter would be looked after instantly and he was as good as his word: within a half hour Father Edmund Moran held the keys to an Alfa Romeo sportscoupe. Its owner assured him that it wouldn't be any problem to pick up the car at Ostia later on. From the time Father Moran turned the ignition switch less than ninety minutes remained for him to get out of the Roman madness and drive to Ostia before the plane left.

"Feeling a little better?"

Lauren Blair looked at Donnellan as he wheeled the car into the Geochron parking lot.

"Yes, thank you."

He had taken her to the Half Shell in the dock area. A converted shed with candles in red globes, lobster traps and netting on the walls, and the best bouillabaisse she had ever tasted.

He knew what I needed, she thought. And it was more than rich hot food. Their gentle conversation had had nothing at all to do with the chalice. It had to do with them, who they were, where they had come from and were going to. She felt more than comfortable with him, something other than safe.

I feel it is right *between us. And what does that mean?*

"Looks like we have company," Donnellan muttered. Lauren caught a glimpse of the car through the rainslicked windshield.

"Leech. That's his car."

Donnellan steered the car beside the elegant black sedan.

"How did he find out?" Lauren asked, more to herself than him. "God, if he thinks he's going to take the chalice before I'm finished—"

She was out of the car and running for the back

entrance, Donnellan at her heels. Lauren pressed the buzzer.

"I have the key," Donnellan said, digging in his pocket. The door opened under his touch.

"Don't move in any farther," he murmured, holding out his arm. Donnellan flicked on the light and beheld the empty corridor.

"Johnny!" he yelled.

The sound of his voice came back to him.

"Press that buzzer again...Doctor Leech!"

Donnellan counted off half a minute, his uneasiness growing with each passing second. He drew Lauren back, fingers undoing the buttons of the trench coat. The communicator materialized in his hand.

"This is Charger One. Do you read?"

"We read, Frank," the Monitor replied instantly.

"We're at Geochron Labs rear entrance."

"We've had you covered all day. Do you want support?"

"Thank you, yes." Donnellan shook his head. There wasn't another team like his.

"They'll be there in less than a minute. I'll keep the channel open."

"Frank, what's wrong?" Lauren asked.

"I'm not sure, colleen. The door's open, no one is answering the bell or our calls, Leech's car out front..."

The communicator crackled. "Frank."

"Still here."

"We have a call coming in from Ostia. Father Moran. Says it's urgent. Very urgent. I'll patch it through to the car."

"Acknowledged."

Gently he steered Lauren outside under the awning. A pair of headlamps pierced the fog, veering from side to side as the car fishtailed to a halt.

"Don't go inside," Donnellan ordered the two agents. "Stay with her. I'll be back in a second."

He slid behind the wheel and reached for the radio

telephone. Through the crackle of static, he heard the police operators relaying the call.

"Inspector Donnellan...Donnellan."

Father Moran's voice was faint but even so Donnellan discerned the anxiety behind it.

"Father Moran, I can hear you, barely. Can you speak up a little bit?"

"Inspector, is that you... is this any better?"

"Yes, this is probably as good as the connection will be. What about Rome? Have you spoken with di Stefano yet?"

A rush of static destroyed Father Moran's words. "Please repeat, Father," Donnellan said.

"Di Stefano will not help us," the priest was saying. "But we can't afford to wait. The things that I have learned about the cup..."

"This is an open line," Donnellan warned him. "But what about di Stefano? Why wouldn't he help you?"

"There is no time for me to explain," Father Moran said. "Please, just do as I say."

"What is it you want us to do?" Donnellan asked.

Quickly and concisely Moran outlined his plan.

"Are you certain you want to play it this way?" Donnellan said, the doubt underlining his tone. "We might be able to come up with an even safer location."

"The advantage of this site lies in the fact that it is isolated," Father Moran replied. "Furthermore, very few people are aware of it."

Donnellan leaned forward, his arms resting on the steering wheel, looking straight ahead into the darkness. He was trying to think of an alternative but was coming up empty.

"Alright, we'll move the chalice right now."

"I may not be able to contact you again before I leave the Continent," Father Moran was saying. "The air controllers have walked out in sympathy with the maintenance personnel. I have found a way to get to Geneva but I don't know what the transatlantic connections will be like."

"You look after yourself," Frank Donnellan said fiercely. "We can't afford to lose you now. Just make sure that Rome doesn't get it into its head to keep you there."

"No one will stop me," Father Moran said with finality. "Rome doesn't understand..."

Another flurry of static broke into the conversation. Father Moran's voice faded; then suddenly Donnellan heard the police operator trying to reestablish the connection. Slowly he replaced the receiver in its cradle.

Donnellan made his way back to where Lauren and his men were waiting. Quickly he explained to them what the priest had told him to do.

"But the chalice is still in there. Leech as well!"

"I'll get the chalice." He turned to one of his men. "Ramon, you get in the car with her. At the first sign of any trouble get her back to the Museum."

"Frank—"

"I mean it. Now go! Martin, you come with me."

"Frank, I can't let you go—"

Lauren's words died on her lips as Donnellan and the other agent disappeared into the delivery entrance. She felt Ramon's hand upon her elbow.

"Please, Doctor..."

Donnellan's Ingram was in his hands. "Safety off," he murmured.

The two men started off down the corridor, running in a low crouch. Within seconds they saw that the door to Lab One was open.

"I'll take the right."

Martin nodded and moved into position. They counted off and simultaneously burst through the opening.

"Oh, dear sweet Jesus!"

Donnellan moved past the agent, running across the lab. He scarcely glanced at Leech, concentrating on the far corners of the lab, gun weaving. All closets were wrenched open, but the doors connecting the lab to other rooms were still locked.

"Whoever did this might still be here."

"Sure, but he's dead too."

Donnellan knelt down and turned Leech's body over.

"Why?" he whispered. "Why in God's name did you have to kill him?"

The horror of Leech's death, the empty eye-socket, the face streaked with rivulets of blood did not diminish Donnellan's fury. He didn't know how Leech had died. Instinct said that the killing was in the same vein as those of Cathy Windsor and Arturo Cardinal Capellini. The body hadn't been dismembered but somehow what had happened was horrible enough.

"What did you want? What had you come for that was so valuable you were willing to kill for it?" he asked Leech rhetorically.

"Frank, what do you want me to do?" the agent Martin said.

Donnellan whirled about and slid the machine pistol into the harness. He came over to the electron microscope. The chalice.

"Damn you!" he whispered, and seized it with both hands.

"Frank, you can't take that!" Martin shouted.

"The hell I can't! Cover me!"

Donnellan moved into the corridor with the chalice, kicking open the door to the outside. He ducked through the rain heading for his sedan.

"He's dead, isn't he?" Lauren said. "They got to him too." She pulled away as he thrust the chalice at her. "It's ugly," she whispered. "God, it's horrible."

"Yes, he's dead," Donnellan said fiercely.

Her terror was so deep she shook herself free of him.

"Frank, I want to get out of here...I don't want to see that damn chalice!"

He moved very close to her, burying his face in her hair, feeling her tremble.

"You know what you have to do," he repeated softly. "Nothing will happen to you, I promise. Lauren, I love you...."

She drew away. "Then why—"

"Because there's no one left!" he said desperately. "Capellini's dead. Leech is dead. You're the only one who can deal with the cup. The only one who can find the truth!"

"The truth is that the chalice kills!" Lauren screamed.

"And it will kill *all of us*—unless we find out exactly what it is! Help me, Lauren, please. I need you...."

She threw herself at him and crushed her face to his neck.

"Give me your strength," she whispered. "Please, just for a little while..."

For what seemed like a long time they held one another. Then slowly Donnellan repeated Father Moran's instructions to Lauren.

"Are you sure you understand?" he finished softly.

She looked up at him, her eyes brimming with tears. "Yes," she said in a faltering voice.

He turned to the agent. "Ramon?"

"No problem, Frank."

"Then move. I'll meet you both back at the Museum." He leaned forward and kissed her hard on the lips.

"Go on, now!" he whispered and got out of the car.

"You want me to call it in, Frank?" Martin asked, coming up behind him.

"Give it a minute," Donnellan said, looking at the retreating sedan. "In the meantime get me Phil at the Hancock. Whatever started here has yet to run its course."

"Where to, Doctor?"

For a moment Lauren did not answer. She was sitting bolt upright, staring straight ahead into the rain, her fingers curled tightly, almost painfully, about the chalice.

"Doctor?" the agent prompted her gently.

She closed her eyes, a shudder passing down her spine.

"Get out onto Beacon Street," she said, the voice hard, flat. "Follow that until Chestnut Hill Avenue, then cut across to Boylston and go west."

The agent wheeled the car about, making for the entrance to the Boston University Bridge.

The metal was becoming warm against her skin, slippery from the sweat of her fingers. Lauren settled the cup in her lap, drawing her hands away.

A hunk of metal. That's all it is ... a hunk of metal crafted into the shape of a chalice. Nothing special about it at all. Nothing! No matter what the Church wanted to believe.

Except for the blood that could not be dated.

Except for the killings of those who came near the cup, handled it, desired it. . . .

In the dark interior of the sedan, Lauren gazed into the smooth concave depths where the golden whorls shone like luminous threads. Her reason told her there was nothing to fear from the cup. It was nothing more than a physical object, which acted as a catalyst for those who wished to endow it with supernatural powers. In itself it was inert, incapable of exerting any influence. One saw in it what one wanted to see, attributed to it those qualities one wanted to. Nothing more.

Then why am I doing what Father Moran asked?

That single question defied reason, opened the door to all the elemental fears locked up in the psyche. If she did not believe, why was she obeying?

What do you believe? she asked herself. *The empirical data you've been taught to accept as evidence? What good is it to you now? The TRACE recorder was proof ... of something. Yet when the needle went off the scale you ceased believing in empirical evidence....What law of the universe are you dealing with here?*

They stayed on Boylston until it crossed with Hamond, then swung south past Holihood Cemetery across Roxbury Parkway and onto Newton Street.

"Turn right here."

The sedan's tires squealed as the car went off the slick macadam onto a dirt road. The agent slowed the car, leaning forward over the wheel, eyes straining for pot holes. Half a mile down the road the gyrating headbeams strayed upon a length of white fencing.

"The entrance should be up here on the right," Lauren murmured. "There it is!"

As soon as the car made the turn the road smoothed out, attesting to the maintenance of the estate.

"Quite the spread," the agent commented. "Do we head that way?" He gestured at the pinprick lights flashing between the trees.

"That's the main house. We want to go in the opposite direction."

At the fork in the road they bore right. The road became narrower, no more than a lane, but still smooth. A body of water shimmered in the crepuscular light.

"Not far now..." Lauren said.

Inadvertently her fingers tightened about the chalice.

Nothing will happen to you, she said to herself. Just do it! Don't think whether it is insane or illogical—do it!

"That's it," the agent said. "End of the line."

He braked the car gently, bringing it to a stop some twenty feet before a small church. The white clapboard shone under the head beams, the brass on the black door glistening. From its design, Lauren guessed the church was at least two hundred years old. But each detail had been lovingly restored and she had no doubt services were still performed here.

"Is this it?" the agent asked her, doubt underlining his question.

"This is it."

The chalice was hot to the touch. Lauren wrenched the door open.

"I'll be back in a moment."

As she stepped out into the night the rain spattered against the chalice. Even from where he sat the agent swore he could hear the sound of something sizzling.

"This isn't a commercial box."

The voice had a distinct twang to it. Maine or New Hampshire suiting the lean pale man who squatted comfortably on his haunches above the *oubliette*. Occasionally he would run the tips of his fingers across the rippled surface, as though caressing a sleeping beast.

"Army," the expert said. "Army issue. Five, six years old. I remember them now."

The expert hadn't introduced himself when he had come up, flanked by two of Donnellan's people. He had smiled upon seeing the safe, then his lips curled back, as though he had witnessed something repulsive. He laid his battered bag at the edge of the trap door opening in the floor of Leech's office and walked around the safe, a scarecrow figure in checked shirt, Wranglers, and eight-hundred-dollar rattlesnake boots. There was a red and white polka dot handkerchief in his hip pocket. He was the best. Phil had assured him of that. He was good and fast and she had gotten him for Donnellan in under thirty minutes.

"Army issue," the expert repeated, shaking his head. "There are two reinforced steel plates up on top, just a hairline fracture separating them. Wires running from the dial up left along to two wires attached to a phosphorous charge along the length of the wall. Touch those and you, the safe, whatever's in it, fry."

"Can you take it?"

"Surely."

"How long? We have a time problem."

"Don't we always?" the expert laughed. "Two minutes, maybe less."

"You want to run that by me again?"

"Two minutes, old son. Course, you'll have to leave the room. Missy didn't tell me you were cleared for this material." He patted the bag.

"What about the damage to the safe?"

"A little pinprick hole. You won't even know it's there."

Laser, Donnellan thought. He's going to burn the connecting wires. "How about *no* damage?"

"Six hours, maybe seven. This thing may be obsolete but it's effective for all that.

"Besides," the expert added softly, "phosphorous is a damn finicky element. No matter how good you are going in, there's always the chance of quick barbecue."

"Do it," Donnellan said, and walked out of Leech's elegant office into the boardroom three doors down.

"A couple of minutes," he said, looking at Lauren and Gerry Samulovitch. The detective, seated at the head of the conference table that dominated the room, pushed the telephone away.

"That, landsman, was the Commissioner," he said wearily. "Apparently the Vatican has informed the State Department that it will be sending over a personal representative to replace Father Moran, who has been relieved of his duties. Further instructions state that when this representative arrives no one— absolutely no one—is to go near the chalice. Of course State doesn't have a clue as to what's coming down. Neither does the Commissioner, Edward Foxx, Esquire. That august gentleman would like to know (a) where the chalice is, (b) what you were doing at

GRAIL

Geochron when you found Leech, and (c) what Leech was doing there." Samulovitch paused. "All questions to which I have no answers.

"To add to our troubles, the FBI has come in on the Capellini killing and is pestering everyone no end. Finally, the media have linked the three murders and are setting siege to the Press Office. Speculation ranges from Protestant extremists through to cult killings à la Manson. Take your pick of anything in between."

Gerry Samulovitch rose and came over to Donnellan.

"The town is scared, Frank. My men are scared. Someone's been passing around the morgue shots of the Windsor girl. The only reason the papers haven't touched them is they're too gruesome.

"On top of everything, you have the Agency in on this...."

"Phil's the only one who could get me the resources," Donnellan said.

"What did you find in his office, Frank?" Lauren butted her cigarette and looked up at him.

"Did you know he had a safe in his office?"

She shook her head.

"We're opening it now. What we find may tell us what Leech was doing at Geochron."

"What about all that fancy equipment the spooks are installing in the fail-safe vault?" Samulovitch murmured.

"Just a precaution, Ger," Donnellan said softly. "Just a precaution."

Samulovitch rolled his eyes heavenward and spread out his hands. "Why me, O Lord?" He shook his head. "I can't give you any more interference, you're going to have to come clean."

"If I find what I think is in the safe, I can buy another twenty-four hours."

"Buy it for what, Frank!" Gerry shouted at him. "People are dropping like flies around that fucking

288

cup. I don't care if they think it's the Grail. It's death."

"That it is, Ger," Donnellan said quietly. "That it is."

"Inspector."

Donnellan turned to see the demolitions expert standing in the doorway.

"She's open. All yours."

"Much obliged," Donnellan said and began to move.

"*De nada.* Say, can one of your people get me back to Logan? They're holding a flight for me."

"You'll be moving out with the others downstairs. Tell Phil I owe her," Donnellan called after him.

"Surely she'll be happy to hear that, Inspector," the expert laughed. "She don't lay me on like this for just anybody. You take care now."

Donnellan led the way to Leech's office. He couldn't discern the holes in the steel made by the laser, but the heat over the vault was still palpable. Once the wires to the phosphorous charges had been severed it had been an easy matter to scan the center lock and leave the microcomputer to ferret out the combination. Donnellan grasped the stainless-steel knob and pulled up. He lifted a sheaf of papers, thumbed through them.

"What the hell are they?" he demanded softly.

The demolitions expert stopped in the doorway of the fail-safe vault. Three technicians, smocks over their blue jeans and sweatshirts, were clustered in the left-hand corner of the vault. The expert peered in for a better look.

The vault was empty save for the pedestal. The demo man picked out the holes bored into the walls where the transmitters for the electronic beams were nestled. As one of the technicians stepped back he saw a bulky rectangular object mounted on a shelf that had been fastened to the far corner, halfway up the wall.

"Give me a second to adjust the mirrors," the technician muttered. He came over to the pedestal and barely touched the shiny mirror suspended from the ceiling at a sixty-five-degree angle. Seemingly satisfied, as he stepped back he made infinitesimal adjustments in the angle of the other two mirrors, one directly above the pedestal, the other high in the left-hand corner.

"Try it now."

Another technician bowed his head over the box. The lens protruding from the short side blinked rapidly several times. "Dead on."

"Give it some juice."

"You fellas still using Zeiss Ikon equipment?" the demo expert drawled.

The technician over the camera made a face and said nothing.

"Then it's got to be Kodak, the new P-2. That's the only one I know of that works on infrared."

The ice was broken, as though he had uttered a magic code.

"Yeah, it's the P-2," the technician said. "Kinda hard to work with in such a small environment."

"Hell, with the optics in that baby, the refracting lens and self-governing image projector, you could shoot from two feet, never mind twelve."

"I suppose," the technician said. "Let's see if you're right."

He peered into the viewfinder and depressed the button.

"Nice to know the stuff works outside the lab too," the technician muttered. "Okay, turn it off."

"What's the time limit on the power pack?" asked the demolitions man.

"Twenty hours, give or take ten minutes. We're using calcium-injected batteries."

"Nifty...very nifty. Christ, I tell you this is a

weird place. Optics, demolitions. This is supposed to be a fucking museum!"

The technician laughed. "Yeah, that's what Phil told us too...."

"Three hundred million, maybe more, depending on how quickly they were to be dumped on the market."

"And that's only the half of it."

Spread out over Leech's desk were the provenances of his hoard. Lauren had kept a running total as Donnellan passed her the files.

"We don't have time for any more," he said.

"Do you know what this means?" Lauren asked him.

"That the exalted Percival Leech was a thief—a grand one to be sure but a thief for all of that."

Lauren flinched at the words, the cold merciless condemnation of the dead man.

"Well, that's what he was, wasn't he?" Donnellan challenged her. "Even I recognize a few of the items on that shopping list."

"It should all have been in the collections of either the royal families of Europe or people like the Agha Khan or the Agnellis," Lauren said. "I know they're *supposed* to be there."

"Have you any idea why they're not there?"

"He could have bought them...somehow. Or they can be on loan."

"Lauren!"

"The man's dead, Frank!"

"He stole them. I don't know how or why, but unless Leech was a closet Howard Hughes, he *couldn't* have bought them."

"What are you going to do with them?" Gerry Samulovitch asked.

"I'm going to take them down to the Commissioner's office," Donnellan said, through his teeth. "I'm going to take them down and have Lauren go through them and tell him what she told us. I'm going to tell him how Leech went to Geochron to steal the chalice. That he killed the night watchman who was the only witness. I'll tell him that we know *why* Leech was there. If he gives me another twenty-four hours I'll know what killed him.... And if I know that, then I can get the killers of Capellini and Windsor."

"Frank, you're losing it," Gerry said, reaching for him. "You said 'what' killed them not 'who.'"

"That's what I meant," Donnellan said savagely. "What. Mack the Knife may be something other than what we thought." He began gathering up the provenances. "Seal the place up after us."

CHAPTER TWENTY

THE COLD froze the blackness onto the cobble-stones. No one was to be seen along Merton Street. Only a few vehicles bumped their way down the incline, tall lights winking as the drivers pumped brakes and skidded gently from left to right then left again. Their windows were rolled up tight, their door locks down. Occasionally a prowl car moved along the street, pausing before the Museum, its search-light playing over the hedgerow, skating along the rain-slicked steps. Then it moved on, carrying away officers with shotguns and automatic rifles in their laps. Anyone walking in the area was scrutinized. In some cases appearance alone was enough for the police to stop and demand I.D. But there were few people out. The terror had set in....

A figure disengaged itself from the wall of the Bennett Museum, its shadow falling across the rough granite blocks for an instant. Seeing it, one would have thought the light had caught a small tree at a peculiar angle, for the shadow did not cast a complete human form. It was hunched over with an arm thrust forward, an arm ending in dirklike talons. Nor did the face have any definition. Then two more figures stepped out. They stood there, the three of them, their backs to the glare of the spot-lamps. They placed their talons in the crevices be-tween the stones set in the wall. One hand came over the other. The vertical climb began, effortless. A grotesque appendage trailed behind each one. Others watched as their kind ascended. They waited.

* * *

"What was that?"

Perlman and Stone were patrolling the gallery that ran above the Grand Salon. They both heard the sound of glass breaking at the same time. Perlman reached for his radio but before he had a chance to open the circuit another sound was heard.

"Let's go!" Stone whispered.

Perlman sent out an automatic signal on his radio and started off after his partner, footsteps muffled by the crêpe soles on their shoes. At the far end of the gallery their pace slowed. Using the classic leapfrog technique one man moved past the other until both were next to the corner where the staircase met the gallery. In one motion Stone jumped across the landing, crouching, then flattening himself against the wall. His eyes met Perlman's, the head nodding up and to the right, in the direction of the staircase. Silently they counted off and pivoted into the landing, their Ingrams pointing up the staircase.

Nothing.

Perlman backed up against the bannister while Stone edged up the stairs, his shoulders flat against the ancient walnut panelling. On the first landing was an office whose door was slightly recessed.

"Behind you!" Perlman screamed.

Stone's reflexes were superb. In the same motion he whirled about and threw himself back, giving both himself and Perlman a clear range of fire. But his finger never reached the trigger. Stone's eyes caught the image of a scaled claw, with long talons gleaming like bleached bone. Then a terrible pain seized his stomach. The talons sank into the soft warm pit of his gut and wrenched upward, lifting him off his feet before they turned back, tearing open his torso. The talons were heavy with gore and entrails, their tips speared with three internal organs. At that instant, Stone's heart, which had only been grazed, burst.

The figure stepped out from the recess, bloodied arm hanging by its side, an intestine trailing along the carpet. Perlman, who had moved up beside Stone, backed away. His brain was seething; the horror paralytic. It was sheer instinct that made him pull back the trigger of the Ingram, the high velocity bullets spitting out of the barrel with enough force to drop a raging steer. But the horror advanced. In the one and a half seconds it took to empty the clip, it seemed not to have suffered at all. Now it was almost upon him. His last step made him fling his head back in pain. His entire back began to burn as though doused with boiling oil. He could hear the vertebrae crack, then the ribs snapped as the daggers drove past his spine.

The creature that had stepped out behind Perlman and extended its claws, causing Perlman to impale himself on its eight talons, now raised the corpse in the air. He was still alive when a fist of razors descended across his face, shearing his features. That same force pulled the body off the talons.

The three did not even pause over their victims but continued down the stairs to the gallery, a trail of greenish grey pus dropping like warm viscous jelly from their wounds. In almost regal procession they walked to the Grand Salon, descending into the maze created by the velvet ropes, passing without regard for the treasures so near their grasp.

The first camera picked them up.

Their leader guided them through the maze and into the corridor that ran behind the Grand Salon. It knelt before the door stencilled MAINTENANCE and without the slightest effort ripped the door away. Twisted metal shrieked through the corridor as the bolts were ripped out of the wood. The alarms hit at the same instant but that mattered not at all.

The leader passed through into the fail-safe vault and came before the pedestal upon which the chalice rested. The electronic beams did not deter him. He passed his hand through them and they disappeared. The claws reached out for the chalice.

And they touched nothing.

The features on the hideous viper skin contracted into an expression of incredulity. The crimson eyes began to burn fiercely, the cracked bloodless lips curling back in hatred. The Lexam glass designed to deflect heavy bullets was raised and hurled to the marble floor with such force that both it and the stone shattered in a myriad of flashing splinters. But the image of the chalice remained suspended over the post.

Slowly the creatures moved back, footsteps scraping over the floor. They turned and walked through the maze, oblivious to the mesmerizing wail of the sirens. When they reached the massive bronze doors one knelt down and pried the two-ton obstructions off their hinges, tearing away at the stone in which they were embedded. They passed through into the antechamber, the front door buckling before their touch, and became one with the wind and the night.

At the foot of the steps they took pause. In unison they turned back to look upon the humankind that was behind them, weapons levelled. On a silent command the firepower was unleashed. A fierce groaning wail of something that could never have been, that was walking away from its own death, filled the night.

PART THREE

"Thou hast drunk the dregs of the cup of trembling."

—Isaiah 51:17

CHAPTER TWENTY-ONE

THE FORENSIC REPORT pertaining to the blood found on Percival Leech's gloves arrived at Edward Foxx's office shortly after three thirty in the morning. The Boston Police Commissioner read the last page in its entirety.

"You were quite right, Francis," he said. "The blood on the gloves matches that of the student. There were also bits of leather scraped off the cinder brick wall against which the victim's head was battered. Redford concludes Leech was the killer."

Edward Foxx was a New England gentleman, meticulous in his speech as in manners. Four hours earlier he had been reading to his wife from Stendhal's *The Red and the Black*. Now he was back in his office, furnished in quiet modern elegance, absently wiping his hornrims. Foxx replaced the Irish linen in the vest pocket of his Brooks Brothers worsted.

Donnellan remembered Foxx as a good detective. Now he was an even better Commissioner. Foxx handled departmental and city politics with a flair all his own. That was his preserve. He left the actual police work to his deputies. He took great pains to keep oil and water separate. Foxx also held Donnellan in great esteem, had fought for his appointment.

"So you have solved one of the two killings, Francis," he continued. "You have provided a motive for Leech's actions, which was to steal the chalice. A good argument has been made to link this killing with those of the girl and the prelate. Under normal circumstances I would gladly take your word that you will very soon apprehend the perpetrator of these crimes. But I do not know if I can give you the twenty-four hours you need.

"Doctor Blair, Francis—there are some sixty rabid newspeople awaiting me in the conference room," Foxx said musingly. "They are literally salivating because of what happened at Geochron early yesterday evening. The links between Cathy Windsor's death, Capellini's, and now Leech's have been made. Certainly what Doctor Blair has had to say about the provenance found in Leech's office would satisfy some of those voracious appetites. But the intrinsic question will have remained unanswered: what happened to Leech and the two others?"

"Promise them a break in twenty-four hours," Donnellan said. "Tell them I've been assigned to the case."

"They will conclude a terrorist organization is operating in this city," Foxx told him. "Do you want that kind of speculation in the street?"

Better than the truth, Donnellan thought.

"Because if you do, then the FBI will pull this case out from under us," Foxx finished. "They are already screaming about lack of cooperation—not to say obstruction—on the part of Lieutenant Samulovitch. Specifically as to where Father Edmund Moran might be. And the Fibbies, Francis, are being pressured by the State Department, which in turn is reacting to Vatican inquiries, and so on and so forth."

"The Feds wouldn't get anywhere in the time I need," Donnellan said. "They need two days just to get their groundwork in order."

"That may be. However the principle of jurisdiction remains, quite legitimately."

"Twenty-four hours, Commissioner. Give me that and I will give you the killer," Donnellan said quietly.

Foxx regarded him steadily. "The following is off the record, Francis. Affirmative or negative responses will suffice. Are we dealing with terrorists?"

"No."

"Do you have the identities of whoever we *are* dealing with?"

Donnellan hesitated. If he didn't put a stop to the killings within twenty-four hours he would gladly surrender the case. It would be out of his depth by then. More firepower, more manpower and security would have to be brought in than he had at his call. He would turn over everything.

"Yes, Commissioner, I have the identities."

"I trust you have a plan for their apprehension?"

"I do."

"Very well. I accept your word on that. As usual, your means are of no interest to me save that I would prefer one of the perpetrators alive. What about the security of the Tour?"

"There is no danger to the exhibit."

"And the chalice, which seems to be the root of all this madness, is *it* secure?"

"Very secure."

"Doctor Blair's safety?"

Donnellan looked at Lauren. "Absolutely secure."

"And the whereabouts of Father Moran?"

"I know where he is."

"Then I will get you the time you need, Francis," Foxx said. "I am sure you understand that when it is gone and the investigation is not concluded, I will have to yield to the FBI. There can be no extensions."

"I appreciate your confidence, sir."

"I do not believe I have ever sensed this kind of mood over the city," Foxx said. "Rank fear...terror... as though the population senses something evil moving out there and is closing its doors at night. Find out what it is, Francis. Destroy it. Perhaps it wouldn't do to take anything alive after all."

Donnellan was rising when the deputy commissioner burst through the door.

"It's the Museum, Frank. Something's going down!"

"Francis, will you be wanting backup?" Foxx asked immediately.

"Thank you, Commissioner, but if there's anything left of them after my people get through with them we're in more trouble than I anticipated."

Donnellan was out of the office before Foxx had a chance to ask the question that had just leaped into his mind: if the chalice had been so important why hadn't it been taken by Leech's killers?

"Oh dear sweet Jesus!"

Donnellan braked hard and the sedan fishtailed to a halt, tires grinding against the sidewalk. In the full glare of the floodlights the Museum resembled a battleground. The massive oak doors, buckled, twisted, the stink of cordite hanging in the air, armed men crouching behind tress, running to forward positions.

"Stay here!" he ordered Lauren.

"Frank—"

"Stay here!"

Donnellan was out of the car, Ingram cradled in his arms, running for the doors. He grabbed hold of one of the security agents who was standing just inside the portico.

"What happened?"

"I don't know..." the man stammered, looking around as though he was waiting for something to come at him out of the mists. "It's worse inside. Perlman and Stone—"

"What about them?" Donnellan demanded fiercely.

The agent shook his head and gestured toward the interior of the building.

"Get over to my car," Donnellan ordered. "Stay with the girl and make sure nothing happens to her!"

He ran inside the Museum.

"What happened?"

The Monitor swivelled in his chair, face drained of all color, the voice low, wooden, signalling collapse.

"We came under attack, three of them—"

"Three of *what*?"

302

"You'll have to see the tapes," the Monitor shook his head. "Otherwise you'll think I'm crazy."

"Casualties?"

"Two. Perlman and Stone. Attacked like the others, Capellini and the girl." He broke off and looked at Donnellan. "We've got to put a stop to this," he said, as though the idea had just occurred to him.

"You said we have the tapes."

"Yeah..."

"Get them out of the camera, now! Put yesterday's in."

The Monitor stared at him.

"Do you believe what you saw on the tapes?"

"No, I can't."

"Then who else will? Make the switch!"

The Monitor leaned over and opened the video terminals. In quick succession he popped five cassettes, handing them to Donnellan.

"There's one more thing," he said. "You were right. They were after the chalice. The hologram worked perfectly."

"And we didn't get one–not one!" Donnellan whispered. "We must have hit *something!*"

The Monitor straightened up. "Nothing, Frank. The guys don't know what to make of it. They were firing at point-blank range. Those—those things just walked away from them. Teams have searched the perimeter—nothing."

Donnellan could not believe what he was hearing. His people were marksmen, all of them. The best could take an eye out at four hundred yards. It was not a question of missing the target. It couldn't have been.

"How did they get in?"

"Through the fourth-level windows. That's where Perlman and Stone met up with them." The Monitor hesitated. "We didn't find any ropes, grappling hooks, no climbing equipment of any kind...."

"It's all right," Donnellan said quickly. "We'll get to that later. I'll call the Commissioner from the car.

I don't want anyone except Samulovitch and foren-
sics on the premises."

The Monitor gestured at the tapes. "What about
the men, Frank? At least five of them saw what's on
the video."

"Not a word," Donnellan said softly. "Tell them
not to say a single word until I get back."

Even as he cleared the front doors he saw his
orders had gone out. The men were moving closer
to the Museum, slipping inside one by one. Donnellan ran for the car, coming over to the passenger
side, tapping on the windows.

"Take these with you," he said, thrusting the
tapes at Lauren."

"What are they, Frank?"

"All the evidence we're ever going to need. Don't
let anyone know you have it and for God's sake don't
lose it!"

"It was them, wasn't it, Frank?" Her face was
ashen, the voice strained.

"Yes." Donnellan leaned past her to the driver.
"Get her home. Don't stop for anything or anyone,
understand? You'll be getting backup along the way.
Everyone stays in the apartment until I arrive."

"Frank, where are you going?" Lauren cried.

"They didn't get what they came for," Donnellan
yelled back. "Who else, who isn't here, knows where
the cup is?"

"Moran," Lauren whispered. "Father Moran." She
looked at the digital clock on the console. The aircraft
bringing the priest back from Rome was scheduled
to touch down in twenty minutes. Somewhere in the
distance the wail of a siren shattered her thoughts.

Father Edmund Moran was the first passenger off
the helicopter shuttle that had ferried him in from
New York. The sixteen-hour journey which had begun in Ostia, had continued through Geneva, Prest-
wick and Shannon had at last come to an end. Hur-

rying through the debarkation lounge, his shoulders aching under the weight of the two heavy bags, he made his way down toward the arrival area.

There was no one to greet him. Donnellan had said he would be here!

"Father Moran!"

He jerked his head in the direction of the voice but the relieved expression on his face paled. He had to look at the man twice before he was certain he recognized him.

The man came up to him. "Father, thank goodness you've arrived. Something quite terrible has happened at the Museum—"

"Lauren—"

"No, she's all right. Inspector Donnellan is with her. That's why I came. Please, the car is out there. They're all waiting for you."

If Edmund Moran had been more alert he would have wondered at how easily his host lifted the heavy bag, how quickly he descended the steps to the arrivals level and made his way to the ramp where the airline limousines and buses idled. But he was too tired. The face was familiar. He was home....

"This way, Father."

The man beckoned to his right then hoisted the bag into the already open trunk. He relieved the priest of the second bag and placed that in the well too.

"Quickly, we'll have a police escort into the city."

Father Moran settled himself in the back seat. He felt his body sink into the soft cushions. Then the door slammed and the car pulled away.

Coming in from the opposite direction, Frank Donnellan thought nothing of the black Lincoln limousine that turned off Neptune Road, heading in the direction of the Boston Expressway.

CHAPTER TWENTY-TWO

"TWO MINUTES! I couldn't have missed him by more than that!"

Frank Donnellan covered his face with his hands, pressing hard against his forehead. He felt her fingers, long and cool, twisting into his.

"Frank, please..."

Suddenly he drew back his hands and gazed out into the mists that lay over the harbor panorama. His ear differentiated between the horns of the ferries, freighter, and tugs that prowled the bay.

"He's been taken," Donnellan muttered. "I can feel it, he's been taken!"

"By whom?" Lauren demanded. "We know what they look like. They couldn't have moved around the airport without causing panic."

"No, that's true, colleen. But who's to say they don't have human servants? Slaves, zombies, those who serve them willingly....Moran knew I would be at Logan. With everything that's happened he wouldn't have allowed himself to be taken by anyone except you or me."

"Or someone he recognized," Lauren said suddenly. "Someone associated with us, whom he would never suspect—"

"Was Tim here when you arrived?"

Lauren looked away. "No, the bed wasn't slept in."

"I'm sorry."

"There's nothing to be sorry for, Frank. It's over. Been over for a long time. But you don't think—"

"I can't take any chances," Donnellan said, twisting around to one of his men. "Have Samulovitch put out an APB for McConnell. Give him all the details—description, office, lecture schedule, everything."

"Do we still have the time the Commissioner promised us?" asked Lauren.

"Foxx will keep his word though God knows I wouldn't want to be in his position," Donnellan said, rising. "The media are baying for his blood after what happened at the Museum. He's got half the force out searching for Moran. The FBI is swinging all the weight it can out of Washington.... The only thing that could break Foxx would be the Vatican demanding the chalice be returned to a representative at once. And that, I fear, is a very likely possibility."

"I want to get back to the Museum, Frank," Lauren said softly. "The bone sample from Cathy Windsor's body..."

"Christ, I had forgotten about that," Donnellan whispered. "But we have the tapes—"

"The tapes' authenticity can be challenged. They *will* be. But if we have supporting evidence, *scientific* evidence..."

"You're right, of course. Not only that but if the residue on the bones of the Windsor girl match that of Perlman and Stone—"

"Then *no one* will be able to dispute the tapes," Lauren finished for him.

He did not feel pain as much as he did an intense terrible cold that seized his entire body. He tried to move his arms and then his legs, but discovered his wrists and ankles looped by leather thongs which in turn were fastened to iron spikes embedded in the floor boards. The best he could do was twist his ankles and wrists.

Father Edmund Moran opened his eyes, staring

at the ceiling. The plaster was the color of ancient ivory, the molding an intricate depiction of the winged Pegasus. Suddenly the priest began coughing. He lifted his head as far as he could and vomited. Now the smell of his own sickness mixed with the stench that had made him gag. When he saw the bile upon himself Father Moran realized he was naked.

"You have awakened, priest."

Edmund Moran let his head fall back against the hardwood floor.

It can't be! It's not possible!

"But yes, it is possible. I told you I would come back for you."

Out in the darkness a reptilian face loomed over him, eyes burning in hatred, in anticipation.

"You are mine, priest!"

Then they were gone. Edmund Moran twisted his head to the right. A few feet away another demon was stooped over, guiding the tip of a thin brush over the floorboards in an unerring straight line. When the priest looked down he saw other lines, coming together to a point, beneath his feet.

"A pentagram, priest," the demon mocked him. "You are in the center of an invocation circle. We will sacrifice you to our Master. After we have stolen your soul. After we have feasted upon your flesh and blood. After you have told us where the cup is to be found...

"Tell me, priest, what have you done with the cup?"

Edmund Moran squeezed his eyes shut. He tried to drown out the voice, and concentrated instead on bringing up the image of Arturo Cardinal Capellini.

"Behold the King!" the demon scorned him. "The great and mighty Fisher King who lies in his own filth. You are a fool, you would-be king! How easily we trapped you. Do you believe you could resist us?"

I must resist! I must!

"You think of Capellini but he is *dead!* As you shall be. I offer you nothing. I do not invite you to our order, for you are a polluter. And I will sacrifice you. But I can do it with great pain or I can offer you oblivion before you are consumed. Which would you rather?"

You cannot yield. You owe it to Arturo, to Lauren and to Donnellan.

"What do you owe, priest? Your own filthy Church does not believe you. Why do you persist in suffering for the cunt of the Virgin?"

Edmund Moran's eyes opened. In one motion he craned his neck and spat as far as he could.

"The futile gesture of the victim," the voice intoned. "But you will be punished for your disrespect."

Simultaneously, cold sharp talons clamped down on his wrists and ankles.

"The pentagram is complete. Bind him into it!"

Our father who art in heaven . . .

The foot-long iron spikes which had served as anchors for the leather thongs were pried from the floor boards. Their sharpened points barely scraped the skin of his palm and instep before they were driven through his flesh. The scream tore out of Father Moran's throat. Then another. Finally the last.

The demon straddled him, watching as the priest twisted his torso, neck muscles straining against the pain, teeth bloodied where he had bitten through his lower lip.

"A foretaste, priest," the demon said. "I shall not touch you. Not physically. But we shall infect your body with things you cannot even imagine. You will scream for release. Beg me to banish the terror within you. . . . Tell me: where is the chalice?"

Hallowed be thy name . . .

Thy kingdom come . . .

"Oh yes, it shall come," the creature murmured. "It shall come now!"

An excruciating pain seized Father Moran's head, a boiling, burning sensation, as though something terrible was being born within his skull. His back arched up, his mouth opened but the scream never reached his lips.

Thy will be done...

The body collapsed into the waste his bowels had released. The pain exploded in his head, as if whatever had been struggling inside were free at last.

A fat hideous maggot, whitish green, slithered out of Father Moran's right ear. Out of his mouth climbed the first of the spiders...

"If I may permit myself an indelicate sobriquet," Edward Foxx said, "the shit appears to have hit the fan."

The three of them were in the boardroom on the top level of the Museum: Police Commissioner Edward Foxx, Lieutenant Gerry Samulovitch, and Frank Donnellan. The curtains were drawn against the paparazzi outside with telephoto lenses. In the center of the oval table was a twenty-inch Sony television and a Betamax unit.

"Do I still have my twenty-four hours?" Donnellan asked, turning to Foxx.

"State has been on the line to the Vatican. The papal secretary, a Cardinal di Stefano, is coming over to take custody of the Tour. According to Washington, di Stefano wants to know two things: the whereabouts of the chalice and of Father Moran. So in answer to your question, Frank, no, you don't have twenty-four hours. As soon as di Stefano arrives, in about seven and a half hours, the case will come under Federal jurisdiction. He is going to demand that. And he will get it."

"I expected as much," Donnellan murmured.

"Frank, what happened to Moran? If we can get to him before di Stefano arrives and the Feds move in—"

"Commissioner, I don't know where Moran is," Donnellan said. "I don't have him. I know who does, but I need time."

"And the cup?"

"The cup is safe."

"Is it, Frank?" the Commissioner challenged. "You assured me about Moran as well. I saw the amount of spent shells around the Museum. What were your people shooting at? Where are the bodies?"

Donnellan brought a video cassette from his pocket and clicked it into the Betamax.

"There are four other tapes like this one," Donnellan said. "You won't want to believe what you see, but at least you'll know what happened here tonight." Donnellan looked away. "I knew they would be coming for the cup. They had to. That's why my people were armed to the teeth.... And still it wasn't enough!"

Donnellan depressed the play switch and the screen flickered to life.

"This is the balcony camera. You're going to see how Perlman and Stone died."

The camera picked up the two security men.

"Here's where they hear something...."

Perlman and Stone began walking up the stairs.

"Oh my God!" the Commissioner whispered. The video faithfully recorded Perlman's last agonies as the talons drove into his belly. Another creature emerged from the recess. Stone was backing away, Ingram level. Because there was no sound, only the slight shaking of Stone's arms showed that the gun was firing. At something that could not be stopped...

Donnellan killed the power and popped the cassette.

"That's why there aren't any bodies, Commissioner," he said quietly.

"What are they?" Samulovitch demanded. "What are we dealing with!"

Donnellan gave them both an edited version of

the Grail story. "And I believe," he finished, "that somehow, through someone, the demonkind got to Father Moran before I did."

"McConnell? Is that why you put out the APB?"

"It had to be someone Moran recognized and to some degree trusted. McConnell's a possible."

"And those...those monstrosities are out there on the street?" Edward Foxx whispered. "Killing at random?"

"Not at random," Donnellan said. "They came for the cup and were denied. In revenge they took the first human they saw."

"Frank, I don't know what to say," Foxx murmured, getting to his feet, hands deep in trouser pockets. "What in God's name are we dealing with? All right, I've seen what in any other case would be irrefutable evidence. But I still can't believe it!"

"Nor will the Feds," Samulovitch added. "They'll try to make this out as some gigantic hoax."

"Elaborate costumes, bulletproof vests, they'll use any excuse to discredit it."

"Or else bury it," Donnellan said. "Which is why I won't tell you where the other tapes are. So you don't have to lie." He paused. "Edward, do you believe me?"

"Do I have any choice—the chewed-up corpses, the video, what you've said about the cup." He paused. "But that won't be enough!"

"It may be if you add this to everything else, Commissioner."

The three men turned round to see Lauren Blair standing in the doorway.

"I've just finished analyzing the fragments of nail on Cathy Windsor's bones. I haven't gotten to the residue on the remains of Perlman and Stone but I'm willing to bet everything that the results will be the same. Gentlemen, the TRACE unit has calculated that the scrapings are 1055 years old. There is no possibility of error."

* * *

"There's nothing more we can do, is there?"

The light behind her cast a sheen on her hair, the black fading into a deep rich blue. Donnellan reached out and gently kissed her on the pale lips, feeling her arm go around his neck, pressing him close. They held each other like that for a long time.

"No," he said. He glanced at his watch. "Di Stefano's plane will be landing in six hours. Foxx will lose jurisdiction. We'll have to give the cup over to him."

"We can't, Frank!"

He rose and went over to the floor-to-ceiling windows of Lauren's living room, looking out at the harbor with its myriad of lights. At dawn the rain stopped.

"No, we can't," he said. "I'll wait another three hours. If there's nothing about Moran or McConnell by then we'll go out and get the chalice." He turned to her. "We will have to destroy it, Lauren, you know that."

She came over to him, slipping an arm around his waist.

"We're next, aren't we?" she murmured. "They took Moran because he knew where the cup was. If he doesn't tell them—and he won't—they'll be coming for us."

"Which is why we must destroy the chalice before di Stefano can stop us."

"How, Frank?"

"We'll take it to a foundry. Take it there and drop it into the furnace. Stand back and watch as the damn thing melts!"

"Then it will be over?"

"There's nothing more we can do, colleen," Donnellan said, lips moving through her hair. "That *has* to be the end of it."

"Yes," she said faintly. "Except for those of us who saw them. Your men..."

"They aren't saying anything," Donnellan shook his head. "They seem to have developed a collective amnesia.... No, we're going to finish it, colleen."

Donnellan opened a hall closet and withdrew his trench coat.

"I have to deliver the test results and the tape to my attorney. If anything happened to me, these go back to you. Between Foxx, Gerry, and yourself, you might be able to convince someone what happened, if the need arises."

"It won't, Frank."

"Forty minutes, no more."

"Frank—"

"It's all right. I have men on the lobby and on this floor. Not guns but flamethrowers and miniature rockets. They're ready this time. I'll be back before you know it."

"I already know it," she whispered, kissing him.

After Donnellan left she ground up enough coffee for half a pot and turned on the NBC news for background noise. Three minutes later the telephone rang. Two short rings indicating the call was from lobby security.

"There's a gentleman by the name of Isaiah Webber," one of the agents told her. "The I.D. checks. Shall I send him up?"

"Isaiah! Yes, of course!"

Isaiah! She had forgotten all about him. God, he couldn't have any idea of what was happening. She opened the door on the first knock to see Webber flanked by two of Donnellan's men.

"Lauren!"

"Isaiah, come in, please. What are you doing out of bed?"

"I'm tired of being ill," Webber said, mounting the stairs. "Lauren, I heard what happened to Leech at Geochron...the fire at the Museum.... What is going on?"

"I don't know where to begin," Lauren said. "Look, Frank will be back in about a half-hour—"

"Frank?"

"Inspector Donnellan."

"Yes, I see." He looked at her carefully. "What's happened to you, Lauren? Where is Tim? He was supposed to meet with me today."

"Isaiah, please—"

"It's about the chalice, isn't it? Something's happened to the cup."

"Isaiah, nothing has happened to the cup."

"Lauren, we are going to the Museum right now!"

"We can't."

Webber's eyes glittered. "I haven't heard from you for almost two days. You haven't returned my calls. You haven't informed me of your progress. That's not like you, Lauren. Now Leech is dead. I hear that di Stefano is on his way over here. I want to go to the Museum, Lauren, and make certain everything is as it should be. But I can't unless you come with me. Do you realize they would not let me in! What is going on?"

Lauren was about to argue but instead reached for the phone. Isaiah was right. He had to know. She and Donnellan would have to tell him everything. If he believed them, possibly he might come up with an alternative to destroying the cup.

"No way, Lauren," Donnellan said when he took her call on the car phone. "Stay there until I get back."

"Frank, he has every right to insist on what he wants. Listen to me, he's heard about Leech, what happened at the Museum. Maybe he can help us."

"Lauren, no one can help us!"

"And what if those things come after him?" Lauren whispered. "He knows about the chalice as well."

A brief silence told her she had made her point.

"All right, I'll ask one of my men to escort you

over to the Bennett. But once there you stay put. Don't tell him anything until I get there."

"I'll be waiting, Frank."

"I, too, colleen." His voice softened. "Pass me one of the men."

Isaiah Webber was silent in the elevator. He held his hands behind his back, head thrust forward, studiously ignoring the armed men flanking him. As the car eased to a halt he shook his head in resignation and brushed past them.

"We'll all go in the sedan," the agent said.

"My car is perfectly capable of conveying us there," Webber said frostily. He stepped forward and opened the door. "Lauren."

"Now wait a minute—"

But she was in the car with Webber sliding in beside her, the door closing and locking. Lauren twisted around to see the agents scrambling for the sedan.

Isaiah Webber leaned forward to the driver. "Destroy them."

Lauren never saw the man's face as he slipped out of the black Lincoln and went back to the sedan. The next thing she felt was a sudden shudder of air that made the heavy car rock. There was the crump of an explosion.

"Now we may go," Isaiah Webber said.

In the rear view Lauren saw the sedan burning behind her.

"Isaiah!" she screamed, and reached for the door handle.

"Please sit back, Lauren. There is no way out for you. None at all."

The driver slid behind the wheel. Lauren wrenched at the handle, then made to leap past Webber to the other door. The car was swinging round the drive, starting off for the entrance onto Atlantic Avenue. She was flung back into the corner.

"Lauren, you will stop that."

The voice froze her. It was so pitiless, so dead.

"Isaiah, what's happened—"

"I ask you once. Where is the chalice? Tell me now and we shall drive there. If you do this I promise you I will spare you the pain."

"Isaiah, you're crazy!"

"I will ask you once."

Lauren drew back, sliding as far away as possible.

"No, no!" she flung out. "God, what do you want—"

"Blasphemy!" Webber said, his furious eyes locking on hers. "You obstinate, silly woman. They shall break you so easily. Even as now they are breaking the priest!"

"Isaiah—"

"Silence!"

Lauren felt as though her skull was on fire.

"You will not say another word," Webber spoke. "You cannot. Your tongue will not move. You can see and feel and hear everything but you cannot speak.... You cannot move...."

Her muscles became flaccid. Try as she did to move, her arms and legs remained lifeless.

Paralyzed! I'm paralyzed!

"Yes, you are that," Webber told her. "I am very sorry for you, that you will not tell me where the cup is. It would mean a great deal to me if I were the one who could bring it to them. Their gratitude would be enormous. They would see that I am worthy of being one of them...."

The car was gathering speed along Atlantic Avenue. The sodium arc lamps flickered overhead, golden drops scarcely penetrating the limousine's black-coated windows.

"But you are like the priest," Webber continued, looking straight ahead. "You do not understand what is about to happen." He twisted around to face her. "The chalice is ours," he hissed. "It is our birthright. How dare you presume to withhold it? What do you understand of the power and majesty of our race? But you don't understand, do you? We are repulsive to you.... Hideous. The stuff of nightmares. Yet we are not that at all. We are the progeny of Lucifer. His children, destined to usher his reign upon this earth. Our earth! What has gone unfulfilled all these millennia will now come to pass. Our rule, our destiny, will be fulfilled!

"Perhaps, in spite of your horror, you will be a part of that rule, for a little while. You are young. Fertile. We will need women to serve as vessels for our race. Many women, thousands..."

Lauren squeezed her eyes shut, unable to look upon the hideously contorted features any longer. Even the voice had changed. Cold, rasping, a snake's voice if a snake could speak.

"Perhaps we might spare you, after you have told us where the cup is. Perhaps when I become one of them, I will be the first to taste you. Would you like that, Lauren?"

She felt his breath upon her face, hot rancid breath. Her flesh recoiled when he laid his hand upon her breast and began to squeeze it. But she couldn't move.

He stayed like that for a long time, kneading her breast....

The car drew past the house on the Post Road and crept up the drive. The rear door swung open.

"I am going to release you, Lauren," Isaiah Webber whispered. His hand squeezed her breast, twisting the flesh, making her cry out silently. "But you will not run. You will follow me. And you will be able to speak."

She gasped and fell forward, vomiting on the floor.

"Why, Isaiah?" she whispered, words choked with sickness. "Why are you with them?"

"Because they gave me back my life!" Webber screamed at her. "Do you understand—life! What medicine held no hope for they cured, within seconds!

I am whole, Lauren. There is no more cancer. I have had everything returned to me. My life, my work. You shall die, Lauren, but I will live on forever. As one of them!" He grabbed her by the back of her blouse, hauling her up.

"Get out!"

Lauren stumbled out of the car, collapsing to the ground, the interlocking brick driveway digging into her knees.

"Come!"

She screamed as Webber gripped her by the hair and began dragging her toward the house. He opened the door and pushed her inside, stepping through beside her.

"I have brought her for you!"

Lauren tasted blood as her teeth sank into her tongue. Standing in a row against the wall were the demonkind, their eyes hungry for her. One of them was in the center of the room. He drew out his claw and pointed a talon at the priest.

"No!"

The viper reared back and struck Father Moran in the stomach, its head digging furiously into the gushing blood, shaking furiously. It withdrew, dragging out a piece of intestine.

The priest lay in a pool of blood. His body was covered with bites, some the size of a fist. A ball of maggots twisted by his right ear while at his groin a crablike creature was feasting upon the genitals. The snake drew back to strike once more.

"Tell us, Lauren: where is the chalice?" Isaiah Webber was whispering. "Tell us and the viper will strike at the heart. His death will be quick and merciful."

Transfixed by the horror, Lauren collapsed to her knees, head swinging wildly from side to side.

The name registered in the recesses of Father Moran's scorched brain. He had lain for hours, listening, feeling, as the reptiles and maggots fed upon

GRAIL

him. He had stopped screaming a long time ago, after
the spiders had infested his mouth. But he had never
lost consciousness. The demonkind hadn't permitted
that. Every so often he would hear one of them ask
the same question...in a dulcet voice he wanted so
much to answer. But he did not.

Now he had heard a different voice, a familiar
name.

*Holy Father, I am Your humble servant. I pray
that You hear my plea in this hour of need. I pray
that You grant me the strength to overcome mine
enemies. I beg You to save the innocent who is trapped
here....*

"Tell us, Lauren."

"No!" The word escaped his lips in a single ter-
rifying cry. Edmund Moran's blood-encrusted eyes
beheld the woman standing above him and a terrible
rage seized him.

*I have never loved you as a man. I never could. But
let me show you my love. Let it come to you from that
which they could not touch. Dear God, I beg of you,
grant me the strength of this love!*

"The Lord is with me this final time!" A brilliant
molten steel coursed through his arms.

The demon pointed his finger and the viper struck
deep into the priest's chest.

Then something happened that Lauren could not
believe. Slowly, exquisitely slowly, the spike driven
through the right palm began to work its way out
of the floor. In one twist the left leg was free, then
the right. As Father Moran rose to his feet the left
arm was free. He reached down and grasped the viper
from his belly. It immediately curled over his arm
but he caught its head in his fist. And squeezed.

"Run, Lauren," he whispered hoarsely. "Run
while my strength lasts...the Lord is with us!"

"Your time has come, priest!" the demon rasped,
and reached for him, talons flashing.

Father Moran turned around and brought both

320

arms around one of the pillars that ran from floor to ceiling. As he twisted it, the wood cried and splintered and the beam was sheared away. Moran drew back and heaved it into the fireplace, shattering the marble, sending hot coals across the floor.

"Run! For the love of God, run!"

Then he reached for the next post and broke that in half. Lauren saw the ceiling begin to crack, plaster pouring down.

"Run, Lauren!"

She drew back step by step, transfixed by the image of this naked man, covered in sweat and blood, head thrust back, muscles straining. Suddenly she felt herself jerked forward.

"You'll go nowhere!" Isaiah Webber screamed.

Lauren twisted around, breaking free of his grip. Something sheared the skin along her forearm. Then she was running, through the library door into the stately hall. Just as she reached the front door she heard another agonizing screech of twisted timber and then a tremendous roar, like that of an avalanche. Above the chaos rose a single voice.

"I bring down the house of the ungodly!"

Smoke, dust, and debris exploded within the library, riding out on hellish screams, borne on some demonic wind. Lauren struggled with the latch, finally managing to open the massive portals. She stumbled on the steps then, falling, gasping, scrambled to her feet and fled toward the gates, her shadow running ahead of her. At the gates she looked back. The house was on fire, the windows a stark orange against the flat gray of the morning sky. She fell against the iron railing, sobbing.

A shadow glided out of the inferno. Then another.

"No," she whispered. "No, they couldn't have survived!"

She scrambled along the gates, oblivious to the underbrush that clawed at her legs, tugging at her ankles as though wanting to hold her back.

Where was the gate?

She saw an opening. A space had been pried between two iron railings. Probably by very young vandals. It was that small. She thrust herself into the opening and immediately caught her shoulder.

"No!"

She looked back to see the demonkind shambling toward her, moving effortlessly through the thinned-out woods. She twisted, feeling the rusty metal tear at her blouse, then her skin. Something brushed her leg and she kicked back viciously.

"You are ours. You shall always be ours."

With a final desperate shove she was through to the other side, rolling down the wet slippery embankment. Her shoulder scraped against an open drain pipe. Clawing at the muddy earth, she crawled to the edge of the Post Road.

Lights.

The yellow foglights of a car.

Lauren crawled into the center of the road on her hands and knees, then staggered to her feet, one arm swinging feebly.

The lights were almost upon her. She heard the squeal of brakes and downshifting of the engine. Somewhere far away a familiar voice was calling her name. Lauren took two steps forward then fell. The last thing she remembered was the insignia on the hood of the car. It was the banner of Alfa Romeo.

CHAPTER TWENTY-THREE

The POST ROAD finished at Milhaven Highway, which in turn ran north into the rolling hills of Clinton County. At the corner of Milhaven and Highway 7 was the Golden Leaf Motel, a simple affair consisting of a diner-cum-office and a row of cabins that ran into the rear of the property. The pool was empty, strewn with leaves and dirt. The slides and swings creaked in the wind.

The owner-manager was sitting behind the front desk, his feet up on a stool, a plate of ham and scrambled eggs balanced on his belly. The portable television on the front desk was blaring out the second hour of *Good Morning America*, when he heard the car pull in.

He swung his feet off the stool as the young man entered.

"Howdy."

He looked all right, dressed for the country.

"Headin' north?"

"Stowe. Been driving most of the night."

The manager grunted, examined the photo on the license, and carefully jotted down the number.

"Fill out the rest, son." He pushed the key to number 12 over.

"Did I guess right?"

"I beg your pardon?"

"Did I guess right. You parked in front of 12?"

"Yes, that's right."

The young man pushed twenty dollars across the counter, taking the key.

"Have a nice rest," the manager called after him and, receiving no answer, added: "And fuck you very much too!"

Tim McConnell opened the door to the cabin and quickly drew the curtains over the front windows. He returned to the car and gently lifted Lauren out and carried her inside, kicking the door shut behind them. He laid her on the bed and carefully peeled away her dirty blood-streaked clothing. Then he ran a bath, laid her in the tub, and gently began to wash her, working away at the dirt on her legs and face with a washcloth.

Lauren remained unconscious but he knew she was all right. Her breathing had steadied, the pulse was even. From time to time she would moan softly, tossing her head from side to side, until he held her and calmed her.

When he was finished, McConnell carried her out of the bathroom and slipped her between the sheets of the double bed. He took her clothing and washed that as best he could, hanging the garments on the shower rod. He opened the window so that the air could get at them.

Tim undressed and slipped in beside her. He leaned over, his lips brushing her forehead, tracing the angry red scars where the branches had raked her face. He heard her sigh, then rolled over and closed his eyes.

Lauren Blair woke up with the night-table lamp glaring into her eyes. She twisted around and saw the jacket—his jacket.

"Tim..." she whispered hoarsely. Her mouth was dry and her face aflame with scratches. "Tim."

He lay huddled across the bed, the sheet pulled up right to the pillow. Disorientation swept over her. Where? How? She made to get out of the bed and the sheet fell away, sliding down to her thigh. Something twisted itself around her calf. Lauren pulled back, but whatever it was only tightened its grip. She flung off the sheet.

And screamed.

Coiled around her calf was a tail, a hideous, scaly tail whose tip flickered like a snake's tongue against her ankle.

The thing beside her moved. What had once been Tim McConnell sat up, grinning at her.

"Tim... Oh God no!"

He reached for her, the talons sinking into her shoulders, the hideous viper mouth drooling to reveal teeth....

"Lauren!" he gasped. A perverted semblance of a smile creased the lizard features.

The talons digging into her flesh, she twisted around and rolled to the floor. Overturning a chair, she scrambled toward the door.

"Lauren..."

The voice was his own again, quiet, hypnotic.

Don't look back!

"Lauren, come to me!"

Don't look back!

"Lauren, look at me."

Her head snapped round, the eyes held in a vise-like grip.

"Come to me."

"No," she whimpered. But her feet took one step, then another toward the source of the foulness that billowed at her.

"Come, Lauren."

She was in the bed, sliding toward him—it—hot tears streaming down her cheeks.

"Lie back."

She felt the talons pull her thighs apart and squeezed her eyes shut.

"Feel it, Lauren...."

* * *

The lights were still on when she opened her eyes. Her womb was burning as though it were a furnace. She smelled her own blood, felt it beneath herself, along her thighs.

"It is time, Lauren."

He came into the room and, standing beside the bed, dropped her clothing onto it.

"Dress."

She rose obediently and reached for her blouse without bothering to wash. He watched her constantly as she dressed and then opened the door for her. They slipped out into the early evening. For a second Lauren looked up at the darkening sky, unable to believe that an entire day had passed.

"You will take me to the cup, Lauren. Where is the chalice?"

"The chalice is at the chapel on the Baldarese estate."

The thing that was McConnell seemed satisfied. He led her to the car.

"You remember how to drive. You will take me there."

"I will take you there...."

The drive to Brookline lasted forty-five minutes, minutes that were lost forever to Lauren Blair. She felt nothing, not the wind in her face, nor the vibrations of the engine through the seat. She drove like an automaton.

The Baldarese estate was on a sprawling secluded plot, bordered by the Hammond Pond Parkway to the north and Barisford Drive on the south. When she had brought the chalice here, Lauren had passed the main house, built on a Norman design, and gone directly to the small white church that had come with the property, blessed by Father Edmund Moran....

"Get out."

As Lauren stepped out of the car she saw figures disengage themselves from the dark woods.

"Where is the cup?"

"Inside the church."

A horrible strangled hiss escaped McConnell's lips.

"Go and bring it to us."

The creature she remembered from the house shambled toward her. "We do not die!" it whispered. "Now go, bring the cup to us!"

Slowly Lauren shook her head.

"Go."

She moved forward, propelled by a force she could not deny. Slowly Lauren mounted the three steps and pushed the doors. She stared uncomprehendingly as they parted.

"Go!"

A low chanting started to rise in the night, creating a wind that swept her along. Lauren entered the church and moved down the single aisle. On either side were the hewn pews and elegant stained-glass windows embedded in cool plaster walls. A hundred candles were burning about the altar around the four magnificent crosses mounted on pedestals, set in a diamond configuration.

And in the center of the holy guardians, the chalice. Exactly as she had placed it.

"Take it for us," a voice thundered in her ears. "Take it and bring it to us!"

She moved past the candles. Past the candles that she herself had arranged according to Father Moran's instructions.

"Take it for us."

Her hands reached out and touched the chalice.

At that instant a blinding light appeared over the sanctuary.

"Take it for us!"

She felt herself being torn apart. The chanting was becoming louder, bearing her away like a leaf on a raging stream. She gripped the chalice and began to walk back. She was just clear of the crosses when the light appeared before her, blocking her way.

The chanting was becoming a wailing, a demonic howling the likes of which is heard in the desert or in virgin mountain ranges. It drew her forward.

The light before her moved forward, blocking the entrance, the doors slamming.

"Please," Lauren whispered. "You're killing me!"

The doors began to rattle violently. Suddenly the entire church was quaking under the pressure of the chanting. The light grew stronger. It spread throughout the church until its radiance was white hot. Then in a torrent of flame it burst forth.

The fireball roared from the church, streaming at the demonkind in a solid mass. For an instant it seemed that the sheet of flame wavered, was thrown back as though hitting an invisible, impregnable wall. Screams born in hell erupted as the church blew apart under the force of the flames. The demonkind faced the fireball in a straight line, heads thrown back, their howls shaking the earth as they sought to protect themselves.

The fire broke through their ranks. One of the demons was consumed by flames, burning like some funeral pyre. The inferno seized the others, hunting them down, scarcely touching them before they became inhuman torches. Its hunger unappeased, the fire raced into the parkland, scorching the woods a hundred feet away from the church. In a violent gust, the flames were sucked into a vortex, drawing everything they possessed into the blazing church.

EPILOGUE

M IDMORNING...*I have come too late, like Arturo Capellini, Father Moran, I have come too late....*

Inspector Frank Donnellan stepped over the fire-hoses that lay in the mud. He gazed around him. It was as though the earth had opened and the flames of hell had scorched the woods. For a hundred feet in a rough circle around the church not a living thing remained. The trees had burned to their roots, the vegetation and underbrush were reduced to ash. Nothing survived.

He had arrived at the Baldarese estate with the pumper. He remembered leaping from the car and running toward the inferno. He would have gone right in, screaming for Lauren, his lungs bursting, had Samulovitch not tripped and pinned him down.

Nothing survived.

The firemen poured water, tons of it, feeding the hoses from the artificial pond. But the flames refused to die. They burned until their work was done. Then, seemingly of their own accord, they began to ebb.

The earth was still hot to walk on but he had tramped over it, sifting through what was left. He found nothing he recognized. Nothing of her. Or the chalice.

Nothing survived.

Now the smoke was still rising as the firemen hosed down the ashes. It drifted over the Baldarese estate in a long pale cloud, obscuring the morning sun.

329

"There's nothing more for us. Let's go, Frank." Samulovitch stepped beside him.

"What happened here?" Donnellan asked. "Why did she have to die?"

"Frank—"

"Why, Gerry?" Donnellan turned to him, tears running unashamedly from his eyes. "She was good. She was so good!"

Gently but firmly, Samulovitch turned his friend away from the devastation. He couldn't answer him. He doubted anyone would ever be able to do so.

"Jesus Christ, would you look at that!"

The fireman behind Donnellan let his hose sag and pointed at the woods. The smoke was still swirling out there but a light was glowing. It became stronger as Donnellan took a few steps toward it.

"God in Heaven..."

Out of the smoke, out of the holocaust, he saw Lauren Blair walking, her face shining, the Grail held aloft in her hands.